~ Michael's War ~

George Mitchell

Tiger Style Publications

For Sylvia and Emily

Cover design by Stephen Mitchell
(mitchybwoy.com)

~PART ONE - TOWN~

CHAPTER 1

September 1938 Chamberlaine a frail sixty-nine-year-old travels to Germany in an attempt to find a solution to the escalating crisis in Europe. On the fifteenth at Berchtesgaden in Bavaria he agrees with Adolph Hitler to the separation of the Sudeten Germans from Czechoslovakia. In return, the German leader agrees to stop short of invasion.

'I can see Betty the Bike'. Whacker was looking out of the bedroom window down into the busy street, his face pressed against the glass so that his breath condensed as he talked. Michael looked up from the comic he was reading but Betty had passed by. To the left, from the bedroom window, they could see over the valley to the Pennines in the distance. This morning the hills, lit by bright autumn sunshine that followed a heavy shower of cold rain, stood framing the Stanbury valley. Wet, shining roofs of terraced houses receded down the hill towards the mills in the valley bottom. Washing, hung out to dry in the early morning, now sagged on the line; shirts, vests and pants dripped sadly on to a backyard. A woman, her hair tight in curlers, scuttled across the hard black earth to collect wet garments into the washing basket that she clutched to her hip; like carrying a baby. A brisk breeze snatched smoke from the chimneys and bent it before blasting it to a grey whirl that twisted and finally disappeared into the rain-washed air. A burst of starlings exploded from the chapel roof and wheeled down the valley.

It was Saturday, no school. Michael liked to sit looking out on mornings like this. He enjoyed the views across the valley and also closer to hand, the busyness of the street outside. He could see the bus stop; people waiting for the buses to Leyden, Hexton or Lumley, they all came past here, mostly double deckers and at this time on a weekend, they were full of shoppers. He could hear the ping of the bus bells as the conductors decided they were ready to go and then the roar of the engines as they strained to begin their climb up the steep hill.

Buses were quite regular but often full; smoking upstairs, no smoking downstairs and more often than not, standing room only. The number of people allowed to stand depended on the mood of the conductor. There were those who packed their buses and then had difficulty collecting the fares, so you might get a free ride, and others who stuck strictly to the official number decided by the bus company. They seemed to take a delight in turning people away. The buses had open platforms at the back and children liked to jump off as they approached their stop; the dare was who could jump off at the earliest point.

Their favourite bus-conductor was Jimmy Quickhand; he had been shell-shocked in the Great War and could not control the movement of his hands. He snatched the fares from passengers' fingers and took several attempts to let them fall into his money pouch; he seemed unable to release the coins. Then, with his eyes screwed tight, his hand jerked over the ticket machine until he finally managed to gain sufficient control to punch out the correctly coloured piece of thin card. The boys liked Johnny, but were also a bit afraid of him because they didn't really understand why he behaved the way he did.

The butcher's shop was next to the bus stop; the raw redness of hanging meat filled the window. Mr. Fletcher, fat and red faced, was inside, slapping chops wrapped in paper on to the weighing scales and shouting out the weight as a question to check with the customer if it was acceptable, since it never quite matched the weight they had asked for. A cowering, yellow dog slunk under the shop window, ears flat, nose twitching, waiting for an opportunity.

Sometimes friends would pass. Whacker lived close by and couldn't wait to get out of the house to avoid his bullying brother or his cantankerous sister, so he was often wandering the street from an early hour. When he saw friends in the street, Michael would rush downstairs, pull open the heavy, black painted door and run to catch up with whoever he'd seen. Sometimes he would return to his bedroom, bringing friends with him, which was why Whacker was there giving a running commentary of his observations. Betty the Bike was noted for being a very friendly girl but the boys were too young to fully appreciate the significance of her name.

Both boys were about the same height but while Michael was slim with his mother's dark hair and grey eyes, Whacker was a solid tousled boy with abundant freckles and spiky red hair. No-one called him 'ginger' for fear of getting a whack in the mouth, which was how he got his nickname. The boy had learned to look after himself in the face of a bullying brother and as a result, was quite happy to take on anyone who bothered him, regardless of their size. He had lived round the corner up Lucy Street for all his life but was proud of his family's Irish Protestant heritage, and sometimes sneaked his father's orange sash out of the house and paraded up and down the street beating an imaginary drum, ignoring the fact that the other children didn't know what his marching signified. Michael admired Whacker's lack of fear and also found him to be a good and entertaining friend, who always had an idea for a new adventure. Michael was a quiet boy; he liked reading and drawing but enjoyed the sense of excitement that his friend brought to life. Whacker said that his friend was a genius because he could read fluently but Michael saw nothing extraordinary about his skill, it was just something he could do. There were other friends of course but these two were close and automatically sought each other out, at school, or when they were playing in the grimy streets.

During the week, when the mills were open, the valley was usually full of smoke, because although the chimneys were high, the fumes were blown back into the town by the westerly winds whipping over the tops of the hills. Consequently, layers of grime covered the streets and buildings, and the air was often full of soot; on particularly bad days, washing, hung out to dry, had to be rewashed.

The carpet mills sounded their sirens at six in the morning to tell the workers that they should be inside the gates. Men and young women could be seen running down the cold, black, cobbled streets, trying to clock-in before the deadline that would result in a deduction from their pay. Michael's father worked as a tuner, looking after looms that broke down. His mother had been a weaver when she was younger but not at this time because it was considered inappropriate for married women to work, even though the income from one wage was only just sufficient to provide for a very basic existence.

Michael hated the family rows that resulted from their lack of money. He could always tell when one was in the offing; the atmosphere in the house started to become oppressive; the looks and words between his parents began to feel wrong. He tried to think of some way of deflecting the impending argument but was rarely successful. He would change the subject by talking about school or one of his friends but was usually ignored by this point in the confrontation. Heated discussions frequently ended with his mother threatening to find a job and Jack, his father, shouting, 'Do you want folk to think I can't keep my bloody family?' The anger in his voice and his staring eyes frightened the boy but he didn't cry; he just felt very sick. At these times he hated Dad because he could see how upset and frustrated his mother was and also that she was frightened, afraid to say anything else.

They lived in a rented, terraced house in the mill town of Stanbury. There was one room downstairs and two bedrooms. In the living room was a black-leaded, iron fire place with an oven at one side and a set pan for heating the water at the other. In the corner they had a stone sink with a gas ring on the draining board. The house had no bathroom and the shared toilet, round the back of the house, was about fifty yards walk through a dirt yard that had other houses round the edge. If the toilet was occupied, they had to wait. Michael would whistle a tune in the hope that the occupant might hurry if they knew someone was outside. During the winter, the water pipes regularly froze and anyone using the lavatory had to carry a bucket of water to flush the system. They were lucky to have a small garden at the front of their house but the sun never reached it so it was made up of bare, hard-packed soil with occasional tufts of rough grass and a sooty privet hedge that didn't grow properly.

Michael didn't fully appreciate the significance of money in their lives; he never thought that his family was poor. He wished that his mother, Kathleen, would wear underskirts without holes in them but it never occurred to him that she couldn't afford to buy new ones. He thought that she was a beautiful and loving woman who should be able to wear clothes that didn't need mending.

It was a time when only a few people could afford cars and none of his friends' families owned one. Like most small boys, however, he was interested in vehicles and tried to learn the makes of those that passed by in the street but never thought of actually riding in one. Whacker's brother owned a motorbike although they never saw it working. He would tinker with it and then, cursing loudly, try to kick-start it into life but without success, apart from oily smoke and a few gasps from the exhaust. Maybe because of this, Whacker was interested in bikes and knew the sounds of all those that would roar through the narrow streets; without fail, he could identify the make and size of engine of every one that passed.

Having wiled away half-an-hour looking out at the street, Whacker as usual became restless, 'let's go down to t' sewage works', he suggested.

'OK', Michael agreed. He nearly always fell in with suggestions of this kind because he knew that Whacker liked to be involved in something physical and he would have plenty of time for reading later in the day at bedtime. Besides, the sewage farm was one of their favourite places and the odds were that other friends would latch on as they wandered down the valley towards the beck that ran alongside the filter beds.

The boys were members of the Lucy Street Gang; a small but exclusive group. They were deadly rivals of the Long Estate gang and frequently fought with them when the insults exchanged or trespasses made went beyond the limits of normal gang rivalry, for example; referring to Whacker as a 'ginger Irish bastard' was sufficient to bring about fisticuffs. Down by the sewage works, the gang had their 'family tree'. The names of all the members were carved into the bark of a huge, old oak, including that of Rags the dog, who although they never knew the name of his owner, followed them everywhere. As the boys set off on their travels around the neighbourhood, Rags would appear and when the gang headed for home, he would leave them around the bottom of Lucy Street. He was a very independent hound and strongly objected to being patted but would allow members to scratch his chest if they first let him smell their hands, then, with half closed eyes, he would enjoy the ecstasy of grubby fingers tickling his front.

With the exception of bicycles, Rags objected to vehicles; if any dared enter his vicinity, he would chase them, growling, barking and trying to bite the rear wheel. This led to many near scrapes and several wounds and patches of missing fur. Apart from these blemishes, his coat was normally dirty and unkempt so that, as a result, he looked like a bundle of old rags, hence his name. Rags clearly enjoyed the boys' company but didn't want to be led by them so he never walked with them. He snuffled along at the side of the street or in the undergrowth exploring the smells, particularly interested in the signs left by his fellow mongrels. Sometimes he would disappear for several minutes but would always reappear to check that he was going in the right direction. In this way he felt that he retained his independence and could imagine that, occasionally, he was leading the pack.

*

The boys wandered up Lucy Street which sloped steeply up-hill, and consisted of rows of terraced houses with ginnels in between leading to further terraces behind. The doors opened straight on to the street. Further up, there was a block of more recently built corporation houses where Whacker lived. These had the luxury of small gardens surrounded by wooden fences. The older houses were built of bricks, which over the years, had become blackened. The action of wind, rain and the heavily polluted atmosphere of the valley, caused flakes of brick to peel off and these sometimes lay in small piles at the foot of the walls. The newer, corporation houses and had retained most of the original colour of the red brick and pebble dashing. They also had indoor toilets and bathrooms and were looked upon with envy by the folk who lived in the old terraces.

The ground was beginning to dry and the boys were able to kick sparks up with their clogs; they didn't use the cracked and uneven pavement so walking on the cobbles it was almost incidental that they would give the old stones glancing kicks to generate the little stars of light under their feet. Some smaller children were playing by the side of the road, sailing sticks in a little stream in the gutter. The leader of the group was Gladys; she was the older sister to two of the others and was telling them not to get too mucky otherwise they'd get a crack when they got home. Michael and Whacker knew Gladys but didn't acknowledge her presence because she was female and therefore had no status. Had Michael been alone, he might have spoken, but to do so in the company of another boy was definitely not acceptable and would have led to taunts suggesting that he and Gladys were in love.

Further up the street they could see Ernest. He was sitting on the step outside his house bouncing a ball between his feet. The boy was small for his age and as usual, dirty, with torn trousers and no socks. His clog irons were worn down almost to the wooden sole. But he was an amiable friend, slow to anger and always cheerful. His hands were covered in warts and Michael's mother said that he shouldn't sit next to Ernest in school but there wasn't much that could be done to avoid this since Michael was too frightened of the teacher to make any special requests about desk arrangements. In any case, he didn't see how warts could walk across from one person to another and he liked Ernest, so he simply agreed to the instruction and did nothing.

Ernest walked across to join them and put him arm on Whacker's shoulder "Ow do, where you goin?'

"Ow do, we're off to t' sewage works.'

Without further words, Ernest joined them; no need for discussion, relationships were easy. Once you were a member of the gang, only the direst of deeds could result in your expulsion and you were fully entitled to join any of the adventures.

A sudden squall splattered cold, hard rain on their heads and they ran up to the top of the street into a ginnel which was overgrown with bramble, rose bay willow herb and other wild plants, and gave some shelter from the shower. The boys paused to squeeze the bottom of the huge, white flowers of the convolvulus that clung to the iron railings alongside. When they were ripe, the flowers came out with a satisfying pop and floated on the wind like parachutes. Sometimes they would find the huge, juicy caterpillars of a hawk moth that ate the plant's leaves. Michael had kept a jar full of these fat creatures, with leaves for them to eat, on his bedroom window sill. They had grown bigger and then eventually turned into hard brown cocoons with a little spike at one end. He had read about their life-cycle and knew to bury the shiny cases over winter in another jar full of soil. His delight when they appeared in the spring as mature adult moths was not shared by his mother who was alarmed when they fluttered, blindly around the tiny kitchen/living room and crashed into the single window, clinging to the glass until they were captured and put outside.

The boys stayed in the protection of the ginnel until the rain stopped and then stepped out on to the track down towards the Barley Field. Why the field had been given this name was a mystery, since barley had never grown there in living memory. The land was rough pasture, used for grazing by small herds of young heifers that stayed for a while and then were driven to the abattoir. The track towards the field was bare ground, covered with loose stones and deep channels where heavy rain had formed temporary streams. Whacker reached the stone stile first and climbed up.

'Any bulls?' asked Ernest, he was afraid of bulls even though he had never encountered one.

Whacker peered at the few beasts nearby; 'yes, a big 'un.'.

'I'm not goin' then', Ernest said. He climbed the stile to see for himself and after careful observation of the cows' immature udders, realised that Whacker was teasing him. Laughing together, the boys clambered over the stile and wandered along the rough pathway that led diagonally across the field. The animals stared foolishly. At this point Rags appeared. He had followed them unseen from the bottom of Lucy Street but wanted to be closer now because he wasn't too keen on cows; they tended to gather round him and snort threateningly, and whilst he would never admit it, he felt that the proximity of boys offered a degree of protection.

Through the next stile, which was a tumbled pile of stones, the path led into a warehouse yard. Men were using a crane to lift huge bales full of shoddy from the back of a flat wagon up to the top floor of the old building. The boys paused to watch as the men stuck hooks on the end of loose chains, into the sack cloth; then a call told the crane operator to raise the bulging sack up to the open door, high near the roof. Two more workers in blue overalls had to reach out, grab the bundle with vicious looking hand-held hooks and then call to the crane man to release the tension so that the bale could be pulled inside. This was the most dangerous part and the men had to be strong to cope with the weight. The Lucy Street gang was familiar with the inside of the warehouse; on days when it was raining, they would sometimes push open a broken window and climb inside to jump about on the great bales, which because they were full of rags, made soft landings for the small bouncing bodies. The occasional warehouse rat made for good sport although the shrieking, leaping boys were too slow and too noisy to catch it.

There was a brief discussion about whether or not to throw stones at the men and then run away but in the end they thought that those on the wagon were too close and could easily jump down. They continued their walk round the back of the warehouse and down past the main factory building; Michael knew that on weekdays they would hear the clattering of the looms and through the grimy windows, see the spinning drive shafts and belts that hung from the ceiling of the huge weaving shed. The noise would be deafening, even outside, while inside the din was so bad that people had to lip-read if they wanted to talk. Michael was aware that his parents sometimes communicated to one another without speaking out loud, usually when they didn't want him to know what they were saying: like the time when they discussed the curious pregnancy of Mabel, who lived next door, but wasn't married. He knew that you were supposed to have a husband and wife to have a baby and so he couldn't understand how Mabel had managed to acquire the tiny red child that they could hear squealing in the night. He did realise from what people said, that this was a big disgrace and Mabel might not be able to go to Chapel on Sunday, which Michael thought was a strange punishment since he hated the weekly ritual of sitting in the hard pew listening to the vicar telling him that he was a sinner and unless he mended his ways, he was going to Hell. He would have quite liked to spend the time reading or playing out.

'She could have got it from the Sally Army' Whacker had suggested, 'They're always givin' stuff away – clothes n' food n' stuff - mebbe they're givin' babies to younger folk.' Michael liked the Salvation Army band, which played at half-time at the football matches but he had never seen them giving anything away and thought that babies came from inside women and had nothing to do with bands, so he didn't agree.

The track now led from the weaving shed out through the mill gates into Cinder Lane and it was here that they came across Brian, another gang member who lived close to the mill because his father was night watchman. Brian had ring worm and had his hair cut off so that the infection could be treated; this gave him some status in the gang since no-one else had had the ailment recently and he was subjected to daily close inspections so that the others could judge the progress of the treatment. Ring-worm was considered more acceptable than nits; to have nits was thought to be an indication of dirtiness. Any one possessing live fleas, however, could provide entertainment since these creatures could be caught and cracked between finger nails.

Brian was bending down near a puddle. 'What you doin?' asked Ernest.

'Washin' me 'ead – it's mucky' answered Brian. 'Tryin' to get rid o' this bloody worm'.

'Won't work, it's in yer 'ed.

'Nurse said I 'ad to wash it to keep it clean.'

'Aye, but not in a puddle, put it under t' tap,' Ernest offered.

After further discussion, it was agreed that Brian's head was looking much better, regardless of how it was washed and the walk continued with another member. Eventually they reached the menacing, dark, brown beck that ran alongside the sewage farm. This had to be crossed by balancing across a narrow metal pipe with a ring of barbed wire at each end – a difficult operation that formed part of the gang's initiation ceremony. This was appropriate since anyone who dare not cross the pipe couldn't reach the family tree that was the centre of gang activity. Even Rags had to cross this way otherwise he would have had to swim the beck which stunk of factory waste and other less easily defined odours. Members did sometimes fall into the water but this did not constitute failure, since the criterion for success was the bravery to attempt the crossing; indeed to fall in the beck provided entertainment for the others and was therefore quite acceptable. Further danger was provided by the fact that entry to the farm was against the law but only a few men worked there regularly and they could easily be avoided. On the few occasions that they had been seen, the gang escaped across the beck before they could be caught. It was thought that no adult would dare to cross the pipe because it was too narrow for big feet and tall people.

Rags particularly enjoyed adventures near the beck because he often saw rats around the stream. Being an expert hunter, he regularly chased and caught these animals, issuing short joyous barks before using his sharp teeth to nip the back of their necks and kill them instantly. The dog usually carried the dead body back to show the boys a trophy of his prowess and was often rewarded with praise, especially if the rat was a particularly big one. Rags didn't know why he hated the rats, he just did. It was much the same with cats but they were more difficult; the cats around Lucy Street were wily town cats, they sought high places to lounge and always kept an eye out for danger. Also, they were equipped with sharp claws and teeth and when cornered, were skilled street fighters who could damage the nose and eyes of even the biggest, fiercest opponent. Nevertheless, Rags knew his duty and would always make a token chase, barking and growling, but would abandon the pursuit when pride had been satisfied. Other dogs were of interest, of course, and much of Rag's sniffing in the undergrowth and around walls was to determine who had passed by. He knew the scents of all the local dogs and immediately sensed when a newcomer was in town; if he detected an interloper, he would take off in search of the owner of the new aroma and offer either confrontation or friendship depending on how he was received. That Rags was the local boss was in no doubt and other canines would usually defer to him, some even rolling on the ground and offering their throats in the time honoured manner. His association with the Lucy Street gang also gave him high status, since to other dogs, he clearly demonstrated by his independent stance, that he was in charge of the boys' activities.

Having wobbled across the narrow pipe, the gang walked through the settling beds towards the big trees at the far side of the farm. Rooks, sitting by their old nests, called a warning from above. As usual, the gang paused to throw the occasional stone into the beds to observe the satisfying plodge as it broke through the crust. No-one was around, which was often the case, so they were relaxed and commented on each stone's effect. Next, the boys came to the sprinkler beds with their slowly turning pipes that delivered contaminated water to be filtered by the layers of increasingly fine gravel. These were natural roundabouts and

Whacker of course, was the first to climb aboard and enjoy the gentle circling motion. There were four pipes so that each boy could have one and soon they were riding round clinging to the supports near the central bearing. For some reason, Michael began to sing. He had read in a book about France, the words of the national anthem and it seemed appropriate to use them in celebration of the fun they were having, despite the fact that he wasn't sure of correct pronunciation.

'Alonsa fon don dee la pateray, la jore de glory est arrive,' he sang at the top of his voice.

What's tha singin'?' asked Ernest. Michael explained and proceeded to teach the words to his friends. Soon, with great gusto, they were all singing the garbled anthem as the booms of the filter pipes revolved sedately in the soft September sunshine that had settled in following the showers.

An angry roar interrupted the impromptu choir; their discordant warbling had alerted the sewage farm workers who were doing some Saturday overtime. The men were immediately intent on capturing the miscreants in order to exact retribution for this transparent affront to the sanctity of their domain. The small, light boys were remarkably agile and quick when it came to fleeing before an enemy; without second warning they were off across the filter bed towards the beck and the narrow escape pipe. Unfortunately, one of the men, having chased the gang before, knew their getaway plan and placed himself so as to block their path. Whacker, very nimble, dodged round him and headed for the pipe but Michael was unlucky he slipped, fell to the ground and was captured in an instant. With one prisoner, the man tried to grab the other two but Michael's struggles made this difficult and they managed to get past. Happy with his capture, the man gripped the struggling captive by his neck. 'Got the little bugger' he shouted to his colleagues – with a note of triumph. Michael's head was crushed against the man's overall, he was held tightly and could smell the stink of sewage and feel the coarse fabric against his cheek, but struggle though he did, he was held fast and escape seemed unlikely. Rags, on seeing one of his gang in trouble, ran round barking and growling making threatening runs towards the man but taking care to avoid kicks aimed at him by the steel toed boots. The boy was beginning to have difficulty breathing and his captor felt his struggles become less vigorous, 'you've 'ad it pal,' he growled, 'we'll get the bobbies to you'. But he reckoned without Whacker and his brave loyalty to a friend. On seeing that Michael was captured he turned, ran back and without hesitation, the little ball of red-haired fury flung itself horizontally at the man's back, knocking the wind out of his body and causing him, with a grunt of pain, to release his prisoner. Before the other workers could arrive, the boys sped down the path, past the barbed wire and over the pipe, followed by a bundle of rags that barked excitedly and jumped up at the boys' hands as they ran. Rags wasn't sure exactly what had happened but felt that he had been involved in something very exciting that deserved to be celebrated.

On the other side of the beck, they paused to look back and shout at the men, who were too big to manage the barbed wire and the narrow pipe. Joined by Ernest and Brian, they hurled insults at the sewage workers, who gestured in fury, describing what tortures they would inflict on any boys who were caught in the future. The gang knew it wasn't wise to stay too long because one of the men could have gone to the bridge and circled round behind them so they set off towards the barley field, arms round each other's shoulders, a brave band of brothers, singing their new triumphant song as they marched along. Out of a clean-washed, blue sky, the autumn sun warmed their shoulders and rejoiced with them.

*

Kathleen, paused in her work; she hated black-leading the fireplace but it had to be done otherwise the neighbours would talk behind her back. It was difficult to have secrets in their neighbourhood, everyone knew everyone else's business, doors were left unlocked and friends would walk into each others' houses with just a call: 'only me', or something similar. Jack had gone to the football match so this was a good time to do the messy work when she had the house to herself. The kitchen/living room was kept spotlessly clean; the threadbare carpet was swept daily and no dust was allowed to rest on the furniture. Her pride and joy, a cut glass vase received as a wedding present, was polished regularly. Michael was not allowed to touch this precious article but he did enjoy looking through it at the multitude of images created by the sparkling facets. Kath wished they had a front room that could be kept for 'best', but with one wage, they didn't have enough money to move to a bigger house. Jack often talked about having a sister for Michael but she wouldn't entertain the idea until they had more room and since there was no prospect of his earning more money, this was another source of tension in their relationship. Kathleen was a practical woman who couldn't understand why Jack was so resistant to her finding a job; she knew that they were looking for weavers down at Finch's mill and her next door neighbour, Mabel said she was definitely going down and her mother could look after the baby but Jack wouldn't hear of her doing the same and got angry if she argued.

The house was dark, even on this bright September day. She worked hard to make the place comfortable but with little money to spend on new furniture it was difficult to make improvements; the suite was old and the table in the centre of the room was second-hand and stained with the tide marks of some liquid that had been spilled by the previous owners. Upstairs, the rooms were small and smelled of damp; marks in the ceiling showed where rain was leaking through the old slate roof. Michael often had a cough and Kathleen thought the dampness might be the cause. So many families lost children at a young age and her love for her son made the thought of losing him unbearable. She asked Jack to complain to the landlord about the leaks but he was worried that the rent would rise if they had any work done on the roof. The long trek to the toilet was also a problem, particularly in winter. To solve the problem they put a bucket behind the front door that could be used if anyone only needed to pee but she hated this and dreamed of the luxury of an indoor toilet and bathroom.

Jack was quite tall with black hair that he flattened to his head with Brillcream. When they first met, Kath thought he looked like Fred Astair. He was polite and friendly with a good sense of humour but as their marriage progressed, he laughed less than before and seemed tired all the time. They had no money for days out and had to save up if they wanted to go to the pictures. She knew that he was always worried about money and that the job in the mill was so tiring, that by the end of the day, he was worn out. Although she still loved him, Kathleen was frustrated by his apparent lack of ambition. He was honest and hard-working, and handed her his wage packet unopened at the end of the week, but seemed unwilling to seek a better job and until he earned more money, they would be unable to look for a better house or challenge the landlord about the poor condition of their own. He wouldn't even let *her* get a job to bring in more money. She felt that the foundations of their relationship were being undermined by the day-to-day grind which left little space for laughter and enjoyment.

Money was in such short supply that Kathleen was unable to visit her parents, Walter and Amy, who had moved to a place called Callthorpe, in the countryside near the market town of Seldown. They had left when Michael was just a baby. He didn't even know what they looked like. To get to Callthorpe required catching three buses and would have taken half-a-day; they simply couldn't afford it. They kept in touch through regular letters but Kathleen knew that both her parents missed her and were sad not to see the progress of their grandson from baby to infant to young boy.

The seeds of discontent grew in Kathleen's mind when she was working in the house and Jack would often come home to find her in a bad mood that he couldn't understand. Now, a new worry was on the horizon: people said there might be a war. She could just remember the last one – all those men dying and for what? The world didn't seem to be a better place, they were still poor and working people laboured for long hours to raise enough money to just about feed themselves from one week to the next. All these notions made her increasingly determined that Michael should not join the legions of mill workers; the grey army of honest people who toiled day-after-day in dirty old buildings for a pittance and one week's holiday with pay every year. Michael was clever; he could talk when he was eighteen months old and could read before he went to school. He had learned by sitting on her lap looking at the words as she read and now loved books even more than she did; he was always at the library and had an unquenchable thirst for information, using a dictionary for words he didn't know. He *must* go to the grammar school, she thought, but what he would do when he left she had only a vague idea – maybe he could be a school teacher, they didn't seem to earn much but they had long holidays and didn't have to wear overalls.

Preoccupied with these thoughts, she was startled by Michael crashing through the door into the kitchen. He was filthy and Kathleen could smell him the moment he entered. 'Where on earth 'ave you been to get so mucky?' Michael looked down at himself surprised by her question, he wasn't aware of his appearance until then so his grazed and dirty legs and the smeared green-brown stains on his trousers came as a shock.

'Er, we've just been up Lucy Street,' he mumbled, knowing well that their trip to the sewage works would not be received kindly.

'You've been with Andrew to the sewage works again, I can smell you.' His mother, as usual, spoke calmly and used Whacker's proper name but Michael knew he was in trouble not least because of his dirty clothes, he knew how irksome it was for washing to be done. The set pan by the fire had to be used to heat up the water, which was then ladled into the wash tub. Clothes, along with washing powder, were then put in the tub and bashed around with the posser on a long stick, after which they were squeezed through the huge mangle and hung out to dry in the little garden. Michael quite liked wash day because the house was warm and full of steam, and the comforting smell of soap, but he knew that his mother found the work tiring and he hated to see her red arms and the drawn look on her face by the end of the day. Also, if the weather was rainy, the clothes had to be hung on the clothes horse in front of the fire which blocked heat from reaching the rest of the house.

'Yes, well … I was grabbed by a man an' Whacker rescued me,' he knew it was no use to lie. He didn't know how but his mother always knew when he was lying. It was an uncomfortable fact and he didn't know how she could tell but he had long realised that the truth would emerge eventually so you might as well tell straight away in the hope of avoiding too great a punishment. The worst penalty was to have his crimes related to his dad, because he was quite capable of cracking legs and he was very strong so legs were left stinging for hours afterwards.

Michael was also quite keen to relate his adventure but his mother was not in the mood to listen and he was sent to his room with the threat of no tea and a possible report to his dad. 'And take off those mucky clothes,' she called up the stairs, 'put your 'jamas on.'

Michael climbed the stairs on hands and knees (his usual method) and went to his room. He took off his clothes, dropped them on the floor and climbed into bed in his pyjamas; this was the only way to be warm in his cold bedroom. He opened the book he was reading called *The Marvels and Mysteries of Science* and was immediately lost in discovering how to make a crystal wireless set. They had an ordinary set in the kitchen but he would have liked to have one that he could listen to by himself. He had heard that it was possible to hear programmes from other countries and thought how exciting it would be to listen to them. The wireless in their house was run from a big accumulator battery that needed to be charged regularly. Old Tom Threlfall who lived at the bottom of Beck Lane, came round to all the houses to collect batteries for charging and left a charged one behind. He was given sixpence for each visit and paid some of that to the shop where the charging was done. Michael was fascinated by this and wondered what electricity was and how it got into the battery. Tom said they pissed on the batteries to make them work but Michael knew this was a joke. Some adults liked to say stupid things to children, thinking it was funny and Tom was one of these. He told a fantastic tale about the headless man who walked down the railway lines in front of the trains and disappeared just as the engine was about to smash him to pieces. Michael enjoyed the stories and pretended that he believed them but really wished that Tom would explain how the electricity got into the battery instead. In some houses and at school there were electric lights but at home they had gas which smelled when the lights were lit and a new mantle had to be bought when the old one burned out. His dad was annoyed if this happened which caused further arguments when he accused Kathleen of using the light too often. Michael knew that a crystal set worked without electricity so, if he could make one loud enough, they could save the sixpence paid to Tom and maybe this would stop some of the arguing. He hated the arguing; his stomach felt heavy and he wanted to cry but held back the tears because he was learning that only softies cried and although in his heart, he thought he might actually be a softy, he wasn't going to show it to other people.

*

'Play up Town'. Thousands of voices took up the words as the club anthem echoed round the ground and rose into the bright, clear air. The players seemed to be motivated by the sound and picked up the pace of the game. Jack enjoyed the flowing, changing patterns as the teams switched the ball around. It was almost as though the men were attached in some way as they responded to the movement of the ball and their opponents. Although he supported Town, he admired the skill of both teams. As a young man he had dreamed of being down on the emerald pitch running till he was breathless under the admiring gaze of thousands of people. Some of the team had other jobs but a few simply trained or played full-time and Jack couldn't imagine a better life; how he would have loved to be out of doors running around building his muscles and his skills in the fresh air rather than stuck for endless hours in the grime of the mill, slumping home at the end of the day with his overalls covered in grease, oil and muck from the looms. For the moment though it was enough to be here; part of the spectacle, a supporter, a member of a huge group of like minded people, responding to the nuances of the contest, groaning, cheering, clapping and shouting encouragement or abuse depending on the state of the game. The supporters were like minute parts of a whole being, their individuality lost in the joint pursuit of a single goal: to win the match. The day-to-day worries of work and home, and the rules that governed individual behaviour were suspended; the crowd and the players were one and they were free to express themselves as they never would in ordinary life.

The final whistle was accompanied by a great cheer and feelings of euphoria; Town had won. Jack climbed up the steep steps of the terrace side shoulder to shoulder with his comrades, the home supporters. The early autumn wind blowing through the emptying arena made them glad to be out-of-doors and from the terraces, they could look up at green fields and trees clinging to the hillside beyond. Jack felt that he would like to walk up the hill amongst the trees and fresh blown air to try to clean off some of the smell of the weaving shed. There were no women in the crowd to break the conformity of the scene. The men were dressed in uniform dull colours and flat caps, with just the occasional coloured scarf to provide a splash of light. But today life was good; no work, a win for the team and the prospect of Sunday sleeping in the chair after dinner. He was sometimes asked to work on Saturdays, if the mill was busy, but never Sundays; everyone rested on that day. Kathleen went to chapel but Jack refused to go, he was sick of listening to the vicar telling him how to live his life; maybe the vicar should try living in their house instead of the fine, large vicarage with its big gardens and then he'd have an idea of what life was really like for most people.

Maybe he should let Kath go back to work; he might be able to persuade the foreman to get her a few looms in their shed so that he could keep an eye on her. He had to admit to himself, even if he would never say it, that he was worried she might be a target for the gigolos if she went back to weaving. He had heard some of the younger men bragging about their conquests: weaving sheds were full of single women, some of whom might be persuaded to allow the men to touch and kiss them and maybe more. Kathleen was tall and slim with long dark hair, beautiful grey eyes and a good figure; he knew that some of the men wouldn't think twice about taking advantage if they were given the opportunity. 'It's not that I don't trust Kath,' he told himself; 'It's the men I don't trust.'

Jack walked out into the main road. There were some cars and buses driving past but the fans just ignored them and spread across the highway. Most had come on bikes which were left in gardens along the roadside; the house owners charged a penny for each machine but left their wives watching out while they themselves went to the match. Pretty soon the road was filled with men, boys and bicycles; the bigger vehicles just had to go slowly to make sure no-one was injured. A boy had been knocked off his bike once and the fans had stopped the car and beaten-up the driver and his passengers. But most drivers were considerate, willing to recognise the rights of the majority.

Today the fans were in good heart; it was amazing how much better they felt when the team had won. A few started to sing the club anthem again and soon the sound grew in strength as more joined in. Jack sang and wished his son was there but Michael showed little interest in football he liked the Salvation Army band at half-time but otherwise just enjoyed running around through the forest of legs of the other spectators. He's always got his head in a book, thought Jack. He even preferred poetry to football! Perhaps he might become more enthusiastic as he got older. Still you can't have everything; he was a clever boy and could even make it to the grammar school if he continued to do well at his lessons. If they had another child, it might be another boy. He had talked to Kath about having a girl baby but she refused to accept the idea until they could afford it, which meant her going back to work in the meantime. Although they were miles apart, Jack pondered the same problems as his wife as he headed home and she sighed finishing off a job she disliked. He watched the shadows on the road made by the wheels of his bike and they seemed to revolve in his mind, mincing up the ideas and turning them over and over. He stood up and pressed hard on the pedals speeding through the crowd to spin the thoughts out into the autumn afternoon. The speed and fresh wind in his face made him feel better. He called to men he knew 'Up the Town!' They stuck their thumbs up and echoed his shout.

CHAPTER 2

*On fifteenth of March 1939, Hitler occupies the remainder of
Czechoslovakia. The policy of appeasement is not working. Chamberlaine
announces that, if Poland is attacked, the Government will feel bound to give
full support to the Polish Government. 3rd September 1939, 11:15: no reply
to Chamberlaine's ultimatum is received, 'consequently this country is now at
war with Germany'.*

School was an interesting yet frustrating place for
Michael. The biggest problem being that he could read fluently
but because hardly anyone else could, all the children used the
same beginners' books which, for him, were boring and too
simple. He was too shy to complain to the teachers about his
problem so he just went along with the rest and when asked to
read out loud, did it slowly, like the others and even threw in a
few mistakes so that he wouldn't stand out. Despite this, Michael
enjoyed being in the classroom with its high windows and
cramped desks because here he learned new facts and ideas. He
particularly liked the Bible stories that started every day and was
fascinated by some things in the classroom, such as the tadpoles
that began to develop legs and then change miraculously into tiny
frogs that could be released back into a nearby pond.

In the centre of the room was a coal-fired stove that was
supposed to heat the room, but in winter, it was inadequate and
children further away from it had to wear their coats, if they had
any. Those sitting near the stove were warm but they were also
closest to the teacher, Mr. Batson, who liked to stay by the heat.
The 'dunce' chair was also near the stove. This was used for
children who misbehaved or did poor work; they were made to
sit in it and continue with their work despite the fact that they
had no desk top and were forced to rest their writing books on
their laps. This made it very difficult for the children to copy-
write or do their sums properly and they were often given further
punishment because of their untidy hand writing. The worst

offenders were made to write on slates with chalk and since these were only usually used by the 'babies' in the nursery, it was the ultimate humiliation and resulted in merciless teasing at playtime. The desks were rigid two-seaters with heavy iron frames and wooden slopes on which to rest the books. Children from previous generations had carved their names or messages into the wood and they were covered with ink blots.

Michael usually sat next to Whacker but occasionally the teacher would move people around if he thought they were talking or wasting time. Michael dreaded having to sit next to a girl since this always resulted in playtime teasing but at least girls usually got on with their work which suited him better than some of the boys who wasted time. Tony Davis liked to trap girls' pig tails in the inkwells while they were sitting up so that when they bent down to work their hair was yanked. He was repeatedly punished for this but seemed unable to resist the temptation.

Michael's classroom was in an old chapel because the main school building wasn't big enough to house all the children who attended. The room was huge with an uneven wooden floor and a high vaulted ceiling. If the weather was wet, the children had to leave their shoes and clogs by the door and walk around in stocking feet or bare feet if they had no socks. Consequently, they sometimes got splinters which could be very painful and had to be broddled out with a needle. A narrow soil path led from the chapel to the main school and children used this to get to the playground and the dining hall. This was fine in summer but in winter the path became muddy and impassable so the children had to stay in the chapel classroom all day. On such days, their dinner was brought across from the kitchen in tin trays and the food was always cold when it arrived. A further outcome of winter weather was a deterioration in Mr. Batson's state of mind: he became morose and bad tempered, annoyed at having to be with his class all the time with no chance to talk with the other adults. This led to an increased use of the cane that hung by the blackboard and which he saw as an essential tool in his battle to maintain the type of behaviour that he required. While Michael was rarely in trouble, he could always sense when the teacher was about to lose his temper and hated to see others hurt and crying, sometimes for very small misadventures, such as when Molly O'Boyle dropped the big ink pot as she tried to fill up the wells. It did make a big mess but she hadn't dropped it on purpose – the girl wasn't really strong enough to do the job. When children were punished or the teacher shouted, it made him feel the same as when his parents argued and there were times when he felt as though he was going to throw-up.

Mr Batson was a tall, stringy man with a grey face. He always wore a suit with a jacket that had leather patches on the elbows. His dislike of children was evident and the Lucy Street gang had discussed many plots to get rid of him, but as yet, had not come up with one that was likely to succeed. The teacher had one entertaining attribute: despite sitting at his desk by the warm stove most of the time, Mr. Batson had a permanent dew-drop on the end of his nose, particularly in winter. The children were fascinated by this and as the drop grew bigger, tension filled the room as they waited for it to fall, either on to the teacher's jacket or on a pupil's work as he leaned over to make corrections. The teacher wasn't aware of his nose problem and looked round fiercely when suppressed sniggers accompanied the escape of another drop. 'Silence', he would bellow, 'that's the last time I'll say it'. Michael wondered what would follow this 'last time' but nothing ever did since the children were too scared to repeat their misdemeanors.

*

'Our Country is now at war children and there are hard times ahead until we have defeated Adolf Hitler and his armies. This morning we shall pray for our soldiers, sailors and airmen and for Great Britain in the fight to preserve our freedom.' The whole school was gathered in the school hall to listen to the assembly led by the head teacher Mr. Sykes. He was a large man with a huge, red face and hair round the edge of his head but none on top. Michael thought he looked like the fat men on the postcards that people sent from the seaside. They were usually shown with young, blond women who had large breasts and short skirts. But Michael had seen Mrs. Sykes and she was much the same shape as her husband. If the children were frightened of Mr. Batson, they were completely in awe of Mr. Sykes; he was rarely seen around the school but anyone sent to his office for misbehaviour could expect to receive several strokes from the heavy, split cane, usually on the hand, or in cases of extreme crimes, on the backside. Gunga Jones, who had thrown a stone through the school kitchen window, had a swollen right buttock for two days after his visit to 'the office'.

Mr. Sykes' voice echoed round the school hall's high ceiling. About three hundred children listened in silence while he went on to explain what the emergency procedures would be in the event of an air-raid. He said they would all receive gas masks which they would have to take with them wherever they went and that in an air attack, they would have to wear the masks while they were going to the air-raid shelter which was to be in the cellar under the chapel classroom. Several younger children started to cry; they were frightened by the things he was saying and didn't understand all his instructions. The head master realised the impact his words were having and tried to reassure them that they would be safe in school but his attempts at calming their fears came too late and the sobbing began to spread. He quickly brought the assembly to an end with '*All things bright and beautiful*' and sent the children off to their classrooms.

He forgot the prayer! Michael was surprised. At Sunday school the vicar had come in to talk to the children about prayer and how important it was. Now here was the head master forgetting what should have been a *very* important prayer for the people in the war. What would God think about that? He wondered. Would He be cross with Mr. Sykes and blast him with a bolt of lightening? Or would He decide not to look after the soldiers, sailors and airmen as revenge? It was all very puzzling;

Michael felt that he didn't understand about God and what He did. The boy was particularly worried about the Lord's Prayer because it said that you had to forgive those who trespassed against you but the men from the sewage farm had shouted that the Lucy Street gang was trespassing and yet they didn't seem likely to forgive them. Would God forgive Mr. Sykes? Was forgetting a prayer trespassing anyway? Trespassing seemed to mean different things. These puzzles occupied Michael through the first lesson of the morning which was called religious instruction. This would have been an ideal opportunity to ask Mr. Batson about prayer, but the teacher didn't take kindly to having his lesson interrupted by difficult questions, so the boy kept quiet and listened.

*

'My brother ses 'e'll go into t' navy.' At playtime, standing in a corner of the yard near to the main school building, they were talking about the war and Whacker was leading the discussion; this was appropriate since he was the best fighter. 'I wish I wer old enough to go 'cos you get to shoot rifles or cannons,' he continued. 'You can kill a lot o' Germans wi' cannon guns 'cos they fire bullet after bullet wiyout stoppin.'

'My dad ses 'e'll get called up,' said Brian, scratching his ring worm.

'I know where Germany is.' This was Gladys, who had dared to join the boys' conversation. 'We went there on 'oliday, it's near Blacksea.' Michael knew that Germany was near France and therefore nowhere near Blacksea but before he could say anything, Gladys continued: 'we saw some nasties; they've got black faces an' beards.' This was impressive information but, coming from a girl, had to be ignored.

'Let's play kick can and 'ook it,' said Whacker. That was the end of war talk for the moment but it left Michael with an uneasy feeling: if men had to go to the war, would his dad have to go? How would he get there? Would he and his mum have to go as well? It was all a big puzzle and no-one had explained it properly. Maybe Mr. Batson would have to go! This idea cheered him up immediately and then all worries disappeared as the can was kicked and he had to escape as far as possible away from the chaser.

After playtime it was physical education. Mr. Batson led his pupils out to the dirt yard at the back of the chapel building. The space was just big enough for the children to stand in four rows facing the school-room door. Round the edge was rough ground, overgrown with brambles and willow weed.

'Running on the spot – begin!' The teacher operated like a sergeant major, any child who moved before the final syllable of the instruction had to stand out by the school-room door and wait for further punishment, which usually involved running round the tiny square of ground until called back into the classroom. The children, in their bare feet, began running without moving forward; some boys had shorts and vests or ran in their underpants but most kept on their normal trousers because they had neither shorts nor underpants. Most girls did PE in their knickers and vests. Fortunately, none of the children had yet been sewn into their winter underwear; this didn't usually happen until the end of October.

'Astride jumps – begin!' Batson continued to change the children's activities but none of the movements involved getting out of line; everything took place in a regimented fashion. The final exercise had the children, with their arms outstretched, twisting their hands round and back until their shoulders ached. No-one dared groan even though the longer the activity lasted, the worse the pain became. But today they never reached the pain barrier because Gladys collapsed to the floor in a dead faint.

'Please Sir, Gladys 'as fallen down.' George Blackwood called out bravely, because you weren't supposed to speak in PE.

'Where? Get out of the way.' The teacher rushed over and picked Gladys up as though she was a bag of feathers. 'Move,' he shouted, as children gathered to get a closer look, 'move.' They scattered before him as he carried the limp body into the chapel room. Here he laid her on his desk, pushing papers and the register out of the way.

'George, fetch Mrs. Parkinson, tell her what happened.' Mrs. Parkinson was a round, grey-haired, mother-hen type of teacher. She taught the babies' class and children enjoyed being with her when they were little because she was kind and helpful and even gave you a hug when you were poorly or sad. By the time she arrived, Gladys had opened her eyes but looked very pale.

'Mebby she's pregnant,' whispered Colin Wormald, whose big sister had fainted when she was expecting.

'Nah, she's too little, she's not ad a period yet.' This was the worldly wise Molly O'Boyle, whose large, extended family discussed natural matters of birth, life and death quite openly.

'What's a period?' Michael, the searcher after knowledge couldn't resist asking.

'It's when yer bleed from down there,' Molly, pointed to her knickers.

'Down where?' Michael was baffled.

'Show yer later,' answered Molly, giving him a funny look.

'She'll have had no breakfast I expect.' Mrs. Parkinson had brought a digestive biscuit and some milk, the usual remedy for fainting, which Gladys accepted willingly, along with the warm cuddle from the teacher's ample arms.

*

Kathleen had gone up Lucy Street to see Mary, Jack's mother, to help with the cleaning. The old lady's arthritis was worse and meant that she had difficulty with some house-hold tasks such as cleaning windows and scrubbing floors. Jack's father George, Michael's Grandad, still worked as a joiner and wouldn't have helped around the house anyway. Lillian, Jack's younger sister, sometimes gave a little help with the washing and Annie, the oldest daughter occasionally made food for her parents because she lived next door. But both of them were quite happy to leave most of the housework to Kath. Mary had a way of finding things for the women to do even when the house was spotless but her daughters had long since learned to ignore the old woman's nagging, doing only what they saw as necessary. So Mary had little control over them and spent her days grumbling about her pain and thinking of jobs for Kathleen.

It was like most of the houses in the neighbourhood: two bedrooms and one living room/kitchen downstairs, with a toilet at the bottom of the backyard. All the chairs had white antimacassars which, like the lace curtains, were Mary's pride and joy and had to be kept spotlessly clean. Kathleen hated going there because the old lady was bad-tempered and very demanding. She seemed to think that she had the right to issue orders and offer no thanks because she was Jack's mother and therefore deserving of respect; a notion that Jack seemed to support whenever Kathleen complained about her treatment.

'Steps need whitenin' now,' Mary ordered. Kath hated this job because it meant kneeling on a thin piece of old carpet placed on the hard pavement outside the front of the house. She had to scrub the steps and then rub whitening on the edges. It was a crucial job because neighbours judged the quality of the housekeeping by the pristine appearance of the outside steps. Sometimes, it took only one woman to begin working on the steps for others to join in. Soon there would be a row of wiggling bottoms along the street as the women scrubbed and whitened in concert.

Michael knew that today he had to go to his grandma's house after school and arrived just as Kathleen started doing the steps. He quite liked going to the little house because Grandma sometimes gave him a penny for no reason and with this, he could buy a sherbet dip or a liquorice bootlace. He also liked the smell of the house: it was a mixture of furniture polish, old wood and tobacco. Despite a weakness in his lungs, resulting from having inhaled gas in the mud-filled trenches of Ypres during the First World War, his Grandad smoked black shag in a gnarled old pipe. He cut shavings off a plug of Negro Head tobacco with his sharp, curved pen-knife and stuffed them into his pipe with his stumpy thumb. Continuing to press the tobacco down as he lit it with a match, he would suck hard and then blow out clouds of pungent smoke. Michael couldn't take his eyes off the thumb which was short with no nail because George had sawn it off with the circular saw in the workshop; there was little feeling left in the stump so it was good for pressing-down the burning tobacco. He would sometimes push the end of the thumb into his nose to make it appear that it was up his nostril, this made Michael laugh. Kathleen thought it 'common' but sometimes laughed despite herself.

'Hello Mam.' Michael paused as he arrived at the little house. He knew that Kathleen hated scrubbing the steps and might not be in the mood to talk but he had a burning question that needed an answer: 'Mam, what's a period?'

'What? That's a funny question; it's like a bit of time - like in 'istory when people talk about the Tudor period.' Kathleen looked at her son to see if this was an appropriate answer but the blank look on his face made her think that it probably wasn't.

Still puzzled, he decided to wait for Molly's explanation. 'Oh ... thanks,' he said and stored the Tudor information away, wondering whether this had anything at all to do with girl's knickers or getting pregnant. He thought it probable that Molly would have a different answer to the one he had just received.

'I'm goin' to play out for a bit.'

'OK, I'll see you at 'ome in about 'alf an hour.' Kathleen didn't want to stay much longer at Mary's house because Annie would be bringing her parents' tea round soon and would start asking nosy questions. Why folk couldn't keep their noses out of other people's lives, Kathleen could never understand. It seemed that, once you were married into a family, they wanted to know all your business and Kath preferred to keep a level of privacy that others thought stand-offish. Her own parents had moved because her father, who was a stone mason, was able to find more work around the farming community and she really missed the mother/daughter chats that she used to have when they lived in Stanbury.

Michael walked up towards Molly's house and was immediately joined by Rags who as usual, appeared from nowhere. He gave a slight wag of the tail, allowed the boy to rub his chest and trotted on two paces in front so as to appear to be leading. Several children were playing with marbles on the pavement, including Molly, who always had to look after the younger members of her family. She looked up as Rags approached, saw Michael and smiled. Now the boy was thrown into confusion; how was he going to broach the subject of periods? He sensed that this was a private matter, since it involved knickers and he really didn't have any experience in this area. He stood, saying nothing, feeling foolish. Molly though was bright and remembered his question. 'Jus come round 'ere,' she said indicating the narrow cobbled passageway between the houses that led down to her house. 'Louisa, you stay 'ere and look after Thomas,' she instructed her sister. Michael followed obediently, accompanied by Rags. 'You ger away,' shouted Molly, aiming a kick at the dog. This was unexpected and Rags, who usually met aggression with aggression, gave a little growl but turned and ambled back into Lucy Street, trying to give the impression that this had been his intention anyway.

Michael found the resulting fifteen minute lesson extremely interesting and while he didn't fully understand the implications of the information, he felt privileged to have been trusted with such an intimate demonstration. 'Don't tell anybody I showed you,' said Molly. He promised, feeling that some kind of bond now existed between them.

*

Still two hours to go. Jack stared at the clock at the end of the weaving shed and willed it to move more quickly. It was the racket of the looms that he hated most; the constant din seemed to reverberate inside his head, dulling his senses and isolating him from the rest of the workers. Everyone seemed to operate in their own zone of silence within the cacophony, occupied by their own thoughts. He lit a Woodbine and inhaled deeply, the smoke tasted harsh in his throat, as the day went by, each cigarette seemed to be less satisfying but also offered some distraction from the grinding noise and intense fatigue that made him feel as though he could fall asleep on his feet.

'It's gone again, bloody thing . . .' Daisy Sykes mouthed at him from the wooden platform next to one of her looms. Daisy was eighteen and an experienced weaver who could manage to look after six looms. She was also a flirt and would walk along the shed with several buttons of her overall open, exposing her underskirt and a shapely knee. According to the younger lads though she was a tease: not beyond a kiss and cuddle but would go no further. 'I'm waiting for Mr. bloody Right and you're not him,' she would say, resisting their wandering hands. Jack liked Daisy, she was friendly and didn't moan at him like some of the others, but he didn't approve of her language: she swore freely and he thought this unladylike.

'What's wrong with it?' He mouthed

'Bloody shuttle's cracked,' replied Daisy. 'Just like before you bloody repaired it.'

Weavers hated to have to stop a loom because they were paid according to the amount of cloth they produced in each shift; a stationary loom meant less money at the end of the week. So the loom tuner was an important figure in the shed, the quicker he was at repairing a fault, the sooner a machine could be restarted. His work was difficult and sometimes involved clambering on top of a loom or scrambling underneath to diagnose a fault, while an impatient weaver waited to press the green start button as soon as possible. When a new part was required, a machine could be idle for days and the tuner was inevitably blamed for the delay and loss of earnings.

Jack examined the shuttle; there was a crack in the back end so the bobbin was loose and the weft had become tangled. 'It'll 'ave to be a new un, I can't repair it agen,' he shouted.

'Oh, bloody 'ell, 'ow long'll that tek?' Yelled Daisy

'Stop swearin',' he yelled back. 'I'll get one from t'stores, it'll be ready in 'alf an hour.'

'Oh, not too bad then.' Daisy smiled, she liked Jack and knew he would do his best. 'You could be my Mr. Right if you weren't such an old bugger.'

He set off for the stores which were run by Simeon Smith, a small, stocky, unhappy man who had once been a tuner. Several years ago, a steel pointed shuttle, traveling at high speed, had flown out of a loom and hit Simeon in the shoulder. The injury was so bad that his arm had to be amputated. The owners gave him a job in the stores because he was familiar with all the machinery of the looms and could order parts as replacements. But he had never gotten over his injury mainly because he was a champion darts player and his throwing arm was now missing; try as he might he couldn't recover his aim with the remaining arm so his social life and status were gone.

'Na' then,' Simeon greeted Jack.

'Na' then. New shuttle for Daisy Sykes.'

'I know what I'd like to give Daisy Sykes,' said Simeon grimly. 'Shuttle Ian.' This command shouted to a tall youth who helped in the stores. Ian did most of the fetching and carrying because Simeon couldn't climb the steps to the higher shelves and also with only one hand, couldn't manage to carry some of the heavier equipment. Jack ignored the comment about Daisy and waited while the shuttle was fetched from the bowels of the stock room. The place was lit by two dim electric bulbs that were barely sufficient to penetrate the gloom of the windowless room. Metal shelves were stacked with parts for the various machines that were used in the factory. Many were covered in layers of dust; Simeon was not inclined to clean up and Ian was too slow and shy to act without instruction from his boss. In fact, left to his own devices, Ian would have been quite happy to spend his time day-dreaming and looking at the women in his Health and Fitness magazines.

Simeon leaned on the counter; 'Another bloody war then.' He paused, inviting Jack's comment.

'Aye, it looks like it. I reckon I'll get called up – it'll be a change from this place at least.'

'You might be OK, I've 'erd that engineers might 'ave to stay be'ind to build guns an' suchlike.'

Jack thought about this for a moment. 'Not sure - they'll need engineers to keep tanks runnin', mebbe they'll call the young uns up first and older ones if it lasts. Some say it'll be ovver in no time. I might volunteer anyway at least it'll get me away from looms and weavers, and if you volunteer, you can pick whether to go into't army, t'navy or t'airforce. But if you wait to be called-up, you have to go where they tell you. Did you know there won't even be any football matches till it's done and t'only pleasure I get is watchin' t'town.'

'Aye, an' t'pay might be a bit better, these're all I can afford.' Simeon took a cigarette from a packet of Will's Woodbines in a greasy top pocket in his overalls and offered one to Jack who took it and lit both with a match struck on his thumbnail. Ian returned with the new shuttle. 'E'll get called up straight away.' The old man gestured, casually towards the tall youth, 'cannon fodder e'll be.'

Jack looked at the boy, 'ow old are you Ian?'

'Eighteen.'

Jack suddenly had an image of Ian on the front line; how would he cope with the change from the warmth and security of the mucky old stock room and the regular, repeating pattern of his life, to the uncertainty and danger of the battlefield? Jack felt cold at the thought and a shiver ran through his body.

'What's up?' Asked Simeon, noticing.

'Nowt – someone stepped over me grave.' Jack shrugged, shook his head, picked up Daisy's shuttle and walked back the weaving shed, unsettled by his thoughts.

CHAPTER 3

In one year, from 1939 to 1940, the price of food rises by 17 per cent and the price of clothes by 25 per cent. The War Office acknowledges that a private soldier's wife with children, living in an urban area with no income other than his pay and allowances, would be unable to manage.

Jack had always found it difficult to talk with his son. Although he loved Michael, their interests were so different that they had little common ground for casual conversation. Consequently, they hardly ever spoke to one another and the boy tended to address any questions he had to Kathleen. Also, Jack's early morning starts and late arrival home meant that they saw one-another only briefly. Apart from when Michael could be persuaded to go to a football match, they never went out together. Kath was worried about this situation. She believed that her son needed a positive masculine role model and was afraid that the two men in her life were in danger of drifting apart. She herself enjoyed Michael's company; like her he was intelligent and sensitive, and they had a very close relationship that they both enjoyed. When Jack had announced his plan to enlist, she was determined that he should speak to Michael about it and not leave it to her to explain to the boy why his father was about to leave them.

As usual, when he was in the house, Michael was in his bedroom, sitting on the bed reading. Completely absorbed in *Alice in Wonderland*, he was fascinated by the notion of her changes in size. He could imagine her frustration at being confronted by a tiny door, too small to get through, that led to a beautiful garden. His mind filled with a kaleidoscope of images and he was totally absorbed by her predicament. He didn't notice the rain pattering on the window but was suddenly conscious of the downstairs door slamming, signaling that Jack had arrived home from the mill. He knew the ritual of his father's homecoming: he would greet Kathleen, complain about the weavers' impatience and then strip to the waist to wash himself in the sink before sitting down to his tea, after which, he would probably listen to the wireless and fall asleep in a chair by the fireside. If Michael went into the living room, they might speak but it was more likely that the boy would just put on his pyjamas and go to bed, calling out down the stairs to say goodnight. Tonight though was different, he heard Jack's boots thumping on the stairs and then he came into the boy's room. 'Hello lad,' he said. 'I've got some news your Mam says I should tell you. It's this er… well, er… I'm goin' to join t'army.' He paused and looked into his son's eyes, trying to gauge the impact of his words.

Michael had already considered the possibility of his father joining the war but was still taken aback by the sudden, dramatic announcement. Before he could speak, Jack continued: 'I think it's my duty to go. I could stay at home but they'd call me a coward and I couldn't stand that … Do you understand what I'm saying Michael?'

Concern about Alice's dilemmas was banished by the unexpected news and questions flooded into Michael's head: 'Why are you goin'? When will you go? 'ow will you get there? Will you 'ave a gun? What do you mean *your duty*?'

'I'll be off in a few days … they'll give me a train ticket to get there … duty's when you feel that you 'ave to do something that maybe you really don't want to do.' Jack tried to answer all the questions. His father's stern face was enough to make the boy realise that this was a serious matter. 'An' when I'm away, you 'ave to look after your Mam,' he continued. 'You 'ave to be the man of the 'ouse.'

The man of the house? This was puzzling; how could he be a man when he was only seven? Would he have to wear long trousers? He wouldn't mind this because, in winter, his legs got cold and the rough fabric rubbed his thighs until they were sore. He decided another question was in order:

'Shall I 'ave long trousers then?'

'What?' Jack was baffled by the question. 'Well I suppose, you'll 'ave to ask your mam.'

Since this had not been rebuffed, Michael tried another: 'will I 'ave to work for money to pay for the bills at 'ome, an' what 'appens if the Nasties come?'

'Nasties? No, you mean Nazis, they won't come, don't worry, we'll be alright. No, no you don't have to work, how can you?' Jack answered sharply; he was beginning to feel the usual frustration of not understanding how his son's mind was working. The boy hardly noticed his father's irritation, he was too busy mulling over the answers. Here was another puzzle; Michael assumed that Nasties could have guns and would try to defend themselves so how could dad be sure that he would be alright? Maybe there was something about war that Michael didn't understand; maybe God would protect the English. He remembered the headmaster said they should pray to God to look after the brave soldiers fighting to save us from the aggressor, which he assumed was another word for Germans. Alright so that was it, how stupid were the Germans? Didn't they know that God was on our side? But then again, he had seen the newsreels at the cinema; huge never-ending ranks of German soldiers marching in their threatening goose-step style – they didn't seem as though they would be poor fighters and they had terrific looking helmets. Were the Germans Nasties? Or were we fighting two enemies? It was all very puzzling.

Jack couldn't work out what was going on in Michael's head. The questions had stopped and the boy was clearly preoccupied with his thoughts. 'You won't worry then? ….And you'll look after Mam?' He decided to try to bring the discussion to a conclusion.

'Yes dad, er…thanks dad.' The boy thought thanks were in order because he had been sort of consulted like a grown up person.

And that was it, after mulling the information over and over in his head, Michael came to appreciate that his father *was* going to war and he had some understanding of the reason why.

He talked to his mother about it and she started sobbing straight away so he knew that dad's leaving made Kathleen sad and thought that maybe he also should feel unhappy but he didn't, for one thing, life without Jack removed the threat of leg smacking and this was fine by Michael. He was puzzled by the whole thing and began to think that there was something wrong with him; that he was a bad boy because he didn't feel upset about Jack's leaving. But Whacker was the same, his brother Jake had been called up and Whacker was really pleased about it and said so. It also meant that the boys could play with Jake's motorcycle, sitting astride and making suitable noises as they roared down imaginary highways. So, all-in-all, apart from the fact that they were sometimes hungry and couldn't get sweets, war-time for the Lucy Street gang, at least in the beginning, was not too bad.

*

'Why did 'e volunteer?' Mary scowled at Kathleen. ''E didn't 'ave to go, engineers don't 'ave to go.'

'I think 'e went because 'e was sick o' t'mill,' Kath replied. She knew that his mother blamed her for Jack's absence but she hadn't wanted him to go; she had pleaded with him to stay in his reserved occupation. But he said that he would be ashamed of walking the street in his overalls when young lads like Ian from the stores would be seen in their uniforms if they were home on leave.

'Look, I'm goin' to do my bit and that's final.' Those were his last words on the subject and now she didn't know where he was; his few letters were censored and he hadn't been home on leave for several months. On top of this, the money he sent home amounted to only just over a pound a week and the grant Kathleen could claim wasn't sufficient to make up to what he had earned before the war. The price of food and clothing was going up and this along with the weekly rent for the house meant that she could barely make ends meet. Working for the demanding Mary was the last thing she wanted to do, Kathleen was seriously considering finding work and not telling Jack until she had to.

Along with the shortage of money, she missed his company. Although they never talked a lot, he was an essential element in the cycle of her life. The pattern of her days revolved around people: Jack, Michael and Mary with the occasional interruption from a neighbour or friend. These folk were the signposts of her existence, the milestones around which she ordered her day-to-day activities. Now she didn't need to get up so early to make her husband's snap, after feeding Michael and herself at tea-time, there was no other meal to make. At night, the cold, damp bed stayed cold longer; she missed the warmth of his body, the regular rhythm of his breathing and even the occasional grunted snore.

Despite all this, Kathleen was secretly proud of her husband; he had made a brave decision to change his life because of something he believed in. Strangely, she didn't expect him to get killed – that was left outside her thinking – an unacceptable possibility, an idea too frightening to even consider. She decided that it was just a case of holding on and keeping calm until the war was over and then maybe they could start again and make a better life. Some folk were still saying that there wasn't going to be a war, nothing much had happened so far, except for shortages and rationing, and people seemed to be able to get things anyway. Mrs. Darnbrook, who owned the little grocery shop across the road from Kath's house, sometimes let her have an extra jar of jam and Mr. Fletcher would give an extra rasher of bacon with her meat ration but she didn't like the way he touched her fingers under the paper parcel as he passed it over; it might be nothing but she knew some women were offering more than pennies for a few lamb chops.

The worst part of Jack's absence was the effect on his mother. Mary became increasingly demanding of Kathleen's time, wanting the house cleaned more often and finding an increasing number of other tasks that ostensibly resulted from her inability to move freely because of her arthritis. She would even, some days, stay in bed, saying that she was too stiff to get up, which meant that the commode near her bed had to be carried round to the lavatory to be emptied. Her bad temper got worse and affected everybody, including Michael's grandad, who spent most of his evenings at the pub to keep out of the way. Kath knew the old lady missed Jack, since she had always made it clear that he was her favourite. His reluctance to write letters made the situation worse and came to a head when Mary accused Kath of keeping his letters to herself.

'You've always 'ated me an' now you've driven Jack into t' army with your naggin'. I know you wouldn't 'ave another baby either – Jack told me, an' 'e wanted one. Where's 'is letters, that's what I want to know? You're keepin' 'em to yourself I bet, you're nowt but a schemer 'iding 'em from me and me wi' all mi pain.'

Kathleen was shocked, she felt as though the old woman had struck her across the face. She was not really surprised that Jack had talked to his mother about the baby but she was still upset by this evidence of his disloyalty. Maybe she was a nag, perhaps she was wrong about the baby but the thought of struggling to raise another child in their tiny house on the money that came in was just too daunting. Yet she couldn't shake the feelings of guilt, particularly as she saw the hate in Mary's eyes – they had never really got on but this was something new – how could she pour out this bile on someone who helped her more than her own daughters. Am I in the wrong here she wondered, are the old woman's feelings justified?

'He hasn't written,' was all she could blurt out.

'You're a bloody liar,' Mary was almost screaming. 'I wish 'e were 'ere so I could tell 'im 'ow you're treatin' me … where you goin' you aven't finished cleanin' yet.'

The walls of the room seemed to close in, Kath felt trapped and her eyes began to fill with tears, 'I'm sorry, I 'ave to go,' was all she could say as she stumbled to the door and out into the street. She felt desperate, betrayed by her husband and hated by the woman in whose company she spent most of her time. Kathleen was a religious woman and knew that she should be satisfied with her lot and respect her mother-in-law. It was her duty to look after the old woman but why should she have to be made to feel guilty when she was doing her best and getting no consideration from another person. Only Michael was a comfort but he was too young to really understand what was going on and it wasn't fair to worry him with her troubles.

*

For months, nothing much seemed to happen, people called it the 'phony war'. Life for the children in school continued much the same; neither Mr. Batson nor the headmaster was young enough to be called-up, much to the disappointment of the gang. Michael and Molly O'Boyle had been moved into standard three even though they were younger than the others in the class, who were eight or nine. The head had decided that since they could both read, write and add up they would be able to cope with the work in the higher class and in any case, it made the numbers even with forty-five in each group. His new teacher was Mrs. Stamp, who kept making the same joke about stamping hard on pupils who misbehaved and then laughing as though it was a new joke every time. But here at least there were some interesting books to read so his 'quiet reading' time, which happened every morning in Mrs. Stamp's class, was more stimulating than re-reading the beginners' books in the old chapel. Also, the new classroom had windows that let in more light, smoother flooring and didn't smell of ancient dust and mouse droppings.

Every week the children had air-raid practice which at least provided a break from the daily routine of school work. When the head master rung a hand bell as he walked round the school, everyone stood to attention by their desks and put on their gas masks. They were then marched out of the main school and down to the old chapel which had cellars big enough to accommodate all the children and adults in the school. The masks were heavy and uncomfortable and as they walked, the children's breath caused the eye pieces to mist up so they couldn't see where they were going and often bumped into one another, much to the annoyance of the teachers. Michael disliked the rubbery smell of the mask but enjoyed the weird spectacle of lines of children with the strange monkey-face attachments on their heads.

Mrs Stamp was tall and thin and as she passed by a faint odour of mothballs mingled with sweat followed her. Her favourite punishment was to pull the ears of children that she judged to be naughty or lazy. Most of Michael's friends were still in standard two so he could only see them at playtime and after school. His new classmates were mostly friendly but the exception was Howard, a tough boy, tall for his age, with long, bony legs and arms. He was a member of the long estate gang and said that he would have to fight Michael to prove to the others he was still cock of the class. Michael had had a few scuffles with members of the gang in the past but wasn't a renowned fighter and didn't anticipate victory against an older and bigger opponent. Nevertheless he knew that as a member of the Lucy Street gang, it was unthinkable to back-down. He sought advice from Whacker: 'Don't be scared of 'ittin' 'im in t' face,' was his advice. 'Some folk don't hit in t' face but that's what hurts most, 'oward won't like it.'

The fight was organised for after school on Wednesday, the place - the back yard of the chapel when the caretaker had left to go to the main school building. A small crowd gathered. Michael looked around feeling very nervous but determined to do his best although he knew that Howard was bigger, stronger and older, and was expected to win. He saw Molly's eyes looking at him. Since her intimate explanation of female periods, they had developed a relationship, founded on Michael's respect for her better understanding of sexual matters; he also liked her dark hair and pretty freckled face. Maybe she was his girlfriend but nothing had been said although her presence here suggested some interest, or it might just be that she wanted to watch the fight, after all there were children here who Michael didn't really know. Nevertheless, he felt pleased that she was there but worried that he might look foolish if he was beaten too easily.

Howard stood at the other side of the small circle, laughing with his friends: boys from standard three who regarded him as their leader and the cock of the class. To Michael, he seemed to increase in size and looked very confident. Whacker, Ernest and Brian stood with their friend. 'Where's thi 'ankerchief?' Asked Ernest.

'What for?' Said Michael.

'To hold on thi nose if it bleeds.'

'I 'aven't got one.'

'Well I suppose tha can use mine,' said Ernest reluctantly.

'He'll not need one,' said Whacker. 'E's goin' to win'.

Michael was grateful for his friend's loyalty but confidence seeped out of him at the thought of spilling his blood in the dusty backyard. He was feeling sick. Was this how his father felt when facing the Germans? But they could kill one another so it must be much worse. Still there was no way out, he clenched his fists and made sure the thumbs were outside the fingers, as Whacker had instructed and stepped forward, arms up in the classic boxer's pose as seen on the newsreels. Howard seemed taken aback by this bold move, suddenly this small compact figure seemed more of a challenge than he had been expecting. He moved sideways, adopting a similar stance. The boys circled one another warily, each reluctant to throw the first punch.

'Go on hit 'im, my tea's ready.' This from one of Howard's supporters caused a general laugh but Whacker marked him for later retribution. The shout did though seem to galvanize the combatants; they moved closer together and made threatening feints. Then Howard, with his eyes shut threw a punch. His longer reach paid off and the blow landed in the middle of Michael's chest, forcing the wind out of his lungs. He gasped for air and allowed his arms to drop, Howard moved in to finish the fight quickly, but reckoned without Whacker's prefight training, Michael, though hurt, remembered the advice and flung a desperate fist towards the approaching face, landing it right on the point of a bony nose. Blood spurted instantly and Howard backed off, giving a yelp of pain and holding his hand to his face with tears filling his eyes. The boys moved apart, one gulping air and holding his sides, the other trying to clear his vision from the mixture of blood and tears. In his breathless state Michael saw the damage he had caused, hoping that the drawing of blood might be regarded as a victory and the fight be deemed finished but Howard was a brave and experienced fighter, he wiped his face with a grubby handkerchief and marched forward, 'I'm not finished yet,' he growled, striking Michael a hard blow on his left ear followed by another to his stomach. He sagged to the ground, his breath completely gone and his head ringing. Howard's superior strength and size now told and the fight was soon over, with Ernest, Whacker and Brian entering the circle to surround their friend and prevent further damage.

The crowd moved off, with Howard's friends slapping him on the back as they walked away. But he paused and went over to Michael, 'You caught me a good 'un, young 'un,' he said, pointing to his damaged nose, 'fair fight 'eh?'

'Yes, sure.' Michael, despite the pain in his head and chest, offered his hand to his opponent, feeling a strange sort of affection for the big bony boy with the blood spattered handkerchief, 'fair fight.'

The Lucy Street gang wandered off to their homes, with their arms round each other's shoulders. 'Next time, try kickin' 'im in the goolies,' suggested Brian. But Michael wasn't sure that he wanted a next time, he was more concerned as to how he would explain his disheveled appearance and dirty clothes to his mother. Some of Howard's blood had splashed on to his shirt. Another thought bothered him; he couldn't shake the image of his father facing a German soldier, like he had faced Howard. Would they shoot at one another or use bayonets? What if the German was bigger and stronger and a better shot? Might Dad lose the fight? Perhaps he could die after all. This was frightening; his own combat had brought home to the boy something of the reality of his father's situation. Suddenly, for the first time he missed his dad and was worried about what would happen to him and his mother if Jack didn't return.

He didn't say anything to Kathleen when he got home because she immediately questioned him about his appearance: ''ow come you're so mucky? I've spent all day at you grandma's cleaning after 'er and listening to 'er complaining about your dad joining the army and now I 'ave to clean you and wash your clothes. I'm just so fed up.'

Michael could see that his mother's eyes were red; she had obviously been crying. He thought maybe she was scared like him that Jack wouldn't return from the war. He felt the rising nausea that he experienced when people around him were anxious or angry and found it impossible to make any answer to his mother's outburst. Kath sat in front of the fire, held her head in her hands and began to sob. This made the boy feel even worse; he was used to his mother comforting him if he was sad or hurt, but wasn't sure how it could work in reverse. The small room darkened and suddenly seemed a frightening place. What was he expected to do? Michael didn't feel able to take charge in a time of trouble. This point marked the beginning of a change in the boy's attitude to his father's absence: he missed the reassuring presence of someone who could handle the day-to-day problems of family life. But he did remember Jack's words, 'You'll look after Mam?' So this was it, now he had to look after his mother. What would dad do? He thought, trying to remember how Jack acted when Kathleen was upset. He recalled the time when her parents left to live in the country and Jack had tried to reassure her that everything would be alright. Michael walked across to his mother's chair and sat on the padded arm beside her, putting his arm round her shoulders. Kath continued to sob but leaned towards her son, comforted by his touch.

'You're a good boy Michael, I'm not really cross with you, it's just that things seem to be goin' wrong, your dad leavin', Mary shoutin' at me and no money.' At this point Kath realised she was in danger of pouring out her troubles on the shoulders of a small boy who she should be looking after. 'But never mind love,' she suddenly smiled through her tear streaked face. 'We'll manage, we'll be alright, don't worry.' She pulled Michael on to her knee and squeezed him tightly till he could hardly breathe.

'Mam, you're breakin' me ribs,' he squealed.

'Sorry love, let's see what we've got for tea.'

His mother stood up and began searching for something to eat in the cupboard above the sink. Michael was amazed by his success; just his hand on her shoulders had made his mother feel better and returned her to her normal self. The small, frightening room was immediately changed, the light through the window seemed brighter and he was suddenly conscious of the cheerful sound of passing people and traffic.

'It'll 'ave to be drip and bread,' Kath smiled from the corner, 'is that OK?'

'Yes Mam, that'll be nice.' Michael would have been happy with anything; now that the gloom had lifted he had a feeling of euphoria, even the painful bruises from Howard's fists seemed to hurt less. He helped to put the cloth on the little table by the window and when it was ready, enjoyed sinking his teeth into the bread covered in the fat from the small beef joint that Kath had been able to get from Mr. Fletcher with their saved up coupons. As usual, Michael had a book nearby; it was a small book that his mother had given him for his birthday, much to his father's dismay, because it was full of *poems* by a man called Robert Louis Stephenson. Michael liked the look of it because it had raised bands on the spine and pages that were roughly cut and uneven on the edges. He enjoyed the way that words were used to create feelings as well as images. The poem was about country life:

'Through all the pleasant meadow-side
The grass grew shoulder high,
Till the shining scythes went far and wide
And cut it down to dry.'*

He had never seen grass that grew shoulder high and didn't know what a scythe was but he liked the rhythm of the words. The poem put pictures in his mind of a landscape made up of large fields with long grass that a boy might hide in from the Germans. It would be better than the old chapel cellar which was dusty and dark and felt more like a place to die than a safe haven from the Nasties' bombs.

CHAPTER 4

Air attacks on mainland Britain increase through 1940, causing considerable damage to docks, industry and transport systems. Civilian deaths are inevitable; over 1000 people are killed in August 1940. The number of casualties continues to grow throughout the year.

After the 'phony war' it seemed now that the air-raid siren went off almost every evening. Kathleen and Michael were lucky, although their little house was cramped, it did have a cellar so they didn't have to rush to the chapel like other people. Mary refused to go out of her house, saying that she would rather die under her own roof than piled up with lots of strangers. Michael's grandfather, who was a constant target for his wife's nagging, preferred to walk out in the open air smoking his pipe and watching the bombers overhead when they were illuminated by the searchlights. The noise they made was either a constant, threatening drone or sometimes a slowly, vibrating beat. He heard explosions from the anti-aircraft guns but it was only rarely that they succeeded in hitting the enemy planes. The whistling of the bombs made him shudder and duck his head, waiting for the flash and crump as they hit. 'Bastards', he muttered, bunching his fists in impotent fury. On one occasion his teeth were so tightly clenched that he bit straight through the stem of his favourite pipe.

Michael and Kathleen sat on the cellar steps. They could hear the noise of the planes and the eerie sound of the bombs falling. Kath, particularly was filled with anxiety until wail of the all-clear siren started. The cellar had no gas light so they had to use candles and huddle round an old paraffin heater that gave off very little warmth. They knew there was a danger of fire if the heater was knocked over but with only the two of them there, they believed that they could be careful enough to avoid such an accident. The town was not near the docks but some of the local factories had been equipped to make armaments and it seemed that the German bombers were targeting the area around Stanbury. In any case, the bombing raids were not always accurate in striking targets of military significance; a bomb had landed in the Long Estate, destroying two houses and damaging several nearby. Luckily the occupants were in the air-raid shelter at the time but several families were now homeless and having to claim from the National Assistance Office to get the wherewithal to manage their lives. It seemed that any area could be a target if it had buildings that could be taken for factories. Most people tried to keep their house lights blacked out but occasional chinks were inevitable and would betray the whereabouts of towns and cities. These provided sufficient evidence for panicky enemy air crew who wanted to get rid of their payload and return to their home base.

Kath looked at her son, his head as usual bent over a book. He squinted in the poor light from the candles and pulled his thin coat round himself to try to keep out the bone-numbing chill of the cellar. She felt an anger rising, this was no way for a young life to begin. Although the boy didn't complain or appear to be frightened, she knew that he was beginning to worry about his dad and she herself was not setting a good example of positive thinking. Added to this, he wasn't getting proper food, his clothes couldn't stand many more repairs, his socks were more darn than original wool and sitting behind blackout curtains waiting for the relief of the siren was no way to spend an evening. We need to get away from this, she thought. The germ of an idea began to form: we don't have to stay near the mill now that Jack's work is with the army. In the last letter from her mother, the old lady had complained that she never saw her grandchild, indeed she didn't even know what he looked like. Kath knew that children from some of the big cities that were particular bombing targets had been evacuated to country places. Perhaps they could evacuate themselves. They would save money on the rent and Michael would be living in a safer environment, plus she would be away from the complaints of her mother-in-law. They wouldn't have a house of their own but when Jack returned they could start again. The idea excited her but she knew there would be problems; not least that Michael might not want to leave his home and his friends.

*

Jack had a love/hate relationship with the desert. It was so different from anything he had ever experienced. The endless sand and blistering daytime heat made anything approaching normal life impossible. The sand got everywhere; in the soldiers' clothes, hair and worst of all, in their food. Meals were not particularly appetising but to grind grains of sand with every mouthful made matters much worse. There was no such thing as a cold drink; water was warm and tasted of the desert. During the daytime the men sweated profusely, their uniforms sticking to them, creating sores on their thighs and producing blistered feet. He often thought about his home town and the family, and cursed himself, wishing he had resisted the pull of the war and his conscience, while still admitting inwardly that he could not have remained at home to leave others to do the fighting.

At night-time, by contrast, he shivered as the temperature dropped to somewhere around freezing. There was some compensation: he was astonished by the number and brilliance of the stars, he had never realised how beautiful the night sky could be and had never before seen anything like the meteor storms that occurred in the autumn of 1940. All the men marveled at the streaks of light that hurtled across the black canvas sky; amazed that none of them seemed to reach the desert floor.

Because of his engineering background, Jack had enlisted as a member of the Royal Army Ordinance Corps and ended up servicing the tanks that were always breaking down, sometimes because they were hit by enemy artillery or aircraft attack and sometimes because the desert took its own toll on machines that were badly prepared for sand storms and baking temperatures. It was heavy, tiring work and he cursed the machines of war in the same way he had raged against the looms. He was given responsibility for recovering damaged tanks. He and another soldier, called Alec Grady, a motor engineer in civvy street, drove a vehicle that consisted of a cab with a trailer. It had tracks that could be lowered in front of a stricken tank so as to form a ramp up which a powerful winch would draw a tow-chain to pull the tank on to the trailer. Broken machines were then transported back to base where they could receive attention. The two men with their recovery vehicle moved with the tanks so that they could be nearby if anything went wrong. An immobilised tank was a sitting duck for enemy artillery and carrying out running repairs was dangerous work, made more difficult because of the lack of spare parts, so the repair base was usually established behind the front line to offer a degree of protection.

During the day the desert heat made any form of physical effort almost unbearable and removing broken parts of machines that were clogged with sand was arduous and energy sapping. Jack surprised himself by the strings of expletives that he regularly directed at inanimate objects. But the most disturbing part of their job occurred when any members of the tank crew were killed: Jack and Alec had to get the bodies out and bury them. The company chaplain tried to attend if possible but in desert war there was little time for ceremony and although they left markers to show where men were buried, they knew that the shifting sands could easily obliterate the sites within days if not hours. At first, Jack was horrified by the damaged state of some of the bodies. He regularly had to throw-up before he could begin to care for the dead in as civilised a way as possible in the context of constant danger. As time went by, they both learned to handle the harrowing nature of the work but Jack never lost his awareness of the reality of their situation: that they were dealing with human beings, who even though lifeless, were worthy of respect and care. Neither of them wished to become hardened to death, even though it was all around them. Jack couldn't believe how loss of life and maiming injuries had become a constant feature of his existence. Broken machines he could manage but he would never be able to accept broken bodies as an everyday matter.

Despite the haste with which they had to act, both men could not help but study the corpses. In them, they recognised the reality of their situation; images of their own fate. In the first weeks after joining the army, everyone operated under the illusion that they could look after themselves; act with caution, follow orders and they would eventually return home unscathed. Confronted by death almost daily, they were forced to recognise that they could be next. It was an inescapable fact that the men that needed burying were ordinary soldiers, nothing special about them just day-to-day blokes, exactly like Jack and Alec, who had probably imagined that they too were immune, invulnerable. Now they were gone, or were they? Jack wondered about the men's souls, the thing the vicar was always on about. Where were they? Did they leave the bodies and rise up to heaven? Were they in the drifting smoke that rose up to the burning desert sky? The two friends couldn't help but study the faces of the corpses to see if there was a clue, an indication of how it felt to be no more. What they found was a strangely peaceful expression on those that had enough face left to recognise. In a curious way this was comforting: the fight was over, nothing to worry about anymore, the struggle to survive had been lost. If these ordinary men could go through it, then there was really nothing to fear. In the light of day, they thought if it happens it happens. At night though, it was different, the dead came alive and in their shattered states marched through their dreams. Despite the cold nights both of them would often wake up with their bodies soaked in sweat.

*

The men knew that, having halted the Italian forces at Sidi Barrani, their next objective would be to advance towards Tobruk. Casualties had been heavy recently; many dead and even more wounded; some seriously. In some ways Jack pitied the wounded more than the dead. He had seen soldiers damaged so badly that he doubted that they would live anything like a normal life in the future. Their only gain was to be taken away from the front line, sometimes back to Blighty. One of the chief topics of conversation was what they would do when the war was over. While they felt great sympathy for the dead and wounded, they tried to shut out the thought that something similar might happen to them, otherwise they would probably have gone mad with fear and anxiety. Indeed this did happen to several of their comrades who simply could not cope with the reality of war; it was not unusual for a deranged man to try to run away into the desert, even though there was nowhere to hide. To an outsider the men's apparent acceptance of death would have seemed callous but they knew that life had to continue in a manner that passed for normal; eating, drinking, playing cards, using the rudimentary showers to ease their stink, all the day-to-day habits that were now integral to their lives. It was important to maintain some pattern to existence otherwise they could loose the daily rhythm that kept them sane. One thing became clear to Jack: you should never get close to anyone because tomorrow they might be dead and the human spirit could take only so much grief. Even so, despite his best intentions, he and Alec became friends. They worked so closely together that they couldn't help but share the occasional humour and regular sadness of their tasks which inevitably drew them into a close relationship.

Despite the challenging and difficult work he did during the daytime, Jack was also required to do guard duty in the desert night. Sometimes there were no enemy bombardments and the desert returned to its normal state of empty desolation. In these moments he was happy to stand guard. He had to stay alert and watch for moving shadows amongst the dunes or in the camel grass. But he could also enjoy the solitude and allow his thoughts to wander back home.

On one night the desert was eerily still. He gazed in wonder again at the aching beauty of the stars. There seemed to be a wide swathe of creamy light from horizon to horizon with millions of brighter stars held in its mesh which was so fine as to appear like a vapour, yet strong enough to support a myriad of heavenly bodies. The quietness was all-embracing; he was deafened by it and almost stopped breathing so as not to shatter its intensity. He tried to think of the words he would use when he returned home so that Kath and Michael might appreciate what he had seen. He determined to tell them about the beauty but not the other things, the other side of his life was too unspeakable and he would have to keep it within himself. He thought how different this place was from Stanbury with its narrow, dirty cobbled streets and ominous mills. He had known that deserts existed but had never appreciated their reality and the enormous contrast with the place he knew as home.

Wandering thoughts brought back his previous life; images of the mill, the football matches and his family, it all seemed from another, distant time. He had never realised how much he would miss Kathleen. He had felt like her that their marriage was not what he had expected but now he longed to see her. His mind was drawn to their wedding day: he remembered how she smiled at him, her long dark hair falling around her shoulders. He regretted the arguments they had had, he felt guilt at his intolerance of her ideas. She was right; they couldn't afford to bring up another child in that house. He mused that maybe, when the war was over, things would be better and he would be able to find a better-paid job, then they could have a little girl. Surely people would be proud of the returning soldiers for the job they had done and would seek to reward them. He determined to be kinder to Kathleen and more patient with Michael; he knew he didn't communicate well with the boy. I'll be more tolerant and take an interest in his reading, he thought. Maybe they might be able to afford a little car and go out places. He pictured the scene; a family traveling to the coast in a Morris 8, chatting and laughing together…

The shell detonated about twenty yards away and blew Jack straight off his feet. He rolled down the dune, his mouth full of sand, his ears deafened and all thoughts of home driven from his mind. His duty now was to raise the alarm and alert his comrades. He started shouting but couldn't hear his own words. In any case, all the men had been blasted into wakefulness, some kept their heads down in their foxholes, while others manned the guns. The beauty and silence of the desert night was shattered; light from exploding shells and firing artillery revealed the silhouettes of soldiers, tents, tanks and guns that had been invisible in the darkness. In the flashes of intense light, movements were frozen in time like terrifying photographs. Even amidst the noise and chaos Jack had time to rage at the stupidity of men who brought death and destruction to this exquisite, pristine wilderness.

*

September 1940

Dearest Kath,

Thanks for your letter and the cake. It was a bit bashed about when it got here but tasted great. I know you used your ration coupons to get the stuff to make it. Please use them for you and Michael instead. We're OK here for food. I can't tell you where we are they'd only censor it. I don't know when I'll see you again but don't worry, I'm not in danger. Mum has written, she sounds poorly and says could you help her a bit more. She's an old woman and she says her arthritis is playing up. Annie and Lillian don't seem to help her as much as they should – I've written to them. You've only got yourself and Michael. Can you find time to call in and help her more often? I know you'll do your best. Tell Michael I'm OK, I'll try to bring him a present when I come home – when this is over. Hope it's soon! There are some good blokes here, some from near us. How are you yourself? I think about you a lot. Don't forget about me will you? Look after yourself and keep writing – it means a lot.

All my love,
Jack XXXXX

The coal wagon arrived. Michael was fascinated by the coal men but a bit frightened of them. He thought they looked like the demons from one the library's fantasy books. The men were unrecognisable, even though they lived nearby. Their faces were black with only the whiteness of their eyes and the redness of their mouths showing through. They wore leather helmets with wide collars that covered the men's shoulders and their upper backs to protect them from the harsh material of the coal sacks. Their steel-capped, hob-nailed boots clunked and scraped on the pavement. The coal wagon was pulled by an old white horse which stood patiently, chewing on the contents of its nosebag and holding the cart still while the men lifted off the great, heavy sacks of coal. Then bent almost double, they staggered towards Michael's house and dropped the sack so that the open top connected unerringly with the mouth of the coal chute. Clouds of dust filled the air, particularly when the men shook the sack to get the last bits of coal out.

Coal was expensive and hard to come by – a lot of young men who might have gone down the mines went into the forces so there weren't enough miners to do the digging and most of the coal that came out went to the factories that were doing essential war work. So the arrival of the coal men was an event that brought out the neighbourhood. Women stood on their doorsteps or in little groups. They mostly wore their wrap-around aprons and stood with their arms folded swapping news and making sure that they received their share of the black gold. Michael listened when the women called out to the men, surprised that they could recognise the coal-covered demons.

'Steady Fred, don't break yer back, Alice'll need yer tonight.' This produced some laughter.

''E can come an' exercise it 'ere if 'e wants.' This produced shrieks.

'Oh Ada, I'll tell your Tom when 'e gets back.'

Kath went inside; satisfied that she had enough coal to keep going. She didn't think she was a prude and knew that the comments were meant to be lighthearted but disliked the way that some of the women talked to the coal men. There were children about and she thought it was wrong to use lewd talk in front of them. Also, despite the seemingly casual nature of the banter, there was a more serious side: Kath knew that a few women were involved with other men while their husbands served abroad. It was likely that these relationships resulted from loneliness and fear of being left alone after the war but she'd made a wedding promise to Jack and believed that nothing on earth would make her break her word.

Michael stayed outside because Whacker had just arrived. He knew one of the coal men and had asked if they could have a ride on the cart. Since this was the last delivery for the day, the men were taking the cart down to the station yard where the horse was stabled and where they collected the coal each day from the train that chugged into the little station most mornings. They agreed to let the boys ride with them down there but said they would have to find their own way back. The two friends climbed on the cart using the huge wooden wheel hub to help them. They sat on the empty sacks which immediately deposited coal dust on their trousers and bare legs. Rags, having observed proceedings from a safe distance, didn't want to be left out of the adventure and having given a token bark at the horse, who was an old friend, jumped up and stood feet astride lolling his tongue and grinning at the boys. The wooden chocks that stopped the cart from rolling down the hill were removed and the old horse responded to the click from the driver's tongue and began to clop slowly down the cobbled street. The men sat up front on the springy seat and smoked woodbines, ignoring the boys who waved at passers by, some of whom waved back, but who mostly took little notice of small, mucky boys riding the coal cart.

The late Indian summer day was fine and the air warm despite a breeze that whisked dust of the cart. As the hill got steeper down towards the town, the horse's hooves began to slip and the driver reined him in, to slow the cart to less than walking pace. The boys enjoyed the bouncy motion of the ride and waved their arms and pulled faces at each other in rhythm to the cart's wheels chattering on the cobble stones. Rags, more alarmed, walked to the edge of the cart and peered over, contemplating an escape route if things got too bumpy.

The horse turned into the station yard without prompting and stopped outside its stable. The men began undoing the harness. Michael, Whacker and Rags jumped down and wandered across to the station entrance to see Colin, an old friend of theirs. He worked as porter, part-time signal man and general factotum, and because he usually worked alone, was pleased to have the company of the boys who sometimes helped him with sweeping out the carriages that were left in sidings off the main tracks. The only other people who worked in the station were the station master, Mr. Ackroyd and Laura Entwhistle, who worked in the ticket office. Ackroyd was a lazy, miserable man, who apart from having the station keys for opening in the morning and locking up when the last train had passed through, did as little as possible, spending most of his time in his tiny cramped office, emerging to shout 'mind the doors,' blow his whistle and wave the flag.

The boys found the station exciting and loved to stand on the road bridge over the rail-track as the trains blasted through, sending clouds of smoke and steam billowing into their faces. They were occasionally allowed into the cab of the shunter that moved the spare carriages around the sidings when they were clean and ready to go back to use. Whacker went on passenger trains for the family's yearly holiday to Blacksea but since the war had started, even these trips had ended due to lack of funds. Michael had been once to the seaside. His only other trip was when he had gone with Jack to see the dog races on Bealby Moor.

Today, Colin's job was to walk along the line to the next station, filling up the paraffin lamps that illuminated the colours of the signals during darkness. 'Tha can cum if tha wants but it'll be a long walk there an' back an' tha'll likely miss tha tea.' He was smiling as he spoke, hoping the boys would go with him, because they could climb the ladders to the lamps more easily than he could. Colin had a game leg, resulting from getting it trapped under a carriage wheel, so he couldn't have been called-up even if he hadn't been in a reserved occupation. It did mean though that he found climbing difficult and walked with a permanent limp that the boys loved to mimic when he wasn't watching. He also smoked heavily and sometimes could be persuaded to give them a puff of his cigarette. As a result, his fingers were stained yellow and his voice was deep and gruff, which made him more interesting to listen to when he told stories of the railway.

The trio set off alongside the line towards Hexton, the next town with a station. The boys walked behind Colin and Rags bounced around, sometimes in front, sometimes behind, foraging on both sides of the line, chasing imaginary quarry and sniffing out the range of interesting aromas in the undergrowth alongside the railway. A hysterical blackbird burst out of the bushes with a barking Rags crashing in pursuit.

'Your mutt should be on a lead,' Colin grumbled.

'E's not ours,' said Whacker

'We don't know oo 'e belongs to,' continued Michael. ''E just comes with us but 'e's in our gang an' we like 'im. Somebody told me 'e belongs to Tom who does the wireless batteries but we don't know if it's true.'

Rags, hearing this fell in behind his friends, just to show that he could behave well, but soon returned to his usual undisciplined approach when they reached the first signal. Michael volunteered to climb the steep metal ladder, carrying the little pot of paraffin with which to fill the reservoir. The metal rungs of the ladder were beginning to rust in places and his hands felt some of the black paint bubbles rubbing off so that his fingers were stained by the red, powdered rust. He poured the paraffin into the lamp and then lit the wick and closed the tiny window. Pausing to take in the view, Michael could see as far back as the little station and down the line to the Hexton tunnel. He could also hear Rags who was not happy to see his friend so high up and barked incessantly until the boy reached the ground.

They continued doing their work until they reached the tunnel. This was about five hundred yards long and consequently, very dark. The summery day was dying and the cutting that led to the tunnel had steep sides which increased the onset of the evening gloom. There was one more signal to deal with before the station so they had to go through the tunnel which was pitch black as soon as they had walked in about ten yards. Colin lit his lamp with its large convex glass lens. It was bright enough to pick out the contours of the tunnel and the shining metal of the lines receding into the darkness. Despite the lamp, they had to walk carefully because the stones supporting the sleepers were roughly piled and sloped steeply near the tunnel edge. The group moved closer together for mutual comfort as the darkness closed around them and the drip of distant water created a mysterious atmosphere that sent a chill down Michael's back. 'Let's sing our new song,' he suggested and the boys began their garbled rendition of La Marseilles.

As they sang the boys became aware of a tuneless accompaniment; 'what's that?' Michael wondered.

'Bloody hell - air raid warning,' Colin sounded worried. 'We haven't got our gas masks.' He knew that he was supposed to carry his around with him, it was in the regulations, but he hardly ever bothered since he had never heard of anyone being gassed.

'We'll be alright in 'ere though,' Whacker suggested. 'It's a bloody good air raid shelter is this.'

'I ought to get you to the proper shelter though, we shouldn't stay down 'ere.'

'It's too far,' said Whacker. 'By the time we get there we could get bombed.'

'Yes, an' we 'aven't done the last signal yet,' Michael joined in. He was keen to stay in the dark tunnel because it seemed more adventurous.

'Alright, but we're staying in the tunnel till the all clear.' Colin could see the sense of what the boys were saying but he still felt uneasy – he was responsible for bringing them down here when he shouldn't really have done it and if anything went wrong, he would be to blame and Mr. Ackroyd would be furious. Still, there was nothing to be done now, just hope that nothing disastrous would happen.

The trio settled themselves with their backs against the curved wall of the tunnel and listened for the drone of the enemy aircraft that might or might not happen. There had been lots of air-raid warnings when the all-clear had eventually gone off without anything happening in between. Colin lit a Woodbine, its point glowed in the dark, the smoke drifted upwards and then, plucked by the air stream in the tunnel, headed back the way they had just walked.

Rags, who thought the tunnel might contain rats, his favourite prey, came snuffling out of the darkness, wondering why they were sitting down. He walked to Michael, putting his head on one side, which was the only way he knew to ask a question. 'We're jus' sittin' down till the planes 'ave gone,' Michael explained. He understood the unspoken question. The dog, with his tongue hanging out, paused for a moment to make sense of this and then, hearing a scuttling down the tunnel, ran off to continue his safari.

'Maybe we'll see the headless man tonight.'

'What headless man!' Whacker hadn't heard the story and listened awestruck as Michael related old Tom's tale. 'It's not true is it Colin?' He said, when the story was finished, his voice a little shaky.

'Who knows?' Colin responded in a mysterious tone, teasing Whacker. 'You get some funny things on the railway, did I ever tell you about the engine driver who got 'is 'ands caught under the engine?'

'No!' Both boys were interested

'He came to no 'arm!' Colin's laugh echoed down the tunnel bringing a sharp bark from Rags in response. He continued to laugh while fending off the boys as they tried to thump him. But as they fought, they became conscious of the ominous low rumble of aircraft. The sound was magnified in the tunnel; it seemed to reverberate down from the sky and along the rails, filling the narrow space with threat. The noise increased until it seemed that the bombers were directly overhead. Colin instinctively put his arms round his two young friends and they felt comforted by his closeness. 'Don't worry lads, it'll soon be over.' But then the long whistling started, followed by the thump of bombs striking the earth. Some seemed close by, causing the tunnel to shake, loosening dust and pieces from the brick walls that fell on to the wooden sleepers or clinked on the rails. Rags emerged from the gloom, his ears down and his tail flat against his backside. He sat next to Michael, leaning close, something he had never done before. Michael tickled the dog's chest and received a big lick in return; for once in his independent life Rags was happy to be looked after and to acknowledge the leader of the pack.

Colin hated the way in which people that he had never met were trying to kill him. Like many others he was frustrated by the war; life was hard enough without the disruption to their lives and constant news of death and injury that was having a depressing effect on family and friends. His shoulders were tense with a mixture of anxiety and anger; it was simply not fair that young lads like Michael and Andrew were having their early lives blighted by an enemy that they neither knew nor understood. They had done nothing to deserve this. He wished that his injured leg had not prevented him from joining up, at least then he would have been better off fighting, doing something to stop this stupid conflict.

The boys, however, didn't feel the same resentment; they had simply grown up with the war as part of their lives. It figured in newsreels, wireless broadcasts, newspapers and everyday conversations; it was simply a fact, a situation that existed. They coped with its impact on their day-to-day existence because there was nothing else to do; they couldn't really recall a time when war wasn't threatened or actually happening. They missed people who were caught up - Michael's dad and Whacker's brother – but it never occurred to them that life could be significantly different from the way it was now.

Although the sound of bombing had stopped, it was half and hour before the all-clear sounded. They had been in the tunnel for several hours and it was now quite dark. Colin said he would service the final signal and told the boys to go home because their families would be wondering where they were.

As they hurried up the steep road back to their homes, they could see fire and smoke beyond the rooftops of the houses and the smell of burning filled their noses. 'Better run,' said Whacker, feeling worried. They often ran when they wanted to get somewhere quickly and were soon back in Lucy Street. Whacker went off home and Michael clicked the latch of his house and pushed back the door and the heavy black curtain that kept light in and wind out. Kath was sitting in front of the empty fire grate with her head in her hands, tears streaming down her face. She looked round at her son as he pushed into the room, his face was black, his clothes dirty and he smelled of paraffin; 'Michael, Michael, where on earth 'ave you been?' Her voice was quiet and full of anxiety.

'We went down the railway with Colin – 'elping with the signal lights, sorry Mam. We couldn't get 'ome because of the bombs.' Michael felt desolate when he saw his mother's face.

'I thought you were dead,' she said simply. 'I thought you were dead, I can't stand this anymore.' A further burst of sobbing increased Michael's feeling of guilt.

'Shall I go to my room?' This was the usual punishment.

'No, no, stay with me,' Kath wept. 'I need you to stay here.' She stood up from her chair and knelt on the rag rug by the fireplace, pulling the boy towards her and crushing him in her arms. They stayed there for a long time; the gas mantle in the ceiling casting a pale light on their shoulders. After a while, they both felt comforted by their closeness and Kath's sobbing gradually ceased.

CHAPTER 5

February 1941 – 130,000 Italians are captured in two months during an offensive by Allied forces in North Africa.

Command of the Afrika Corps passes to Rommel. One of his tasks is to support the collapsing Italian Army.

March – Rommel begins siege of Tobruk.

Michael watched his mother scraping the paper to get the last vestiges of margarine for a jam sandwich that she was making for breakfast. The room was dark in the mornings because the sun only shone through the window in the afternoon.

'Why ….. why should we move to the country?' Michael had received the idea badly, as Kathleen had expected.

'Because I can't stand to live 'ere any longer, your Grandma wants me to work for 'er all hours that God sends; even your Dad says I should do more for 'er and we get bombings every night and people killed all around us and we 'aven't got enough money to live on, we've not enough food. Your other Grandma says we can live with them where it's safer and they can get more food in the country because of the farms. I know you'll 'ave to leave your friends but you'll make new ones and the countryside is nicer to play in – better than the sewage works and the railway.' Kath spoke calmly and kindly, she was determined but knew it would be a big wrench for her son so she wanted to persuade him to agree rather than force him to go against his will.

'What about school?' Michael wailed. 'I'll 'ave to go to a new school with new teachers an' what about Rags, who'll look after him?'

'Rags has looked after himself since 'e was born,' answered Kath. 'An' you're good at school they'll like an intelligent new pupil.'

'I can't go without Rags, 'e follows me everywhere….. I could stay 'ere an' live with Whacker – 'e won't mind. You go an' I'll come in a bit.' This seemed a good idea and the boy warmed to it: 'I could come an' visit, I can catch a bus so's we can see one another, an' I could bring Rags…. although 'e won't like the bus…. so maybe not …. but I could still go to school, I could sleep in Whacker's bed – 'e wouldn't mind an' ….. His ideas drained away as he looked into his mother's eyes, realising that his argument was not being accepted and that there was probably nothing he would be able to say to change her mind. He tried defiance: 'well I'm not goin' I'm jus' not goin' an you can't make me.' Tears of frustration began to well but he fought them off, determined not to cry, 'I'm not a 'vacuee, I'm stayin', you go, I'm stayin'.'

'You can't stay 'ere by yourself Michael, you have to trust me, life'll be better and you'll soon settle down and enjoy it and Grandma and Grandad will be pleased to see you.'

'Well I don't like them, I don't know them an' I'm not goin' an' that's that.' He tried to bring some finality to the discussion with the phrase that adults used to him, then ran upstairs to his room and fell on the bed at last giving way to tears. Kath followed and sat on the bed, unwilling to leave alone the son that she loved so much and hating the upset that she was causing, but nevertheless determined that their lives needed the change. She had spent precious money on a bus journey to Callthorpe and spoken with her parents who were both delighted by the proposal, for they too loved their grandson and his mother and would be happy to see more of them. The house was big enough to accommodate two more people and they agreed that country life would be better for Michael.

*

Rags didn't know what to do. He lived an independent life most of the time, hunting for the enemy (rats and cats) and foraging for food. He had many human acquaintances, some gave him food others just said hello and there were times when he simply came across food in unusual places and took advantage of the situation. He didn't understand the concept of stealing and was surprised by the way some folks reacted when he took what apparently no-one else wanted. This was particularly true of Mr. Fletcher the butcher who had once thrown a sharp knife at him because, on one hot summer's day, the lure of red meat hanging in the shop had proved too much to resist.

Although he was mostly independent, the dog did have an owner – old Tom Threlfall the battery man. They had a loose and informal relationship. Tom wasn't sure how he had acquired ownership of Rags; he only knew that he had known him since he was a puppy. They wouldn't meet up, sometimes for days on end, but Rags knew that, if he was hungry, thirsty or needed a place to rest, there would be food, water and shelter available at Tom's little house. The old man had never patted the dog which may have been why Rags responded badly to anyone touching his head. Tom and Rags existed together, they were not friends just souls with a mutual dependence; Rags for doggy needs and Tom for the occasional company that the hound provided.

But now there was a problem. The dog turned into the cart track leading to Tom's home only to find it blocked by an ambulance, fire engine and a large number of people. The house was a pile of rubble: broken and charred wood beams, piles of blackened stone and shattered window frames. There was a fire still burning from somewhere inside the mess. A fireman was using a hose to direct a stream of water towards the flames but the pressure was poor and the water hardly reached its target. Home guard men and local people were pulling stones off a crumpled body with its head covered in blood and a leg sticking up at a peculiar angle. Rags heard Tom groan then cry out as they tried to lift him. He thought he should go to his old friend, but although Rags was a brave dog, he was scared by the noise and all the people and he definitely didn't like the fire engine.

The dog circled the remains of the house, keeping out of sight as far as possible and looking for the bowl that usually contained his food but it was nowhere to be seen. He sniffed the shattered stones seeking a scent to follow but his nose became full of acrid smoke, causing him to sneeze.

'Gerrout of it, bloody dog.' An angry call was followed by a lump of debris hurled in Rags' direction. He barked defiantly as the stone missed but the scene he witnessed was enough to persuade the wily hound that he could no longer rely on Tom to provide sustenance and shelter. Hardly anyone knew of the relationship between man and dog so he was regarded as a nuisance at a time when people around were deeply upset by the events that were now part of everyday life. Tom was a popular old man who did a worthwhile job that was simple but essential in the community. There was anger and frustration in the air so a tatty old dog provided an outlet for these as the people joined forces to drive him away from the scene of destruction.

Rags left hurriedly, his tail down and his heart low. He didn't understand what had happened but realised that he was now, more than ever, left to fend for himself. These were strange and frightening times, he headed for the old warehouse where he could hide and think things over. He jumped up to the broken window that the Lucy Street boys used to get into the building and pushed it open. As usual, the warehouse was full of bales of shoddy; pushing his way behind one of these, he settled down to consider his options.

*

The day was hot and dusty, the sun poured mercilessly onto the men's shoulders. Dust devils whirled, sometimes rushing through the ranks of soldiers, causing them to turn their heads away and raise their hands to cover their eyes. The Italian prisoners looked defeated; their uniforms seemed shabby and dusty and their faces were crumpled with dead eyes, they had an air of utter weariness. Jack watched without emotion. Despite the fact that these men had been trying to kill him and his comrades, he couldn't muster any feelings of hatred. He had an almost kindred feeling because he shared their exhaustion; he understood why they shambled along in loose ranks, resigned to the end of their war, no fight left.

The British guards walked alongside about twenty yards apart, holding their rifles loosely, quite aware that their captives were unlikely to offer any kind of resistance. The tank crews watched mostly in silence with the occasional jeer directed towards the 'bloody Eyetie bastards.'

Jack wondered if it was all worth it; they had captured Tobruk, the Italians capitulated and those not captured had retreated but it had cost a lot of lives. The place seemed to be miles from anywhere and at first sight, didn't seem as though it would be an important town but he guessed that the deep water harbour made it significant as part of a supply chain. The local people originated from nomadic tribes which had spent much of their time traveling the desert on ancient caravan routes. The war had seriously disrupted their lives; it was no surprise when they greeted the troops with surly indifference. Nevertheless, Jack couldn't help but be interested in the architecture; it was like nothing he had ever seen before. The buildings, set along narrow streets, were flat-roofed and made from mud-brick with tiny windows. He felt as though they were full of mystery, harbouring secrets behind beaded curtains. The tall minarets of the mosques looked alien but somehow more elegant than the steeples of churches back home. He thought that the town had a biblical feel, reminding him of stories from his Sunday-school childhood.

Now they understood that they were to dig in and protect this place from the German Afrika Corps, which was expected to provide tougher opposition than the Italians. They were thought to be better armed and there were rumours of a new and inspirational field-marshal called Rommel.

Thoughts of home were never far away. Jack was disturbed by Kath's letter about moving to her father's house. The kernel of jealousy prompted questions: 'Was she leaving to see another bloke?' He knew that these things happened; several soldiers had received 'Dear John' letters from wives or girl friends who were finding the loneliness too difficult to deal with, particularly when there were men remaining behind who could provide the extra luxuries that made war-time life bearable. In his heart he knew that Kath was very unlikely to be unfaithful but her letters had become increasingly glum, he couldn't shake the feeling that something serious was wrong. He also worried about his mother, knowing full well that his father would rather spend his time in the pub than play the loyal and helpful husband. He wanted Kath to stay around and make sure that Mary was cared for because he knew that his sisters avoided ministering to their mother's needs if they possibly could. He had expressed these thoughts in a letter home but Kath had studiously ignored his request when she replied.

A barked order interrupted his reverie. He refocused his eyes on the bedraggled echelons. 'What do you think they're goin' to do with all these prisoners?' He asked Alec.

'Dunno, some say they're bein' sent to England.' Alec scratched sand out of his hair. He was usually a reliable source of information because he spent a lot of time in a card school where a mixture of rumour and hard fact was discussed. 'I've heard they're buildin' camps for them out in the countryside.'

This information didn't help lighten Jack's mood; the thought that these scruffy Italians might be housed near to his in-laws house made him more determined to make Kath stay at home. He decided to write a more authoritative letter demanding that she stay put and forget about moving to Callthorpe.

There was a sudden kafuffle along the line of prisoners; they were fighting amongst themselves for some reason. A cloud of dust was raised by the kicking feet. One of the guards used the butt of his rifle to restore order. The Italians shouted and waved their arms, Jack thought their language sounded pleasant, even when they were angry. A prisoner had blood running down his face caused by a blow from the rifle butt. One of the others, a big man with a luxuriant black beard, rushed and put his arms round the injured soldier, protecting him from further attack but the soldier who had used his rifle stepped forward to deliver further blows, striking the large Italian about the shoulders and head.

Jack could see that the English soldier had lost control; the anger and frustration he felt about the war, sudden death and the extreme conditions that he had to face, were boiling over. He hated the Italian prisoners because they were a physical manifestation of the factors that were controlling his existence; he would carry on hitting out until his anger was spent by which time someone would be badly injured or dead. Jack didn't like the Italians any more than anyone else but he couldn't stand by and see a helpless man brutalised. He ran down the line of prisoners, his feet slipping in the loose sand, until he reached the scuffle. He gripped his comrade round the arms to prevent him from continuing the beating: 'hold on lad,' he said. 'No point in killin' 'im, you'll only end up on a fizzer'. The soldier struggled to get free but Jack's arms were locked and he wouldn't let go.

'Bastards, they're all bastards,' the soldier screamed.

'I know lad, I know but you can't kill 'em this way.' Jack kept his voice calm and gradually the soldier began to relax his struggles until his body sagged and he began to sob; huge breath-wrenching sobs. Others arrived and using comforting arms, led him away. Jack straightened, dusting his clothing and looked at the large prisoner who was still protecting the smaller man. 'You alright?' He asked.

'Tante grazie senor ... sono Rodolpho ... sono Rodolpho.' The man put out his hand towards Jack who didn't know what to do; this was a prisoner – an enemy – offering his hand; you weren't supposed to shake hands with these people. Yet there was something about this bloke; the gaze from his black eyes was steady and unafraid despite the fact that he was a prisoner and his shoulders and neck must have been in agony from the beating. He was clearly saying his name; Jack couldn't understand his words but recognised that Rodolpho was like Rudolph – a name. He met the Italian's calm gaze and knew for some reason that here was a kindred spirit – a man doing his duty but still hating the conflict - almost automatically he raised his hand and felt the warm, firm grasp of a fellow human being not an enemy.

'Jack, I'm called Jack,.' he mumbled.

'Gracie, senor, lei è molto gentile.'

'Get the bloody line moving,' the sergeant's voice was angry. 'Get out of there Spencer, let's get these buggers shifted.' Jack stepped back, releasing his grip on Rodolpho's hand. Their eyes flashed a last message; something almost like friendship had passed between them. Jack was disturbed; how could this be? This was the enemy, they were trying to kill him and the others, they were supposed to be evil and yet here was a man, a man who had warmth and humanity in his eyes and his hands, who had taken a beating to protect another and could still turn to the enemy and show thanks and gentility. He watched the sad ranks of men trundle off in the dust and wondered where all this mess would end, how could they ever get back to something like normality?

10th February

Dearest Kathleen,

Thankyou for your letters, they mean a lot to me. I can't wait for this business to be over, then I can see you and Michael again. We can think about having a little girl when I get back. How is Michael doing at school? I bet he's grown, can you send me a new photograph? The one I have is all crumpled. We're alright here so don't worry. I've met up with someone from Long Estate he told me some news about one of the men from our town but I can't put it here – it wasn't good. How's Mary and dad? She hasn't written for a while, I'm worried about her. You know she depends on you. I don't want you to go away from our house. I know things are tough but I promise things will be better when we get back so don't worry, try to stick it out.

I'll write again soon, all my love, Jack

*

Whacker tried again to kick start his brother's motor bike but the ailing machine simply spluttered and coughed, it clearly did not intend to spring to life. The gang had congregated in what could loosely be called Whacker's garden. There were no plants growing, only a pile of high weeds round the edge, with rough grass and patches of bare clay earth in the middle. The family had tried to cultivate some vegetables in response to the 'Dig for Victory' campaign but these had disappeared due to a combination of lack of care and games of football, cricket and wrestling. Working together, the boys had taken the bike apart and managed to reassemble it with only a few parts left on the ground. 'Mebbe those bits should be in,' offered Brian, scratching the remains of his ringworm.

'I'm not takin' it to bits agen,' said Whacker. 'It jus' takes too long an' it might not work anyway.'

'We could get a book from the libry.' Michael's solution to problems was to try to find an answer in writing. He knew that Whacker wasn't keen on books because he didn't read very well. 'I'll read it an' you an' Brian can be the engineers.' This division of labour seemed to please Whacker but Ernest wasn't happy:

'What'll I do then?'

'You can be t'foreman.' Michael wasn't altogether sure what a foreman did but he knew it was an important position.

'What does a foreman do?'

'I think 'e 'as to help an' give advice an' make sure everybody's doin their job.'

This mollified Ernest because it sounded a bit like being the boss. So the team was formed and Michael, who had the only library card, set off in search of a technical book about the construction of motor bikes.

*

The librarian, Elizabeth Simms had worked in the local branch for many years and had considerable experience in dealing with scruffy kids. She was a tall, thin woman of indeterminate age, disappointed with her life and suspicious of children. She wore pince-nez spectacles and viewed Michael and the others over the top of the lenses. She knew Michael as a regular visitor but had never seen his associates before and regarded them with distrust.

The library had shiny, parquet floors, high, arched windows and tall shelves full of books, each section labeled by subject and from A to Z according to the author's name. The rooms smelled of disinfectant and damp cardboard. Whacker and Brian began searching through the shelves for a book about motor cycles, with little hope of success largely because they were in the fiction section. Michael, who knew his way about, made straight for the card index that listed non-fiction books according to subject and found the titles of three books that might be useful in dismantling their machine. He and Ernest found only one of the books present: '*Service Guide: BSA Bikes*' by Arnold Makepiece. They took it from the shelf and went to the quiet reading area to peruse its contents. Whacker and Brian arrived and since they were to be engineers not readers contented themselves with sitting at the table waiting for Michael to pronounce on the book's suitability.

Unfortunately, sitting still and quiet, as expected in a library, was not their forte. It began with Brian suggesting to Whacker that they could go and look at Health and Fitness magazines while they were waiting. Ernest decided to join them and the resulting giggles and squeals of delight began to reach the ear of Miss Simms. The noise confirmed her expectations of what would happen when four scruffy boys entered her establishment so she had been waiting to pounce. Striding purposefully to the magazine rack, she took Whacker and Brian by their ears and without a word marched them out of the library and deposited them on the pavement. She then returned to Ernest and with a sharp 'out!' indicated that he should follow his colleagues, which he did, wilting under her steely gaze. She then returned, satisfied, to her desk. She didn't trust boys and was not prepared to tolerate even the smallest disruption to the sanctity of her domain.

On the pavement the boys recovered their dignity and began to discuss retribution. 'She's urt my bloody ear'ole,' moaned Whacker, rubbing said member.

'Mine as well.' Brian copied the rubbing. 'I'm tellin' my Mum, she can't chuck us out the libry it's meant for us to use.'

Whacker knew that telling his mother would have little effect, indeed it might result in a clout for causing trouble and bringing 'shame on a good Irish family.' He rethought his strategy: 'No, we should go back an' tell her she can't pull our ears an' get away with it.'

Ernest and Brian were not sure that they wanted to go back in; they were not regular library goers and Miss Simms was formidable and nearly as frightening as Mr. Sykes their head teacher. 'We could chuck some muck at the windows,' Ernest suggested.

'Or mebbe shout 'old bag' through the door.' Brian's idea.

'Let's do both.' Whacker was determined on revenge. The library had a small garden in front with ragged lupins growing in it along with tufty clumps of coarse grass. They pulled up sods of grass with soil attached and crept back to the main door. On the count of three they pushed open the heavy double doors and simultaneously threw the sods into the library shouting 'old bag' at the tops of their voices. Without waiting to see the effect of their actions, they ran round the corner and headed off back to the sanctuary of Lucy Street.

Had they stayed to see, they would have been gratified by the results. One particularly heavy and mucky clod landed on Miss Simms' desk, scattered books and file cards, and covered the polished wood with heavy, black soil. The accompanying screech of anger would have delighted the trio; the librarian rushed to the door but saw only the rapidly retreating backs of the miscreants. Turning in her frustration to look at the damage, she spied Michael looking with horror at what his friends had done. 'You little swine,' she screamed, almost beside herself with rage. Miss Simms marched to Michael's table and using her favourite grip on the ear, dragged him to the door. 'Out, get out and never come near this library again.'

'But, but I've done nothin', nothin' at all, I was 'ere reading'.' The boy tried to wriggle free while protesting his innocence but it was useless, her grip was iron and she wasn't in the mood to listen. Michael was forced to follow his pals albeit at a slower pace but with the same painful ear and dented pride. The outcome was, of course, more serious for him; he was a regular visitor to the library and gained considerable pleasure and information from the books he borrowed. Miss Simms was unlikely to forget him even though he was completely innocent so it looked as though this side of his life, for the time being, had ended prematurely. Added to this he had not been able to gather enough information to help with the repair of the motor bike.

*

The gang reassembled in Whacker's garden. After considerable thought in the sanctuary of the warehouse, Rags had decided that Michael, with whom he had shared so many adventures, was most likely to provide the occasional source of shelter and food that he required. He arrived and sat down with the boys while they considered the next stage of their attempt to coax the old motorbike into life. Michael tickled the dog's chest and Rags thought that he had made the correct decision although the boy was not yet aware of his new responsibility.

Molly, walking by, decided to stop and see what was going on. She leaned on the remains of the old wooden fence that surrounded the garden, looking but saying nothing.

'It's yer girl friend,' said Ernest, grimly. Michael coloured. He liked Molly but it was an unspoken rule that girls were not allowed in any of the gang's activities and leaning on the fence watching, almost constituted a breach of etiquette. He decided to ignore both the remark and the girl.

'You'll never get it to work.' Molly, unaware of the rule, was not going to be ignored.

'What do you know?' Asked Whacker, scathingly.

'Well you've got all those bits left, they should be inside, it's obvious it won't work without all its bits.' Molly's logic was penetrating and difficult to rebuff.

'Look you, bugger off.' This was Whacker's desperate response, knowing that the girl was probably correct but unwilling to acknowledge the fact.

'I can stay can't I Michael?' This was the ultimate challenge to the mores of the select community. Michael was flummoxed; on the one hand was his best friend's instruction to leave, on the other his embryonic relationship with a girl who had been very instructive and placed a lot of faith in his discretion. But gang loyalty was paramount;

'It's Whacker's fence,' was his feeble response.

He could feel the power of Molly's eyes fixing him with a look of disgust. She believed that he had shown cowardice. The girl didn't appreciate that, for boys, steadfastness to the group's beliefs was essential to maintain your reputation and status.

'You can't make me go,' she said stepping back from the fence. 'This isn't your road an' I can stand where I want.' Molly folded her arms and stood, refusing to move. Michael had a very uncomfortable feeling; a mixture of guilt and sadness. He decided that he must try to take charge of a difficult situation so that everyone would feel OK:

'Look there's no harm in 'er watchin' is there? An' she's probably right about the bits we've left out.'

Whacker looked hard at his friend. Was he arguing in support of a girl? This could initiate a problem in their relationship. Fortunately, before an argument could begin, Brian joined in:

'Oh ignore 'er. I think we could run it in. I've seen people push a car down a hill to get it started an' when it got fast enough, it started. Let's push it up to the top of the street an'let it run down; it might start on its own.'

Disagreements were forgotten because this idea clearly offered a new strategy and after much tugging and pushing, with Rags getting under the feet, the machine was poised at the top of Lucy Street near the ginnel. Since it was his brother's bike, Whacker was nominated to steer. Brian, seeing the steep slope before them, decided to offer the pillion to Ernest who, after all, was the foreman. At the count of three the other two pushed and the bike with its nervous passengers, was soon gathering pace down the hill. The poorly inflated tyres meant that the riders felt every bump on the cobble stones and their bodies were bouncing like broken puppets. Whacker valiantly pulled the clutch and brake levers hoping that the engine would spark miraculously into life but it remained stubbornly dead. Small children shouted and clapped at the sight and Rags, who hated motorized vehicles, decided that this was an enemy even though it made no engine noise and ran after it barking and trying to bite the back wheel. Seeing the speed of travel and realising that there was no means of slowing down, Michael and Brian were now worried for their friends' safety. The machine careered down the centre of the street, with Whacker clinging to the handle bars and Ernest clinging desperately to his friend. The front wheel hit a hole created by missing cobbles and the bike swerved to the right, headed over the pavement, past Molly - who shrieked - crashed through Whacker's fence and ended in a pile of bramble, willow weed and bits of broken fence.

The rim of the front wheel was bent out of shape and the tyre completely flat. The boys, though somewhat bewildered, were scratched and bruised but otherwise unhurt. Michael and Brian arrived breathless;

'That wer great,' Brian puffed out, 'can I 'ave a go now?'

Whacker, aching, looked at Brian with disgust, 'We're never touchin' that bloody thing agen.' Michael agreed and Molly walked away nearly crying with laughter.

CHAPTER 6

In July 1941, Italian prisoners of war begin to arrive in the English countryside. The men are housed, on the edges of towns, in camps made up of Nissan huts. After settling in, many are sent out in small gangs to work on local farms. Those from farming backgrounds find the jobs similar to their working lives in Italy. Most of the men co-operate well and eventually the rules are relaxed and small groups are allowed to work with individual farmers, having been delivered in the morning to be picked up and returned to their camps in the evening.

A soft summer rain refreshed the air as Kathleen set off to Mary's house. Three young women dressed in their work aprons were walking arm-in-arm down Lucy Street on their way to the mill for the early shift. They had been menders, looking for flaws in the suit cloth that the firm made, but now they were involved in making canvas rigging for aeroplanes. They were careless of the rain as they chatted about the letters they had received from their boy friends in the army. Kath envied them their easy relationships and wished she too was going to work, doing something more interesting than attending to the needs of a cantankerous old woman.

Jack's letter had made her cry with frustration; he never seemed to understand, or care, how she was feeling. His main concern appeared to be the welfare of his mother. Kath knew that, because he was the first born son in the house, he felt a responsibility for the whole family and particularly Mary. She could appreciate that he wouldn't ask his father to do women's work but couldn't understand why he didn't ask his sisters to take more responsibility. It was as if he felt more comfortable giving his own wife instructions than in making demands on his siblings. Kath would have liked to talk the situation over with him but long distance letters were inadequate for such discussions. In any case she could imagine how difficult it was for the soldiers; she had seen the newsreels and read the newspapers so didn't want to increase his anxiety by worrying him with troubles at home. Also, she had to concede that Michael was happy living in Stanbury where he had good friends. He didn't want to leave and begin a new life in Callthorpe. As a result, Kathleen had just about decided to accept her lot; she would have to put up with it and forget her feelings of discontent for the sake of the people who were most important in her life.

She opened the door of her mother-in-law's terrace house with the usual feelings of trepidation, wondering what sort of a reception she would receive. Mary was sitting in her rocking-chair as usual, huddled in a shawl in front of the coal fire, which was burning despite the warmth of the July day. The house smelled of the Wintergreen that she rubbed on her joints to ease the pain.

'Oh, there you are, about time too, I was beginnin' to think you weren't comin'. Me arthritis is killin' me today, an' nobody cares ..... I wish Jack were 'ere e'd look after his old mam.' Kath ignored Mary's moans – she had learned to do this – realising that answering back only gave the old woman opportunity to pour more bile on her head.

'What do you want doin Mary?'

'Well there's some washin', George's vests, underpants and shirts need doin' an' some of my stuff, an' the bedroom could do with a clean, an -' Mary seemed inclined to continue the list but Kath cut her short:

'OK, I'll do the washin' but I've got to go out this afternoon so that'll be all today.' Kath had nowhere to go but knew that Mary would keep her busy all day if she stayed around.

'That's just typical of you, leavin' me 'ere with jobs that need doin'.'

'Mary, I can only do so much – I've got my own 'ouse to look after as well as Michael. Why can't Lillian or Annie help you more?' Kath knew the true answer to this question was that her daughters had long since learned to resist Mary's demands and were actually doing less than they used to because they were tired of their mother's bad temper. She also knew that the old woman would never criticise them in front of her daughter-in-law since this would have been to admit their apparent lack of concern.

'They do as much as they can – they 'elp me a lot – more than you. My Jack said you'd look after me while 'e were in't army. 'E's told me in 'is letter you want to move away but your not to, Jack says so. 'E said to tell you to do what I want.' Mary was angry at the implied criticism of Lillian and Annie and would never admit what she knew in her heart: that her daughters avoided her as much as possible and were quite capable of refusing to obey her demands. She knew that Kath would not resist her because of her loyalty to her husband and secretly enjoyed the power she had over the younger woman. There were times when she deliberately pushed her daughter-in-law to breaking point just to see how far she could go, then used Kath's angry response as an excuse for redoubling her complaints. 'You don't know what pain I'm in an' you don't care,' she continued. 'I'm goin' to write to Jack an' tell 'im you're bein' nasty to me.' Her voice had risen and her eyes were wide with anger.

Just like her son when he gets cross, Kathleen thought. She had almost stepped outside the argument because she knew the outcome would be the same as always. She decided to stay silent knowing that protestations would simply feed Mary's fury. It was almost like a game replayed over and over. Kath also had some sympathy with the fact that Mary's arthritis was painful and bound to affect her temperament as well as her physical condition. But this sympathy was diluted by the old woman's attitude: she seemed to hate Kath no matter how hard she worked; her efforts to help never received any thanks or a kind word. It was expected that the daughter-in-law would be subservient to the matriarch without question or reward. There was something feudal in Mary's attitude and the problem lay partly in the fact that Kath was unwilling to play the serf. She could not bring herself to just obey; her inner pride told her that this was an unhealthy relationship, that she deserved more consideration and occasionally, a word of thanks.

Deciding that further comment would only prolong the diatribe of complaint, Kath started work. She ignored Mary's continued moaning, collected up the washing and began to separate it into different piles. 'I'll make you a cup of tea in a minute,' she said. Mary didn't respond, frustrated that Kath wouldn't rise to her anger. She sat looking into the fire, the rhythmic motion and slow creak of her rocking chair gradually lulling the old woman into a doze. Kath didn't mind this, at least when she's asleep she's not nagging, she thought. She began to ladle hot water from the set pan into the wash tub and the steam rose, combining with the heat from the fire, to create a densely humid atmosphere.

*

The classroom had high, rectangular windows and faded cream upper walls with brown wooden boarding about a yard high beneath. Sunlight filtered through the outer grime on the windows and lit the display board, on which were some examples of neat handwriting. Mrs. Stamp was very keen on handwriting, she regarded a neat hand as the main attribute that children should have after they had been in her class. She was particularly pleased when other teachers or Mr. Sykes commented on this quality in pupils who had been in her care. Unfortunately, this meant that handwriting practice was a regular feature of her lessons; the children had to copy, from the blackboard, long sections of meaningless prose. Her particular favourites were verses taken from Gilbert and Sullivan operas; the fact that these were often unintelligible to the children was not considered important, since all they had to do was concentrate on correct letter formation, letter size and correct spacing. These skills were considered so important that only minimal time could be given to the development of children's expressive or creative skills. Those who were the most 'successful' writers sat at the front of the class and the untidy ones were at the back. Michael, although able to read well and capable of producing imaginative and grammatically correct writing, wrote so quickly that his handwriting was messy and often punctuated by ink blots. His pen had a broken nib and so the marks it made were quite thin. 'Just like spiders,' said Mrs. Stamp. 'I hate spiders, ugh, creepy, black, ugly things.' This was clearly true since every time a spider dared to enter her sanctum, Howard (who was a very neat writer and sat on the front row) was ordered to catch the creature and remove it from her sight. Michael found himself relegated to very back row of desks but didn't mind this since it meant that he was not constantly in Mrs. Stamp's field of vision.

The school year was coming to an end and Mrs. Stamp was content; she had several fine examples of quality writing on her display board and felt that she had fulfilled her duty with these children. She was so satisfied that she made a very unusual announcement. Sitting on the high stool behind her tall narrow desk, glaring at the children, daring any of them to speak or make an unnecessary movement, she said: 'we're doing art today.' This was extraordinary because Mrs. Stamp had often indicated that she regarded such trivialities as art and music as a waste of time. Consequently, they figured only rarely in her rigid timetable of religious education, followed by arithmetic and reading in the mornings, and writing in the afternoons. The occasional PE lesson was taken by Mr. Batson when they swapped classes and Mrs. Stamp went down to the old chapel to teach handwriting to his class.

At the front of the classroom she placed a white pottery vase containing five red roses. Each pupil was given a small piece of blue sugar paper and several tin boxes of broken crayons were distributed to those children who were thought sufficiently responsible to monitor their use. Following the instruction to 'draw these flowers and make sure to fill the paper and get the colours correct', the children began to work; the sound of crayons rubbing on the coarse paper was accompanied by the occasional whispered request for a colour to be passed over.

Michael enjoyed drawing and looked carefully at the subject to try to get the shapes and colours. The vase was fairly easy but the roses were more difficult and it was hard to get a good view from the back of the class. Also, the box that he could reach had only a small, broken piece of red crayon that was soon used up by other children. What to do? He had seen wild roses before, down by the sewage works, they had been yellow and there was a half stick of yellow in the box. But he knew that Mrs. Stamp's instructions had to be obeyed to the letter. He could see that the box on Molly's desk had a bit of red crayon, he tried whispering but she couldn't hear, so he stood up quietly and crouching to avoid being seen, tried with bent knees, to get to her desk.

'Michael Spencer, sit down and get on with your work.'

The boy froze at Mrs. Stamp's shriek. He considered explaining but realised the futility of such a course and crept back in his desk. There seemed only one answer: the roses would have to be yellow. Unfortunately, blue sugar paper imparted a greenish tinge to yellow crayon, so the flowers were nothing like their original hue. When he had finished he blew the powdery residue off the paper and sat up straight with his arms folded – this was the drill required to indicate to his teacher that he had completed the task. She didn't notice him at first so he surveyed his work; the vase and flowers were close to the shapes of the original and he had used up most of the surface, as instructed, but he felt uneasy about the colour of the roses. Mrs. Stamp approached; 'Spencer, could you tell me what is the colour the roses in my vase?'

'Please Miss, they're red,' Michael's voice shook a little – he knew he was in trouble.

'And pray tell, what colour are you're roses?'

'Please Miss they're yellow.'

'YELLOW! Are you colour-blind? They're GREEN. Have you ever seen GREEN roses? Has anybody in this class ever seen GREEN roses?' The children remained silent, recognising a rhetorical question.

'But Miss . . . .' Michael attempted an explanation about the lack of suitable crayons.

'Don't you *but miss* with me. This is a waste of materials. Don't you know there's a war on?' Now at full volume, Miss Stamp recognised insubordination and this must not be accepted. With an aim built from years of practice she aimed a flat, bony, right hand at the back of Michael's head, followed by a left to the other side. The blows sent the boy spinning from his desk on to the floor, his head dizzy with the force of the attack. 'Go and stand in the corner.' This final instruction was accompanied by a push in the back as he staggered to his feet. 'And face the wall – I don't want to see you!'

Now a deathly, breathless silence descended. The pupils, with their heads down, scratched away at their drawings, trying to minimize even the noise of the crayons. No-one dared look up for fear of catching the teacher's eye and being swept into the maelstrom of fury that had arrived in their midst. Michael was not by any means the first to suffer the teacher's wrath; in the past, many children had been hit for minor misdemeanors and she was not averse to using a thin cane hanging by the blackboard if the crime was sufficiently serious, or if she was in a particularly bad mood. Miss wanted red roses and red roses she would have, even if it meant scratching their arms to draw blood.

Only Molly O'Boyle was not working; she sat with tears of mixed anger and frustration coursing down her freckled cheeks. She felt that Michael, like others in the past, had been unfairly treated. We've got to do something about this she thought, but what? To speak out would simply bring the wrath of Stamp down on her head, no, something more subtle was required, something that would upset the teacher but avoid the resulting in retribution. Molly decided to wait and consider a strategy of revenge when she was not so upset, perhaps the Lucy Street gang could be involved. She had heard about their antics at the library and thought they might have ideas. Molly was mature beyond her years and Mrs. Stamp had attacked her particular friend and consequently, made a determined enemy.

Whacker, Ernest and Brian were still in Mr. Batson's class but they met up with Michael during playtimes and like today, after school.

'The old bag!' Whacker's immediate response, on hearing the news, was supported by the others.

'Yer, she ain't fit to be a teacher, Mrs. Parkinson's the only decent teacher in this school.' There was agreement with Brian's statement.

'Let's chuck some sods through 'er window.' Ernest remembered with some delight the battle of the library.

It was at this point that Molly joined the conversation: 'No you'll get caught if you do that, everyone will see you an' then you'll get caned.'

The boys were taken aback, this was not the first time Molly had tried to join in and they were not quite sure how to deal with it. But Michael respected her and decided to listen to what she had to say: 'go on then what do you think we should do?' He had mixed emotions about the events in the classroom. He thought that he had made a mistake using the wrong colours and deserved to be punished but on the other hand, to get slapped on his head twice and then pushed into a corner was too severe, even his dad only slapped legs and that only when Michael had done something terrible. Also, the others clearly thought that he, like many others, had been badly treated and were even talking about taking action. Maybe what had happened was unfair and something needed to be done. 'What's your plan Molly? What can we do?' His obvious regard for the girl impressed the others and they gathered closer to listen to her idea. Even Rags who had, unnoticed, joined the group, moved between Michael's legs to hear the plan.

*

Rags was having a bad time; the loss of his 'owner' was proving to be more of a problem than he had expected. He had decided to adopt Michael but the boy had not yet realised his new role and a regular supply of food, suitable for a dog, was not forthcoming. Rags appeared regularly at the door of his new owner's house, but although greeted with friendliness and a tickle on the chest, neither Michael nor Kathleen realised that they were required to provide food. The dog thought that he would try a howl now and then to indicate his hunger and desire to be let into the house but this only resulted in him being shooed away.

He returned to his hiding place in the shoddy warehouse to rest and think things over. He was quite comfortable there; the place was dry and warm, and he liked the smell of the old cloth. Also, there were a few rats that provided sport but they weren't good to eat so he had to resort to loitering near Mr. Fletcher's shop in the hope of a bone or something better if the butcher relaxed his usual vigilance. This was unsatisfactory because the pickings were thin and there were other dogs to contend with. These were lower order mutts who deferred to Rags' high status – he had only to growl and they fled - but this was another inconvenience in his vexed situation.

The ragged hound lay between to huge shoddy filled sacks and pondered. It was clear that these humans were slow on the uptake and needed a clear message as to their responsibilities; the only thing to do was to give them his full attention. He would stay by Michael's side at every possible opportunity until the boy understood that he was the dog's new owner, friend and food provider. In return Rags would behave like a proper *pet* (a word Rags hated) then, when everyone appreciated their roles, matters could be placed on a more normal footing leaving the dog to return to the more eccentric life that was his custom. Satisfied with his plan he snuggled down for a well earned sleep – this thinking was tiring work.

*

It was the afternoon of the last day of the summer term. Mrs. Stamp was looking forward to her holiday; she was going with her mother and her two children to Nethersea. Her husband was in the army and had been evacuated from Dunkirk in 1940. Like everyone, she was worried that the war wasn't going well, but at least he was safe somewhere on the South Coast so life wasn't too bad at the moment. She had done a good job with the unruly children in her class; some of them now had a fair hand with pen and ink and they all knew how to behave because she had 'stamped' on any indication of disobedience. The lady allowed herself a thin smile as she walked down the corridor after supervising school dinners, pausing at the office to collect the register for her class. Mr. Sykes was in there talking to the secretary. 'Good afternoon Mrs. Stamp,' he said, returning what he took to be a smile of greeting on her face. 'Ready for a well earned rest?'

'Good afternoon Mr. Sykes,' she replied. (These two were always scrupulously polite to one another and never used first names even though they had worked together for several years.) 'Yes, but it won't be the same without Harry, I'll be glad when this awful business is over.'

'I agree, Mrs. Stamp, there never seems to be any good news, I hear that the Germans have taken Smolensk and are advancing through Russia.'

'Dear, dear, where will it all end? Still, better get on, the little darlings await.' She walked out of the office with a reedy, humourless laugh.

Mr Sykes was quite happy to see the last of Mrs. Stamp for several weeks, since she had repeatedly challenged his authority after it became clear that he wouldn't be called up. She seemed to take the unfair attitude that he was somehow avoiding his duty. He, in turn, would have liked to suggest a more enlightened approach to her classroom practice, but in truth he was afraid of her, particularly now that she had become less respectful of his status. He had decided to take a non-confrontational approach, in other words, to do nothing.

She strode purposefully into the classroom and was surprised to see the children sitting up straight in their desks.

Goodness, she thought, I've been more successful than I imagined, what an excellent response to my discipline. Proudly, she gave a slight nod of appreciation to the pupils and marched to her high desk, only to encounter a further surprise: on the desk, neatly wrapped in red tissue paper, a rectangular box with the words 'to Mrs. Stamp from her class' printed neatly on the outside. This was extraordinary; she had never received a present from her pupils before and regarded this as the understandable result of her firm approach to discipline. 'Well, what a surprise children, thankyou.' (She decided not to raise the matter of tissue taken from the paper drawer without her permission.) Picking up the present in her left hand, she began to remove the covering. How exciting, she thought, perhaps they've used their coupons to get me some chocolates. Disappointingly, the container turned out to be an old chalk box but still, it could contain a bar of chocolate which would be quite acceptable. As she opened the container and put the fingers of her right hand inside, something black and quick came out and ran up her arm. 'Oh!' She said in surprise and then 'oh my God,' as more of the creatures collected by Michael from the Lucy Street ginnel made a break for freedom. What followed could be heard all over the school: a blood curdling scream that shook Mr. Sykes to the core. He immediately raced to discover the cause.

It was at this very instant that Rags had chosen to demonstrate the new close association with his owner. Having followed the scent of Michael to school, he found his way past the entrance hall, down the corridor to the door behind which his master was waiting. The door was slightly open and he could see his quarry and also other children, some of whom he knew, sitting in strange seats with boxes on the front. He took the scream as a signal to enter but at the same time found himself trodden on from behind. Taking this as an attack on his person, Rags bit deeply into the offending leg. Then, barking joyously, flung himself onto Michael's desk and began to lick his face. Mr. Sykes' yelp almost matched the first scream of the woman who was now covered in spiders and just about hysterical. She stood, paralysed by the arachnid attack, unable to move, a second but silent scream lodged in her throat. Mr. Sykes rolled on the floor grasping his ankle and mouthing obscenities that should not have been voiced in front of young children. This seemed an appropriate moment for innocent pupils to leave; at a given signal from Molly, the whole class stood and intoned 'have a good holiday Mrs. Stamp,' then marched in a very orderly manner out of the room to begin their summer holiday a little early.

Their control fractured as they reached the playground and groups of children could be seen holding on to one another doubled up with laughter. Molly was the centre of the hilarity, patted on the back and congratulated for the success of her plan. Whether there would be some sort of repercussion after the holidays, no-one cared at the moment, the weeks of summer stretched out before them and September seemed light years away. Only Michael did not seem happy with the outcome. 'What's up?' Said Molly, 'it was a laugh wasn't it? You look as if you'd lost a pound and found sixpence.'

'She screamed, did you 'ear 'er scream? An' 'er face, she was real upset.' Michael hated to see anyone unhappy; it gave him the same feeling in his stomach as when his parents argued. 'I wish we 'ad'nt done it.'

'Oh you're a big softy, she'll get over it. Mebbe it'll teach 'er a lesson, mebbe she'll be kinder in future.' Molly tried to make him feel better but his face was still long and so she held his hand and Michael liked it; he liked the warmth and softness of her skin and the way her small fingers held his firmly.

Are you two courtin' then?' Howard called out but Molly ignored him and Michael just stuck out his tongue. He felt that the girl was a real friend like Whacker; one who could be relied on. He knew that she had formulated her plan because of his treatment by the teacher and although he now felt sorry for Mrs. Stamp, he was, at the same time grateful to have someone who cared for him, even if she was a girl. He decided to suggest that she become a fully fledged member of the Lucy Street gang.

*

When Michael arrived home Kathleen was upstairs making the beds. Hearing the sound of movement he called out from the bottom of the stairs, "ello Mam, you alright? Did we get a letter from Dad?'

"Ello love, I've been to Grandma's doin' her cleanin'. There's a letter from your Dad on the table. I'll make some tea in a minute.'

Michael picked up the folded letter and read it. He was pleased that Dad said they should stay in their house, maybe Mam would stop talking about it now. But he had the same mixed feelings about this as after the bating of Mrs. Stamp: he wanted to stay near his friends but he knew his mother was unhappy, mainly because of Grandma but also she felt their house was in a dangerous place, near to factories that the German bombers were targeting. He hated anyone to be unhappy and was frustrated that he couldn't find a solution to their problems.

While he was mulling things over he heard a scratching at the door followed by a plaintive whine. He found Rags outside, sitting on the step looking mournful. Michael bent down and tickled the dog's chest, 'what's the matter, you hungry?' Rags stuck out his tongue and breathed quickly, clearly indicating that he was indeed looking for a meal. The boy turned putting his head round the door and called up to his mother, 'Mam, Rags is 'ere can 'e come in? I think he's hungry.'

'Oh Michael, that old dog stinks,' Kath called down, 'He'll go away if you leave him outside.'

'I don't think so Mam, 'e came to school today an 'e follows me everywhere now. I think 'e wants to live with us.'

'Well 'e can't, I've enough on feedin' us an lookin' after Grandma.' Kath tried to sound definite but she knew that her son loved the old dog.

The boy looked at Rags: 'sorry pal, you'll 'ave to find somewhere else,' and he closed the door. Rags was baffled. Why didn't they understand that he now belonged to them? Hadn't he fought off an attacker to keep Michael safe? Didn't he follow the boy everywhere like a *pet*? He tried another whine and scratch on the door but nothing happened. Well he was determined not to end up back in the warehouse; it was a warm evening so he decided to stay by the house until these humans realised their new responsibilities.

Kathleen came down and started to make baked beans and chips for tea. Michael put the wireless on and they both listened to the news broadcast. A posh voice told them about the war and warned that more air-raids were expected, giving everyone advice about using the local shelters or the Anderson shelters in their gardens. Michael liked the idea of a shelter in the garden, he thought it would be like an underground den and better than going down the cellar which, even with the paraffin heater, was cold and damp, with only the candle to provide light. He wasn't frightened by the raids although they happened quite regularly. He always felt that the bombs would miss their house. Even when they had been trapped in the railway tunnel, he wasn't afraid and had enjoyed the adventure. He knew that bad things happened and was sad when old Tom the battery man had been killed but always felt that his family would be alright. His father had said not to worry about him; he would be alright, so if his Dad was not worried about actually going to the war, why should Michael worry about their safety at home?

The evening light began to drop but they didn't put on the gaslight and because it had been a warm day, the fire was not lit; it was pleasant to sit and chat quietly. The traffic on the road outside stopped and just a few people were walking out. The air raid wardens were patrolling, ready if anything happened tonight. There was a strange quietness in the air, no wind, no sounds; even their own voices became hushed. Michael looked at his mother, the light was dim but he was sure that she was crying. 'What's the matter Mam?' He asked.

'Nothing love, I'm alright, I just miss your Dad and when it's quiet like this I think about him and wonder what's happening.'

'Don't worry, Dad told me he'd be fine. Mebbe the war will be over soon and he'll come home.' Michael tried to sound encouraging but he felt that his words were inadequate; he wasn't old enough to fully understand the nature of his parents' relationship. The adult world was a mystery to him; they seemed to be obsessed by money, which he didn't worry about at all. He thought their house was fine, just big enough for the three of them, close to shops and buses, and with plenty of people around who were friends. He didn't feel the need for a bigger house and although a sister might be nice, he now had Molly as a friend which was probably nearly as good. He could understand why Kathleen was worried about Jack but *he* knew that it would all be fine in the end; he just didn't have the words to convince her, although he kept on trying.

The air-raid siren whined through their quiet conversation. 'Oh not again,' Kath's voice was tired and strained; she hated the noise almost as much as the threat to their safety. 'Close the curtains love.'

Michael stood on the table by the window and pulled across the heavy black drapes, making sure that there was no gap to allow the light through. Kath lit the gas lamp so that they could see to collect the things they needed to take into the cellar. She could never find the ration books when they were wanted. There was a loaf of bread in the cupboard by the sink and she still had a jar of homemade jam; they might need food because you could never tell how long they would have to shelter from the attack. At least it's was a warm evening, she thought, so we don't need to take the paraffin heater. Michael picked up two cushions that they used to keep the cold from the stone steps from penetrating their behinds, along with his current book: *Swallows and Amazons* by Arthur Ransome. He liked the story about the children having adventures on the lake but objected to one of the girls being called 'Titty' which he thought was a stupid and slightly rude name. Reading in the cellar was a problem because he needed to sit near the candle otherwise he couldn't see and Kath said he blocked all the light and she had difficulty with the sock darning jobs she took with her.

Rags also hated the siren; he didn't really understand what was happening but he sensed danger from the way the people behaved and in the tunnel, had sought out Michael's closeness to provide security. But his new master wasn't around. They were obviously not going to open the door and let him into the house and he knew that the warehouse was too far away, now that the heavy drone, that heralded the arrival of loud explosions, had begun. He decided to cross the road and hide behind the butcher's shop; it might even be that an old bone could be found, or failing that, the smell of meat would make him feel better. A stray cat had the same idea and there was a minor confrontation when the dog crept behind the wooden shop. Back arched, the cat spat defiance at Rags. But this was not the moment for a fight; he simply turned his back and snuggled down in the protection of the wall. The cat's fur slowly sank to its normal position and still keeping an eye on the dog's back, the frightened animal flattened itself into a hollow in the ground. So the human war forced two natural enemies to an uneasy peace for the time being at least.

In the distance the sound of ominous whistling began, followed by the dull thump of bombs striking the earth. The air-raid warning continued to sound and the air was soon filled with the clatter of police-car bells and the howl of fire engines. Anti-aircraft fire blasted into the sky following the bright pathways of the searchlights. Rags smelt acrid smoke and put his paws over his nostrils to try to keep it out but he couldn't avoid the flashes and stunning explosions that made him wince and whimper.

His master, unaware of his friend's plight, listened to the same sounds getting progressively nearer. He looked at his mother's face etched with fear in the candle light; a trail of tears ran down her cheeks. He reached out and took her hand. Kath smiled; here she was, being comforted by the child that she should have been protecting. She looked at Michael's attempted smile and whispered a silent prayer, asking God to look after him. The racket outside was the worst she had heard and seeking greater safety, she took the boy's hand and led him down the cellar steps on to the cold paving stones at the bottom near the coal room and there they stood with their arms around each other.

The bomb came at an angle and exploded against the rear of the house. The impact was sufficient to tear the old brickwork apart. The back wall collapsed and the windows at the front were blasted out before the whole front of the house crashed into the black soil of the garden. Wooden beams groaned as they were unable to support the heavy slate roof; the entire structure fell in upon itself as years of soot and dust mingled in a dense, choking cloud. In minutes, a home that had stood for decades, was reduced to a pile of rubble, the only part left standing was the iron fire place and a small section of the chimney. The staircase fell in one piece, covering the cellar, sealing mother and son in a hole about three metres square.

Deafened by the noise of falling masonry and the impact of the bomb, Kathleen and Michael were plunged into complete darkness. Their candle was extinguished by the blast of hot air and they were instantly choked by the thick dust of generations that swirled around them. The force of the explosion picked them off their feet and flung them against the stone wall of their shelter. The boy had been protected by his mother's body but she lay unconscious as a result of her head hitting the wall of the cellar.

After what seemed like hours, but was actually only about five minutes, Michael, confused and hurting, started to try to move. He could feel Kath's body lying on the floor but she was completely still. The boy called to her but got no response. He felt for her face and realised that her eyes were closed. In a moment of panic he thought she was dead but then became conscious of her laboured breathing. 'Mam …… Mam, wake up, wake up, wake up.' He pushed her inert body but still got no response. Michael coughed and then couldn't stop; it was a cough that came from deep within him as his lungs tried to shift some of the choking dust. His found breathing difficult – gasping for some clean air – but there was none. He could also smell gas and knew that this was bad; the gas would soon fill the cellar and if there was a fire it would explode. We've got to get out quickly, he thought. He felt his way on hands and knees to the cellar steps and began to crawl upwards, counting the steps because he knew there were ten of them. As he reached the eighth his head hit the collapsed staircase. He scrabbled forward but nothing would move; the way was blocked.

'Maybe we can get through the coal chute.' He spoke aloud and his croaking voice surprised him. He scrambled backwards in the blackness to the bottom of the steps and then crawled across the flat floor area to the thin wooden door of the coal house. Touching his mother's feet as he passed, he shook them in the hope that she was awake but there was no movement. He pulled at the side of the door and it moved gradually with a scraping sound and then fell on top of him; it had been blown off its hinges. He could feel the pile of coal and pulled himself upwards, sometimes falling backwards as the loose pile collapsed under him. The metal grate, when he found it, was immovable, he knew it should open and it wasn't too heavy for him to lift because he had taken it off when the coal men came but now it wouldn't shift at all. He cried out, as loud as his dust filled larynx would let him then listened, but nothing happened. He called again – nothing - and again – nothing. He shook the grate, trying to loosen it but his boyish strength had no effect. Sitting on the pile of coal Michael cried and coughed in frustration. He cried out again to his mother but received only silence. The smell of gas was getting stronger and Michael's optimism began to fade; maybe they wouldn't be able to get out and then what.......?

*

The detonation across the road was unlike anything he had heard before and frightened Rags into a panic. He ran, whimpering, without any destination in mind, trying to get as far away from the din as possible. The cat, hissing, its ears flat and its fur once more standing on end followed the only living thing it could see, frightened of being alone in this madness. They ran with incredible speed as debris crashed around them, they heard the window of the butcher's shop shatter and the reverberation of another explosion blew them off their feet.

Rags found himself rolling along the ground, unable to control his movement. A flying stone glanced off his side, cutting through his fur and leaving a bleeding gash. As he lay, panting and beside himself with fear, in the depths of his canine brain, the old dog remembered Michael: he had adopted the boy as his pack leader and here he was running away. This was no good, a dog must return and protect his master, otherwise like old Tom, the boy might disappear. His side hurt, but with great courage, Rags turned and limped back towards the house. The cat, by now, had vanished into the night.

*

'All these folk 'll be in' t shelter up at t' school.' Two air raid wardens were standing in front of the two terraced houses that had been almost completely destroyed by a single bomb. 'There's not much we can do here till morning.' Still they stood looking at what was left. Half the shared wall remained, some of the bricks hung loosely almost ready to drop. Slates, wooden beams and scattered bricks covered what had once been the kitchen. Everything was blackened, but for some reason, there was no fire.

'What's that bloody dog doin'? Gerrout of it.' He shouted at Rags who was pawing at a pile of stones and barking. The man, frustrated by the futility of war and the blind havoc created by indiscriminate bombing, rushed at the dog and aimed a kick.

Rags backed away but, keeping low, circled back to the same spot, still barking.

'What's he found?' The other warden was calmer and saw the gaping wound in the dog's side. 'He's hurt look, but he's found something.' They scrambled over the ruins to where the dog continued to scrabble at the debris. Rags looked at them, barked, and redoubled his efforts. The men joined in. Better equipped to shift rubble, they cleared the coal grate. Lifting it easily now they shone a torch into the eyes of a coal streaked, tear stained face.

The smell of gas made the wardens step back. 'Come on son let's get you out of there quick, I can smell gas.' The calmer one held out a hand to help Michael but the boy started to scramble back down the pile of coal.

'Me Mam's down 'ere – help me Mam, she's gone to sleep.'

Knowing the urgency of such a situation, the men squeezed through the narrow hole and scrambled down the pile of coal following the boy who had now disappeared. Kathleen was still unconscious and her breathing was shallow. The stink of gas was even stronger in the cellar. By the light of their torches, the wardens could see that the pipe leading to the gas meter had snapped off. One of them picked up Jack's hammer from the stone shelf and prepared to flatten the pipe. 'Careful don't make a spark,' the other one called out.

'It's OK I know what I'm doin'.' He took out his handkerchief and wrapped it round the end of the pipe before flattening it to seal the end.

Michael watched as Kathleen was half-lifted, half-dragged up the coal chute and into the open air. The sight made him weep; his mother's dress was torn and he could see her tattered underskirt. At the back of her head the hair was matted and looked black with blood from the wound. They laid her on the ground and the boy went over and pulled her dress straight and touched her dust covered face. He looked at the wardens, 'will she be alright?'

One began: 'We don't kn....'

'Sure son, sure, she'll be fine, don't worry we'll get 'er to 'ospital an' they'll sort 'er out,' the other one interrupted quickly. No point in worrying the lad he thought, he's got enough to put up with at the moment.'

*

5th August
1941

Dear Jack,

First you must not worry. Kathleen and Michael are well but they are living in my house because yours has been bombed. It happened just as the school holidays began. Kathleen got a bang on the head and had to go to hospital. Michael's breathing was bad for a while but he's OK now. But I say again, do not worry, they are fine now. Kathleen is going to write to you soon. I think she might talk to you about going to her mother's place but I want them to stay here, then when she gets better she can help me. Will you tell her to stay here? I'm sure they'll be fine when they settle down and Michael gets back to school. Your Dad's not so well he's fed up with the war and it's getting him down. My arthritis is playing up something shocking. We will all be glad when this thing's over. How are you? Write to us soon.

Love Mam

*

For once the desert night was hot because a warm wind blew steadily, lifting baked air from the surface of the sand and wrapping it round the resting soldiers. Only a few men wanted to sleep under the vehicles. The others decided to lie down in their fox holes to try and get as much relief as possible from any movement of air, believing that they could easily run to hide if the nightly barrage came close.

The first shell made no sound until it demolished Jack's recovery vehicle. Others followed hitting two tanks and yet more exploded harmlessly on the desert floor some distance away. The shock waves exploded in the men's ears even before they had chance to be alerted by sound of the initial firing from the enemy guns. The recovery vehicle's cab was totally destroyed and the trailer was smashed beyond recognition rendering the whole thing useless. Worst of all, Alec, having decided to sleep underneath, was killed instantly. Once again the night was floodlit as shells burst, each one providing a still image of men scurrying to take cover or to man the guns. The booming noise of the allied artillery now added to the violent cacophony. Jack's mind screamed at him in protest, unable to cope with what was literally a hell on earth.

*

When he learned of Alec's fate, Jack was desolate. Despite his misgivings about forming deep friendships, he and Alec had become reliant on one-another for both work and comradeship. They were an excellent team, drawn closer together partly because they were alike in many ways, but also, as they carried out their more daunting duties, each came to recognise the bravery and humanity of the other. Now in the cold grey dawn, with the stink of battle still lingering, he had to stand beside his friend's grave, listening to the harassed chaplain mouthing the well-practised last rites. Even though Jack had to some degree, become inured to the horrors of war, he wept grievously for his pal and made a silent vow never again to allow anyone else to get so close.

Mary's letter arrived in Tobruk by the middle of September. It was delivered thanks to the Royal Navy's support for the British 70th Infantry Division, which had replaced the 9th Australian Division, who had held the fortress for over five months. With his vehicle destroyed, Jack and some of the tank-crew members found themselves operating as infantry. They knew they were lucky to be alive and in some ways, he was happy to leave the old machines behind because he was sick of trying to repair the aging mechanisms that were wearing out and constantly affected by the billowing sand. His engineering skills, however, were still in demand but now he was required to repair anything vaguely mechanical: machine guns, rifles, vehicles and even catering equipment. He would happily have left Tobruk to the Germans but the place was regarded as an important port that needed to be held so as to inhibit the enemy's supply lines.

The letter was very unsettling, despite Mary's assurances, he knew that Kathleen would not want to live with her, they just didn't get on. He wondered about asking for compassionate leave but couldn't face the inevitable arguments that would occur when his wife recovered her health. No, better to stay here, thought Jack. Kathleen is capable of sorting out her life. My presence might simply cause more friction because they would both be expecting my support and one of them would inevitably be disappointed. In truth, he had very divided loyalties: as her only son, he felt obliged to support Mary but being absent from his wife had made him realise how deeply he cared for her. He felt that he was probably the worst person to try to sort out their conflicts. Jack also worried about Michael; his young life was already being blighted by the war, he didn't need troubling by disagreements in his family life as well. There just didn't seem to be anything practical that he could do to help his son. He found the entire situation extremely frustrating.

Jack was also wearied by the traumas of war in the desert. He had experienced the rawest outcomes that occur when nations fight: what appeared to be a total disregard for human life with men, dragged from their normal lives, then required to live like animals, scratching shelter out of the sand and spending their days and nights trying to slaughter the enemy. It offended his beliefs about the nature of humanity. He was sure that not all Germans and Italians were evil war-mongers; he knew that they must be working people, like him, with children they loved, who would be happy just earning a living and enjoying family life. The one thing that the war had done for him was to make him appreciate what he had at home; he could hardly believe the dissatisfaction he had felt before he enlisted. He did not believe that he was a coward, but in his heart, he knew how difficult it would have been for him to take compassionate leave and then return to this living hell after being at home.

*

Over the next weeks, the situation in Tobruk became increasingly perilous for the Allied troops. They were surrounded by German infantry and armour and there seemed no prospect of relief or support. The only way out was by sea; if the navy convoys came under attack and couldn't make land, then the soldiers would be trapped like rats; desert rats as they had been christened by the enemy radio broadcasts. Despite his intention to avoid close relationships, Jack had become friendly with a corporal called Bob Gunn. It was simply impossible to exist in a vacuum. He needed to keep in contact with other men. To exist as a loner was the way to madness. Bob was a resilient character who usually gave Jack feelings of confidence, but who had recently become more pessimistic about their chances: 'We're stuck here in this damned town and nobody gives a shit about us. We're expendable, cannon fodder. All we're doin' is delaying the inevitable.'

His words were unsettling, Jack's state of mind was already troubled; events at home and around him in the desert were beginning to persuade him of the unacceptable: that the war might be lost. But he dismissed this as unthinkable: 'there's no point in talking like that,' he said. 'The sergeant told me that the Eighth Army is tryin' to get to us an' we've got to hold out till they arrive, we've got to be determined an' resist, I don't think there's any alternative.'

Those in power appeared to think in the same way for the next day, the British began to extend their defensive lines, more minefields were laid, the Royal Navy provided gunfire support and the Desert Rats dug deeper into their holes. For the time being the German advance was stalled.

CHAPTER 7

*German Stukas use specially constructed bombs with fuses that
cause them to explode just above the desert surface in order to detonate mines.
Tanks bearing black crosses lumber through the safe channel and on the 21st
June 1942, the siege of Tobruk is over. The navy has been forced to
withdraw its support and the British soldiers are trapped with their backs to
the sea.*

Jack watched through his binoculars from the roof of one
of the white painted houses standing alongside the main route
into town. He had ammunition but recognized the futility of
firing; it was time to move out. The engineers had been ordered
to place charges to destroy any equipment that might be useful to
the enemy and then make their way to the beaches about a mile
away. He went to find Bob who was working in the power
station and they both climbed aboard one of the three ton lorries
that were filling with troops. 'Mebbe the navy will come back,'
Bob suggested but there was hopelessness in his voice.

'I doubt it,' Jack replied. 'An' we're too far away for the
little ships to come like they did at Dunkirk.'

The battle raged on into the evening and then fell quiet as
night drew on. Flames lit the sky above the town but only the
occasional sound of shell fire suggested continuing conflict. The
cooks had managed to bring some rations and produced tea that
was some comfort to dispirited men. Bob had an idea: with a
group of comrades they tore the wooden planks from the side of
a lorry and began to fashion a primitive raft but soon realised
that there wasn't enough material to make even one vessel
capable of carrying men across the Mediterranean.

They huddled in their greatcoats as the desert night
dropped cold around them. Some fell into fitful sleep. Others,
too anxious to relax, talked quietly and smoked. Jack looked
again at the stars which never ceased to attract him. The same
broad band of milkiness stretched from the horizon, over his

head and down the sky at the other side. Why couldn't he see this at home? He wondered what Kath and Michael were doing. Could they see the stars? Had they moved to Calthorpe as expected or had Mary persuaded them to stay? When would he see them again, if ever? He felt a strange calmness; there was nothing he could do, his fate was to be determined by others. He had seen men die; he had seen others badly injured to the point of wishing for death. He was tired - an all embracing lethargy. After months stretching into years of the hard grind of existing and fighting with nerves stretched to breaking point, he had nothing left. Let someone else make decisions; maybe he would be killed, perhaps imprisoned. He thought about the Italian prisoners – they would be in England, safe from bullets and shells. He remembered, what was his name? – Rudolph. Yes that was it, a big kind man who had shaken his hand. Where was *he* now? Probably safer than me, he thought.

The first light drifted sneakily, unexpectedly, across the shoreline. It was a night that they didn't want to end – the men feared what this day would bring. A few still fiddled with planks from the lorries, more to keep themselves busy than with any hope of escape. The sea was calm. A small, white-painted, Arab fishing boat lay still on the surface; a local pursued his peaceful, day-to-day work in a battlefield. There was no movement of large vessels, nothing as far as they could see. No rescue in sight. Jack Spencer saw the slow swell of the waves, heard the water kissing the shore. I only ever took Michael to the seaside once, he thought. We could have gone more often, we should have gone. Will I ever get the chance to go again now? His spirits slumped. How could this desert place with its beautiful nights and the calm, blue, seemingly limitless sea be a place of conflict and death? The violent actions of humans were totally incongruous, how could men be so stupid?

It was Sunday – a day of rest. Sounds of a bombardment came from the harbour; the Germans anticipated resistance but none came. Smoke drifted across the beach – it was a familiar smell. The men ate, for the sake of eating: tins of bully beef and large biscuits that were tasteless. Nothing happened. Then around midday, two tanks appeared high above on the escarpment, looking down on the beach – just watching. Then, for several hours, nothing. Jack and Bob talked quietly, Jack kept touching his rifle; 'never let it leave your side,' the sergeant major had told him. They didn't know what to expect next. Jack was determined that, if it came to it, he would sell his life dearly. He picked up the rifle and tested the mechanism, he knew that heat and sand could affect its operation and wanted to make sure that he could use it to defend himself. Some men discharged their weapons into the sea. 'Why they doin' that?' He asked Bob.

'They've got dum dum bullets; the kind that make a bloody big hole in a body. They've heard that the Germans don't take kindly to findin' those so they're getting' rid.'

There was a sudden stirring, the men looked up and saw a German officer walking from the direction of the tanks, holding a white flag. 'Mebbe the buggers are surrendering,' Bob muttered grimly. One of their officers used a piece of driftwood and some white fabric to fashion a similar flag, then walked up the beach towards the enemy.

*

No. *WAP/NS/589*　　　　　　　　　Army Form B 104-3
If replying please quote number above

Infantry Records Office

　　　27ᵗʰ June 1942

　　　　　Dear Sir/Madam,
　　　I regret to have to inform you that a report has been
received from the War Office to the effect that 3651287
(Rank) *private*
(Name) Jack Spencer
(Regiment) 70ᵗʰ Infantry/RAOC
On the *22ⁿᵈ* day of　　　*June*　　　　　　　19　　42

　　　　IN NORTH AFRICA

　　　Is missing but assumed to have been captured by
enemy forces. It has not been reported where he has been
taken, nor are any other particulars known. In the event of
any information being received by this office, you will
immediately be informed. I am to express to you the
sympathy and regret of the Army Council.

　　　Yours faithfully, *Richard Ainley* Officer in charge of
records

　　　IMPORTANT　Any change of address should
immediately be notified to this office.

　　　Kath couldn't speak when Mary asked why she was
crying. She just held out the telegram which had been delivered

by a youth on a motorbike. He had a young fresh face, his cheeks red from the wind created by the speed of his bike. Kathleen remembered his blue eyes, they were like Jack's. He seemed such an innocent boy to be bringing such bad news. She had read the telegram several times before she began to fully understand its implications. She had thought at first that it was going to be like the one Mrs. Sykes from the top of the Long Estate had received telling her that her husband had been killed in action. This one seemed almost worse; leaving her uncertain of Jack's condition, as though he was neither dead nor alive. 'No other particulars known' . . . what does that mean? She wondered. Could he be dead and they don't know, or does it mean that he is still alive? She finally focused on 'captured by enemy forces'. Well how dare they? What right have these Germans to take him away and not tell anyone where to? Anger and fear mingled and then dissolved into tears. It seemed that the present chaos of their lives was building upon itself. Human beings tried to hold on to the notion that normality would eventually return but there were times, such as those that Kathleen was experiencing, when the long, dark night of war appeared to be endless; when the only conceivable outcome was oblivion.

Kath became aware of Mary touching her which was a thing she never did. It felt strange and inappropriate. She shook the old woman's hands off her shoulders and stood. 'I've got to find Michael and tell him.' She looked round wildly as if expecting to find him somewhere in the house but the boy went out as often as possible; he didn't like living in Grandma's house any more because he was constantly being told off. According to Mary, he tore his clothes too much, got dirty too often, spent too much time reading and had unpleasant friends, just to mention some of his shortcomings. No friends were allowed to visit, particularly Whacker, mainly, it seemed, because he had red hair. But all members of the Lucy Street gang were thought to be unwashed and undesirable. Essentially, Mary didn't like children; she wanted a quiet life in a tidy house and to be looked after in her old age. She wasn't really happy when Kath went out, unless she knew exactly where her daughter-in-law was going.

There was also the question of Rags and how to get rid of him. The dog's action at the time of the bombing demonstrated his loyalty to Michael and although she had been unaware of it at the time, Kath recognized that his scratching at the pile of rubble had probably saved their lives. Another few minutes in the cellar and they would both have died from asphyxiation. From that point on, Rags had been fully adopted by the boy and his mother. They insisted that he should live with them. Mary, however, hated 'the nasty smelly creature'. 'Get it out of my house,' she had screamed as the dog tried to follow his master. Ears down, tail between his legs and growling softly, he had turned back on to the street.

'But 'e's my dog and 'e saved our lives,' exclaimed Michael.

'That's right,' Kath added, 'if he goes then so do we.'

'Well 'e's not coming inside.' Mary was adamant. 'E'll have to live on the street.'

'But 'e'll get cold at night an' die.' Michael felt sick at this treatment of a true friend.

Eventually grandad solved the problem. Without a word, one evening, the old man arrived home carrying a wooden kennel under his arm. This was put near to the outside door and demonstrated to the dog that he was, after all, accepted. Michael was delighted; he put his arms round George's thigh and thanked him. They found a piece of woollen carpet big enough to cover the floor and two old tin bowls from the second hand shop. These helped to make life more comfortable and although the dog continued his normal transient existence, he now had a home and a family that could be relied upon for regular food, shelter and company.

Now though, all thoughts of Rags were dismissed, Kathleen had to go to Michael. 'Where are you goin'?' Mary called after her retreating back. 'You don't know where to find him, better to stay 'ere till 'e comes home from school ....' But it was no use; Kath was half running, almost blindly, out into the street in search of her son.

*

Mr Sykes had decided that, although they were amongst the most advanced pupils, they were also the youngest, so Michael and Molly had to remain in Mrs. Stamp's class. One advantage of this, from the boy's point of view, was that he was again in the company of his best friends. Whacker, Ernest and Brian were also pleased that the Lucy Street gang was reformed. Molly, on the other hand was appalled when she found out. The thought of spending another year with a bullying and uncaring teacher filled her with dread.

Michael's optimism soon diminished as he realised that he had read all the books in the classroom and added to this, it soon became clear that Mrs. Stamp was going to put them both through the same lessons they had experienced the previous year. The teacher had a year's programme of lessons and saw no reason to make any alterations. She was irritated by the head's decision to leave these two children in her class and further, had a strong suspicion that they were behind the spider fracas that had haunted her through last year's summer holidays. This did mean, however, that she treated the two of them warily and neither was spanked or treated unfairly. It would have been difficult, in any case, to criticise their work since both remembered very well the expectations of each exercise, having performed the tasks required just a few months ago.

The lack of challenge and new learning was beginning to tell on Michael. He became dispirited and retreated even further into his own reading. This was helped by his groveling apology to Miss Simms at the library, which persuaded her to remove his ban, but was not sufficient to expiate the sins of the others who had been involved in the attack on the sanctity of her domain. He could once more borrow books and took full advantage, carrying to Grandma's house, piles of books on a wide range of subjects from poetry to science. So, when he wasn't out on the streets with the gang, he retreated to the cramped bedroom he shared with his mother to devour as much information and enjoyment as possible from his beloved books.

The room became a sanctuary for the boy; here he was able to escape the worries about his father that were a constant topic of conversation between Mary and Kath and also, he could avoid Mary's constant nagging about his appearance and habits. He tried to be polite and do what was expected of him but he sensed his mother's unhappiness with their lodgings and knew that she too was regularly criticised, even though she now carried out all the tasks that the old woman demanded. It seemed that, because they were under Mary's roof, they had to accept her as the head of the household. Grandad George went out to work early in the morning, returned for his tea and then went to the pub until he came home and went to bed. He occasionally chatted with Michael, but only when they met out in the street. He would sometimes bring home wooden swords or pistols that he had made for the boy at the joiners' shop, but he rarely spoke to Kath and seemed to communicate with Mary by differently intonated grunts that meant 'yes, no, hello,' or sometimes 'be quiet'. He never made any kind of decision and his rarely voiced opinions were confined to the iniquities of war and the condition and price of beer.

*

Kath stopped at the school gate and tried to calm herself, suddenly aware that rushing into Michael's classroom in a hysterical state would simply upset the boy and create a scene and she didn't like scenes, which was one reason why she tolerated her mother-in-law's demands. She sat on the low wall by the gate; it had once had railings but they had been removed so that the metal could be used for the war effort. The remaining stubs of iron stuck into her backside but she felt nothing. Thoughts swam in her head: she had no house, she was not even certain that she had a husband and both she and Michael were unhappy living with Mary. She also knew that Michael was frustrated at school. It was clear that something had to be done; it wasn't possible to delay the decision. The two of them were on their own and would have to solve their own problems. Waiting for Jack's return was no longer an option.

Rags appeared from nowhere. It was uncanny how the dog would turn up when there was trouble about, thought Kath. He licked her hand and leaned against her leg. 'How'd you like to live in the country?' She asked him. This sounded OK to Rags, he didn't understand 'country' but he was happy to go anywhere with his family. He gave a short, sharp bark of approval. Kathleen looked into his liquid brown eyes, wondering if he understood anything that was happening. She conjured-up an image of Michael and his dog wandering happily through the fields and hedgerows of Callthorpe. It may have been a romantic vision, made all the more appealing by the stress caused by Jack's situation, but it seemed the right solution to their problems. She was aware that there was an element of flight in her plan; an attempt to escape that wouldn't necessarily provide a complete solution but it was a step away from the stress of their life with Mary towards, what she hoped would be a safer and more stimulating environment for her son. And so the decision was made.

~PART TWO - COUNTRY~

CHAPTER 8

The 1929 Geneva Convention states that prisoners must be treated no worse than the capturing power's own troops. Permanent camps are to be inspected by the International Red Cross. Officers cannot be made to work and NCOs can only act in a supervisory role, but private soldiers may be put to work, provided that the work is not of military importance.

In contrast to the cordiality of surrender proceedings between the officers, Jack and his comrades were not well treated as they were lined up ready to be moved. He understood how the Germans felt; they too had lost comrades but it seemed a cowardly act to kick and beat men who were unable to defend themselves for fear of being shot. It was very clear that some would have liked to kill the prisoners there and then but satisfied their anger with occasional hits from rifle butts and kicks from heavy army boots up the backside. Jack recalled seeing the bedraggled line of Italian prisoners and how some of the British had been quite happy to treat them badly. He had long realised that war returns many men to a primitive, brutish state and only the strong and humane can rise above it.

Seeing the enemy at close quarters evoked peculiar emotions in Jack. He felt small and insignificant; of no importance. In contrast, the Germans seemed confident, well organised; totally in charge of the situation. They appeared to be bigger and stronger than the English and behaved as though capturing large numbers of men was an everyday occurrence. Their contempt was casual yet obvious. They didn't expect any resistance and got none. Jack felt humiliated and angry with himself and the others for giving in with such apparent meekness.

'Hey Tommy, for you the war is over,' some shouted, or, 'England is kaput, we in London soon, to see your wives.' Jack spun round at this and looked for the eyes of the caller. Bob, standing next to him grabbed his shoulders and turned him away.

'Don't be an idiot; they're just lookin' for an excuse to put one through yer brain.'

They were searched and all belongings confiscated. Jack managed to hold on to a photograph of Kath and Michael by hiding it in his underpants. He tried to keep hold of a wrist watch that Kath had given him for a wedding present but the jab of a rifle was enough to persuade him to let go.

The prisoners were then formed into threes and marched off to a hastily erected compound, surrounded by barbed wire. It was not so secure that the men couldn't have broken out but they were too weary to try anything and simply fell on the ground in search of rest. Now they had only their clothes to keep them warm in the desert night. They were given nothing to eat or drink. Despite this, many slept through sheer exhaustion.

Jack looked for solace in the night sky, so long a quiet and beautiful friend during his time in the desert. Kath won't know what's happened or where I am, he thought while he gazed at the heavens that appeared untouched by the inconsequential trials of men. Michael was interested in the stars and planets he often looked out of his bedroom window and could recognize some of the constellations. When I get back I'll get him a telescope ... but then I might nev ... He left the thought unfinished. His life was on hold, no-one knew what the next days, months or even years might have in store. The officers had been moved to another stockade - it seemed that they were to be separated. This left the men leaderless and insecure. Their leaders may not have been popular and were often criticised for the orders they gave but all significant decisions were left to them and now they were not around, their influence was missed.

The night seemed long, particularly for those like Jack who couldn't sleep. Next morning it was as though a switch had turned on the sun. There was no gentle dawn to gradually remove the night's chill; a sudden blast of heat overwhelmed the sad group, rendering them extremely uncomfortable, hot and hungry with raging thirsts. The patrolling guards looked at them with cold eyes. There was no indication of food or drink being available. One of the gunners had a little German: 'bitte trink und essen,' he tried.

The guards laughed and mocked him, 'trink und essen, wo ist Mr. Churchill?' One threw a half-smoked cigarette over the wire, 'Cigaretten, Tommy,' he called. Most of the men smoked but no-one picked it up.

Eventually, when the burning sun was high in a yellow sky, the prisoners were lined up and given a tin cup which was then filled with warm, ill-tasting water. They also received a thick crust of bread smeared with something that might have been margarine but which by then had melted. These were consumed rapidly but went nowhere towards satisfying empty stomachs.

Trucks began to arrive in clouds of dust and the men were marched forward and put on board. Mercifully the wagons had canvas covers that shielded those inside from the worst of the heat. A German officer walked round checking the trucks and spoke to the prisoners in good English: 'settle down and be comfortable, you will be go to the ships and then to permanent prison camp. Do not think of escapings or causing troubles, my men have orders to shoot anyone problem causing. And you have nowhere to go, the German Army controls everythings.' They did not doubt his words; the enemy had demonstrated their ability to overcome the best the British had to offer at Tobruk and seemed in complete, confident control.

Later, crowded together below decks on the small vessels that were to transport them across the Mediterranean, many of the men were seasick. The throb of the engines, the rocking rhythm of the boats and the heat and stink of bodies combined to create iron-clad, Turkish baths that were simply unbearable for men who were already weak from hunger, thirst and exhaustion. Jack saw several, near him, who lay down and had all the appearance of the dead bodies he had seen during the desert conflict. Comrades tried to rally them even though they themselves were weak and deathly tired. As they disembarked, some were dragged along by their friends, others seemed beyond help and were left behind. Jack never found out what happened to them.

*

The hardest thing for Michael was saying goodbye to the Lucy Street gang.

'Why you goin', an' where you goin, an are you comin' back?' Whacker couldn't understand why his best friend was leaving. Life wasn't too bad; they had the sewage works and the black streets to play in, occasional fights with the Long Estate boys. Sure, school was a pain but there were the holidays and you would have to go to school wherever you lived. So, what if Michael had to live with his grandma? Whacker's grandma was a kind and loving old lady, who sometimes gave him a penny and he assumed that Mary was just the same, even though she had banned him from her house. Whacker was quite used to being punished and thrown out of his own home so he didn't consider this to be extraordinary.

'We're goin' to live in Callthorpe with my other Grandma and Grandad. Our house has gone an' I 'ate school with Mrs. Stamp teachin' and Mam's not 'appy livin' 'ere anymore,' replied Michael, trying to answer all his friend's questions.

'How far is it to Callthorpe, I've never 'eard of it?' Brian joined in. 'Can we come over an' stay?'

'Yer, that's a good idea.' Whacker was enthused. 'We'll come an' stay, OK?'

Michael wasn't sure. 'Well I don't know 'ow far it is but we 'ave to get three buses an' there might not be enough bedrooms.'

'I'll sleep on t' floor.' Whacker was not going to be put off.

Ernest had listened to the discussion. 'Will you come back when t'war is over?'

Michael thought. 'Probably yes, cos dad will be home then an' he'll want to be 'ere near Grandma Mary.'

'That's no good,' Whacker dismissed Ernest's thought. 'It could be years till it finishes, we could be grown up an' old and 'ave forgotten what he looks like.'

So it went on but there was no escaping the inevitable; Kathleen and now Michael were both happy with the idea of living in the 'country'. The boy wasn't sure exactly what this meant but he was fed up with school and the constant tension in his home life. He could no longer bear to see his mother frustrated and unhappy. He was a bit worried about his Dad, after the capture but the boy had a peculiarly unshakable faith in his father's ability to survive. For Michael, it was unthinkable that the war could be lost.

The deciding factor had been Kath's agreement that Rags could go with them. It appeared that both his grandparents liked dogs and were quite happy to accommodate even a scruffy mongrel. He would miss the Lucy Street gang but his mother assured him that he would find new friends in Callthorpe and they might be able to come home to visit Mary from time to time, so he could see his old mates at those times. 'So you see I'll come back sometimes an' we can play together then,' he explained.

'I bet you won't never come back.' Whacker was not happy and the promise of occasional visits was not going to appease him. Michael didn't know what else to say. He noticed Molly standing in the background. He left the others arguing, to speak to her.

'You goin' away?' She asked.

'Yes, we're goin' to live with my other grandma in the country.'

'Which country?'

'No not another country, in the *country*, where there are lots of fields but still in this country.'

'Will you come back?' Molly, usually in good humour, looked sad. Michael didn't like this; he felt a sick feeling in his stomach.

'Yes, we'll come back sometime.' He decided not to get involved in the same discussion again.

'OK, see you then.' Molly turned and walked off slowly.

'Molly,' he called.

The little girl turned and looked at him with her steady green eyes; 'what?'

'Err, see you.' It was all he could think to say.

*

Kath found the parting with Mary more difficult than she had expected. She had grown to dislike the old woman but was surprised by the guilt that she felt at their final meeting.

'You're leavin' me then. I wonder what Jack would say if he was 'ere.' It wasn't so much the words as the crumpled look on Mary's face as she spoke. Behind her usual grim face there was a sign of genuine regret. Kathleen had to harden her heart at this moment and force herself to bear in mind the reality of the situation. Mary had two daughters who could easily help her out. They had been quite happy to leave everything to Kath, now they would have to accept more responsibility for their aging parent.

'I'm sorry Mary but it's just not working. You must be aware that we don't get on, we're always arguing. Michael's unhappy at school and its dangerous living 'ere with the bombs. We nearly died once – it's just not safe.'

'What about me!' The old woman's face filled with anger. 'I could get bombed. George is never in, 'e's useless, doesn't look after me properly.'

Kath was in tears now and angry with herself for letting Mary get to her. 'I can't take responsibility for everyone. I've got to look after my son first an' I think that's what Jack would want me to do.'

'You don't know or care what Jack wants – he would want you to help me, that's what. Wait till I tell 'im, 'e'll 'ave something to say to you my girl.' Mary was almost screaming now and Kathleen realised that they were getting nowhere with this argument it was just upsetting them both.

'Look, I'm sorry we can't leave on better terms but we're goin' an' that's the end of it. You've still got Lillian and Annie, they can help you.' Kath turned to leave but couldn't avoid a final salvo from her mother-in-law.

'Go then. He should never 'ave married you. I told 'im it was a mistake. You've never been a good wife – wouldn't even give 'im another child. You're selfish, through and through.' The final insults made it easier to leave. She felt liberated; a weight had been lifted. Kathleen was suddenly filled optimism; this was the right thing to do and she knew it. Her step was light as she walked up Lucy Street carrying her suitcase, on her way to fetch Michael from Whacker's house.

*

Rags stood with his front paws on the bus window sill and watched the road disappearing under the double-decker that bounded along the broad trunk road leading from the busy city of Ludstow towards the Minster town of Seldown. Needless to say he had never ridden on a motorized vehicle before and had to be persuaded to get on in the first place. He backed away with his hackles raised, growling at this great beast that was about to eat him in its huge cavernous mouth. Kath told Michael to get on board and call him. When the dog saw that his master had not been devoured, he decided to take a chance and leaped onto the platform. Keeping his body low and tail between his legs, he clambered up the stairs to the upper deck. Upstairs, the bus had a well along the right side and passengers walked along it and then climbed up a little step to the bench seats that stretched across to the left. The seats could take five people but there were not many passengers so Michael, Kath and the dog had the front seat all to themselves.

For a while the mongrel was unsure about this bus-riding business but gradually came to enjoy watching houses flying by alongside and when he looked out front at the moving road, he was entranced and gave a little yelp of pleasure. From time to time checking that his family was still around, he spent the whole hour and a half journey looking out. Seeing other dogs in the streets below made him feel superior and a flock of pigeons fleeing from the noise of the bus caused him to bark with delight and charge to the side window to watch them soar away behind.

Michael was feeling pleased with himself because he had on his first pair of leather boots. He knew that they were second hand, from the market, but to him they were the best boots ever. He kept looking at them and rubbed off any scuffs that appeared. He had shown them to Rags who had sniffed them appreciatively. He was also excited because he had rarely been on such a long journey and was fascinated by the changing scenery. His visit to the seaside when he was little had all but vanished from his memory.

He had been to Ludstow before and felt at home in the city with its busy streets and shops. He remembered going there before the war and looking at the beautiful toys in the windows of Sampsons but now there were hardly any toys on display and a lot of the other shops were boarded up. Some had been destroyed during air-raids and were now piles of rubble with warning notices telling people to keep clear. The bus station was busy with people, many in uniform, traveling to destinations all over the country. Michael looked at the posters; one read: *Is your journey really necessary?* And another: *Dig for Victory*. How could you do that? He wondered. His mother told him it was about growing your own food to save money and maybe he could do that when they got to Grandma's.

*

The landscape changed as they traveled; houses, shops and factories gradually gave way to fields surrounded by wooden fences and hedges. Farm houses and barns sat comfortably in the countryside and seemed to be the only buildings. The bus stopped at little villages on the way and passengers climbed aboard or disembarked. Sometimes the bus waited a few minutes because it was ahead of time and needed to wait for people. I wonder if this is what *the country* looks like, he thought.

The bus terminus in Seldown was not as busy as the one in the city. They climbed down the steps and because they didn't want him to begin his wandering ways, held Rags by the new collar and lead that Kath had bought. He hadn't liked them at first but Michael explained that he could take them off when they reached their final destination, so for the time being he accepted the indignity of being led by the neck.

The bus was parked in one corner of a big market square. There were small shops and houses round the edge with windows made up of small panes of glass which had the usual white crosses intended to prevent flying fragments in the event of explosions. There were more people in uniforms around, mostly waiting for buses. When they walked, their boots made crunching sounds across the cobbled square. There were several ponies and traps parked at the far end of the square, outside a pub called the Rising Sun. Other people in civilian dress were walking about or standing talking in small groups, some of the women had wicker shopping baskets slung over their arms.

Michael took in the look of the town and felt good. He liked the atmosphere; the people didn't look as anxious as those in his home town, there was a much more relaxed air about the place. Buildings around the square looked cleaner and there was no taste of soot in the atmosphere. Rags was interested in the horses waiting outside the pub and but for the lead round his neck, would have gone to sniff at them. He was good friends with the coal men's horse back home and thought these new slimmer creatures might be interested in forming a relationship. He gave a little experimental bark but they ignored him.

At the furthest corner of the square stood the Minster; a beautiful gothic building, finer than any church that Michael had seen. 'Oh! Look at that – can we go in?'

'We've got forty-five minutes before the bus to Callthorpe comes but we need to be in the queue in good time because it will be full.' Kathleen knew that there were only two buses each day and they were well-used, particularly on market days, when the local farmers brought some of their produce to sell. 'We can just 'ave a quick look inside but you can come again on another day if you like. We'll 'ave to tie Rags to the gate because I don't think dogs will be allowed in.'

The Minster was one of the few buildings to have retained its iron railings. Having fastened the reluctant pooch by the gate they walked to the huge, imposing wooden doors. Rags whined his displeasure at being left and then contented himself with looking around for potential adventures. He was sure that this new town would offer up some new and exciting places to smell-out. Kathleen twisted and pushed the heavy iron ring on the door and it moved surprisingly easily to reveal the worn stone slabs of the entrance. Moving to the door on the left of a wooden screen they stepped into the Minster and paused, both of them staggered by the scale and majesty of the interior. Carved oak pews receded into the distance towards the high altar and the choir stalls, while the vaulted ceiling seemed to emphasise the pair's insignificance. 'Look at the colours,' Michael pointed to the rose window behind the chancel. 'And there and there,' as he spied more of the stained glass. 'It's just beautiful.'

'Glad you like it.' The voice startled them. 'Sorry, didn't mean to make you jump.' The man had a long black cloak and a dog collar, like their own vicar. He was tall with dark tousled hair and brown eyes. His voice was soft but clear; ideal for talking in the great space of the Minster. 'I'm one of the curates. Would you like to see the choir stalls? They're famous you know.'

They were both quite pleased to be received as though they were of some importance and followed him down the aisle. The stalls were in fact extraordinary; the carving was incredibly detailed and the filigree screens behind could only have been the work of highly skilled artisans. ''ow could they do that?' Michael couldn't believe that people had made these things.

'You must go and see the workshops. You can see the craftsmen carving like this when we need some repairs.' The curate was about to lead them outside but Kath stopped him.

'We 'ave to catch a bus to Callthorpe soon and we mustn't miss it.'

'Oh, I see, yes it will be the last one today. Anyway you can come again sometime. Ask for Michael and I'll come and show you round, it's nice to find a young man who's appreciates fine work.'

'That's my name,' Michael chimed. 'You've got t' same name as me.'

'Well then we'd better be friends,' said the curate, smiling and holding out his hand. This was strange to the boy; he wasn't used to being invited to shake hands with an adult. He took the hand gingerly and found his small fingers held gently but firmly. 'You'd better call me Mike and then we won't get confused, said the man. 'And what do we call your sister?'

'She's not my sister,' Michael replied, laughing. 'She's my Mam, an' she's called Kath.'

Kathleen found herself blushing, 'Kathleen Spencer,' she said, shaking hands. 'We must get goin' or we won't get a seat.'

The curate took them to the main door and waved as they collected Rags and walked quickly to the bus stop where there was now quite a long queue for the Callthorpe bus. 'I like him, an' he's got the same name as me. Can we come back and see't carvers?' Michael said, looking his mother straight in the eyes to see how she felt.

'Oh we'll see.' Kath wasn't sure what to think for she had a natural reserve and didn't really trust people who were familiar too quickly. But this time she agreed with her son, there was something about the curate; he had nice brown eyes and a friendly smile, but more than these things, he had a comforting aura of extraordinary warmth. Even after this brief meeting, she had a peculiar feeling of loss at leaving him. She felt she would like to see this man again. 'We'll see.'

The bus, when it arrived, was a single decker and quickly filled up. Michael sat on one side of the aisle and Kath sat on the other, further back with Rags, held by his lead, crouching fearfully under her seat. They seemed to be the only people who didn't know anyone. There was a lot of chatter with conversations sometimes held in loud voices across the bus.

The boy was fascinated to find himself sitting next to an old woman who carried a leather bag with a duck's head sticking out of it. At first he thought the bird might be dead and then it made a soft quacking sound and shook its beak. He looked at the woman who smiled and seemed friendly so he put out his hand to stroke the duck's head. 'You mun be careful boy, 'e'll 'ave yer 'and off,' she warned. Michael withdrew quickly and she laughed displaying a mouth with only four teeth at the front and these brown as conkers. 'Only jokin' boy, you give 'un a stroke if you want, it'll be the last 'e gets, 'e's for the pot tonight – roast duck for tea.'

'Oh!' Michael was dismayed; he didn't like the idea of the live bird being roasted.

'You come round an' I'll give 'un a leg.' The old woman cackled. He couldn't take his eyes off her teeth.

'Are you jokin' again?' He asked which made her laugh even louder. The boy was baffled.

'Leave t'boy alone Maisie.' A voice from down the bus called. ''E's only a little duck hisself.' This caused general laughter at which point Michael decided just to look out of the window because conversations were too difficult. He realised that the nature of the landscape had changed again. Now the little bus was lumbering down much narrower lanes with high hedgerows on either side, he could hardly see over them. There were very few other vehicles, which was fortunate, since anything approaching would have had little space to get by. Occasionally, gaps in the hedgerows revealed tracks leading off the main road, but these flashed by so quickly that he couldn't see where they were leading.

After half-an-hour the bus emerged into an open space. It was like nothing Michael had seen before. There were small cottages, a pub, a church and a few shops set round a green area with a large pond in the middle. Several white ducks floated on the water, some with their heads tucked down their backs. There were also a few on the grassy bank. The place seemed to be deserted.

'Anybody for Timpney?' The bus driver called out over his shoulder and several people started to extricate themselves from the crowded bus. Since nearly everyone was carrying parcels or shopping baskets, there was a lot of pushing and chatter. The woman next to Michael put the duck in the bag on his knee, scrabbled under her seat and to his amazement, pulled out a small wooden crate full of tiny, yellow chickens. 'You carry yon duck for me young man an' I'll bring t' chickens.'

'But we're not gettin' off 'ere,' he said, looking back at Kathleen for verification. She smiled and nodded.

'It's alright young un',' said Maisie, ''e'll wait for you, won't you Stan?'

'Come on Maisie, stop messin' about,' the driver replied.

Michael did as instructed, holding the now loudly quacking duck in both arms and struggling down the central aisle of the bus. He could hear Rags barking and his mother explaining to the dog that he wasn't leaving them behind. He waited outside while Maisie said goodbye to her friends and then he handed over the bag. 'Thanks young 'un, come an' see me sometime an' I'll give you a duck supper.' This was followed by a cackling laugh and another display of four brown teeth then, to his horror, a big smacking kiss on his cheek. 'Bye, bye my little duck, see you soon.'

Michael, red with embarrassment, climbed back aboard and hurried to sit with his mother who had moved over to Maisie's seat. She was smiling when she saw his confusion. 'Don't worry son, she's just havin' a bit of fun.'

'She 'ad chickens under the seat – did you see 'em? An' she's goin' to eat the duck!' Rags, sensing his master's excitement and pleased at his return, jumped up, put his front feet on Michael's legs and gave his face a big lick.

'Yes, not like home is it?' Kath looked at her son. It was *not* like home, everything was going to be very different for him. She knew he had been sad to leave his friends and although she had assured him that he would find new ones, she was aware that children in small country communities could be insular and suspicious of strangers. Still, things had started well, the curate and Maisie had been friendly and he had seemed to enjoy meeting them, although, the kiss had been unexpected. The curate though – same name as her son - Michael had liked him and he was a very attrac ......She quashed the thought. Don't be stupid she said to herself, he won't remember you for more than ten minutes. Kath turned her head to look out of the window at the flying hedgerows. The thought recurred and she again squeezed it out of her mind. Guilt washed over her; here she was thinking stupid thoughts when her husband was in deep trouble, probably very frightened and maybe even dead. She felt a surge of adrenaline deep inside and experienced a sudden longing to have him here, next to her, holding her with his strong arms. Tears began to trickle down her cheeks – a sob escaped, unbidden. Michael looked, 'you missin' Dad?' he asked. 'Don't worry mam, he'll be alright, I know it, he'll come back to us.' Kathleen pulled her remarkable son and his dog towards her, squeezing them tight.

*

Three days after capture, they reached French soil and were loaded on to railway cattle trucks. Packed tight and with no food or drink, the journey continued to be extremely uncomfortable. After what seemed many hours, the train shuddered to a halt and they were ordered to disembark. Lined up on what seemed to be a temporary station with no real platform, just a long grassed area, flat enough for a lot of men to stand on, they were given two or three potatoes that had been boiled in their skins and a cup of water. Some prisoners rushed to the longer grass and started to relieve themselves; many had diarrhoea. Others had already used the cattle trucks for this purpose because there appeared to be no other option. It seemed at first as if the guards might try to stop them. They raised their rifles and shouted, but an officer called out orders and the guards froze, and contented themselves with keeping the prisoners covered until they returned to the queue.

'I stink and I've got bugs in my hair,' Bob said.

'Yes, me too, said Jack, 'I 'aven't 'ad a wash for at least a week.' He looked at his friend's face, the tan from the desert sun had gone, he was a sickly grey colour and his hair was matted. God do I look like that? He thought. Looking round he realised that all of them looked ill and dispirited. He wondered if they should have fought on and got it over with, it looked as though many of them were going to die anyway, it might have been better to die the soldier's way.

His home seemed to belong to another time and the prospect of having to live-on in these conditions filled him with dark, desperate thoughts. He contemplated running out of the queue and escaping into the long grass but it was an idle thought. He knew in his heart that he would try to stay alive and wait for something better to arrive. At this stage though, Jack had no idea what that might be.

Ordered to get back on to the trucks, the prisoners felt a little better for the food and the chance to stretch their cramped limbs. The trucks had been hosed out but still stank of old cattle smells and human excreta. Some men were in pretty bad shape; they just collapsed on the floor and tried to sleep.

Jack peered through the wooden slats on the side of the truck and watched the passing countryside. He knew that France was occupied and wondered how life was for the people. He gained no clues from what he saw. The train rattled through fields and farms which looked huge to Jack. At occasional level crossings, vehicles waited for the barriers to rise and he saw people standing alongside but they looked quite normal. Some of the vehicles were army wagons and there were soldiers riding motorbikes waiting to cross. He wondered if they knew what was in the cattle trucks or of they didn't care and just wanted to get on with their lives. How he envied them: to have a life that was not totally controlled by someone else.

After several hours, the train slowed and came to a staggering halt in a station; clouds of steam burst from the engine and obscured the scene. It was getting dark now and there were only a few overhead lights. But as the steam cleared, he could see more soldiers, they were lined up as if waiting to travel, then he realised that they were relieving those who had been guarding the prisoners. There were plenty civilians around, all seemed to be carrying suitcases or cardboard boxes. He noticed that they didn't look at the soldiers. A woman in a bright headscarf walked along the edge of the platform, she was carrying a basket containing long loaves of bread. Jack had never seen bread like this before. Without thinking, he called out 'hello Missus, where are we?' The woman was startled but paused and looked through the space between the slats straight into his eyes. 'Hello,' he said again, 'where are we?'

'This is Artieul,' she said in clear English and then, 'who are you?'

'We are English prisoners,' he replied.

'Halt,' a voice screamed, 'gehen Sie, schnell, gehen Sie, nichts sprechen!' The guard rushed towards the woman pointing his rifle and then reversed it as if to strike her with the butt. She turned in panic and fell, spilling her bread over the platform, at which point the soldier kicked her in her side.

Jack was incensed. 'Leave her alone you bastard,' he shouted. 'Leave her alone you bloody coward.'

The guard turned and pointed his rifle straight at Jack's eyes, 'English tod - kaput.' It looked as though he was ready to fire and then he laughed and turned his attention to the woman who was slowly picking herself up. He grabbed her arm and dragged her roughly to her feet, then kicked the bread all over the platform, some of it fell under the train. 'Gehen Sie,

Frazösiche Schwein,' he yelled and delivered one last kick to her retreating back.

'Bastard, German bastard.' Jack was beside himself with anger and he hammered on the wooden walls as he shouted. The Guard looked once more; his eyes were cold, filled with hatred. He smiled, drew his index finger across his throat and walked away. A chill ran through Jack's body. Did this German know something? Were they traveling on this train just to be exterminated?

'You're determined to get yourself shot you silly bugger.' Bob Gunn pulled his friend away from the side of the truck and pushed him into the middle. 'For God's sake, calm down.' But Jack was frightened now. The soldier's casual cruelty to the woman and his contemptuous dismissal of Jack's reaction filled him with dread. What was to become of a train-load of English soldiers in a situation where they were at the mercy of a callous enemy? His fear mingled with guilt; he knew that the woman had been kicked because he had spoken to her. It was his fault.

He felt a surge of loneliness. In the past days he had been a member of an army, with a structure to his life determined by those in command who, while sometimes making stupid decisions, were nevertheless, on his side. He had been amongst men who were fighting to attack the enemy and to protect themselves and him; they had a clear purpose. Now, those in control had no reason to protect him; their intentions were impenetrable and yet he was completely at their mercy. He was surrounded by comrades but none of them had any power; a fighting unit had been emasculated. He might as well have been alone in the cattle truck heading for an uncertain fate.

His feet slipped on the sodden floor as the sudden, juddering movement of the train took him by surprise. He sat down on one of the men who was trying to sleep and was instantly regretful; 'sorry mate, sorry.' But the man was too far gone to care and simply grunted and rolled over.

The train clattered on for several hours. It was very dark when it finally stopped and they were ordered out once more. An officer, standing on the roof of one of the trucks, spoke to them. He explained that they were to stay here for a few days until moving to a more permanent camp. The buildings to which they were marched turned out to be an old French army barracks which had been fortified to form a temporary holding for prisoners of war. The beds, made of wooden boards, were uncomfortable but the men were given hot soup and coarse bread, just about the best meal they had had since they were captured.

*

Michael tickled Rag's chest and looked round at his first sight of Callthorpe. He thought it looked bigger than Timpney but much smaller than his home town. There were no large buildings like mills and all the houses were built of the same warm, red brick which glowed comfortably in the evening sun. He wondered if the houses back home would have looked like this if they hadn't been covered with the black deposit from the factory chimneys. The road round the village green where the bus had stopped was cobbled but some of the small roads leading off looked as though they were just made of hard earth. Up one of these he could see where the rows of houses ended, leading to fields that stretched unendingly into the distance. Trees in the graveyard of the small, ancient church bent protectively over the gravestones. There were a few shops: a butcher smaller than Mr. Fletcher's, one that had men's clothing along with women's dresses and hats in the window, a co-op grocery shop and a greengrocer's with a wooden trestle table outside on which were cardboard boxes holding sorry-looking fruit and vegetables. Two old men, one with very bent legs, were strolling towards the Brown Cow pub at one corner of the green. He could see the landlord drawing the blackout curtains. They knew about the war then; he could have imagined that there was no war because the place seemed so peaceful.

The boy felt uneasy; this was strange, it was fine to sit in a bus watching countryside go by but now he was in a place where he would live. Where were the warehouses and mills? What about the sewage works? That low stone building with piles of sandbags around the entrance looked like a school but it was very small and where was the train station? There didn't seem to be any hills; the fields were huge and flat and receded to a distant, misty horizon. The sky was massive, arching right over tiny people and low buildings. Michael felt lost. I don't know where I am, he thought. His stomach lurched. In that instant, he wished to go back to the streets and hills that he knew. He watched, anxiously as the bus turned laboriously to face the way it had come. It stirred up the dust as it gathered speed back down the narrow lane. It was the last link with his old life and he didn't want to see it go.

'Here you are, here you are. We saw the bus. Stan would have dropped you off by the house if you'd asked him.' A small man with a rugged, weather beaten face, startling blue eyes and totally white hair had spoken. He had a huge smile on his face.

'Dad! oh yes, I just didn't think,' Kath put her arms round the man and gave him kiss. 'Michael, this is your grandad he's called Walter.'

Michael looked into Walter's eyes. Behind the blueness he saw love, friendliness and something else, a quiet sadness. He was to learn later that the old man, like Grandad George, hated the war, because he remembered the horror and pointlessness of the last one.

The man put out his hand. Michael thought that this was the second time that day that he had been invited to shake hands with an adult, maybe he was growing up. He shook hands with his grandfather for the first time and the hand he felt was cool and rough to the touch. It was a capable hand that belonged to a man who could be trusted. Michael had no idea where these feelings came from but he was learning to trust them; he knew, instinctively, that he was going to like this man and would be able to talk with him.

'Nice to meet you Michael and thankyou for looking after Kath since your dad left.' Walter smiled and put a friendly hand on the boy's shoulder. 'Now who's this old boy?' He bent down and tickled Rag's chest. The dog looked at his master, to check that this new person was acceptable and then wagged his tail.

'You're lucky,' said Kath, 'he doesn't usually allow people to touch him until he's got to know them.'

'I think I might have two new friends,' Walter replied and Michael thought he was probably right.

*

Walter led the way from the bus stop, across the green, to a dusty, narrow lane surrounded by a high hedge with trees behind. They followed it for about half-a-mile to Birch Tree Cottage. The house had a wooden gate, in a hedgerow, which opened on to a long pathway that twisted through a garden to the low, stone-built house with two windows that stuck out of the roof. Just like eyes, thought Michael. The roof was made up of red terracotta tiles like the other houses in the village. The house sat comfortably embedded in a garden that was filled with a riot of summer growth. Michael had never imagined that such a garden could exist. There were elegant silver birch trees, beneath which a vegetable patch was set with neat rows of carrots, cabbages, radishes and others things that the boy had never seen before. The flowers though were not organised neatly but grew everywhere in great confusion as though they were just left to get on with their lives as they wished. Rags, who was now released from his lead, gave a yelp of delight and disappeared into the undergrowth to explore. The boy felt as though he was being drowned in a profusion of colour and was almost overwhelmed by the heady perfumes. A soft, sweet sound came from a dense bush near the path. 'What's that?' He asked Walter.

'It's a turtle dove; they're nesting deep in that bush where they're safe.'

'Why does it make that noise? It's beautiful. Why is it called a turtle? They swim in the sea.' Michael had heard pigeons at home but this was a gentler, more melodious sound.

'That's just the sound it makes, but I don't know why it's called turtle,' said Walter. 'If you like birds you'll find plenty round 'ere.'

Michael didn't know whether he liked birds or not, he was interested in everything. 'What are these?' He asked pointing to a group of smiling flowers that glowed with rich colours.

'They're sweet Williams.'

'What? No I'm Michael, not William.'

'I know your name lad, it's the name of the flowers: sweet Williams.'

Michael laughed, 'Oh, I see. An' what're these?'

'They're called dog daisies.' Walter smiled and spoke carefully to avoid another misunderstanding. 'Let's go inside, plenty time for questions later, your Grandma'll think we've got lost.'

But Amy, having heard their voices in the garden, knew where they were and was standing at the door of the cottage. She also was small and grey haired with a button nose and twinkling grey/green eyes just like Kath's. Her dress, covered with a pattern of tiny blue flowers seemed to match the country garden. It was as though she was a natural element of the scene; totally in keeping with her surroundings. 'Come on, come on, the kettle's boiled and I've made the tea.' She put out her arms to receive the grandson she had last seen when he was a baby. Michael was not ready for a cuddle with someone he hardly knew, he put out his hand to shake but Amy ignored this and gathered him up in gentle hug and murmured, 'Oh, love I'm so glad you've come.'

The kitchen had a red tiled floor with multi-coloured, rag mats scattered around. A heavy, pine-wood table sat comfortably in the middle of the room and there was a smaller table with thin legs under the window. The fireplace was set in a huge stone arch and there was a metal spike that allowed a black kettle to swing over the flames. In the hearth a large brown teapot sent out a trickle of steam. Alongside the fire was a large oven with an iron door. A creel hung from the ceiling near the fire and several garments were hanging there to dry. The warm, comforting smell of fresh baked bread permeated the room.

After tea, Michael was shown to his room. It was built in the roof space and had a little window that enabled him to see out over the garden to the fields beyond. There were no buses and shops here, no people walking by indeed he could hardly make out the lane beyond the hawthorn hedge which surrounded the garden. He could though, see a meadow full of grass taller than he had ever seen and he remembered a poem:

> 'Through all the pleasant meadow-side
> The grass grew shoulder high,
> Till the shining scythes went far and wide
> And cut it down to dry.'*

So this was what it meant. Maybe he would see the scythes cutting this grass; it looked long enough already. He decided to ask Grandad if he could watch when they cut this field.

*

The boy examined his new room. There were no damp patches on the ceiling and he had a cupboard, a bookcase full of books and a wash-stand with a basin and jug covered with a printed flower pattern. He went to pick up the jug and was surprised at its weight because he hadn't realised that it was full of water. Next to the basin he found a bar of soap in a little dish and there was a towel hanging on a rail fixed to the stand. It seemed that he was expected to wash himself here rather than at the kitchen sink. Michael noticed the electric light bulb, covered by a pale blue glass shade. He looked for the switch and found it by the door. Carefully, he pushed it down and was delighted to see the bulb light up instantly. Switching it on and off several times, he couldn't believe how quickly it responded to such a simple movement.

There was a sharp, impatient bark downstairs. In the excitement of meeting, everyone had forgotten the dog. Rags had discovered several mice, a fat wood-pigeon and a multitude of new smells and although he was happy to continue his exploration, he needed to check that his master was safe and close at hand. By the time Michael had reached the door, Amy was bending down talking to Rags, assuring him that everything was fine and explaining that the wooden kennel by the door was his home. She also pointed out the two bowls, one with water and the other containing a mixture of meat and dog biscuits. 'These are for your food and we expect you to keep guard and let us know when anyone comes. But don't bite anybody unless we tell you to.'

The dog put his raggy head on one side and listened. He leaned on Michael's leg when the boy arrived and looked up to make sure that the instructions he had received were bona fide. The boy nodded and smiled agreement but had to explain to Grandma that his dog would sometimes wander and disappear for days because he was still very independent. So they shouldn't worry about this and couldn't expect Rags to be on constant guard. He would, however, bring a present, usually a rat or similar, when he returned and Amy shouldn't be alarmed if such a gift turned up on the doorstep. When it was clear that all were in agreement with the contract, Rags licked Michael's hand, gobbled some food, had a drink and then returned to reconnoiter his new domain.

Alone in his room again, Michael sat on the bed. Once again realization that his life was going to be very different returned. He felt disoriented; what shall I do now? He wondered. At home he knew the pattern of life: where the shops were, how to meet his friends, which chair to sit in, how to get to the library, the way to school. Here he knew nothing, except where he was supposed to wash his face. The garden was beautiful, much better than the one at the bombed house and Grandma

Mary had no garden at all, but what lay beyond? Could he walk through the grass field? Were there any children nearby? Would he have to stay in the garden all the time? Might this house be bombed as well? Where would they go if it was? Where was the air-raid shelter? He lay back on the bed, thoughts flying around in his mind. I wonder what Whacker's doing? Where's my Dad? Will we stay here forever? At last, exhausted by the traveling, he fell asleep and dreamed of walking with his father in long, deep grass, not able to find their way back home.

*

Another long train journey took the prisoners right across Germany into Poland to a town called Dopplenz. They were then marched for about half-a-mile uphill to a forbidding, old castle which they learned later, was named after the town but known to the Germans as Stalag 111Z. This was to provide more permanent accommodation.

The men were in bad shape; lack of food, water and basic hygiene had left them hungry, thirsty and dirty. They were covered with lice and many had dysentery. They were ordered to strip and walk into cold showers; their first proper wash for about two weeks. Their clothes were put into steam ovens and then returned to them, although they were mixed up with the result that many now had ill-fitting uniforms. After showering they had their hair shaved. Jack endured the indignity of this process with feelings of relief; he felt that the Germans would not go to the trouble of cleaning and delousing them if they were to be executed.

From the shower block, they were taken to wait in a cold, stone corridor until they could have their photographs taken and be issued with a POW number. They were then assembled in a large courtyard with a damp, stone paved floor and surrounding it, lichen covered high stone walls with tiny windows marking the ascending storeys. The summer sun touched the castellated tops of the fort but its warmth couldn't reach the men gathered below. The fragment of blue sky made Jack ache to be outside of this threatening place. They were addressed by the camp commandant, Ludwig Balheim, who explained, in clipped but accurate English, that they were now under the protection of the International Red Cross and might, at some time in the future, be eligible to receive food parcels from this organisation. 'The Red Cross will also see that your families are informed of your whereabouts. So you see that Deutschland will treat you well unless you cause trouble, in which case, you will have to be punished. I must also tell you that when we have won the war you will be employed in repairing any damages that your RAF has caused.' His next words were drowned by a spontaneous cheer from the prisoners. Now his composure slipped and he shouted, 'you will be silent when I speak!'

When the men were quiet, they were split into groups and taken to the dormitories inside the fort. The officers were kept together. They heard that the senior officer, Colonel Edward Johns, had been appointed as CO and was responsible for liaising with Balheim in matters relating to the welfare of the prisoners. He was given a small room to himself. Everyone was given a postcard on which to write the name and address of their next of kin so that they could be informed of the prisoners' whereabouts. The card told their relatives that they were in German captivity and also had a section in which the men could indicate whether or not they were wounded.

The beds were wooden double bunks. On each was a small sack containing a spoon, knife and fork and a cup and bowl, all made of thin metal. There were also pyjamas made from a rough fabric. The beds had two rough blankets and an empty mattress which they had to fill from straw piled up near the door. Jack and Bob had stayed close together and were in the same dormitory with others from the same unit. Two guards holding rifles with fixed bayonets stood near the door and watched grimly as the prisoners sorted themselves out. Eventually, the Germans indicated that the men had to move to a large hall where they were given soup and bread before returning to their rooms. As soon as they were all inside, the door clanged shut, bolts slid across on the outside and the lights went out.

'What a God-forsaken place this is.' The loud voice came from across the dormitory and startled everyone because conversations had been hushed since they arrived in Dopplenz.

'It's the best we've seen since Tobruk,' another disembodied voice called.

Emboldened now, talk started all around. It was as though, having at last reached a more permanent home, the prisoners felt a degree of security and began to discuss their situation. Some started to move around, searching in the dark for the single lavatory or seeking out friends to talk with.

Jack lay back and stared through the blackness at nothing. His mind went straight home. What are they doing? How will Kath be coping? Do they know I'm alive? An aching tiredness overcame him and he drifted off to a troubled sleep. Father and son, hundreds of miles apart, slept and dreamed the same dream.

CHAPTER 9

The U-boat campaign in the Atlantic begins to affect supplies of wheat from Canada which are destined for Britain. War Agriculture Committees are established to address extreme food shortages. These are made up of Ministry of Agriculture officials and prominent local farmers. Their purpose is to increase production of grain in an attempt to counteract the loss of imports. The 'War Ags' have considerable power. They control every aspect of farm operations and have the authority to evict farmers who they think they are not complying.

After his first night of deep, exhausted sleep, Michael had some difficult nights. He heard a regular air-raid siren in the distance and woke up immediately, sometimes shivering with fear at the thought of his new home being reduced to rubble. The siren also roused his grandfather and together, they stood at Michael's bedroom window. Looking out over the flat fields, they could see great distances and watched the flashes as the bombs hit and heard the delayed sound of explosions. They could see the searchlights occasionally picking out German planes and hear the pop of anti-aircraft guns but never saw a plane come down. 'Will they come over 'ere?' Michael asked. 'What would we do if they come? We've got no cellar now.'

The old couple had been given an Anderson shelter made of corrugated iron but it had never been erected and lay in pieces, under the hawthorn hedge at one side of the garden. Neighbours said that these shelters were dark and damp and since air raids focused on towns, were hardly ever used. A neighbour, Mr. Perry, who was a keen gardener, used his to store potatoes.

'Don't worry love, they're trying to bomb the docks and the factories. We've only got fields and farms. They can't see us because it's so dark round here.' Walter put his arm round the boy and felt him shivering. 'Try not to get upset, I'm sure that this house won't get bombed, you're safe here.'

Michael's day-time anxiety began to fade but was still beneath the surface. For many months he still had dreams about being in the cellar of the old house as the bomb hit. He regularly woke up calling for Kathleen and struggling to free himself from an imaginary pile of bricks.

*

The grass in the field that Michael could see from his bedroom window was actually a good crop of wheat. Walter agreed to take him when it was being harvested. He told the boy that this was an important local event and most of the villagers would turn up, some helping and others just watching, keen to be part of village life. The war made these activities even more important than usual as people held on to key points in the cycle of farming life which helped them to maintain a sense of normality.

It was now a fortnight since they had arrived in Callthorpe. The day of the harvest dawned dry and bright. Michael was awake as the early light crept into his room. He heard a strange mechanical sound coming from the lane outside, pulling back the curtains he saw, for the first time, a Fordson tractor pulling a bizarre piece of machinery towards the gate leading into the field. He rushed to the wash stand and splashed water on to his face, rubbed himself partially dry with the towel and charged along the landing to his grandparents' room. 'Grandad, wake up, I think they've started the harvest,' he shouted, diving on to the big double bed, only to find that it was empty.

'Michael, we're down 'ere,' Amy called up the stairs. 'Come and get your breakfast.'

Down in the kitchen, waiting for him, were thick slices of toast and a *boiled egg*, something he hardly ever had at home. He cut the toast into strips and used it to dip in the bright yellow of the yolk, gulping hot tea in between mouthfuls. Rags was down by the gate barking at the huge, growling monster but not venturing into the lane. Michael could hardly sit still and kept rushing to the kitchen window to see what was happening. 'Calm down, you'll not miss anything; it'll be a while before they get started.' Amy smiled; she was pleased to see his childish enthusiasm for something that she took as just a regular feature in the cycle of rural life.

When breakfast was over they walked across the lane to the field. Walter explained that the machine being pulled by the tractor was used to reap and bind the corn. They stood together at the edge of the field, near the gate, keeping out of the way of the farm workers. Rags had decided that, since his new family was brave enough to enter the field containing the monster, he would investigate and after standing watching for a few minutes, disappeared into the hedge bottom.

Everyone seemed to know his grandad and Michael was pleased when he was introduced to the people who arrived. He asked why there were so many people coming to the field and Walter explained that everyone helped at harvest time. 'They move round each farm in turn and then they all make use of the village threshing machine to separate the wheat from the chaff. You can see that later if you wish. Some farmers are usin' combine 'arvesters now but 'ere in Callthorpe they still use the old methods.'

There were some children around but they ran together in a group and he had no opportunity to speak to them. They looked lively and fit with red, sunburned faces and scruffy clothes. 'They're gipsy children, Michael,' said Walter. 'Some folks don't like the gypsies but I take 'em as I find 'em. Some're good and some're bad, like most other people round 'ere. They're hopin' the farmer will give 'em a penny for helping collect the sheaves.'

A group of men arrived and Michael was surprised to see that they were carrying guns, which they held loosely over their arms with the double barrels pointing down. 'Are they soldiers?' He asked.

'No lad,' Grandad laughed. 'They're just local blokes, waitin' for the rabbits and hares. You'll see what they do later. There won't be much for them to do yet.'

The tractor started into life with a great roar, pulling the strange machine into the wheat. As it moved forward the sails began to turn, pulling the long stems into the cutters. Michael was fascinated to see the machine send out sheaves already bound with rough twine. 'How does it do that?' He had to shout because of the noise of the engine.

'I don't know lad, you'll 'ave to ask Donald later on.'

'Who's Donald?'

'He's the farmer driving the tractor - Donald Gant.' Walter pointed at the large man in blue overalls sitting with bare, muscular arms steering the noisy machine. 'They used to use the great shire horses for this job but he got the tractor after the War Ags started up.' Michael thought he would have liked to see horses pulling the reaper and imagined what it would have looked like. As he watched the machines turned round the top of the field so that only the flying sails and the top of the farmer's body could be seen. The boy thought that the farmer looked magnificent riding above the wheat.

People, including children started collecting up the sheaves and leaning them in groups so that they stood with the grain at the top. They looked like a line of Red Indian tents; in fact some children crawled through the holes at the bottom until they were reprimanded by the adults. A large man with red hair threatened to hit them and raised his clenched fist. The children ran away to another part of the field. 'Can I help?' Michael asked.

'Sure you can. Just watch and follow what the others do.'

Michael ran to find a sheave and with a good deal of straining, carried it to where one of the men was making a pile. 'Thanks young 'un,' said the man. 'Just lean it agen these an' it'll stand firm.' Michael was delighted to be taking part and rushed off to find another one, staying close to the man because he seemed friendly. He enjoyed the rough feeling of the wheat stems and the comforting smell of seed heads. He was glad to have on his new boots because it was difficult walking over the spiky stubble left behind by the reaper. He thought that his old clogs wouldn't have suited the task. He started to take off his shirt because he was getting very hot but Walter called to him to keep it on. 'You'll get scratched and itchy if you take it off.'

A lemon-yellow sun rose through the calm, blue sky and a long, late summer day passed slowly. The tractor continued its lazy progress bringing down the wheat and shunting out sheaves. Flocks of swallows zoomed around harvesting the myriad of insects that rose as the crop was disturbed. The helpers settled into a steady rhythm, collecting the sheaves in teams, occasionally standing to rest, leaving the work to another group. Michael's muscles ached but he felt intense pleasure that he was able to do this hard work in a strange environment. This was like nothing he had ever experienced before; he enjoyed the calm purpose of the activity and despite being away from his normal life, began to feel at home. Thoughts of war and bombs seemed to be from another distant dream-time.

The tractor noise stopped. Michael looked up to see what had happened. Everyone was walking towards the gate and he was surprised to see Kathleen, Grandma and some other women carrying heavy baskets into the field. 'Time for snap lad,' Walter called. 'You've earned it.' The women were soon surrounded as they passed out huge chunks of bread and cheese, accompanied by pickled onions and apples. There were bottles of beer and jugs of home made lemonade. The boy was suddenly aware of his raging thirst and gulped down the cool, bitter-sweet liquid before devouring crusty bread and a block of cheese.

Kathleen's heart swelled at the sight of her son: his hair was tousled and his face red and dirty from the dust of the field, sweat trails ran down his forehead and cheeks but he had the aura of a boy in heaven. She had not seen him so contented for months and was sure that she had made the correct decision to move to Callthorpe. 'Mam, I've been helpin' – look at all those sheaves, we've done all those!' She couldn't reply and just locked him in her arms, her heart bursting. Michael struggled to get free, thinking that a 'farm-worker' was too grown-up to be cuddled. Amy and Walter watched and smiled. Rags, his coat full of seeds and sticky buds, appeared from nowhere and rubbed against the pair, eager to share the moment.

After snap, the reaping continued with the standing wheat getting smaller. Villagers returned to their task and the field filled with conical stacks of sheaves set in windrows to dry in the sun. Michael, now an experienced labourer, had developed the knack of lifting the wheat and was as quick as anyone to do the work. 'You've earned your penny today,' said the man he was working with. 'Make sure you get it, ol' Donald will likely forget.' The boy was so pleased to be involved that he had never thought of being rewarded.

He was suddenly aware of a feeling of tension around the field and noticed that the men had snapped their guns and were carefully watching the diminishing area of wheat. He was startled by the explosion as one was fired. The hares, which had made their shallow burrows in the field, had been driven away from the noise of tractor into the remaining uncut area. As the standing wheat got smaller, there came a point when they were forced to make a run for the safety of the hedgerow. It seemed that, when one broke cover, the rest followed and soon the animals were running wildly from all points. Michael was amazed at their speed. He had seen rabbits before but hares were new to him; he admired their long back legs and the pace they were able to generate, with instant changes of direction. Some were too quick for the guns and disappeared into the hedge bottom where Rags tried to intercept, with joyous barks, at having found such a worthy target.

Michael watched now as the men broke their shotguns and spat out the used cartridges with a puff of smoke. They were very quick to reload and soon the field was littered with dead bodies. Now he felt distressed to see these beautiful animals cut down and bleeding. Some were not dead and had to be beaten with the butt end of a gun. He turned away and buried his head in Walter's trousers. 'Oh, don't take on lad,' said Grandad, bending down, 'it's how things are in the country. Too many hares and there would be no vegetables in t' gardens. Anyway, the fastest ones always get away. Besides, times are hard an' we're all short of meat. A nice jugged hare is welcome on any table.'

'Well I'm not eatin' any,' sobbed the boy. Grandad smiled and ruffled his Grandson's hair; 'come on, let's go home, it's been a long day an' we're all tired.' Michael protested, rubbing his eyes, but allowed himself to be led towards the gate. A descending sun drenched the scene in gold as shadows lengthened across the stubble and an old man, a boy and a dog walked together down the field and across the lane to birch tree cottage. Michael forgot about his wages but would never forget his first harvest.

*

Life in Dopplenz was boring. Time did not seem to progress, days just revolved around one-another. The prisoners were able to exercise in the courtyard but it was small and even impromptu games of football were restricted with so many men in a limited space. Every few weeks, the Germans printed a small newspaper, in English. It described terrible events in Britain with towns such as Coventry and Bristol reduced to rubble and Londoners on the verge of surrender. They became increasingly disheartened by the news and frustrated that all they could do was wander, anti-clockwise round the depressing, uneven stones of the castle yard.

Regular food was provided but it didn't amount to much; a bowl of soup, a few pieces of bread, each day and a small knob of margarine and a spoonful of jam maybe once or twice a week. All the men were losing weight and had little strength for vigorous activity even if there had been space for it. A few determined souls tried to organise the men for regular exercise and the others watched as a small group bent, stretched and ran-on-the-spot every morning after roll call. Jack and Bob thought it was good to keep as active as possible and joined in. Gradually the group grew and before long nearly all the prisoners were taking part every day.

The summer of 1942 was coming to an end and days began to shorten. The chill of early autumn made the prisoners shiver in the early mornings and exercising was sometimes done wrapped in great coats or blankets. Their lives were brightened one day, however, when they received the first delivery of red-cross parcels and messages and gifts from home.

The CO spoke to the men after the morning roll call: 'Men, I am pleased to tell you that we have received news from home and from the Red Cross. Mail and personal parcels will be delivered to your billets but we will share out the contents of the Red Cross provisions now. I'm sorry to tell you that I believe that our captors have withheld some of the items that we should be receiving. Oberst Balheim denies this but I fear that he is not being entirely truthful. Unfortunately, there is nothing we can do at this stage. Perhaps we should be thankful that our families know where we are.' With this the prisoners were ordered to line up to receive tins of jam, chocolate, packs of cigarettes, pipe tobacco and other items that they never expected to see again.

The Red Cross provisions proved to be a considerable morale boost, enhanced by letters and parcels from home that left many in tears. Jack poured over Kath's letter and his heart clenched when he read about the move to Callthorpe. He had thought that his family was secure in his mother's house but now he felt as though he had lost control. It was difficult for him to accept that they could take decisions without consulting him. His life was in limbo and somehow he had expected his family to remain the same until he could rejoin them. Inside he knew that this was unreasonable but the news made him feel even more frustrated and cut-off from normal life. His feelings of jealousy also resurfaced; what if Kathleen met someone new in this village? Would she be faithful, with him being so far away? The best part of the letter was at the bottom where Michael told him about the harvest and said he wished that Jack could have been with him. At this point the sadness that had been kept inside welled-up and overflowed and Bob found his friend, sitting on his bunk, sobbing uncontrollably. There was nothing to do but put his arms round Jack's shoulders and wait for the release of emotion to subside.

After a while the two friends shared their letters. Bob had been called-up on his eighteenth birthday when he was still living with his mother. He had neither wife nor children but expected to get married to his girlfriend Liz when the war ended. He, like Jack, was depressed by their situation. While they realised that the news they received from the Germans was laced with considerable propaganda, they nevertheless feared that the Allies might lose the war and that life would never return to normality. Liz had written a passionate letter which made Jack feel slightly embarrassed. 'She certainly loves you,' he said.

'Oh sure,' said Bob, 'but she's a very friendly girl and I worry that any blokes around might think she's available.'

'Yes, you're worried like me but there's nowt we can do so we've just got to hope they'll be faithful. It's not that I don't trust Kath, it's those buggers at 'ome I don't trust.'

'Yes, I think ….' Their talk was interrupted by cries of alarm, sounds of confusion and running feet echoed from the stone walls outside their room. They hurried out of the billet and found men rushing to the end of the corridor where a small window overlooked the courtyard. 'What's up?' Bob asked of the others standing around the window.

'It's Gunner Blake, he's topped himself,' one of the men shouted.

When they eventually got through the press of bodies and stretched their necks to look out of the window, to the left, they saw the slack body of Private Blake hanging against the cold, stone wall of the old castle. He had used his blankets and towels to make a noose and simply allowed himself to fall from the tiny window of the toilet block that served his dormitory. His head was twisted at a strange angle and his eyes and mouth were open. The body swayed gently and his boots scraped against the wall dislodging powdered, fragments of stone. Jack groaned, he had seen dead bodies before but this one seemed so much sadder than the others. He could almost feel the weight of despair that had driven this man to end his life.

All around, prisoners were reduced to silence at the sight. Then someone shouted, 'for God's sake get 'im down.' But no one could manage to get sufficient purchase to pull the body back through the window. It must have taken the strength of a desperate man to squeeze through the small space.

It was then that objects began to rain on to the courtyard: books, plates, mugs, paper, bits of uniform, whatever the men could get hold of was thrown into the air to drift down and patter on the stone paving below. This seemed the only way that they could demonstrate their empathy with Gunner Blake. There were no words, just a quiet clatter as their belongings hit the ground.

They found out later that the soldier had received a letter, from his mother, which described the affair that his wife was having with an American airman. The men agreed that it would have been better for Blake to remain ignorant; there was enough frustration in their present predicament without bad news from home. It was doubly agonising to learn that American troops were stationed in England while they were stuck in a God forsaken castle in Poland. The thought of slick talking cowboys impressing his wife gave Jack another cause for anxiety, although he thought that they were unlikely to be stationed near a country place like Callthorpe.

CHAPTER 10

The Geneva Convention decrees that POWs should be allowed two letters per month for 'other ranks', while officers should be allowed 3 and 4 postcards a month on stationery provided. Prisoners should also be allowed to receive relief parcels. Throughout the war, there are many complaints about mail and parcels not being received or arriving very late.

Kath read the despair in Jack's latest letter. He tried to sound hopeful but phrases such as 'hope for the best' and 'make the best of it' were out of character. When he enlisted, she had seen a brave and determined man, keen to do his bit, now, even though the letter was brief and lacking detail, she could sense that his spirit was diminished. Still it was good to hear from him and she was pleased to have evidence that her own letter had reached its destination.

Michael read the letter and was full of questions: 'where is he then?' 'Can I send him a present?' 'Will they let 'im come home?' 'Can we go ….'

'Oh! Enough Michael, we'll just 'ave to be patient and hope the war will end soon love. I can't answer your questions, I just don't know. We just 'ave to be pleased to hear from 'im and know that he's alright. It's time you were off to school now, or you'll be late.'

The school was a single storey building built of old stone. It had high arched windows with many small panes each with the inevitable cross of sticky-tape. Around the doorway, the local home-guard had stacked sand bags. There was an intention to use the school as a centre for civil defence if the Germans managed to get as far as Callthorpe.

It was Michael's second day at the village school. The first had been chaotic. There was only one class of about thirty children ranging from four to eleven years old. The teacher Miss Newby, because it was the beginning of term, had to cope with the new little ones, some of whom made a fuss because they didn't want to leave their mothers. She also had to look after those who were returning, ready for new work and full of stories from their holidays.

Michael didn't really fit into either category but had no idea about the classroom practices so just sat quietly. He selected an encyclopedia from one of the shelves and began reading, resting it on his gas-mask box. Consequently, it was not until late in the morning that the teacher really noticed him and called, 'oh yes, Michael Spencer, we'll need to find out what you can do. Can you read or are you just looking at the pictures? Come and show me.' He went and sat by Miss Newby and demonstrated that he could read fluently. 'Marvelous,' she said. 'We'll have to find some more difficult books to keep you on your toes, I can see that.'

The boy didn't see why he should have to stand on his toes but was pleased to receive some praise on his first day. He had taken an instant liking to his new teacher. She was young, about twenty-six, with fair hair, blue, smiling eyes and smelled of lavender. She seemed calm and kind, dealing with new pupils purposefully, shooing the parents out and provided interesting activities to take the children's minds off their troubles. Unusually in Michael's experience, she used the *first* names of the established pupils, greeting them with interest and humour. They responded to her with respect mingled with affection and were very keen to tell her their news.

Only one child held back. He was small with bright red hair. His clothes were ragged but that was not unusual, many of the children had garments that looked old and were either too small or too big as though they had been passed down from older siblings. Michael noticed that the boy had on a pair of boots, without laces and with the sole of the left one hanging off, but no socks.

Like Michael, the boy seemed happy with his head in a book and didn't want to join in the general conversation. Perhaps he's new like me, Michael thought. So he went over and said hello but the boy turned away and continued looking at his book, clearly not reading or taking any interest in the pictures. Michael wanted to find out more about this strange boy but decided not to bother him anymore until he understood why he was so unsociable. Whacker was the only other boy that he knew with red hair and he was always friendly so it was all a bit of a puzzle.

He watched as Miss Newby tried to talk to the boy but he turned away from her as well. He shook her off when she tried to put her arms round him and started to cry. She walked away shaking her head. When playtime arrived, the boy took no part in the other children's games and just stood by the wall fiddling with loose pieces of mortar.

Michael had an idea; he remembered that Brian's ring worm had made him feel poorly and depressed, so he went to the boy and asked, ''ave you got ring worm or somethin'?' All he got in reply was a shy look and a shake of the head.

'Don't bother with him,' another boy called. 'He's weird. Never plays with us or anything. He's a German.' Michael didn't understand this but left the boy alone, determined to get him to talk and be friendly at some time in the future.

Now, on his second day, he was looking forward to his new school. It wasn't as big as his old one but he liked the feeling of the old stone building with its small entrance hall that served as a cloakroom. There was a little office where a part-time secretary worked. The lavatories were in another stone building at the bottom of the playground. The school was set on one side of the village green straight opposite the Church. Michael was going to have to learn in a class that included much younger children but the teacher seemed livelier than those he had experienced before and he began to think that this school was likely to be a more interesting place. His mind flew back to Mrs. Stamp and he shuddered when he thought of the bleak desert that was her classroom and the old books that he had to read over and over again.

Michael couldn't believe what he was seeing; even at the beginning of the year, Miss Newby's classroom was full of interest. There were books everywhere; some on bookshelves, others displayed with their pages open to show interesting pictures. There were displays about local history and a collection of autumn leaves, fruit and fungi on a table with reference books to study propped against the wall. There were also maps showing details about the war and advice about helping the war effort and keeping safe. This made the boy think about his father and he thought that he would tell Miss Newby about Jack when he got the chance.

'Because there are so many children at different ages in this class,' said Miss Newby, 'I'm going to let the older ones decide on a personal project that they can study but I would like you to work in pairs. I need all of you to think about something that you would like to work on and let me know tomorrow what you would like to do and who you would like to work with. Then, for an hour each day, you can concentrate on your project and I can help the younger children with their reading and writing. The librarian from Seldown has said that she will let us have books that fit in with your topics when she knows what they are.' Michael was delighted to hear of a library and wondered if he might be able to become a member. His own books had been irreparably damaged when their house was bombed. Searching the ruins when it was safe to do so, he found only tattered remnants and all he had now were the books belonging to Walter and Amy that were in the bookcase in his bedroom. A buzz of conversation followed Miss Newby's announcement. 'Alright, don't discuss it now because we've got work to do but I'll give you some time to think this afternoon.' The children settled down and the day's work began. Michael thought to himself that he had been right; the work in this school *was* going to be more interesting. He already had a good idea of what he wanted to study.

*

Kath sat by the kitchen window looking out at the garden. Rags was asleep by her feet. He wasn't supposed to be in the kitchen, but when Michael wasn't around, he liked to stay close to Kath. It was as though he needed to be near to one of them. The dog wasn't as independent as he had been when they were in Stanbury and although he would sometimes stay out by himself for a morning or afternoon, he didn't disappear for days at a time.

The leaves were beginning to turn towards autumn. Her father had already dead-headed the roses and the other summer flowers were drooping towards the end of their lives. There was still colour to enjoy: a great fuchsia bush was still full of blood red flowers and the Michaelmas daisies with their yellow eyes were beginning to open. She loved the garden and the house, and regretted stalling on her decision to move here long ago. She thought about Mary with some tinges of guilt but knew, in her heart, that she had done her best for the old woman and that now, her priority had to be her son.

Amy was in the kitchen too, making plumb jam. There was a warm comforting smell of fruit and sugar as the heavy iron pan bubbled on the stove. 'What're you thinkin' about?' She asked. 'Not broodin' about Jack I hope. There's no good worrying, it'll all come right in the end, you'll see.'

Kath didn't answer. She listened to her mother's words of comfort but knew that that's all they were; things *could* go wrong. They had been lucky when the house was bombed, if it hadn't been for Rags they would be dead now. She bent and tickled his back as she remembered his bravery. He woke immediately and looked up with his head on one side and his long, red tongue sticking out. His tail thumped on the red-tiled kitchen floor and he stood up and stretched, ready for a walk. 'Yes mam, you're right' said Kath, looking into the dog's trusting eyes. 'That's the way to think about everything at the moment. I'm just takin' Rags for a walk, is it alright, I feel like some fresh air.'

'Sure, you do that, I've got plenty to do. Will you call at the co-op and get some sugar please? My ration book is in the top drawer, I've got some coupons left.'

They had tried in the past to keep Rags on a lead. He tolerated it in the towns and on buses but in the countryside he pulled and twisted his head so much that it was just a waste of time so he was allowed to trot along, sometimes with them and sometimes pursuing interests of his own. He had always loved the rich aromas in ditches and hedgerows and now enjoyed the greater variety of country animal smells. While the sewage farm rats had provided good sport, he now chased rabbits, hares, weasels and the occasional grouse although the latter were impossible to catch and hares were too speedy unless they were caught unawares. He gave a bark of delight when he realised that they were going out and flew down the long pathway to the gate, jumping up, he lifted the latch and with his paw, pulled it open. Kath followed, knowing that he would reappear at some point just to check that she was alright.

The lane was quiet except for a colony of rooks that complained and argued from the high sycamores. A late autumn sun warmed her back. She thought how different this was from the urban environment with which they were familiar. The red tiled roofs of the village seemed suspended in a cluster of trees. A few fires had been lit and grey smoke stood straight against the deepening blue of the sky. A comforting smell of burning wood hung in the air. Kath could see the church tower reaching above the village with a union jack hanging limp from the flag post. It was all achingly beautiful.

I suppose we're fighting to protect places like this and the home that we used to have, she thought. Why did human beings allow themselves to be driven to killing and hatred? Surely there were places like this all over the world where people just wanted to get on with their lives. She had never been to Germany or Italy, had never met anyone from those countries so why were they trying to kill her and her family?

She reached the village and headed for the Co-op to get sugar for Amy but found herself drawn to the Church. Kathleen had secure religious beliefs. She tried to live a Christian life, attending their chapel at home out of commitment rather than habit. She had begun to wonder why, despite everyone's prayers, God wasn't playing His part in bringing this conflict to an end. The events of the war seemed to her to be completely contrary to the way in which people ought to behave towards one-another. 'Thou shalt not kill' was, in Kathleen's opinion, such an obviously fundamental rule of life, that she couldn't understand why the huge number of killings was being allowed. It had all happened before, she could remember how worried they had been when Walter went to fight in Belgium during the First World War; the look on her mother's face every time there was a knock on the door – was it the news she dreaded? Now it was all happening again – why? Perhaps we're not praying hard enough, she thought. Maybe we're not saying the right things.

The Church in Callthorpe seemed a much more appropriate place for prayer than the chapel at home. It was considerably older, more intimate and had a tangibly spiritual atmosphere. She had a feeling that prayers offered in the peace of the village might be more likely to be heard than those emanating from the forbidding Victorian pile of the chapel she had attended in a noisy industrial town. She knew that this was an emotional response; Kath recognised her own lack of logic, but it just felt right.

Turning in through the lych-gate, she followed the winding path through the graveyard to the door. The ancient, finely carved stone arch of the entrance felt like a gateway from everyday life into a world of faith and belief in a power beyond her understanding. The door, she knew, was always open, so twisting the heavy iron ring, she pushed hard on the ancient wood, which moved easily and quietly, and stepped inside. The interior was cold but sunlight streaming through the stained glass made it feel warm. The eagle on the lectern reflected a mellow glow that dripped gold on the pulpit and the altar rail. Running her fingers over the carved oak of the first pew, Kath felt for a hassock with her other hand and pulled it out. Kneeling, she began to whisper her prayers. A cloak of quietness descended around her. The whole building paused to listen. She prayed with all her heart for an end to the war, trying to find the right words that might be heard.

Afterwards, she sat, silent for a while. Her prayers, as usual, had made her feel peaceful and relaxed, but now more so than she had felt for months. 'Jack, Jack, keep believing love, stay strong, don't give up.' Kath spoke out loud.

'Oh, I'm sorry. I didn't know anyone was here.' The male voice startled her. She spun round reddening that someone might have heard her prayers. The man had emerged from the bell ringers' room. She could see the coloured ropes hanging behind him. There was something familiar ...

'Hello, how nice to see you again. It's Michael, oh no we agreed on Mike, remember, because of your little boy's name, we met in the Minster.'

*

The school day ended. Michael walked from the classroom and out into the playground. Just as at his other school, the railings had been cut off so that the metal could be used to make armaments. Now a small stone wall was all that separated the playground from the pebbly road that wound round the village green. The stubs of the railings had been covered over with cement to prevent children from scraping themselves on the remaining rough edges.

Several children were already sitting on the wall; they seemed to be waiting for Michael. Two of the bigger boys stood up and blocked his way. 'Now then city boy, can you fight?' Thomas Gant, a farmer's son, spoke threateningly. He was about the same age as Michael but taller and he looked strong. He had the red complexion of a country boy with wild, sun-bleached hair.

Michael sighed inwardly. He had been here before. He remembered his fight at the other school and more importantly, Whacker's advice. Stepping forward, without hesitation, he stood on his toes and hit the boy hard, right on his nose. Blood spurted immediately. Thomas Gant squealed and fell backwards over the little wall, scattering the other children.

Michael had mixed emotions at this point: he was pleased by the successful strategy but upset to have hurt someone. He stepped over the wall and knelt down by his adversary. Pulling out a rather grimy handkerchief, he tried to stem the flow of blood which made Thomas squeal even louder. 'Gerrim off me,' he shouted, trying to sit up.

'Don't sit up,' said Michael, 'put yer 'ead back and 'old this 'andkerchief to your nose, it'll stop the blood.' Thomas, recognising good advice, did as he was told and remained lying down. The other children were surprised by the events, having fully expected the strongest boy in the school to have made short work of the smaller newcomer; they simply stood and watched, not without admiration.

At this point, Miss Newby came out to see what was happening. 'Thomas, what's happened to you, you're bleeding!' Michael thought he had better own up and started to speak but was interrupted by the boy on the ground.

'I fell over the wall Miss and bust my nose.' The cock of the school was not about to admit that a smaller boy had got the better of him. Besides which, there was an unwritten law that you didn't tell tales.

The teacher took her injured pupil inside to tend to his wound, while Michael was left rather nonplussed by this outcome. The others, with slightly amazed looks on their faces, drifted away but he decided to wait for Thomas so that he could offer his apologies and thanks. He didn't want to have ill-feelings when he had only just arrived and with a school so small, he realised that it was best to get along with the other children wherever possible. Here was another puzzle though he thought; I want to make a friend of this boy, even though we've been fighting. Howard back at the old school, despite the fact that he was from the long estate, had become a friend and he wondered if the same might apply to Thomas. Maybe, he thought, this will happen with the Germans; after the war was over they might become friends!

When his opponent eventually escaped the teacher's ministrations, the two boys set off to walk home. Thomas's nose had stopped bleeding and apart from a slight reddening, looked fine. He lived at Gant's Farm which Michael passed on his way back to his grandparents' cottage.

'I think it was a lucky punch,' Thomas opened negotiations.

'Yes, I 'ave a friend who's a good fighter an' 'e told me to get a punch in first so that's why I did it. I didn't want a fight but you challenged me.'

'Yes, that's true but I think I could beat you if we fought again.' Thomas looked at Michael for confirmation or further argument.

Michael thought for a moment about the best strategy. He didn't want to make an enemy and he certainly had no ambition to be the cock of the school. He was happy that he had demonstrated his bravery so decided to agree with reservations. 'Yes I think you could but you're bigger. If I was your size I might win.'

Thomas too paused to consider and then agreed; 'OK. Mebbe I could still be cock an' you could be second.' This appeared to be a reasonable compromise so they agreed and solemnly shook hands.

Peace established, Thomas invited his new friend to visit his farm. They walked together up the rutted track to an old farmhouse, covered with Virginia creeper the leaves of which were beginning to turn to their autumn colours. 'Do you want to see my rabbits?' Thomas asked. 'They're in the barn.'

'Yes please, 'ow many 'ave you got?'

'There's four does and two bucks an' eleven little uns.'

They walked to the barn and pushed open the great doors. Inside the floor was covered with hay and there were four stalls, two containing horses, one empty and one with a variety of home made hutches. Michael could see rabbits looking out through the wire mesh on each cage. On the floor of the stall was a bigger hutch with just a door in the side and a wire mesh fence that cut off about four square yards of the floor. Here young rabbits, mostly black and white, ran around, but as the boys entered, they disappeared inside the hutch. The barn was filled with the warm, sweet scent of hay. In the far corner, a wooden ladder led up to a hay loft that was full of piles of dried grass. Gaps between the boards of the barn wall allowed late sunshine to send dust filled rays through the air.

Michael was entranced. He had never seen anything like this before. The old warehouses that he and the Lucy Street gang had played in were about the same size but they were filled with the smell of shoddy and sunshine never penetrated the grimy windows. The only animals they might have seen were scuttling rats. 'Are they all yours?' He asked, amazed.

'Sure. I've got some hens too and I look after the geese.' Thomas was pleased by Michael's obvious admiration. 'You can help me feed 'em if you like.'

'Can I?' Great, what do they eat?'

'Well, the rabbits like dandelion leaves an' carrots and the 'ens and geese eat corn. There's food for the rabbits in this sack and the grain's in that big box over there.' Thomas pointed at the appropriate containers. They spent some time giving the animals food and then watched as they ate. Michael was fascinated by the way dandelion leaves disappeared as the rabbits nibbled and he enjoyed being surrounded by clucking hens when they threw grain on to the floor. All was peace; the calm, trusting animals made him feel peculiar – a strange tingle ran up the back of his neck. I would like to have this feeling at my house, he thought.

'These baby rabbits, could I get some do you think?' Michael asked.

'You can 'ave some next time the big uns get a litter.'

Remembering his lesson with Molly, Michael asked, 'do they 'ave to shag when the female's 'ad a period?'

Thomas wasn't sure about the 'period' business but agreed that the male had to mount the female when they were old enough to do it. 'The hens and geese do the same. One cock can manage as many as twenty hens, an' when the hens are ready to sit they get broody an' they can keep as many as a dozen eggs warm till they hatch. You can have some of those as well if you want'

'Some of what?'

'Some chickens – they come from eggs you know!'

'Oh! Yes, well I knew that. I don't know about 'avin chickens, I'd 'ave to get somewhere to keep 'em.' Michael was beginning to get confused by this generosity. He had never been offered anything so valuable before and felt that he needed to give something in return. 'I'll 'ave to ask my grandad.' This sounded a bit lame but was the best he could think of at the moment.

The boys continued their tour of the farm. Thomas proudly pointed out the fields nearby. 'And we've got more further over, near your house.'

'Is the cornfield yours?'

'Yes.'

'I was there when they did the 'arvest. I 'elped to stack the sheaves.' Michael was pleased with the connection. 'Your dad's called Donald isn't he?'

'Well I was there as well and …'

'**Thomas, your tea's ready**.' A female voice interrupted, calling from the door of the farmhouse.

'And Donald's my dad and that's my mum,' said Thomas. 'I'll have to go. See you tomorrow – don't forget who's cock of the school will you?'

'No, it's agreed. See you.' Michael watched his new friend run to the house and then set off down the track to the lane. He wanted to tell his mother about his very interesting day and broke into a mixture of quick running and skips as he headed to the cottage.

*

'Oh, yes I remember, sorry I wasn't expecting to see you here.' Kathleen felt her face flushing. Nevertheless, she was pleased; he did remember me after all, she thought.

Mike explained that he was sometimes called out to the villages around Seldown if a local vicar was ill or needed some help with a particular project. 'The vicar of Callthorpe has a few ideas for his harvest festival – he's thinking about inviting some of the local Italian prisoners who've been helping on the farms but he's worried about the reaction of people who's sons and husbands have been called up. He doesn't want to cause trouble. The bishop asked me to come and talk with him about it. I had to say that the Bishop's not keen – he thinks it's too risky at the moment. Personally, I'm not sure, most people round here seem to get on well with them and say they're doing good work. What do you think?'

Kathleen was still coming to terms with seeing the curate so unexpectedly, particularly at a moment when she was feeling vulnerable. 'I don't know what to say. We've only recently arrived 'ere as you know and I've not even seen any of these prisoners. I couldn't say what local folks will think but I wouldn't come to the harvest if prisoners were here you see my husband's been captured by the Germans.'

Mike looked shocked. 'I'm sorry I didn't know, please forgive me.'

'It's alright, you couldn't know, how could you?'

'Still, I think the vicar should know about your husband, it'll help him make up his mind.'

'Please don't say anything to him,' Kath's eyes were welling up. She didn't want this intrusion into her affairs. 'It doesn't matter whether I come to the harvest or not – he doesn't even know me.'

'No, of course you're right, I'm sorry I'll just suggest that it's not a good idea at this time. I'm sorry I seem to making a mess of this. I didn't mean to ….'

'Please stop saying you're sorry,' Kath interrupted. 'I'm just upset at the moment, please don't wor….' Suddenly it was all too much. Seeing him had been a shock and now the conversation was becoming an embarrassing mess. She turned and half stumbled, half ran towards the church door and out towards the village green. Not looking back, she continued towards the lane back home. Rags appeared and ran with her, wondering why they were in such a hurry. Mike stood in the doorway of the Church, scratching his head, watching, but with no idea of what to do.

*

Amy couldn't imagine what made her daughter run through the kitchen and upstairs to her room without speaking but thought that it would probably have something to do with Jack. She carried on with fixing the tops on to the jars of the jam that she had made, using grease-proof paper and strong rubber bands to make an air tight seal. She had made far too much for their own consumption but knew that she would be able to exchange some for other spare foodstuffs that her neighbours might have. Everyone tried to find ways to supplement the limited goods that could be obtained through their ration books.

After a while she made a pot of tea, cut some thin slices of home baked bread and put some of last year's jam on to a small porcelain dish. Carrying these on a tray, she climbed the stairs to Kath's room, knocked quietly and pushed open the door. As she had expected, her daughter was sitting on the bed with her head in her hands.

'Come on love, let's have a cup of tea and cheer ourselves up.' Amy put the tray on the dresser and sat on the bed. She put her arm round Kath's shoulders and gave her a cuddle. This produced a fresh wave of weeping.

'Oh Mam, what's going to happen?' She sobbed. 'It's lovely here and I think Michael loves it now but it's just an escape it doesn't solve anything. We've got no real 'ome and God knows where Jack is and what he's goin' through. When will we ever be right again?'

'Kathleen, there's nothing we can do. We just have to hope and pray that things will turn out right. In the meantime you've got a lovely son to look after an' you've got to make sure that he's alright for when 'is dad gets back.' Amy decided that firmness was required. It was no good brooding. She sympathized with her daughter but it was no good feeling sorry for yourself, you just had to get on with life as best you could. She could remember the last war and they had come through that so they just had to do it again.

They heard Rags barking and then the sound of Michael bursting through the kitchen door, calling out excitedly, 'Grandma, are you here? Can I 'ave a rabbit? Thomas says I can and some chickens if I want. Where are you? They've got a huge barn with rabbits and horses. And I know his dad because I was at the harvest with Grandad. Are you in?'

'We're here, upstairs in my room,' Kath called, quickly dabbing her eyes to try to remove signs of tears. 'What's this about a rabbit?' They heard his footsteps thunder up the wooden stairs. He burst in, face red, breathless because of his run from the farm to the cottage.

'It's Thomas at the farm. I made 'is nose bleed an' now we're friends an' we went to his farm an' he's got rabbits an' hens an' geese an' he says I can 'ave some if I want an' I said I'd ask you an' can I? Please.' He paused and looked carefully at his mother. 'Ave you been crying?'

When the boy had calmed down they managed to get the full story. Both women were pleased that he had made a friend but sad that he'd had to hit someone. Decisions about acquiring animals were deferred until Grandad had been consulted and consideration given to housing them and relationships with Rags, who quite enjoyed chasing smaller animals and might consider new creatures as fair game.

*

Whacker missed his pal. Brian and Ernest were good friends but they were followers and left all the thinking to him. Michael had been quiet, most of the time happy to follow the natural leader, but there were times when he had good ideas that helped to make life more interesting. Then there was Rags; he was only a scruffy old mutt but it was nice to have him around as part of the gang. Molly seemed to have joined up and had some good ideas, but in the end, she was only a girl and not an acceptable replacement for his best friend. They had sent letters to one-another at first but Whacker was not much of a writer and although he still thought about his friend, he gradually stopped writing. Michael continued to correspond for a while, but it's no fun writing to someone who doesn't reply, so his letters got shorter and shorter until they eventually stopped altogether.

The autumn term had started at school. All the Lucy Street members were in the same class. Their new teacher was a man, Mr. Gunson, who looked like a boring old man with grey hair, a grey suit and rimless spectacles. But when he spoke to the children he came alive, making them feel that he liked them and was interested in their ideas. He managed to get a lot of new books and even some scientific equipment. He encouraged his class to observe and keep information about the weather and living things such as plants, and a family of mice that were kept in a big old fish-tank at the side of the classroom.

The new teacher was particularly keen on model making and before long, the classroom was full of cars, buses, tractors, gliders, model boats and aeroplanes, all made out of scrap wood, cardboard and paper, some even fitted with rubber band engines. Several children stayed behind after school to work in the 'model club'. Mr. Gunson was ahead of his time.

To Whacker's delight, his new teacher arrived at school every morning on a Triumph motorcycle. During one of the model-making sessions Whacker told Mr. Gunson about his brother's ailing motorbike. 'It's a 250cc two-stroke Triumph,' said Whacker. 'Same make as yours but yours is 498cc Speed

Twin an' I know it'll go up to 90 miles an hour.' The teacher was pleased by the boy's interest and surprised by his knowledge.

"E knows all about motorbikes Sir,' Ernest joined in. "E can tell the make and engine size just by listening.'

Whacker was not usually an interested learner so Alan Gunson was pleased to have an opportunity to encourage this reluctant student: 'Well I tell you what', he said. 'I'll ask Mr. Sykes if we can bring your brother's machine into school and try to repair it. Maybe we could keep it in the coke store, there's lots of spare space in there and it won't be in anyone's way. If we can get it going, it would be a good surprise for him when he comes home after the war.'

At first, the boy wasn't sure what to make of this. His previous experience of people in authority had suggested that they were only interested in getting him to behave himself in what they thought was a suitable manner, now here was someone who seemed to be taking an interest and offering to help. It was Brian (who continued to scratch his head even though his ring worm had long since healed) who suggested they had nothing to lose because Whacker's brother would be furious when he saw what they had done to his machine, so if Gunson could make any improvement to its condition, it would be worthwhile.

Pushing the old machine up the hill to the school was very difficult. It took all the combined strength of the Lucy Street gang to manage the task. Alan Gunson was a bit dismayed when he realised the nature of the repairs that were needed as he surveyed the rusting wreck. 'Well Andrew,' he said, 'it's a big job. We'll need new forks, the petrol tank's bent out of shape and one of the wheels is buckled. And that's before we start on the engine.' He noted Whacker's downcast face. 'But we'll try our best,' he added trying to sound positive. 'You never know, we might succeed. Shall we give it a go?'

Whacker nodded but felt that it was a hopelessness situation. Nevertheless, he was beginning to trust this unusual teacher who appeared to be genuinely interested; 'OK Sir, thanks for 'elping anyway.'

*

It was the day when the ten older children in Miss Newby's class had to decide on the title of their personal project. There were several ideas, many related to the war. Soon most pupils had found partners and subjects they agreed on. Prompted by Miss Newby's wall displays, Thomas Gant was working with one of the girls, making a history of the war so far, with the intention of keeping a record as new events unfolded. Michael would have liked to work with Thomas but didn't want to think about the war because it reminded him of being bombed out of his home and made him remember his father's unhappy situation.

Since arriving in Callthorpe he had wanted to find out more about farming. It was so much part of the life of the village and his interest had grown as a result of his experiences at the harvest and visiting Gant's farm. He wondered whether, if they stayed in Callthorpe, he might someday work on a farm and determined to find out as much as possible so that he would be prepared to get a job. He certainly didn't want to go back home to work in a mill. He had found a different rhythm to life. The day-to-day grind of industrial towns changed little during the year, the weather had some impact: winter working made all the more arduous when it was cold and dark but essentially, life went on to the same timetable. In the country however, work and living changed significantly according to the time of year. The pace was slower but seasonal changes to the style of life were more intense and identifiable. To the boy, this felt like a more natural way to live, here he became more in tune with a vibrant and stimulating environment.

Most of the children in school were from farming backgrounds, or had lived all their lives in the area. Consequently, they would have been more interested in studying city life. No-one wanted to work on a project about farms. The only other person who had not chosen a topic was the boy with bright red hair whose name was Reuben Kruyf (which explained why the others thought he might be German), but when the teacher asked what he would choose, he simply shook his head and looked away. 'Reuben, how about working with Michael? She suggested, hopefully. 'You live on a farm and might be able to give him lots of good ideas to help with the project.'

Anna Newby got on well with the other children but was at a loss to know what to do about Reuben. He must have been about seven years old when he started school and she wasn't sure whether this was because he had been to another school or that he had simply not attended, which was not unheard of in country places. In fact she knew that many country people regarded schooling as a waste of time for children who would inevitably work on the family's farm. It was thought that they could learn all they needed to know at first hand.

Reuben hardly talked to either her or the other children and was making very slow progress in learning to read and write. She had tried to speak with his mother when he first arrived but she seemed to think he was alright. In fact after the first few days, the boy came to school unaccompanied. Several notes sent home had been ignored or, what was more likely, not delivered.

The father of the family, a large man with the same red hair as his son, was occasionally seen driving through the village on his tractor. He helped with the harvest on other farms and received the same courtesy from other folk but was regarded as a bit of an enigma and didn't respond to friendly overtures. He never came near the school. Anna was beginning to think that she would have to visit the Kruyf's farm if she was to have any proper communication about this boy.

On this day, she wondered if maybe, just maybe, working with Michael might provide a breakthrough. He was a bright boy, keen to learn and she had seen him approach Reuben before. Perhaps the two of them might get on and start to communicate. 'Well Reuben, what do you think?' She asked, smiling encouragingly. The boy shrugged and looked at his battered boots. 'Fine, that's settled then.' Anna decided to adopt a brisk approach and pretend that he had agreed to the arrangement.

'They can visit my farm if they want,' Thomas called across the room. 'Michael's been up lots of times, they could both go together.'

'Thankyou Thomas,' the teacher replied, 'that's a very kind offer.'

'Reuben's got a farm of his own. They could go there to find out things' one of the other's suggested. This brought an immediate facial response from the boy: his face crumpled and it looked as though he might weep.

The teacher noticed. 'Well we'll see, no need to worry about such details yet. I'm sure these two will be able to get plenty of information.' Reuben seemed reassured and the look of alarm left his face. 'Now you'll need to plan your projects so I'm going to work with the little ones and you can talk to one another and write down a few notes to show what you will do. Talk quietly, here are some pencils and you know where the paper is.' With a final look to reinforce her instructions, Miss Newby collected the younger children from their play activities and started to work with them on their reading.

Michael went to sit with his partner. 'D'you want to get some paper and I'll do the writing?' He asked. Without speaking Reuben walked to the paper tray and got a sheet. 'Let's start by making a list of the different types of farm.' Michael looked at Reuben and waited for him to say something but the boy showed no sign of making a contribution. 'OK, well why don't you start? You know more than I do so you can write the list.'

'Can't write,' Reuben muttered – almost inaudible.

'What?' Michael couldn't hear.

'Can't write.' Again Reuben muttered but this time Michael got the message.

'Oh, well, don't worry, I'll write but I need you to tell me what you think should be in our list.' The two sat in silence then and tension grew. For several minutes, which seemed like hours, they sat, not looking at one another and not talking. Michael sat with the pencil poised over the paper, finding it difficult, but determined not to be the one to break the silence.

'Them's dairy an' arble.' Reuben spoke!

Without saying anything, for fear of breaking the mood, Michael wrote 'dairy' and 'arble' at the top of the paper. 'That's good,' he said, 'we'll start with those two. What type's yours?'

'Im's dairy.'

'Right, what happens on a dairy farm?'

For a few moments there was another silence, then Reuben began to speak, slowly and in a very quiet voice, but with Michael listening carefully and writing quickly, he told the story of a dairy farm from dawn to dusk. From the other side of the room, Anna Newby watched and smiled to herself; perhaps this was the breakthrough – the first step on the road to a proper understanding of this puzzling boy. She was sure that there was some significant problem or experience underlying his reluctance to communicate. Michael's success might lead to an eventual solution that would see Reuben learning and playing a proper part in the life of the school.

She turned to one of her small charges; 'Now Glenda, what word is this?' The child, with matted hair, dirty smudges on her face and a dress at least two sizes too big, looked at the word and the picture beside it. She was just beginning to realise that the pictures near to the incomprehensible smudges called words were related to the words themselves. Turning her beautiful, clear blue eyes on her teacher, she said, 'it's a cow miss.'

'Oh Glenda! It *is* a cow, well done.' The child received a huge hug out of all proportion to her level of success.

CHAPTER 11

January 1943: German Army withdraws from the Caucasus.
The Soviet Army begins an offensive against the Germans in
Stalingrad.
In Casablanca, Churchill and Roosevelt hold a conference.
Montgomery's Eighth Army takes Tripoli.
The first bombing raid by Americans is at Wilhelmshaven.

At home: from May 31ˢᵗ 1941, the BBC's Home Service begins
broadcasting 'Workers' Playtime' from factory canteens 'somewhere in
Britain'. The show helps to raise morale amongst the civilian population.

The winter weather in Dopplenz was harsh. A bitter wind
moaned through the towers of the old fort and frosts were
severe. Limited coal supplies for the stoves in the billets meant
that the prisoners had to wrap themselves in blankets or
greatcoats even when they were in their bunks. The washrooms
were small and inadequate, with only freezing cold water on tap
but more often than not, there was no water supply so getting
thoroughly clean was impossible. The men knew that they stank
but since everyone smelled the same they just had to tolerate the
constant lack of proper hygiene. Freezing temperatures resulted
in the abandonment of early morning exercises, except for a few
very hardy men who needed to keep the pattern of their lives
stable. They kept going partly for fitness and partly for the
mental release that vigorous exercise provided.

Unfortunately, Gunner Blake was only the first suicide.
Several men couldn't stand the monotonous regime and the
uncertainty of their lives, and decided to make an end. Two
soldiers hanged themselves and one simply jumped from one of
the high, narrow windows down to the stone courtyard. The
Germans reacted by fixing iron bars across the windows so that
it was then impossible for the windows to open and in any case,
there was no way that a man could get through the narrow spaces

that remained. The captors also established a new role: one soldier was appointed to be a representative for each dormitory. This person had to hand out letters and parcels, and manage the coal ration. He was also to be held responsible if anyone committed suicide. It was made clear by Balheim that these Grenadiers, as he called them, would be punished if any future events occurred. The prisoners were incensed by the unfairness of this strategy but they had learned that the commandant often chose an expedient route rather than considering a more moral approach to a problem.

Jack and Bob Gunn found the situation just as difficult to cope with as everyone else. It was the sameness that got to them. All the days ran together with little distinction, they never rose from their beds and commented on the quality of the sunshine or even the severity of the rain, their world consisted of the walls of their billet and the exercise yard. The high ceilinged hall where they ate was just as depressing as the rest of the fort and was not enhanced by the execrable quality of the food which was barely sufficient to keep them alive. The nights were the worst: hopes raised by dreams of home and friends were dashed as the cold, grey light brought them awake surrounded by the same dread environment. Jack repeatedly moaned that they should have fought on at Tobruk. 'We'd 'ave been better off fightin' and dyin' than stuck in this hole like cowards.'

Bob didn't agree. 'We live to fight another day. Who knows we might get the chance if the allies get here and let us out, or we might escape, there's several plans I've heard about, we could ask to join one.'

'Waste of time,' said Jack. 'If we got out of here, we're hundreds of miles from England. We'd just be captured an' shot. Look at those who are talkin' about escape, they're all bloody nut cases. I wouldn't go across a road with any of 'em.'

Similar conversations were held all over Stalag 111Z. Word reached Balheim that frustration amongst the prisoners was growing and that before long he might have a riot on his hands. In discussion with his officers and Colonel Edwards it was decided that the prisoners would be happier if they had something with which to occupy their time.

The Germans instructed local Polish farmers that they would be expected to make use of prisoners sent out on work detail. In fact the farmers were quite happy to make use of extra labour. Following a visit from Gruppenführer Schmidt from Berlin, it was also decided that a new camp for Polish dissidents could be built in the countryside nearby. Prison labour would also be used for this projects but it was thought that the nature of the camp should be kept from the British CO and his men.

As the idea reached fruition, the Germans realised that the men could also be used to repair roads and clear waste ground. Apart from those involved in building the new prison camp, working parties would be small and because the Germans didn't want to run the risk of prisoners absconding, they were to be well guarded. Jack and Bob were pleased to be selected, with two others, to work for a local farmer.

On the first day that the working parties left the camp, Jack's group was marched out of the huge front doors of the prison. They got their first sight of the countryside around: the fort had been built on the edge of the small town which was set in a valley surrounded by tree covered hillsides. The houses were small and huddled together as if for warmth. They were built of uniformly grey stone and in the early light of this cold winter's day, the place looked unwelcoming. The windows reflected the steel grey sky and all the doors looked black and sealed shut. It was as though the buildings themselves didn't wish to look at this strange, bedraggled group of alien creatures.

Still it was good to be outside. Jack was pleased to see a huge, open sky after months of looking at the small rectangle that was all he could see above the walls of the fort. His eyes feasted on the view. It made him feel like a human being rather than detritus spewed out by the events of wartime.

They marched, after a fashion, on a rough, steep road up the side of the valley, out of town and on to a dirt track leading through a stand of pine trees. The aromatic scent from the trees was almost overwhelming for men who had not been in the open air for many days. Almost in unison they took a deep, satisfying breath, luxuriating in a simple pleasure. A rustle in the trees caught their attention and their eyes met those of a small herd of deer hurrying to get away from potential danger. Jack was amazed; he had never seen deer before. He saw their liquid eyes and sure, quick movement and was entranced by their beauty. I am seeing different countries, unusual environments and strange animals, yet I am a prisoner, he thought, wondering at the paradox of a life that resulted in these contrasting experiences. How strange that his involvement in a desperate conflict could still reveal new and wonderful things: stars in desert nights; a soft, rolling, dawn sea and now pine forests with shy, wild, delicate creatures.

The farmhouse was set in an open area with its back against a steep hillside. To the right was a large wooden barn and beyond, they could make out a cleared pasture. A group of about ten cattle were gathered around a great pile of fodder. Some of the beasts turned their heads as the men arrived, their animal breath forming clouds of mist in the chill air.

The farmer, a stocky, strong looking man with a beard came out to meet them. Apart from 'gut morning', he couldn't speak English. The prisoners had no Polish and their guard spoke only German. Nevertheless, by dint of hand signals and miming, the farmer managed to convey that he wanted logs chopped and then stored outside the house. Then, pointing to a stack of dusty roof tiles and a ladder, indicated that his roof needed some repair. Jack smiled and using the same system of gestures, indicated that he and Bob would work on the roof.

Climbing up the ladder to survey the damage, they found that they had a view down the track and could see beyond the pine trees to the fort and the town in the valley bottom. The surrounding trees and hillside sheltered them from the biting wind and suddenly, life seemed a little better. The single guard settled himself on a pile of logs near the top of the track and lit a cigarette. He looked relaxed and clearly wasn't going to be too officious. The men knew that he was called Hans and that he was one of the friendlier guards. The sound of chopping began and the two on the roof began pulling out broken tiles and throwing them down to the ground. The farmer appeared in the middle of the open space, rubbing his hands together and calling to the guard, 'is gut, is gut.' Hans nodded and smiled.

After about three hours, the farmer's wife appeared carrying a tray with a jug of hot soup and some thick slices of brown, crusty bread. She had red cheeks, smiling eyes and wore a colourful skirt with a woollen shawl wrapped round her shoulders. She was the first woman that the prisoners had seen for weeks. Jack could have wept to see the normality of this couple he had almost forgotten that people were still living relatively ordinary lives.

The farmer called to the men, 'com, com,' and waved his hands to indicate that the food was for them. They waited until Hans, using the tip of his rifle, showed that they should come to eat. The prisoners, farmer and guard stood together in the yard drinking soup and taking hungry bites from the bread. It was by far the best soup they had tasted since their capture; it actually contained lumps of meat and potato. After eating Bob passed round a pack of Red Cross cigarettes. This was extraordinarily generous since smokes were in short supply but the outing was creating a positive mood so there was almost a feeling of camaraderie as they stood blowing smoke in the cold January air.

They heard the sound of an engine. A grey German army vehicle sped up the farm track and came swiftly to a halt, spitting gravel from its wheels. Hans immediately dropped his cigarette, ground it with his boot and started shouting and waving his rifle, almost pushing the prisoners back to their work.

Ludwig Balheim stepped from the passenger seat and strode purposefully towards the guard. Taking off his leather glove he struck Hans a stinging blow across his face and shouted angrily. Jack was learning to loath the guttural sound of the language which seemed so full of hate and anger. While the men didn't understand the words, the meaning was clear; Hans had been fraternising with prisoners and this was 'verboten'. Having delivered the rebuke, the commanding officer strode back to the jeep and was driven swiftly back towards the town on his way to check on other working parties. Hans stood still, his face red from the blow and a mixture of anger and embarrassment. The farmer made to approach him but was waved away, 'gehen Sie, schnell,' Hans yelled.

From that point the prisoners worked quietly for the rest of the afternoon. The cold deepened, until without gloves, the men's hands couldn't grip properly. Eventually, the guard indicated that they should form up to march back to the fort. No-one looked at his face. They shared his resentment at the unfair treatment but had no way of sympathising; he was the enemy after all.

Back at the fort, the prisoners gathered under the light of the single bulb that provided gloomy illumination in the dormitory and related the day's events. Some had worked on farms, like Jack and Bob, others had repaired roads and one group of three men, working with men from other billets, had begun to erect massive wooden stakes in the hard, frosty ground in an area not far from the fort. They were actually making the first steps towards the creation of the Polish prison camp but didn't at this stage realise the purpose of the construction. More interesting for them was that they had been working alongside some Polish prisoners. They had managed to communicate about the war and it seemed that things were not going as badly for the Allies as the prison newspaper had suggested. They were also made aware that many Poles hated the Germans and that the British prisoners were regarded as friends. These pieces of information cheered the men, leaving them with some feelings of optimism. Taking everything into account, this was one of their best days since the surrender.

*

Snow had fallen silently during the night. Michael had seen heavy falls at Stanbury. The whiteness even made the roofs of the mills look attractive. Black streets were transformed and in the early mornings, the untouched surfaces were so beautiful that footprints or the tracks of a passing vehicle seemed to mar a perfect scene. Soon though, traffic changed the whiteness to brown slush which sprayed on to the pavements and reduced wonderland to grubby reality. Children tried to keep the magic going but their snowballs became hard packed ice and snowmen in the street were destroyed by passing vehicles or kicked down by residents wanting to walk to work.

In Callthorpe it was different. Trees hung with magnificent white candelabra, fields were covered by endless blankets and some of the hedgerows disappeared under deep drifts like frozen waves. Enormous, dagger icicles hung from eves and windows.

The only vehicles that could move were farm tractors. Buses couldn't cut through the deep drifts on the country lanes and were cancelled. Since most people had outdoor jobs, these were put on hold while paths were dug to enable folk to get to their work or as far as the shops in the village. On the farms, milking still had to be done and animals supplied with fodder.

The boy had to blow on the glass before he could rub frost off the window of his chill bedroom. Peeping through the tiny clear hole in the icy pane, he marveled at the sight and thought how different it was to the view from his last home. Michael felt as though he could open the window and fling himself on to the garden and be caught safely by the soft whiteness. He tried to open the catch but it was frozen hard. Thinking now to wash his face he found that he had to break a layer of ice in the jug before splashing bitter, cold water on his cheeks.

With the log fire burning brightly, the kitchen was warm. Kathleen and his grandparents were already sitting round the heavy oak table, eating breakfast. 'Want an egg young man?'

Walter peered over his spectacles which, as usual, were on the end of his nose.

'Yes please.' The pullets that Michael had been given by Thomas had grown well and were now beginning to lay. Grandad had made a hen run with a wire mesh fence behind the house and repaired an old hen house that he had used in the past. He was quite pleased that the boy was interested in animals because it gave him an excuse to renew an old hobby. Besides which, the eggs were very welcome in these hard times. Michael loved opening the nest boxes and taking the still warm eggs to Amy. They had decided not to accept Thomas's offer of rabbits because Rags regarded them as his natural prey and would have made their lives a misery.

The dog didn't really understand the purpose of hens any better than rabbits. As far as he was concerned they were excellent chasing material; he particularly enjoyed the squawking noises they made as they ran. But Michael had explained to him that they were to be left alone. While he found this difficult, the old dog respected his master's decision, but would sometimes sit for several minutes staring through the wire mesh. At first, the hens clustered as far away as they could, but eventually got used to him and wandered around scratching and pecking without concern. This the dog found intensely irritating and it was with great difficulty that he resisted the impulse to take revenge on the stupid clucking creatures.

Two land girls lived and worked on Gant's farm. They had proper names but had become known as Gert and Daisy after characters on Workers' Playtime. This was partly because they never stopped talking. Thomas' mum was happy to have two lively young women around but they drove his dad wild with their endless chatter; he just wanted them to get on with their work.

Apart from working on the farm, the women also helped by taking milk deliveries round the village. They were collected every morning by Andy the milkman. He drove a wagon with wooden side flaps. It was pulled by a huge, white Shire horse.

Their first job was to collect milk churns from the farms nearby. These were left on wooden platforms by the side of the roads near the farms. As they collected a full one, they left a clean empty one behind. The full churns were taken to the dairy, which was behind the pub and then sent out on delivery all around Callthorpe and the other villages.

Michael liked to chat with Gert and Daisy when they called. They came from the Midlands and he enjoyed their accents. This morning he heard Andy call his horse to stop and went to the door to collect the milk. Gert was there. Soft blond hair peeped out below her woollen hat. She had rosy cheeks from the cold air and her blue eyes twinkled with good humour. 'Now then my love, are you takin' me out tonight?' She asked, grinning.

Michael, used to the banter, which had confused him at first, said, 'if you want, where shall we go, to the pictures?'

Gert called back to her friend who was sitting on the wagon, 'Oh Daisy, I've got a boyfriend, we're walkin' out.'

'No you don't, he's mine,' shouted Daisy. 'He promised to marry me last time I called. You 'aven't forgotten 'ave you my love?'

Michael laughed. 'Sorry I'd forgotten. Can I 'ave two girlfriends?'

'Just listen to him, typical man. You're mine an' I shan't share you with anyone else.' Gert smiled and tousled the boy's hair. She emptied the milk into the enameled container that Michael held and set off down the path. She wore khaki trousers, a sweater and gloves with no fingers, which looked as though they wouldn't keep her hands warm. 'See you tonight then darlin'. Meet me by the village green an' don't be late.'

'Michael, come in out of the cold and shut the door. Don't take any notice of those silly girls.' Amy called from the kitchen. 'It's a wonder the milk isn't frozen this morning, the time they take.'

*

After breakfast, Walter peered over his spectacles again; 'what you thinkin' of doin' today boy?' He asked.

'I might read my new book,' answered Michael. 'I've not started it yet.' He had received the book as a Christmas present along with a bike (second hand) and some nuts, a bar of chocolate and an apple in the sock that he had hung over the end of his bed. The book was 'Oliver Twist'. Kath thought that he was now reading well enough to be introduced to some classic authors.

'What about doin' some sledging?'

'I'd like that but I've got no sledge,' said the boy.

'Well we can improvise. When I was a boy, we used to slide on an old tin tray. I think there's one in the attic. What do you say grandma?'

Amy frowned. 'I think there is but I wouldn't know where to look.'

'C'mon Michael, let's see what we can find.'

They went upstairs and pulled down the ladder that led to the attic. It was very dusty in there and because there was no light, hard to find anything. Walter rummaged around until, with a cry of triumph, he emerged carrying a battered tin tray with a picture of a quaint village scene printed on it. 'This'll do,' he cried. 'Big enough for both of us if we squeeze together.'

Wrapped up in scarves and wooly hats, and accompanied by an excited Rags, they set off across the fields looking for a hill steep enough to allow a sledge to slide down. Rags ran ahead, occasionally disappearing in deep drifts and then jumping up to see if his friends were still with him. His tongue hung out with his exertions and his coat was soon full of globular lumps of snow. 'Nearly human that dog,' said Walter.

'Apart from Whacker, he's my best friend,' said Michael.

'What about Thomas?' Grandad wondered.

'Oh yes, he's a good friend,' Michael answered. 'But Rags saved our lives you know. We wouldn't be here but for him digging in the rubble at our old 'ouse.'

'Yes I know,' said Walter, putting his arm round the boy's shoulder. 'An we're very glad he was around.'

They walked, taking giant steps to get their feet clear of the deep drifts. There was no talking for a while because trudging through deep snow took a lot of energy and they were both breathless. Occasionally, Walter had to pull Michael out of particularly deep snow. Finally they reached rising ground and slipping from time-to-time, climbed up to the top of a small hill. The scene before them was magical; a low sun in a flawless blue sky sent golden rays across the surface of a pristine landscape. The tall, still trees were elegant black sculptures with their branches coated in white. Dark hedgerows echoed in negative colours outlined the fields, while a frozen mercury stream ran alongside one of the meadows. They could have been the only people on earth; the only sign of life was an occasional crow that flew like a sweep's handkerchief through the crystal air. Even the dog sat for a while, impressed by the beauty of the view.

'OK, let's see how this magic sledge will go.' Walter set the tray at the top of the hill and Michael sat on the front with Rags between his legs. Settling himself behind and wrapping his arms round his grandson, Walter gave a gentle push on the snow but nothing happened.

'Push harder Grandad,' called Michael. Rags barked agreement. The second push released the 'sledge' and it gradually slipped over the edge and down the slope. The small hill now took on a different aspect; it seemed to tilt and a gentle decline became a precipitous drop. The front of the tray clipped bumps in the snowy surface and sprayed icily into their faces. Michael yelled with exhilaration, the dog barked excitedly. Walter joined in and soon they were screaming like banshees as the sledge hurtled down, gathering speed. At the bottom an unseen drift waited; as the tray cut through it, it flipped sideways and into the air. The sledge went one way and three bodies went another. Performing half somersaults, they landed some distance apart and disappeared from view.

Laughing, with icy tears rolling down their cheeks and snow down their necks and in their Wellington boots, the two humans fell into each others' arms while Rags leaped around barking like a mad dog.

Then the noise intervened. They paused in their joy. A low growling sound gradually increased. They stood still clinging to each other and looked to the sky behind the hill. The roar increased, making them crouch. Walter reached to enclose his grandson in his arms for protection. Rags gave a curious whine. A flight of Handley Page Halifax bombers, impossibly close to the frozen earth, thundered overhead. They were so near that the camouflage colours were clearly visible and the pair could see the guns sticking out of the rear turret. It seemed that the planes were traveling too slowly and would surely fall to earth but they continued their inexorable progress in the direction of Timpney village. The awesome image of these huge flying machines made Michael gasp while the immense, deafening sound caused him cover his ears.

'Look at those!' Michael shouted. 'Where are they going?'

'They'll be landin' on the new airfield at Timpney.' Walter too was staggered by the sudden cacophony that smashed into the beauty and happiness of the snow covered meadows. 'We can never be allowed to forget there's a war on.' He was both sad and angry that a simple pleasure had been marred in this violent way. They watched the great machines get lower in the darkening sky and eventually disappear. Walter tried to recover the mood; 'C'mon let's climb up and do it again.'

They continued their sledging for a while but somehow the atmosphere had been eroded. The boy couldn't help but remember the bombing of his house and the thought of the machines he had just seen dropping bombs on other people, filled his head. The old man was sensitive to his grandson's change of mood. Finally, the pair trudged back home with a wet and subdued Rags following behind, staying close.

*

186

By the time Sunday came around, the snow had been cleared from most of the country lanes but still lay deep along the hedgerows and ditches. Kathleen and her mother were able to make their way to Church for the morning service. Although she had been brought up as a member of the Church of England, Kath had attended the local Chapel in Stanbury, because Jack's family were Congregationalists and Mary had insisted that his wife should worship with them. Now she was pleased to return to her former habit and found the services comfortingly familiar; having her mother around gave added peace of mind.

The winding pathway from the lych-gate to the main door had been cleared of snow. Trees reached their sloping branches protectively over the worshipers as they approached and the church building stood blackly against the whiteness. The scene had a melancholy air and Kath shivered as they walked towards the ancient building.

Folk from the village greeted one another by the west door but fell silent when they entered the nave, offering only a muted greeting to their neighbours. 'People seem quiet today,' said Kathleen.

'The vicar's poorly,' answered Amy. 'They're wondering who'll be taking the service.'

Kath knew the answer before Mike stepped out in front of them. She met his eyes momentarily and quickly looked away, spending the rest of the service glued to the hymn book or examining her gloves. The closing prayer was said and notices given out. The congregation started to wander to the door. Kath would have liked to make a quick escape but Amy was chatting to friends so she had to wait with her.

Mike was standing by the door shaking hands and receiving praise for his interesting sermon of which Kath had heard very little. She tried to walk behind a group of parishioners but he saw her and called, 'Oh, Kathleen, could I have a word please?'

She felt heads swivel and eyes turn in her direction and would have liked to make some excuse but Amy said, 'It's alright darlin' I'm going to talk with Mrs. Brewer. You have a chat with the vicar.'

The last few people walked down the path and they were left alone. 'I just wanted to apologise for the other ...' Kath cut him off:

'No, no need, it was my fault I was just a bit upset that's all. Please don't worry about it.'

'But I just seemed to make matters worse and I was trying to help. Could you please forgive me?' Kathleen looked into his eyes for the second time and saw his concern and genuine sorrow.

'Of course,' she smiled. 'Please forget about it, it was just a silly moment. I was worried about Jack and Michael and the war. Everything seemed to be piling on top of me but I feel better now.'

'Alright, that's grand,' he said. 'I wouldn't want to start on the wrong foot with one of my parishioners. It looks as though I shall be here for a while, the vicar's very poorly and we can't get a locum to come out here. I'm lodging in the village for the moment so we might run into one another now and then.'

'Oh.' Kath wasn't sure what she thought about this. Why should she be pleased with the news? She dismissed the feeling. 'That's nice,' she said and immediately thought how daft that sounded. 'I mean good and ..... well I'll have to go now, my mother'll be waiting.'

'Yes, of course.' He held out his hand which she took, feeling an electric tingle from his long, cool fingers; she almost gasped at the sensation. Turning, she hurried down the pathway, angry with herself. What's the matter with me? I'm like a silly schoolgirl.

*

Michael had not gone to church because Reuben had said that he could go to visit their farm. 'My dad's going to Ludstow on Sunday, so you can come and we'll do the project.' He said after Friday school. The boy was talking quite freely to Michael now but was still reluctant to communicate with other children or the teacher. Indeed, sometimes people would ask Michael what Reuben had said because his words were so indistinct. But Miss Newby was happy that some progress, albeit slow, was being made. Being invited to visit the farm was also a breakthrough; Reuben had coloured and given no answer when Michael originally suggested that it would help with their work if he could have a look round. Today then was an opportunity not to be missed. Rags, of course, wanted to go with him but Reuben had expressly requested that the dog should not be brought along.

Michael left the cottage and walked for about a mile through cold, winter lanes and up a long track to reach Kruyff's Farm. When he reached the main buildings he immediately realised that conditions on this farm were totally unlike those he had seen at Thomas Gant's. The house was built of the same warm red brick as some others in the village but the paint on its windows was peeling and the roof had several broken or dislodged tiles. The cow sheds nearby were in need of repair with wooden planks missing and one of the great doors hanging loose from the bottom hinge. Inside he could see black and white cows, with their heads sticking through the fences of their stalls, eating hay from a long trough that stretched the length of the shed. One lifted its great head and looked at the boy as he arrived into the farmyard. It gave a loud bellow and several others gazed with their out-of-focus eyes. A barking sheep dog rushed from the barn only to come to an abrupt stop as it reached the extent of a chain fastened to its collar. The barks turned to snarls as it strained to break loose. Michael now understood why bringing Rags would not have been a good idea; a fight with this aggressive animal would have been inevitable.

Reuben appeared in the doorway of the house. 'Down Ben, down,' he shouted. The dog stopped barking and squatted, keeping its eyes on Michael and growling softly. 'It's alright, he can't reach you. You can't make friends with him. He can smell your dog.'

A thin, grey haired woman came to the doorway behind Reuben. 'Hallo Michael, my Reub has told me about you. I tink you are good friend to my son. You come in the house, have tea.' Michael was surprised by her strange speech and thought that she seemed nervous but he was pleased by her welcome. He walked over to the door and put out his hand which he knew was the polite thing to do when meeting someone. Mrs. Kruyff looked and then rubbed her hands on her apron before taking hold of his. 'Velcome, velcome, come have tea.'

In the kitchen a great black iron range filled up half of the kitchen wall. A kettle sat comfortably on top and bubbled merrily. Using a cloth, Mrs. Kruyff picked it up and emptied the boiling water into a shiny, brown teapot. Around the walls there were many pictures, some of canals and windmills, with people wearing clogs standing around. One showed a frozen lake with people skating. She saw Michael looking at them; 'pictures from Holland, where ve come from. Some round here tink ve from Germany but is not true. Ve Dutch people, ve come many years ago before Reuben born, he is English you see. I still not talk English very good, makes people think ve German. Dirk say they don't like us.'

Michael looked at Reuben. His head had sunk down into his shoulders as it sometimes did in school; he was embarrassed by the way his mother spoke. Then he felt Michael's eyes and looked up. 'Dirk's my dad,' he said.

They sat around the table drinking hot tea and eating bread with butter. 'Ve have good butter here. You take some for your mama ven you goes,' Mrs. Kruyff smiled as she spoke, revealing several missing teeth. 'Now you go look round and do your vorks before Dirk come back, OK?'

Michael thanked Reuben's mother for the tea and the boys set off to look around the farm. He had brought a little notebook and wrote down ideas and sketches for their project while they were walking.

Michael was interested to learn, first hand, about the day-to-day workings of a dairy farm. Reuben led him to the cow shed after first tying the sheep dog to a fence post outside. 'He's a good guard dog,' he said. 'But he's not a pet, he's too fierce with strangers.' The cows were still munching on the hay. 'All they do is eat and then moo when they're ready for milking. Would you like to see how it's done?'

'Yes, but I thought you did it in the morning and evening.'

'It's OK to just show you.' Reuben seemed pleased to be demonstrating his skill to his friend. He fetched a small stool and a metal bucket. Sitting under the nearest cow and resting his head against the animal's huge flank, he started to squeeze a teat. The white stream squirted into the pail, making a fine ringing sound. 'Do you want a go?' He asked Michael.

'Yes please.' He took Reuben's place and was amazed at the warmth flowing from the cow's body. He tried to copy the action but nothing happened.

'Start at the top and squeeze downwards, you won't hurt her.' At last a small squirt of milk came out but missed the bucket which made the boys laugh. The cow flicked her tail into Michael's face and he fell over which produced more hilarity.

'Let's try one of these,' said Michael pointing to cows further down the shed.

'No, they won't give milk yet, they're heifers.'

'What's a heifer?'

'It's one that hasn't had a calf yet.' Reuben grinned, realising how little Michael knew. 'They can't give milk till they've had a calf. There are some calves in the other shed. Do you want to see?' They walked through frozen ruts of the yard to another barn that was even more broken down than the first one. The half-grown animals were not in separate stalls but wandered about in a big open space. They cowered together when the boys entered, looking with the same unfocused eyes that the cows had. 'They have their mother's milk when they're little but we can take it when they start to eat grass.'

'What do you do with the calves?' Michael asked.

'We keep the females and sell the males. We only need one bull. He has to be in a shed of his own. Come on we'll go and see him.'

Michael was astounded at the size of the bull. He stood, completely filling his stall, tethered to the wall by the ring through his nose. 'We have to be careful of him,' said Reuben proudly. 'He can kill you with his horns if he's annoyed.'

The sound of many feet outside startled the boys. Michael asked who was there. 'Is it your dad?'

'No, it's the Italians,' said Reuben. 'They're helping to repair the sheds.' They stepped outside and in the muddy yard, saw a group of six men in bedraggled uniforms being handed tools by a soldier while another one stood with a rifle on his shoulder.

'OK you lot, get crackin',' said the first soldier. 'Kruyff wants that barn patched-up by dinner time, an' woe betide you if it's not done properly. You know what he's like. Then you've got church parade this afternoon.'

One of the prisoners spoke: 'sono Domenica, iss Sunday no-one work iss day to rest.'

'Look Rodolpho, you'll bloody well work when I tell you to. You're bloody lucky to be out in the fresh air. Now get on with it and stop complaining!' The guard with the rifle unhooked his weapon as a little threat but made no attempt to point it at the prisoners.

'OK, Inglese, I work.' The Italian turned towards the boys with a smile. 'Buon giorno ragazzi, come sta?' He was a large man and had a big black beard. He seemed unafraid of the guards; it was almost as though he was in charge of the working party. Michael liked the twinkle in his eye and would have answered but didn't know what the man had said so he just smiled.

'Gerron with it, stop wastin' time.' Now the armed guard spoke. He felt as though the prisoner was laughing at him by talking to the boys. He lunged forward aiming the butt of his rifle at Rodolpho's back but the Italian was too quick and simply swayed out of the way. The other prisoners laughed which made the soldier even angrier. He shouted, 'you Eyetie bastard I'll bloody teach you.' He stepped towards Rodolpho, his face red with rage.

'Vat in hell's name iss going on here?' The huge man, with red hair, that Michael had seen on the day of the harvest strode round the corner of the barn. 'These iss suppose to be vorking not fooling. Get thems vorking or I throw them out! I report this to CO.' His bellow was so loud that everyone stopped and stared at him, except for Reuben who turned his back on the scene and crouched down low to the ground. Michael looked at him and wondered what was going on.

'And who iss dis?' The farmer turned his glare on Michael.

He was about to answer when Mrs. Kruyff rushed into the yard, her face contorted with fear. 'Come now Michael iss time to go, come now.' She grabbed him by the hand and pulled him towards the farmhouse.

'But I need to ....' Michael tried to object, he was enjoying his visit and the boys hadn't finished their work.

'No, iss no more visit, iss time to going.' The woman, shaking with anxiety, continued to pull his arm, taking him to the top of the track leading out of the farm. 'You go now but take vith you.' She pushed a rectangular blue paper packet into his hand. 'Is butter, gif your mother. Please be Reuben's friend iss good for him. You come back other time ven Dirk not here.' With this she pushed Michael's back and propelled him on his way. He could still hear Mr. Kruyff's angry shouting even when he had reached the lane at the end of the farm track.

CHAPTER 12

The Handley Page Halifax is a four engined, long range heavy-weight bomber, carrying 5.4 tons of bombs. It is similar to the Lancaster, which has a greater bomb load and a longer range. It is the first bomber to be equipped with HS2 navigation targeting radar.

'How far is it?' Thomas had suggested that they could ride their bikes over to Timpney to see the bombers at the airfield.

'It'll take about half-an-hour,' Thomas replied. Most of the snow had cleared and although the lanes were still wet, it was safe to set off without fear of getting stuck in a drift.

'Alright, I'll go. What about Reuben? 'E might come with us.'

Thomas looked doubtful. 'I don't think so. He never plays-out with us; he's always got jobs to do for his dad. Anyway he never talks to me, you're the only one. He doesn't even talk to Miss Newby.' Michael knew that this was true and decided not to press the matter.

They set off wearing sweaters and gloves, with gas masks slung over their shoulders. In their saddle bags they carried a packet of jam sandwiches and a bottle of home made lemonade. Thomas was a strong rider but Michael had never had a bicycle before and had only just learned to ride so he kept falling behind. His father had once tried to teach him to ride but Jack's cycle was too big and the boy's feet couldn't reach the pedals. Rags, who had decided to accompany them, had no trouble keeping up with Thomas but most of the time he stayed with Michael running easily alongside, his tongue hanging out and his breath condensing in the cold air.

They passed close to Kruyff's Farm and Michael looked up the track to see if he could see Reuben. He was still puzzled by what had happened when his father had arrived and shouted at the Italians. Reuben wouldn't give an explanation about his own or his mother's behaviour and didn't want to say why

Michael could only visit when Mr. Kruyff was away. The events of that day had set back their friendship. Reuben seemed to have lost his trust in Michael and was once again reluctant to speak. Michael was worried about this and so was Anna Newby. She had a feeling that Reuben might stop going to school like some of the other farm children.

The track to the farm was empty so they continued to pedal towards Timpney. The air was cold but refreshing and on the flat roads, they could keep up a good speed. Michael quickly improved and soon the boys were speeding along side-by-side. Michael began to sing his version of the Marseillaise.

'What're you singing?' Thomas asked.

'It's the French National Anthem. We used to sing it back in Stanbury, me, Whacker an' the others. Shall I teach you?'

'OK.' Thomas was a good singer; a member of the Callthorpe church choir. They rattled along singing; feeling exhilarated by the noise of their voices and the fresh country air blowing round their heads. The bare winter hedgerows flashed by and the journey passed quickly; soon they were riding through the first houses of Timpney.

They didn't know how to find the airfield and had determined to ask someone for directions. An old woman, who looked vaguely familiar to Michael, was walking along the edge of the lane carrying a basket. When they stopped and asked the way, she began to explain and then laughed and shouted out, excitedly, 'it's my boyfriend, don't you recognise your old Maisie?' Michael immediately recalled the bus journey and Maisie's duck sticking its head out of her bag. To his horror, she grabbed him round his shoulders and planted a big kiss on his cheek. He looked at Thomas, who was barely able to contain his glee and explained how he and the old lady had met.

Maisie wasn't going to let her 'boy friend' escape and insisted that the boys go with her for some refreshment. They explained that they had sandwiches to eat but these were dismissed. 'I know young boys,' she said. 'Appetites like 'orses. You follow me an' we'll see what we can find. I might have a bone for this old boy,' she added, pointing at Rags whose tail wagged in response to what he thought might be an offer of food.

They walked to the village green, the boys pushing their bikes and Maisie chattering continuously. There were still ducks on the village pond and Michael wondered what had happened to the one Maisie had brought back from Seldown. At the edge of the green, they came to a tiny cottage with a brown door, dark-red brick walls and a thatched roof. The garden was small, surrounded by a white wooden fence. The black earth had been dug over ready for the planting of spring vegetables.

'This is my little 'ouse, it's one of the oldest in the village, even older than me.' Maisie pushed open the unlocked door and ushered the boys inside. 'Now let's see I've got Dandelion and Burdock and some of my homemade fruit cake, how does that sound?' They politely agreed that this sounded fine and indeed it was; the cake was delicious and the drink cool and strange but refreshing. Rags lay on the kitchen floor chewing the remaining meat off a bone that Maisie found for him. The old lady asked about their families. She had heard of Gant's farm and knew Michael's grandad. 'He's one of the best stonemasons around here.' she said. 'I think he was asked to do some work on the Minster in town.' This was news to Michael and reminded him of the other Michael who had shown them around. 'I've heard of another farm in Callthorpe, it belongs to a Mr. Kruyff,' Maisie went on. Michael was about to say that he had been there when she added, 'nobody likes old Kruyff, don't you go anywhere near him. Some folks think he's a German.'

''E's not German, they're Dutch. Reuben goes to our school, we know 'im,' Michael said. He went on to explain that he was working on a project with the boy and they were sort of friends.

'Well that's as may be but don't you go near that man, he's a bad lot.' Maisie was so adamant that Michael decided to say no more but wondered exactly what made Mr. Kruyff such a 'bad lot'.

Thomas remembered the purpose of their trip; 'can you tell us how to get to the airfield?'

'Sure I can but you won't be able to get near, it's very well guarded.'

She told them to ride straight on through the village and out on the Seldown Road for about a mile and then turn off left at the first crossroads. They would see the airfield in the distance but would need to go for another mile down this road.

*

As they approached the aerodrome they found themselves riding alongside a wire mesh fence that sloped inwards at the top where it had strands of barbed wire. They could see low buildings in the distance one of which had a curved corrugated iron roof that met the ground on both sides, while each end was closed off by a brick wall. All the buildings were painted in wavy camouflage patterns. There were several buildings with huge doors. One of them had its doors open and they could see the tail of an aircraft sticking out.

The boys got off their bikes and walked down a track by the fence until they could see the end of a runway which was quite close to the wire. Near to the fence there was a huge, circular turning area with tarmac tracks leading off towards the buildings. The runway itself stretched into the distance. They could now see several planes standing near the hangers. Men, some in overalls and others in uniform, were working on the aircraft. Bombs were being loaded and long hosepipes carried fuel to the tanks.

They decided to sit on the grass verge and eat their sandwiches in the hope that something exciting might happen. The afternoon was moving on and they had promised to be back for supper but didn't want to leave until they had seen more of the bombers.

After a while, Rags' bark heralded the noise of a vehicle and a jeep appeared speeding down the rough track towards them. In it, a driver and two soldiers looked quite threatening. They had red caps and one wore three stripes on his arm. The vehicle pulled up sharply, its brakes squealing. The hair on the dog's neck rose and he adopted an attack pose. The boys themselves were alarmed at the speed of the jeep's approach and stood up sensing trouble.

'Now then lads, what're you doin' here? A bit of spying is it?' The sergeant spoke. His peaked hat sat low on his head so that they could hardly see his eyes. Michael and Thomas felt threatened; maybe they shouldn't have come here. Rag's growled. All three soldiers looked very fierce and were heavily armed. 'No sir,' said Thomas. 'We were just looking.'

'We come from Callthorpe,' Michael added. 'We came to see if we could 'ave a look at the planes.'

The sergeant's tone was angry, 'Oh, so you're from the Callthorpe spy ring then.'

'No sir, no, we're not spies at all,' Michael was beginning to feel really worried.

'Leave of sarg,' one of the other soldiers joined in. 'You're scarin' 'em.'

The sergeant smiled. 'Alright boys but you're not supposed to hang about here you know. This is a secret place and we have to guard it day and night. But I'll tell you what, you look like good lads to me so you stay here with us for a bit and you'll see them take off. They always fly at dusk you know, so they'll be over Germany at night-time.'

Thomas and Michael felt relieved and pleased to be treated with respect by these men. The sergeant stayed with them, smoking a cigarette, while the other two walked along the fence checking that it was still secure.

'Shouldn't be long now,' he said, pointing to the planes. The engines were being started and they could see the propellers moving, slowly at first and then quickening until the roar indicated that take-off was near. Exhaust smoke billowed out of the vents on the engines. With stately slowness, the bombers began to move towards the waiting watchers.

'They're comin' this way,' said Michael. His voice quivered with excitement.

'That's right, they have to take off against the wind. You can feel it blowing in our faces.' The sergeant held up his hand to feel the cold breeze heading straight down the runway.

The engine noise grew to a crescendo as, one by one, the huge machines rumbled to the turning circle. Soon, the first one was close enough for the boys to see the aircrew in the cockpit. The gun turret on top was too high to see into, but as the plane turned to prepare for takeoff, they could see the rear gunner sitting in his Perspex bubble. To their delight, the airman waved. The boys waved so vigorously that they were in danger of dislocating their shoulders.

When it was in position, pointing down the long stretch of tarmac, the bomber paused as if waiting for some signal and then, even though it didn't seem possible, the engine noise grew even louder. Rags, his ears down and his tail between his legs, stood behind Michael, his fur flattened by the wind from the propellers. The watching group covered their ears as the massive metal beast accelerated away from them. Before it was airborne, the next one had turned, ready to begin its journey. The boys stretched to see the first one rise into the cold, winter dusk. It seemed too slow; they couldn't believe that it would stay in the air. One-after-another they came and roared into the distance, rising inexorably into the evening sky. Michael counted them; eighteen climbed and disappeared from view. 'They've all gone.' He sighed, wishing to see again the magnificent, yet frightening, spectacle.

'Not yet,' the sergeant spoke. 'Wait a while and they'll return. They have to head east to Germany. They took off into a west wind.'

Minutes later like huge grey birds, they passed overhead, now in three groups of six, on their way to join up with bombers from other airfields. Their noise reduced to a steady drone. The boys waved. 'Good luck,' shouted Thomas. Rags looked up and gave a whine followed by a sharp bark. He couldn't understand what had just happened and was a bit ashamed of himself for being scared.

'Aye, they'll need that alright,' said one of the soldiers. 'Rather them than me.'

Michael couldn't believe what had been said. He would have loved to be inside one of the bombers. He tried to imagine the views that the rear gunner would have as they headed for the coast and the flat fields rushed away behind giving way to the dark depths of the icy, unforgiving North Sea. His imagination flew with them; he could sense the mixture of fear, anticipation and excitement that the men were experiencing as the winter night swallowed them. Then he thought about their mission; they would be dropping bombs on people. The memory of his experience was vivid. He didn't want anyone else to have to go through that, but, equally, he didn't want the airmen to be harmed. 'Return safe,' he whispered to himself.

'Time to go boys, your mums'll be wondering where you are. Better set off now.' The sergeant smiled he had enjoyed their enthusiasm. 'If you want to watch again, call at the guard post and ask for me: Sergeant Ferris. If I'm on duty, I'll come and see you but if I'm not you won't be able to stay so close to the fence.'

'But we want to see them come back, to make sure they're all safe,' said Michael.

'You can't do that, they'll be landing before dawn and before you lads are out of bed.'

They stood and looked at one another, trying to think how they might be able to get to Timpney in time but there seemed no solution. It was school tomorrow and they didn't think that either of their mothers would let them ride out in the night.

'Well mebbe we can come another night. Do they fly every night?' Thomas wondered.

'Look boys I shouldn't really tell you anything but I can see you're honest, sensible lads. You must remember that everything about the aeroplanes is secret. You musn't tell anyone else, understand?' The boys nodded their enthusiastic agreement. He continued: 'no, they don't fly every night, bombers might need repairing and also, they must wait for their orders. It would be too much for them to go every night. Now listen, if you are able to come very early one morning, go to the guard house on the day before and make sure I'm on duty. Then we'll see what we can manage. OK?'

The boys thought this was a great idea. They thanked the soldiers and set off back towards Callthorpe, switching on their battery powered lights because it was now quite dark. They had black sticky tape covering most of the lenses but thin beams of light picked out the road ahead. Dark hedgerows with black, witches' fingers, pointed at two boys and a dog, as remaining adrenaline powered their pedaling and they too, like the bombers, were swallowed by the night.

*

Work parties outside the fort made a welcome change for the prisoners. Following their first visit, Jack and the others returned to the same farm to continue with repairs to the roof and other winter jobs that needed doing. They learned that the farmer was called Stanislaw and his wife Marietta. These two had links with the prison because they supplied meat and vegetables but had no love for the Germans who they regarded as invaders. Using sign language and odd words of English and German, the prisoners learned that many people in Poland had been imprisoned, particularly Jews, some of whom had been moved to ghettos in Warsaw and Krakow. They said there was also a place called Birkenau where terrible things were being done but no-one had ever been there so the stories were a bit vague.

Hans, the soldier who had guarded them on their first visit was replaced by Günter, who was not popular in the prison. He had been known to use the butt of his rifle on the backs of prisoners who moved too slowly for his liking. He barked orders at the men and shouted at Stanislaw if he didn't keep them busy.

They could easily have sabotaged the repairs by doing sloppy work but because they liked the farmer, they did the work properly albeit at a slower pace than they could have achieved.

'Might as well make this last as long as possible,' said Bob. 'It's better than being stuck in that damned hole.' Jack agreed. Life in the fort was becoming unbearable: the food was poor, the heating inadequate and the regime oppressive. Increasing numbers of prisoners were being sent to the 'cooler' for minor misdemeanors and the supply of red-cross parcels and mail from home had all but dried up. Christmas greetings from their families had only just reached the men even though it was nearly March.

The poor supply of food left the prisoners weak and prone to illness, and the one army doctor among them was overworked and had minimal medicine and equipment with which to treat the growing number of patients. This situation exacerbated the already low morale and arguments and fights were increasingly common.

The need to get away was overwhelming for some men and various escape plans were developed. All such ideas were supposed to be vetted by the escape committee, made up of some higher ranks, but individuals and small groups sometimes acted alone, leading to a few surprising events. The roofs of higher dormitories were above the height of the surrounding walls of the fort and by scrabbling through the ceiling of their room, two airmen made their way out to where they could see the surrounding countryside. Using thin slats of wood from the damaged ceiling and blankets from their bunks, they improvised wing-like structures that could be fastened to their shoulders. One moonless night, after waiting for an appropriate breeze, they launched themselves into the air and managed to float beyond the top of the outside wall.

The fort had originally been built on a slope which was intended to provide defence against attack. This made landing difficult and on reaching the ground, the two men toppled forward and rolled down to the bottom of the incline. Their 'wings' shattered as they rolled, one suffering a broken arm as the structure was wrenched from its fastenings.

The noise of their landing attracted the attention of the guards and despite trying to make the cover of the pine forest, they were quickly recaptured. For several days they were held in the cooler and then, according to Balheim, transferred to another prison camp. Edward Johns, the CO, was unable to get any information about the treatment the airman received for his broken arm.

There were several other escape attempts but none were known to be successful and those recaptured were not returned to Dopplenz. Rumours abounded: there was huge suspicion that escapees were killed. Whether true or not, this notion was enough to discourage all but those who were either very brave, very desperate or both.

Jack and Bob had wondered if they might be able to slip away on their trips to the farm. Both of them felt frustrated by their situation and Jack, in particular, continued to be angry with himself for surrendering so meekly. His mind kept recalling Ian the youth who worked in the stores at the mill. He wondered how he had coped with the rigours of war; was he alive, dead or captured? Jack couldn't imagine the boy acting bravely in the face of the enemy and yet people had hidden strengths. He had seen acts of bravery from the quietest and most unassuming characters and cowardice from some who exhibited loud bravado.

On this day, they clambered up the wooden ladder to continue their roof repairs. They removed the tarpaulin from the hole they had made and Jack climbed through it into the loft space to work from inside. There was very little space and he had to work doubled-up while Bob passed materials through the hole. Eventually Jack's back was aching so badly he decided to lie on the floor of the loft to get some relief. Lying down, he found his head close to the manhole which provided access to the loft from the bedroom below. The board covering the hole had shifted slightly and he could see Marietta standing in front of a long mirror. She looked at herself and then turned sideways to view her dress from a different angle, holding her hair up and then letting it fall on to her shoulders.

Jack heard the door of the bedroom open and saw Marietta turn towards the sound. He couldn't see her face but the tone of her voice was strange. She spoke in Polish but seemed to get no answer. Now clearly upset, she backed away towards the large bed with its elaborately carved headboard. A figure moved towards her and Jack could see that it was Günter. The German said nothing but continued to move towards the woman who was by now standing against the bed. She put out her hands to resist his advance and was about to call out but the soldier stepped forward quickly and grabbed her with one hand round her back and the other across her mouth. His intention was clear and Jack was immediately filled with feelings of horror and anger. He looked towards the hole in the roof and motioned Bob to come through, putting his finger to his lips.

Bob was about to speak but the look on his comrade's face stopped him. He clambered through the hole and bent double, walked over to look into the bedroom. His action was immediate, pulling the loose board out of the way he dropped into the bedroom, closely followed by Jack. The German immediately released his hold on the woman and stared at the prisoners who stared back and then his eyes swiveled to look for his rifle which was on the floor by the bed. Marietta lay on the bed, her face pale; a mixture of fear and anger in her eyes.

Jack saw the guard's intention and stepped forward to put his boot on the weapon. Time stood still; no-one moved or spoke, the tension was palpable. They could hear the incongruous sound of the other prisoners talking to Stanislaw in the yard below.

Marietta took charge of the situation: she stood, straightened her dress and then stepping towards Günter, slapped him hard, across his face. The sound was like a gunshot and must have hurt but the German didn't flinch or speak. She smiled at the prisoners. 'Dziekuje.'

They were impressed by her dignity and stepped back to allow her to leave the room. Günter stepped forward and pointed at his rifle his face asking the unspoken question. The two friends looked at one another. 'What do you think?' Jack asked.

'I'm not sure, mebbe we should shoot the bastard. What'll he do if we give him the gun?'

'We can't kill 'im Bob. Even if we escaped, they'd take it out on Stanislaw and Marietta. Remember what they've done to other Poles.'

They stood, unsure of their next move. Günter sensed their indecision. He walked towards the weapon and made to pick it up. Jack stayed with his foot holding it down. 'Ist gut,' said the German, holding out his hand, 'freund.' His face indicated embarrassment and a wish to end the impasse without enmity. Jack refused the offered hand but bent down and picked up the rifle, handing it back. 'Ist gut, danke.' Günter was clearly relieved. He turned and walked from the room and then down to the door of the farmhouse, his heavy boots pounding the stairs.

The two friends couldn't get back through the access hole on to the roof so they too walked down the stairs and out into the farmyard. Marietta had clearly not spoken to her husband about the incident because he looked startled to see the men, who should have been on the roof, coming out of his front door. He was about to speak when Günter started shouting at the prisoners indicating that they should line-up ready to return to the fort. The other men were surprised because, although the sun had dipped behind the hills, there was still clear daylight and they didn't usually finish work until it was nearly dark. Jack and Bob knew that the German wanted to get away from the farm as quickly as possible before Marietta said anything to Stanislaw.

The group formed up and trudging rather than marching, followed the road back to Stalag 111Z. On arrival, as the huge gates closed, the prisoners went back inside to their dormitory and Günter disappeared. As usual, the men were tired after their work and lay down on their bunks waiting for others to return and tell their stories from the day. Jack and Bob were in a subdued mood: while they had prevented harm coming to Marietta, they felt that Günter had got off lightly but couldn't think of any other course of action that would not have caused a great deal of trouble.

Bob voiced their thoughts: 'he's a bastard but what else could we have done?'

'I don't know but this is not right, 'e should be punished. What's goin' to 'appen when we go to the farm tomorrow? Mebbe 'e'll try again…. Should we tell the CO?' Jack wondered, his voice full of anger.

The other men from the farm wanted to know what they were talking about and Jack began to relate the events of the afternoon. As he began, the door of the room swung open violently and four guards, including Günter, barged in. They walked straight over to the friends' bunks and dragged them to their feet, shouting loudly and aggressively in German.

As they were pulled up, both friends knew immediately what was happening. 'You bastard, what have you said?' Jack shouted into Günter's face. The German responded by smashing the butt of his rifle into Jack's stomach which doubled him up as it drove the breath out of his body. Bob struggled to help but received the same treatment. Now hardly able to stand, the two were half-dragged, half-pushed out of the room, down the stone stairs and across the courtyard to the solitary block below ground-floor level. Without speaking, the guards threw them on to the floors of separate cells and closed and locked the heavy metal doors. The prisoners found themselves in small spaces which were completely dark and stank of dampness and urine.

For some minutes, Jack, still gasping for breath, lay on the floor feeling sick. Then he heard Bob calling out, 'Jack, Jack, can you hear me? Are you alright?' Before he could answer, Jack heard a key rattling in a lock and a squeal as the door of a cell opened. He heard Bob's voice again: 'you bastards, you …' and then the sound of thumps and groans.

'Nicht sprechen English, nicht sprechen Tommy!' A harsh voice almost screaming and then silence.

In the darkness, the pain in Jack's stomach seemed to increase in intensity. He was painfully aware that Günter had decided to cover himself against any allegations by accusing them of some misdemeanor. He knew then that they should have taken some other course of action at the farm but they had been foolish enough to think that the German was sorry for what he had tried to do and that the incident might be forgotten. 'What the hell's goin' to happen now?' He whispered to himself, 'what a bloody mess.'

*

Kathleen was crying too often. Amy was worried about her daughter's state of mind. When they had arrived in the cottage it had seemed as though she would settle down to the country ways and feel a bit more contented with her life but over the next few weeks, Kath had become increasingly gloomy and regularly burst into tears without any warning. Michael did his best to cheer her up, but although she smiled at her son and cuddled him, the good humour didn't last long.

Kath had talked about doing some work, maybe joining the land army to help out the farmers, or volunteering to support the home guard but nothing had been arranged. Amy decided to use her initiative and get her daughter involved in village life. They were badly in need of someone to teach at the Sunday school. The previous teacher had joined the Women's Auxiliary Air Force because she was determined to help with the war effort, so there was a vacancy.

Amy went to speak to the new vicar. (Everyone called him vicar even though they knew he was only a curate.) He agreed immediately saying that he considered Kathleen to be a very suitable person to take on the role and Amy hurried back home to break the news.

In the kitchen, Kath was preparing mash for the hens and Michael was waiting to take it out. Rags sat by the door sniffing the air and wondering if there might be some food for him. Amy came in rubbing her hands from the cold. She made herself a cup of tea, sat at the table by the window and explained her idea.

Far from being grateful, Kathleen was upset. 'I can't do it Mam, I don't know how to teach. The children won't like me. I've never done anything like that. You shouldn't have gone to see him without telling me …. I can't do it….. It's no use, I ….' The rest was drowned as tears welled in her eyes and she pulled her apron up to her face.

Amy was surprised by this reaction. 'I'm sorry; I thought you'd enjoy it. You're so good with Michael; you've taught him all sorts of things. I thought it might take your mind off worrying about Jack,' she said.

'I don't want to stop worrying about Jack, don't you see? Kath spoke angrily. 'What sort of a wife would I be if I forgot 'im? 'Im out there, lonely and frightened…'

'I don't want you to forget him, don't be silly. But you've got to think about yourself as well - and Michael. How do you think it makes him feel to see you crying every day?' Amy was cross now. 'Life goes on Kathleen. You have to be strong for your son and for yourself. Jack knows you haven't forgotten him – goodness me, you write nearly every day.'

'But 'e doesn't write back,' Kathleen responded, tears still flowing.

'No,' Amy knew this was true. She was sure something had gone wrong with the post. 'I'm certain that Jack's still alright or we would have been told. It's just difficult to get letters through from over there. In any case, what's the good of moping?'

Her daughter went quiet. She knew that Amy was right; she *had* been crying too much. Worry about Jack was her constant companion. She couldn't separate her life in Callthorpe from his in a prison that she could only imagine. In her darkest times, she found herself almost wishing he was dead, so that she could find relief from the unending anxiety, so that there might be an ending – a finality. But as soon as the thought had entered her head she recoiled from it in horror and felt deeply ashamed.

She also knew in her heart that there was more to her upset state than her mother understood but she couldn't talk about this. Anyway, I wouldn't be working with him, she thought and I would like to be with the children. 'You're right Mam but I need to think it over. Thankyou for thinking about me anyway.' She walked over and kissed Amy who immediately started to cry.

'Look at us, what a pair of soppies we are,' she said. Michael walked over and joined the cuddle which made them both laugh.

'Sunday school'll be a lot better with you as teacher,' he said. Rags barked his approval and went out to find a rat or other token; he felt that everyone needed cheering-up.

CHAPTER 13

March - April 1943   Montgomery's Eighth Army breaks through the Mareth Line in Tunisia. Axis forces withdraw as American and British forces join together.

The German 17th Army begins attacking to eliminate the Russian beachhead at Novorossiysk but fails and is forced to withdraw.

The Warsaw uprising begins, organised by the ZOB, a Jewish fighting Organisation. It is sparked by German troops and police entering the ghetto to deport surviving inhabitants

Two days after the events at the farm, Jack and Bob were taken to stand before Balheim to hear the charges against them. The British CO was present but not allowed to speak. They were charged with attempting to rape a member of the civilian population; a despicable act only prevented by the brave actions of Gefreiter Günter Schmidt.

Both men tried to protest their innocence but were told to keep quiet since this was not a court of law and the evidence against them was irrefutable. They looked desperately at their CO for some support but he stared stonily ahead and wouldn't even meet their eyes. The sentence, death by firing squad, was duly pronounced and the men were returned to their cells to await execution.

For almost three weeks nothing happened. The prisoners waited in fear of their lives, but as time passed, began to wonder at the delay, almost wishing to get it over with and put an end to their dread of the final act.

Their living conditions were miserable: very little light or warmth permeated the cells, the beds were hard wooden boards and the food they were given was even worse than that served up in the canteen. They became gradually weaker and Jack developed a lung wrenching cough. Their eyes were running and sometimes, after fitful sleep, they had difficulty in forcing the lids to open. Sores developed on their backs and legs. They were unable to wash themselves, the Germans deciding that an occasional shower of cold water from a hosepipe was sufficient. There was no question of them receiving letters or Red Cross parcels.

For want of something to do, Jack explored his cell, realising that it was centuries old and probably had evidence of previous occupants. His fingers found thin marks carved into the old stone of the walls. For a time he didn't recognise them but, closing his eyes and imagining the shapes as a whole, he recognised a name: Zamoyski, the same name as Stanislaw and Marietta. He wished now with all his heart that he had never gone to the farm. Alongside the name he found other words in Polish and groups of three scratches crossed by a diagonal line: someone had marked off the months of their incarceration. The marks almost filled one wall of the cell. Some poor devil had spent years stewing in this hole. He decided not to start counting the days since he probably had little time left but he couldn't help but think what man or woman had made the marks. What had they done to deserve their captivity? Did they get out alive?

Finally it seemed that the day had arrived. A party of guards arrived outside the cells with the Camp Commandant and the British CO. Bob was brought out first and stood in the middle with guards on both sides. He was in a weak state and could hardly stand. When Jack had taken his place the group moved forward and climbed the steps up to ground level. Instead of turning out into the courtyard where the execution was to take place the prisoners were marched to the Commandant's office and told to stand in front of his desk. Balheim sat behind the desk and with his head down, not meeting their eyes. He announced that they were to be returned to their billets.

'What? Why? What's going on?' Jack was incredulous. He looked at Edward Johns, who in turn looked at Balheim.

'Herr Commandant, I think they deserve an explanation,' he said.

The Commandant, still staring at his desk, looked angry but spoke: 'the charges have been dropped, we have new evidence.'

'What evidence?' Bob demanded. Johns shook his head slightly to indicate that further questioning might prompt an adverse reaction.

Balheim looked up for the first time and to their surprise, had a sad expression. 'Your CO will explain. You must be aware that we are not barbarians we do not punish innocent men. Now return to your rooms, there are some important changes that we need to organise. It is finished.'

Back in their billets, the two were immediately surrounded by the other prisoners and told the full details. It seemed that while no working party had returned to the farm, other groups had told the story to Polish people that they encountered around the town. News of Jack and Bob's plight and the reasons for it had reached the Zamoyskis. After deliberating for some days and at considerable risk to themselves, they had visited the fort and insisted on speaking to Balheim. At first the guards had resisted and denied them access, saying that they would convey messages. But Marietta was particularly determined and said she would fetch all the local people to the gate unless she was allowed to speak directly to the Commandant.

Balheim recognised their bravery and knew that they would not have risked angering the occupiers unless they were telling the truth. Needless to say, Günter lied to the end but had now disappeared from Dopplenz and was rumoured to be on his way to the harsh conditions at the Russian front.

The two friends were amazed their good fortune. Balheim was a hard man but had acted honourably. News went round the prison population quickly and while he was still regarded as the enemy, the commandant gained a degree of respect.

Jack and Bob tried to get back to their normal routine but were still shaken by their ordeal. Jack, in particular, was considerably weakened by the lack of proper food and exercise.

They were due for further disruption, however, as a few days later they found out the nature of Balheim's important changes.

*

The countryside moved towards spring. Michael was amazed by the suddenness of the change as primroses, sweet violets and celandines began to appear in the hedgerows. The woodland floor began to fill with bluebells, while daffodils, tulips and wallflowers brought startling colour to Walter's garden.

The old man was delighted by his grandson's interest in natural things. He enjoyed helping the boy to remember the names of the plants and explaining that the distant mysterious call was from a cuckoo. They explored, always accompanied by Rags, down hidden pathways and through the spring meadows, each one of them enjoying the sense of rebirth and new energy flowing from the land.

This morning they decided to take sandwiches because Walter had promised to go to a lake which might contain water birds getting ready for their migration to northern countries. They set off through the back garden, past the hens and two apple trees, through a gate which led into a coppice of willow trees. Fresh green shoots were bursting from slender branches. A low morning mist that presaged a fine sunny day hung close to the fields. The ground around the coppiced trees was covered with coarse grass that made walking difficult because their feet slipped down holes between the tussocks and they had to be careful to avoid a twisted ankle.

Rags had no such problems and bounced around full of excitement at being outside. He was maturing now and had, by persistent but unobtrusive infringement of the rules, managed to establish a presence on a rag mat in the kitchen, near to the fire. Even at night, when the weather was cold, he was allowed to remain inside. He enjoyed this quieter life and spent more time sleeping but as soon as anyone made a move to the door he was awake and ready to offer his protective accompaniment. Once in the open air, he transformed into the intrepid hunter of his youth.

His energy was rewarded this morning when he startled a pair of pheasants hiding in the coppice. They flew off, flying low, making their alarmed chuckle with Rags in hot but fruitless pursuit. 'They must've managed to escape from the guns eh? Lucky ones those two.' Walter laughed. He told Michael how he occasionally worked as a beater for the people who owned the big house at the far end of the village. They had a lot of land and a big area of woodland where they bred pheasants for shooting. But, since the war had begun, most of the men, including the gamekeeper, had been called-up so the few remaining birds had been allowed to run wild.

They broke out of the coppice and continued along the edge of a field where the corn shoots stood straight and vibrant green. A breeze moved across and caused a wave to ripple over the surface. 'It's alive,' called Michael. 'Look grandad, it's just like flowin' water.' Walter nodded and smiled, Rags barked; ready to attack the hidden prey that lay beneath the fresh green covering.

At the end of the field a rickety wooden stile allowed them to climb through the spiky hawthorn hedge, down a muddy slope to a little stream. There were stones set at intervals so that anyone could cross with dry feet. The water reflected dappled sun and shade and rippled musically between the stepping stones. They paused to investigate and saw several small fish hiding in the pebbled bottom of the stream. Michael bent down and tried to grab one but they slipped easily out of his reach. They had slender bodies but large heads. 'What are they?' He asked.

'They're called millers' thumbs because of their flat heads,' answered Walter.

Michael remembered Grandad George's flat thumb: 'they could be called joiners' thumbs,' he said and explained why.

'Yes, I remember seeing George's thumb.'

The boy was surprised; he had forgotten that when Jack and Kathleen had been first married, both families had lived in Stanbury. Walter and Amy seemed so much part of the life of

214

Callthorpe he couldn't imagine them living anywhere else. 'Why did you leave Stanbury?' He asked.

'There was plenty of work for a stonemason,' the old man explained, 'but we wanted to get away from the mills and I was offered some work on the Minster in Seldown which I thought would be interesting so we came out here. We missed you all though and Amy couldn't wait to get you over here as soon as your house was destroyed. We were both worried that Stanbury was too dangerous. Your grandma wasn't happy when you went to live with Mary.' Michael knew why they hadn't come straight away but decided to say nothing. He thought that his mother wouldn't want him to tell how unhappy she had been.

They passed through a field of cows. The animals moved together for protection when they saw the dog. Their warm, sweet breath rose in the air and they stared with anxious eyes at the trio that had invaded their space.

The walk continued. Michael watched a small bird climb steadily higher into the sky, singing as it went, then suddenly dropping to earth. 'It's a skylark,' Walter answered the question before it was asked. 'You might think that there would be a nest where it lands but it runs through the grass to its nest so that a predator won't be able to find it.'

'There weren't any skylarks back 'ome,' said Michael. 'We only saw sparrows, rooks an' starlin's. It's great 'ere Grandad,' he added, putting his hand into Walter's rough fingers. The old man's heart leapt at the boy's pleasure in a simple yet beautiful thing and at the obvious trust they shared.

He wondered about Michael's relationship with his father. 'Do you miss your dad?' He asked. Then immediately thought it a stupid question but it did serve to open the subject.

'Yes. I didn't at first but now I do, I wish 'e was 'ere. He might not come back you know.' Walter was surprised at the calm manner of Michael's statement but before he could speak words of comfort, the boy went on: 'people get killed in war 'an you never know who's next. Mam an' me could 'ave been killed when the house was bombed. I don't know why we're fightin'. I don't understand it at all.'

Walter paused, what could he say that would make sense to a small boy? 'Wars are fought for different reasons son,' he began. 'Most are pointless and could be avoided. The last one that I was in started because one man was killed and people in power were too stupid to realise where their arguments and demands could lead. In the end huge numbers of men died and countries were wrecked because the thing got out of control and nobody knew how to stop it. This one's different; a mad man has driven a country into a war because of his own greed for power.'

'That's Hitler isn't it?'

'Yes lad, he's the one who started it. I don't know what else our country could do. The Germans were attacking other countries and we could have been next so we were almost forced to fight. But the German people themselves could have stopped it if only they'd seen how wrong Hitler was. They should have thrown him out. But sometimes people get carried along by the mood of the majority; the louder and angrier you sound, the more people seem to follow, then a kind of mass madness takes over.' He looked at the boys face to gauge the impact of his words and saw that he was listening intently. 'Does that make sense to you?'

'Yes it does,' Michael had a serious look in his eyes. 'Mam said that dad had to go because it was 'is duty an' she's proud of him for goin' an' so am I but I want 'im to come back soon.'

'We all do Michael, we all do and God willing he will.' There's God again the boy thought. If He can control things, why doesn't He stop this? It was very difficult to understand. He remembered fights he'd had with other boys and knew that sometimes a conflict was unavoidable. He also recalled the other children who had gathered to watch his fight with Howard and no-one had tried to stop it so maybe this was a bit like the mass madness that grandad had mentioned.

From this point, both were occupied by their own thoughts till, after half-an-hour of walking, they reached the edge of the lake. Rags was called over and told to stay with them and be quiet. He responded appropriately, crouching down and going into hunting mode. They could hear the chatter of the birds. The ground rose slightly and there were several large boulders to hide behind as they approached so they were able stay out of sight of any creatures on the surface of the water. Their caution was rewarded: as they peeped through tall reeds at the edge of the lake, they saw a rich variety of water birds floating on the lake and many others seeking food around the weedy margins.

Michael gasped as two descending swans flared their wings as they skidded on to the surface of the water and then proceeded to swim together, tipping themselves up to reach the underwater plants. There were mallards and several variously coloured groups of ducks that he couldn't identify. Two particular birds were behaving strangely; they swam together, each mirroring the movements of the other. They had very long necks and crests that rose and fell as they danced. At one point they appeared to be standing up on the water, facing one another. 'Look at those,' he whispered. 'They've got hats on and they're dancing.'

Walter whispered back, 'They're grebes, great crested grebes. They dance when they're going to mate. They build a nest that floats on the water and the male stands guard while the female keeps the eggs warm... Those swans over there are called mute swans because they don't make a noise... And see those grey/brown birds on the bank, they're pink footed geese. We're lucky to see them; they'll be off soon up to the northern countries. They only stay here over the winter. They breed in Norway or Denmark and then, in late autumn, they come back, bringing the young ones with them. Then we can see them again. They come back to the same lake – I don't know how they do it, they're just marvelous birds.'

Michael listened intently and thought about the flight the geese would make. He imagined them heading north cutting through the cold air, driven by some strange, primitive force. Compared to the bombers he had seen lumbering towards their laborious take-off, the geese would fly with ease and grace. The air truly belonged to them not to men. Magnificent though the planes were, they could never belong in the sky in the same way as these wild, mysterious creatures.

It must be very tiring to fly over the sea to another country. He thought about his father: will he see them as they fly? He wondered. He listened to the birds chuntering to one another. Lots of different noises, he thought. Each type with its own language, just like us and the Germans but the birds get along together, why can't we?

For about half-an-hour the three friends watched the comings and goings on the lake, when, suddenly, as one, the birds rose. Alarm calls and the sound of bustling wings filled the air. Loose feathers drifted down to the water. 'Oh, no!' Michael called. He looked at Rags thinking the dog might have moved. He was growling softly, but apart from looking upwards to see the birds, he was quite still.

The crack of a shotgun, followed by a second, startled them all. One of the geese dropped through the air twisting as it fell, its feathers all awry. 'It's farmer Kruyf,' said Walter. 'What's he doing out here?' The large man strode like an angry giant along the edge of the lake, his red hair hidden by a flat cap. He carried a smoking shotgun, broken over his arm; a binocular case hung from his neck. 'Strange, why 'as 'e done that? He's got plenty birds on his farm if 'e wants food. Why kill a wild 'un?' Michael looked at his grandad's face, it had an angry look.

Michael was about to stand but Walter put a hand on his arm; 'let's stay where we are, he's not a pleasant bloke, let him get on his way.' The boy stopped and settled back down. Rags stayed quiet. Kruyf walked to where the bird had fallen, picked it up and fastened to his belt. He strode off the way he had come, satisfied with his kill.

When Walter looked, the boy had tears in his eyes. He knew immediately why Michael was upset. 'It's the country way lad, some animals are seen as food round here. The others have to do useful jobs, even dogs and cats have to do their work. Once they're too old they're put down.'

'But it was such a fine lookin' bird. . . An' it was ready to fly off with its mates. . . It was free . . . he shouldn't have killed it . . . . it's wrong, it's just wrong! I feel sick.' He sobbed and rubbed his eyes with muddy hands which made him look even more sorrowful.

'I know Michael, I agree really. Some animals are bred for food but the wild ones should be left alone.' Walter put his arm round the boy's shoulders but Michael wriggled free.

'I don't think they should kill anything at all. Cows give us milk an' 'ens give us their eggs, why do we 'ave to kill them?'

'Well people like to eat meat. Maybe we need it to make us grow properly.'

Walter spoke from the heart: he loved to eat meat. But Michael could not be convinced; 'I'm never goin' to eat animals again, never, never.'

The day had been marred. The three bird watchers shared their food and then set off back to Callthorpe. Michael was quiet and Walter didn't know how to cheer him up. Rags managed to start a hare that was crouching in the new corn but its rapid changes of direction were too much for him and he returned to his master breathless and disappointed. 'It's alright Rags,' Michael said, 'you're not doin' any more killin'.' The dog thought about this and wondered whether rats were excluded but hadn't the words to ask.

*

Mary died on the 14th April 1943. She was 67. Since Kathleen and Michael had left for Callthorpe, the old woman had been left to the ministrations of her daughters. Like their mother, they were basically selfish and had little inclination to be at the beck and call of their demanding parent. They had been controlled by her when they were children but had rebelled as teenagers and once having left home to form their own families, they had no intention of allowing her to once more dominate their lives.

This left Grandad George to bear the brunt of her complaints. His strategy, as before, was to say as little as possible and to spend as much time away from home as he dared. He missed Michael particularly. Although they hadn't talked much, he felt that they had got on well together and he loved the boy. His daughters were childless at the moment and since both their husbands were overseas, they were unlikely to provide him with the distraction of another grandchild.

The old man enjoyed his work, so with this and his daily visits to the Royal Oak, he had a tolerable life. Annie still brought food in for his tea and Lillian managed to do his washing. His only problem lay in the fact that Mary had no-one else to talk to, so when he arrived home, she recounted the day's annoyances and nagged him to do the little jobs that he repeatedly forgot. Her constant moaning about her daughters, the neighbours, the shortages and that selfish bitch, (Kathleen), nearly drove him crazy.

Unfortunately, Mary's health was deteriorating but her approach to people meant that her constant complaints were regarded as being the rantings of a cantankerous hypochondriac. No-one took her seriously because she had always enjoyed telling people how ill she was.

Following her death, George was full of guilt; he knew that he had not given her the attention that a wife should have. He was inconsolable and now spent more time in the home on Lucy Street than he had done for years. His daughters tried to support him; they were worried that his health would suffer but he wouldn't listen. In his own mind he had been a bad husband. He also realised that the news of his mother's death could have a devastating effect on Jack. They had always been close and the old man knew that, without his son's insistence, Kathleen would not have stayed as long as she did after her house had been destroyed. Even from the distance of a foreign prison, Jack had shown more concern for Mary than anyone else.

They buried Mary behind the chapel. Kath managed to raise the bus fare but Michael was left behind. The weather was appropriate; steady rain fell from a steely sky and the little group round the family grave stood close together making a roof of black umbrellas. Afterwards, they ate soggy potted meat sandwiches in the Co-op restaurant and discussed what to do about Jack.

Kath looked out of the window. Apart from a few more bomb sites, Stanbury hadn't changed. The dark mills remained, clustered in the valley bottom and people still walked with hunched shoulders. It seemed as though the rain always fell here. She felt that she must get away as quickly as possible or the place might suck her back to her previous life. It was hard enough to cope with Jack's absence. This place and Mary's death served only to make her even more anxious and depressed.

'I think we've got to tell him,' she said. 'He would want to know and how would you explain not tellin' him when he gets back?' Kath knew that Jack had been involved in some sort of trouble but his letters recently had contained no details and had been very brief and sad. If she had known how sick he was, she might have thought twice about sending bad news.

'He might not ...' Annie received a sharp kick under the table. Lillian looked at her and frowned.

'Yes I think you're right Kath,' she joined in, hoping that her sister-in-law hadn't noticed.

But Kathleen knew immediately what Annie had meant: 'Yes, I know, you're right, he might not come back,' she said, trying to hide her emotions. 'But I've got to keep on hoping.'

'Of coure you must.' George said. 'But you're right he's got to know. Do you want to write or shall I?'

Eventually they decided that the old man was the one who should send the letter. Kath left as soon as it was decent to do so, making the excuse of the long bus trip. She wept on and off for much of the journey but as she was carried along the lanes from Seldown both her sorrow and the day's rain began to die away. The countryside worked its magic, helped by a late evening sun that painted a deep red on the roofs of the passing villages as they rested amongst the new spring trees.

CHAPTER 14

May – June 1943: *Allies take Tunisia and German and Italian troops surrender in North Africa.*

Jewish resistance in the Warsaw ghetto comes to an end. Himmler orders the liquidation of all ghettos in Poland.

Dönitz suspends all U-boat operations in the North Atlantic.

At home: supplies of wool and cotton are down to 20% of pre-war levels. There are hardly any goods in the shops. There is little chance of replacing broken or damaged household items.

News spread quickly round the prison: there were to be no more working parties sent out from the fort. All prisoners were to be moved to a camp somewhere near the German border. The men saw this as an indication that things were not going well for the Germans; it could be that they were being forced to withdraw in order to consolidate their defences. They also realised that such a move would place them in greater danger since, if the Germans were to be defeated, it was likely that the war would eventually be concentrated on their home ground. But on the whole, the British welcomed the indication of their enemy's weakening situation. Undernourished, depressed and frustrated by their situation, they were pleased to see any glimmer of light at the end of the wartime tunnel.

Bob Gunn was worried about his friend. Jack's spell in the cooler had left him weak and dispirited. He had a terrible cough and seemed to have all but lost the will to survive. He definitely wasn't in a fit state to endure a long journey in a cattle truck. The medical help Jack had received in Dopplenz was minimal: essentially, advice from the one medic who had been captured, along with whatever medicines they could scrounge from the Germans, or items that turned up in Red Cross supplies.

Bob went to see the British CO who had been given use of a small room on the ground floor as his office and living quarters. The furniture was basic: two wooden chairs and an old desk along with a cot and a wash stand but he was, at least, able to sleep alone and perform his ablutions in private. He could also request an audience with Balheim although this was not always granted. Nevertheless, his living conditions were much better than those of his men and it was rumoured that he received some items from Red Cross parcels that were appropriated by the Guards. This was actually true but he usually handed out most of the goods to other officers, believing that they deserved better treatment than the other ranks.

While Edward Johns was a basically decent man, who conducted himself with dignity, as a representative of the prison population, he was a failure, being too frightened of upsetting the Germans. He was not prepared to make a stand against injustices. He had made a tentative complaint about the missing parcels and the unreliable mail service but had not pursued the matter when rebuffed by Balheim. Men had made regular complaints to him about the standard of the food they received and the insanitary living conditions but more often than not, he was too nervous to communicate their dissatisfaction.

When Bob raised the issue of Jack's poor condition, Johns simply dismissed any suggestion that anything could be done to alleviate his suffering: 'Balheim is busy making arrangements for the transfer; he won't have time to bother about one prisoner. Besides, corporal Gunn, you two have caused him enough trouble already he'll not be inclined to make any special arrangements for either of you. I suggest that you do all you can to make your friend comfortable but there's nothing I can do to help. Dismissed.' Bob was about to protest but could see from the CO's face that, as far as he was concerned, the matter was closed.

Fortunately, the day of the transfer dawned bright and warm. Guards rousted the prisoners at dawn and instructed them to gather together their meager belongings. No food was provided; the men had eaten nothing since late afternoon on the previous day. Each billet in turn formed up by the main gate and began the trek to the railhead. They were supposed to march but few were fit enough to manage anything better than a shambling walk. Bob and a sapper, Ginger Davidson, held Jack up and virtually carried him down the steep track from the fort to the railway.

As expected, they were loaded on to cattle trucks with armed guards sitting on the roofs. They laid Jack on the floor with his back against the wooden sidewall. His face was grey and his breathing laboured; he looked close to the end of his strength. One of the guards that they didn't know looked in and saw his condition. He passed over his water bottle and broke off a square of dark chocolate from a bar in his pocket. Not used to such kindness, Bob didn't know how to respond but Ginger remembered a bit of German: 'Danke, vielen dank.' The guard nodded, took back his flask and walked on.

The uncomfortable journey, with frequent stops, took about three hours. The men were transported to an area close to the Polish/German border known as Silesia. They learned later that this was known as the air-raid shelter of Germany because the allied bombers were not able to carry sufficient fuel for the length of the return flight.

From the train the prisoners walked about a mile on good roads to a purpose built camp with a double wired fence, watch towers and about twenty wooden sheds as billets. There was another adjacent camp that already housed Russian prisoners.

Each shed was about twenty-five meters long with double bunks for forty men. In the centre of each billet was a wood-burning, pot-bellied stove and near to the main door, a wash room with showers and toilets. Once inside, the men felt warmer than they had during any of the months they had lived in Stalag 111Z. Some men were actually smiling. This appeared to be a much more comfortable place than the damp, cold, filthy fort they had left behind.

Their first impressions proved to be correct: they were supplied with new uniforms and army boots supplied by the Red Cross, food parcels arrived more regularly and the men had a reliable supply of water and could use the showers. The parcels of food proved to be vital since the Germans kept cutting back on supplies for prisoners because their own food was getting scarcer.

The humanity of the passing guard seemed to have helped Jack to find new sources of energy. The chocolate, washed down with cold water, had tasted like the sweetest food he had ever encountered. He still needed to be supported on either side but his spirit was much improved. On arriving in their allocated billet, he slumped on to his bunk and almost immediately, fell asleep, only to be awakened minutes later by German guards ordering everyone outside for a roll-call.

After they had been counted and the total verified with the prison lists, they were addressed by Balheim who had traveled with them and was to be in charge of the new camp. He explained to the prisoners how lucky they were to be given a new camp which had been arranged for them through the good offices of the Führer. He also told them that victory by the forces of the Fatherland was inevitable and they should forget all ideas of release by the allied forces which, it seemed, were being driven back on all fronts. They were advised to settle into life at Stalag X1BC (which they found out later was near Leipzig) and wait for the end of the war, when they could become members of the glorious Third Reich. In the meantime, he explained, they would be given opportunities to work outside the camp so long as they behaved well.

To their surprise, the men then listened to their own CO telling them that he would do his best to make their lives as comfortable as possible and that he had agreed with the camp commander to try to prevent any escape attempts. There was some muttering in the ranks at this news but most thought that Johns was just saying this in front of the Germans to make them relax their vigilance. Bob Gunn wasn't sure he felt that their CO was basically a coward who was looking after his own best interests.

After a few days of settling into the routine of the new camp, the first work parties were organised. Those involved found that they were no longer working on farms or in carrying out repairs to the local infrastructure, instead they were working on bigger projects. Knowing that the Allied planes couldn't reach Silesia, the Germans had decided that this was a suitable place to build new factories that were intended to produce armaments. Prisoners of war and other displaced persons were being mobilised for this task so Americans, Russians and some Jews were involved. The British and Americans were fortunate in that their countries had signed-up to the Geneva Convention so they were treated roughly within the guidelines set down. The Russians and Jews had no such standing and were treated badly; forced to work even though many of them could hardly stand. They were guarded by the SS troops who were much harsher than the regular army which was responsible for the Allied prisoners.

Initially Jack was clearly too ill to work and was moved to the camp 'hospital'. This was little more than another shed with the lone medic in charge. He still had insufficient medical supplies but at least the beds were clean and there was sufficient food to help, to some extent, to renew wasted bodies. Jack was beginning to show signs of progress when he received George's letter. The day it arrived, he was almost overwhelmed with sadness. Devastated that he would never see his mother again, his sorrow was mingled with feelings of anger towards those back home who had allowed this to happen.

His mental and physical condition began to deteriorate and the medic was seriously worried that he would not last much longer. It seemed that Jack had lost the will to live. The end of the war appeared to him to be further away than ever. He felt increasingly detached from his former life; things were happening to his family that were beyond his control. In his weakened state, anxiety mingled with depression to the point where the easiest option was to simply lie still and die.

The turning point came with a letter from Kathleen and more importantly, some sentences written by Michael.

Birch Tree Cottage,

May 28th 1943

Dearest Jack,

I know you will have received your dad's letter by now. We were all saddened by Mary's death but I must tell you that she was more ill than either she or the rest of us realised. The doctor said that there was nothing that anyone could have done. We have not heard from you for such a long time, I pray that you are as well as can be expected. Please write as soon as you can then we will know to send a parcel. We are all well and Michael is thriving in the countryside. Amy and Walter send their love and we all look forward to the end of these terrible times when we can be together again.

All my love, Kath

Dad,

I'm sorry about Grandma. I have got a new friend here, he's called Thomas. He lives on a farm. School is OK. Rags the dog came with us and he likes it here. I want to show you a lake with wild birds and we can sledge in the winter and there are lots of good walks we can do. I'm taller now, Mum says about up to your shoulder. Grandad is looking after us but I want you to come back. There are lots of things we can do here.

Love Michael

PS We've got some hens.

PPS I can ride a bike now like you.

His son's words tore into Jack's heart. In his mind's eye he had a picture of them striding through the fields together or riding bikes down the country lanes; his whole being ached to be away from this God forsaken existence. Catching sight of himself in a cracked mirror, he looked into the eyes of death; his face gaunt, his head almost skeletal. From deep within he summoned a new determination to get home somehow; to last through to the end, which must surely come in time. I can put up with this, he thought. I have to be strong for my boy, he's depending on me. It was this goal that sustained him through the remaining harsh days of his incarceration.

*

Michael's project work with Reuben was nearly finished. They had written, drawn pictures and collected photographs all about the farms in the district. They had been able to visit Gant's farm with Thomas. Mrs. Hare, who owned the biggest arable farm in the village, had welcomed them to her establishment with fruit cake more beautiful than they had ever eaten before. Kath wondered how she could afford the coupons for the rich ingredients but she had learned that some things were possible in the country that would have been out-of-reach for town folk.

Miss Newby was delighted by the work that the boys had done but most pleased by the way in which Reuben's friendship with Michael had blossomed despite suffering the occasional setback. He was still reluctant to communicate with her and particularly wary of any physical contact but he was more settled in school and he came every day, usually on time.

The boys had spent a lot of time at Reuben's farm but always when his father was away which seemed to be quite often. Michael was always hurried off when it was time for Mr. Kruyff to return. Reuben was friendly now but would never talk about his father or where he went and Mrs. Kruyff, although pleased to see Michael, never mentioned her husband except to warn him not to go near the shed round the back of the farm house. This seemed to be Mr. Kruyff's special domain; not to be violated. Michael, being inquisitive, asked Reuben why the shed was so special but the boy just shook his head and made no comment.

The Italian prisoners worked on the farm every day. They seemed to have no thoughts of escape and their good behaviour and willingness to work resulted in them becoming trusted to stay at the farm without a guard. A wagon picked them up at the end of the day and returned them to the prison camp which was just outside the village.

They clearly liked children so the two boys sometimes sat with them when they were resting to eat their snap. The leader, Rodolpho, said that he was learning to speak English and was pleased to have two clever 'ragazzi' to help him practise.

'I from Genova,' he said. 'How are you today?'

'I am very well,' answered Michael. 'I come from Stanbury.'

'How is your name?'

'No, what is your name,' Michael corrected.

'My name is Rodolpho.'

'No, you should say *what* is your name.'

'I tell you, my name is Rodolpho.' It was clearly going to take some time for the big Italian to master the subtleties of the English language.

Michael laughed, 'OK, my name is Michael and this is Reuben.'

'Ah! I call you Michelangelo.' Rodolpho smiled and clapped the boy on his back, nearly knocking the wind out of his chest. 'And you I call Reubens,' he cried, smiling. Reuben backed off to avoid the congratulatory back slap. 'Due bene ragazzi - my frens.'

From this time forward the prisoners and the boys *were* friends. Whenever their visits to the farm coincided, they sat together to eat. Rodolpho's English improved and he never missed an opportunity to reaffirm his regard for his 'ragazzi'. Michael sometimes brought food for the men: Amy's baking was very well received and in return the prisoners showed their skills by presenting him with things they had made: tiny aeroplanes and ships produced from scrap wood and very realistic English shillings and half-crowns that looked to be shiny metal but were actually made from cardboard. Reuben didn't say much of course but seemed happy just to sit with the men and listen to the musical mixture of Italian and English.

Rodolpho told them about his family back home, saying he missed them very much. He also surprised the boys by saying that he didn't like the Germans but couldn't explain why. They all agreed that they wanted the war to be over.

Once, when Reuben was in the farm house, Michael told Rodolpho about Jack and about him being a prisoner. This interested the Italian greatly. 'I also like football,' he said. 'Maybe I meet your papa after war and we watch football. Eh? You have good papa I think but not Reubens,' he said quietly. 'I think he is bad man to family. I sorry for little ragazzo.'

'Attenzione!' One of the others called Leonardo pointed to Reuben emerging from the house and the conversation ended.

*

The countryside bloomed as spring moved towards summer. Welcome daylight lengthened; a relief from the dark days of winter when it had seemed that they had only just opened the curtains in the morning when they had to start drawing the blackout in the evening. Kathleen loved to see new life emerging: wild flowers, vegetables in the garden, the noisy rooks squabbling over nest material in the high trees but best of all was the light. She marveled at the huge, hemisphere of sky that soared above the flat landscape; at one time full of infinite blue with delicate cirrus clouds whipped into mares' tails and next packed with rushing cumulus that sent shadows chasing across the growing cornfields. The regular cycle of seasons was reassuringly normal against the backdrop of a world torn apart by war.

She was enjoying the work at the Sunday school. The children liked her although they couldn't always understand her accent. Kath had found a beautifully illustrated book that retold the old testament stories in simple words and the children listened intently when she read them out, often asking her to 'read it again'. The work took her mind off Jack's situation although he was never far from her thoughts. His last letter had sounded more optimistic but there was an edge of great disappointment when he wrote about Mary's death. Kath had the feeling that he hadn't forgiven her for leaving his mother's house.

This week, it was Amy's turn to do the Church flowers but she had been invited to visit Mrs. Hare at the big farm. They were good friends and Amy didn't want to miss seeing her. She knew that her friend was very busy running the farm and that she might not be able to arrange another meeting for some time. Kath said she was quite happy to take the flowers and put them in the fine cut-glass vases but wasn't confident about her flower arranging skills. Amy was sure that her daughter was quite capable but agreed to call at the Church on her way home to make sure everything was alright. Kath accepted this offer and her mother set off early to enjoy a cup of tea, some of the famous fruit cake and a chat.

Kath finished her chores and went into the sun-filled garden. She cut a basket full of early roses and some greenery for background, then walked down to the village. There was no-one inside the church but streams of sunlight flowed through the stained glass to produce a tranquil and welcoming atmosphere. It reminded her of her first visit. She sat for a while in one of the back pews and let the peace and quiet of the place wash over her. A feeling of lethargy spread through her body as she allowed herself to completely relax. Time stopped. She felt to be cocooned in an individual capsule where the slightest movement would break the invisible skin and allow the world to penetrate. She remained as still as possible, her mind empty, hardly breathing.

The curate pushed open the old wooden door, humming quietly to himself. He knew immediately that he had once again startled Kath by his entrance. 'Oh, sorry, I didn't know there was

. . . .' He paused and laughed. 'This is déjà vu, we've done this before.'

She laughed nervously, feeling foolish. She was frightened of his use of 'we', it threatened the familiarity which in her heart she actually craved. 'Yes, … I was just sitting a moment… I've come to do the flowers.'

'Please don't let me disturb you Kathleen. Sit as long as you want. The flowers look beautiful,' he said, pointing to the basket. 'I've got a job to do in the vestry. And, by the way, thank you for your work with the Sunday school, the children are really enjoying themselves.'

'Oh, thank you, so am I.' She picked the flowers and started to fiddle with them. Mike walked down the aisle, nodded to the crucifix on the altar and disappeared through the door to the vestry.

He moved quietly but it was no use, Kath's mood was broken. She began to sort the flowers into three bunches, her hands shaking; one by the door and two for the altar. Their heady perfume filled the air and she almost drifted into a different daydream. 'Come on, get on with it,' she said to herself and then remembered that the vases for the flowers were kept in a cupboard in the vestry. 'Oh, God,' she said aloud.

She was worried that she might appear to be following him if she went in there but waiting was not an option; she had no idea how long he would be and he would wonder why she hadn't got on with the flower arranging. She walked to the door which stood half open. He was moving around, still humming to himself. What's the tune? She thought and listened for a moment but it was unrecognizable. She knocked. 'Excuse me, I need the vases.'

'Oh, sure, come in. I think they're in the cupboard.' Kath stepped through the door. The room was small and she had to pass close to him. He smelled of soap and the black cloth of his cassock. She hoped he wouldn't talk so that she could get back into the church. 'Kath, I meant to ask you, have you heard from Jack? How's he doing?'

She stopped, a glass vase in her hand. 'We had a letter, he's feeling OK, as well as can be expected, he's ...' Kath felt the warm prickle of tears. She felt a sudden desire to be held. She looked at his arms.

'I'm sorry, I didn't mean to upset ... I've done it again, I just seem to say the wrong thing. I ...' He stepped forward and put a hand on her shoulder. This was too much, Kath stepped forward and his arms were round her. The dam that had held back months of anxiety burst, she wept freely, her body shaking, sobs echoing round the old stone walls. He touched her hair. Tears made a dark pool on his cassock. The vase slipped from her fingers and shattered on the stone floor.

They stood for a few minutes that seemed like an hour. No words. The crying stopped but they didn't move.

'Hello, cooee, anybody there?' Amy's voice was like an electric shock. They sprang apart. Kath dropped to her knees and started picking up pieces of glass.

'Yes here,' she called, stepping to the door, waving a shard of glass as if it were a trophy. 'I dropped a vase ... sorry.'

Amy looked at the tear stained face and was about to speak when Mike appeared. 'Hello, Amy aren't the flowers beautiful? We were just having a chat and the vase broke. I think we've got a spare.'

Amy was nonplussed. 'Oh, yes, well I've just been to see Mrs. Hare.' She looked quizzically at Kathleen who wouldn't meet her eyes. Mike went back into the vestry.

'You can help me now.' Kath walked to the pew and started to push roses into a rough bunch.

'Yes, alright but be careful, you'll scratch yourself.' Amy took the flowers and began to sort them.

'I'll leave you to it then,' said Kathleen, brusquely, 'now you're here.' Without waiting for agreement, she walked quickly to the door and out into the graveyard. Amy was about to speak but her daughter's exit was too swift. She looked helplessly towards the vestry but Mike didn't appear. 'Well I never,' she whispered to herself, shaking her head. 'What on earth's going on?'

*

Mike stood looking at the broken glass littering the floor but made no attempt to pick it up. His mind was in turmoil unable to understand what had just happened. He had known Kathleen Spencer for a short time and from the beginning had been aware that she was a very attractive woman. He had also recognised that she was troubled: her husband was a prisoner, her house had been destroyed and she had been forced to uproot her son. Moving to Callthorpe had completely changed her life. He felt that he should offer her a supportive relationship, as he did with any of his new parishioners who were worried about the future.

But what had just happened? As she stood with him in the vestry, he had felt her need for comfort. The power of it had been overwhelming. To hold her had been irresistible, automatic; something that could not have been avoided, like cuddling an upset child. But in the moment, there was something else: he had felt her vulnerability and her femininity. The fabric of her dress, her hair against his cheek, her slenderness, they had disturbed him and beneath these physical elements was an underlying, primitive core; his body had responded.

He had always tried to live his life as a Christian. There were times when his determination had been tested but he had always been able to hold to his principles. He felt that, at some time in the future, he might get married and have a family but his life had been full without these things and he had not yet met anyone to whom he could commit. The war had also intervened. He had volunteered at the beginning but the heart that was, even now, performing its irregular rhythm, had prevented him from being accepted. Despite his lack of involvement in the war however, these were still not good times for seeking to a wife.

Yet now he found his defensive wall of spiritual and moral beliefs under attack from within. He was sure that Kathleen had simply needed comfort but here he was coveting another man's wife.

Amy knocked on the vestry door. 'Oh, Mrs. Green, come in, no need to knock, I was just …'

'I'll sweep up this broken glass,' Amy interrupted him. She opened a tall cupboard that held equipment for cleaning and took out a dustpan and brush. 'I need the vases as well,' she added without looking at him.

Mike needed to think: 'Thankyou, Mrs. Green,' he said. 'I'll get out of your way.' He walked through the church down the aisle to the bell ringers' room. Then, climbing the narrow stone steps, went up past the bells hanging silent from the dusty beams of the gantry, to the wooden stairs that led up to the door which opened on to the roof of the tower. He stepped out into a fresh breeze blowing from the distant sea and walked to the surrounding wall, resting his hands on the cold stone. He could see the toy village below. It was playtime at the school; children's voices. Grass on the green responded to the wind. A dog barked. The local ARP man sauntered towards the co-op, his gas mask swung casually from his shoulder.

*

Mrs Gant had talked to Amy and Kath to see what they thought about the boys' desire to watch the bombers returning in the early dawn. It had been agreed that they could go but had to be back before school started.

As arranged, they rode over to Timpney the previous evening and found Sergeant Ferris to make arrangements to meet him by the guard house. To make the start of the day easier, Michael stayed overnight at the farm. Thomas had a large bedroom and a bed big enough to accommodate two boys. They were sent to bed early to make up for the sleep they would miss but spent most of the time talking or wrestling. In fact they slept very little and were wide awake before Mr. Gant knocked on the door of the bedroom.

With a breakfast of hot tea, and jam and bread inside, they set off in darkness with only the tiny slits of light from their bicycle lamps to guide them. The adrenaline of excitement powered their pedaling as two dark shapes ripped along the silent lanes through the early morning chill. They were not surprised to be joined by a ragged, panting shape running alongside; Rags knew where Michael was even when they were apart. He had sensed that something was happening and was determined not to be left out.

Sergeant Ferris was waiting. 'Now remember you two, this is a secret arrangement – no-one else must know about this or I'll be on a fizzer.'

'What's a fizzer?' Michael asked.

'Never you mind. Now who's this?' He said pointing at Rags who was peeping through Michael's legs. He was watching the sergeant's boots, remembering kicks aimed at him in the past.

'It's Rags, he's come as well but 'e'll be good an' do what I tell 'im.'

'OK, but he's your responsibility.' The soldier bent to stroke the dog, but as usual, Rags backed off with a warning growl. Michael put his arms round Rags and told him that Sergeant Ferris was a friend. The dog licked his master's face and smiled at the soldier. 'One man dog eh? Right come on, we'll go to the place you found last time, they're just about due.'

A soft drone could be heard as they walked beside the fence. Soon they thought they could make out dark shapes in the sky. 'How do they find their way in the night?' Michael asked. He thought that Thomas and he had needed lights to ride to Timpney, how on earth did big bombers find their way through the dark sky to another country and back?

'You'll have to stop asking questions lad. Just take it from me, they have a special way of doing it but I can't tell you how. After the war, maybe you'll find out then.'

Suddenly, lines of lights outlined the runway. 'Gosh,' said Thomas. Rags gave a little bark. In the gloom, they could see wagons, jeeps and green fire-engines and hear their engines start-up. There was an immediate increase in excitement. The air crackled with electric anticipation.

The Bombers were coming in from behind. The boys instinctively crouched down as the first one roared overhead, accompanied by a great whoosh of air. It dropped quite suddenly, tyres squealed as its wheels touched the runway and a cloud of smoke burst from each side. The stench of burning rubber filled the air. The dawn was lightening and they could see the rear gun turret. Michael wondered if the same man who had waved at them last time was inside. The plane swerved slightly and then recovered its equilibrium and sped down the tarmac, disappearing in the dawn light. Before they had lost sight of the first one, another was down and then the next. The noise and commotion was too much for the dog, which lay down between Michael's feet with tail and ears flat, growling quietly.

The boys' senses were pounded by the noise and visual spectacle. Mouths open, they were staggered by the skill of the pilots who managed to drop these huge, rattling machines out of the sky on to a tiny surface, while controlling the incredible speed at which they arrived. They were so close together; no sooner had one landed than another roared in. Some landings were further down the runway, some almost landed on one wheel, others bounced but they all got down safely. Michael wished they would slow down so that he could concentrate on every detail.

The sergeant was counting them as they arrived: 'thirteen … fourteen … fifteen. Three missing. No! One more. The next one, lagging some way behind the others, was making a strange noise; not the usual drone building to a roar as it got nearer but a more staccato sound. The sky was now light enough for them to see that two propellers were turning but one of the others was nearly stopped and the fourth one had flames licking round the cowling. There was damage to the wings and a gaping hole through the tail plane. 'Oh God! Can he make it? Get down

boys, get down.' He was shouting now. The boys and Ferris
hunched down and backed towards the hedge behind them.

The plane was too low; its undercarriage seemed almost
to brush the hedge. They could feel a blast of heat from the
flames as it passed over. With a deafening racket it landed several
yards before the runway began and the left-hand landing wheel
collapsed as it hit the ground, folding underneath the fuselage.
The huge plane swiveled round tearing up mounds of grass and
earth, accompanied by the sound of tearing, screeching metal. It
missed the runway completely and continued its slide across the
grassed area towards the hangers. It seemed that it would never
stop, but quite suddenly, it did. The wreckage continued to creak
and flames from the engine started to spread across the wing,
licking towards the cockpit.

'Get them out, get them out.' Ferris was shouting towards
the fleet of vehicles that had arrived close to the stricken
machine. Almost immediately hoses run from the fire-engine
started spraying. At first the spray fell short but then the power
increased and water started to splash on the flames but with no
visible effect. A door in the side of the plane swung back with a
bang. Smoke billowed from inside and men dropped on to the
grass and rolled away. Ferris was counting again: 'one, two, three,
four ..... come on where are you? Five, six ... come on ....
seven. All out, thank God!'

Through the clouds of smoke, the boys could see figures
rushing towards the airmen and helping them to get away from
the burning wreck. Flames were beginning to reach the main
body of the aircraft, licking round the very door through which
the men had escaped. Vehicles and men started to withdraw
from the scene, beaten back by the intense heat; the water from
the hosepipes ineffective now that the fire had taken firm hold.

'Come on now, quickly, let's get you away from here, she
might explode.' The sergeant gathered both boys in his arms and
pulled them and their bicycles away up the track towards the
main guard post by the road from Timpney. Rags needed no

further bidding but still stayed by Michael's side. 'Run lads, quick as you can.'

They ran together, not looking back, until they reached the far corner of the protective fence, not far from the guard house. There, Ferris thought they would be safe and stopped. Now the boys looked back but could only see black smoke rising behind trees that edged the winding track they had run along. Then an explosion blasted their ears and flames flew upwards. 'The fuel tanks,' explained the sergeant, 'they would be nearly empty but still full enough to blow us to kingdom come if we'd been nearby. Don't worry, the aircrew was out and everyone else has got clear.'

People were beginning to arrive from the village. They had heard the impact of the stricken bomber and rushed out of their houses to see what was happening. The boys were surprised to see the huge figure of Mr. Kruyff standing on the edge of the group. What's he doing here? Michael thought but decided not to approach the man for fear of making him angry again. In any case Kruyff turned quickly and walked off with a grim smile on his face. Then Maisie arrived in her dressing gown, with her hair in curlers, amazed to see the two boys. 'What on earth are you doing here?' She demanded. Michael and Thomas looked at one another and then at Sergeant Ferris, remembering what he had said.

'We were just passing,' answered Thomas. He knew that this sounded rather lame but was unable to think of any other reason.

'Just passing,' Maisie was incredulous. 'What are your parents thinking, letting you out at this time in the morning? You'd better come with me.'

'No Maisie, no thankyou,' Michael joined in. 'We need to get back in time for school. We've got to set off now.'

The old woman was reluctant to let them go but finally agreed, extracting their promise to visit her soon. The boys walked over to the sergeant, and without speaking for fear of giving something away, shook his hand, then rode off with a nervous dog trotting alongside. The sounds had reminded Rags of the time when he hid behind the butcher's shop – a time when he had been very frightened.

*

This experience strengthened the already firm bond between the two boys. The images would remain fresh and clear in their minds for the rest of their lives. In the excitement of the moment, they didn't immediately realise the significance of Sergeant Ferris only counting to fifteen before the final crash-landing. Two planes were missing. They learned later that both had been shot down and it was not known whether any of the aircrew had survived. Michael thought that if they had bailed out, they might be in the same prison camp as his father. He decided not to discuss this idea with his mother since Kathleen was horrified that they had been so close to such a potentially hazardous event and agreed with Eileen Gant that they should not be allowed to visit the airfield again.

CHAPTER 15

Summer 1943   The Allies have some success in southern Europe: they land in Sicily and by the middle of August the Germans evacuate the island. In July, Mussolini is arrested and the Fascist government falls. Marshall Badoglio negotiates with the Allies. On September 8th, the Italian surrender is announced.

At home: rationing continues to produce hardship. The stealing and forging of coupons and books is a problem. There are thousands of claims by people reporting that they have lost ration books.

'We need to talk.' Amy sat with Kathleen in the kitchen. Michael had hurried his breakfast and then rushed off to play with Thomas. Walter was out building a wall round Mrs. Hare's large vegetable garden; she was tired of the damage caused by rabbits and thought a stout stone wall might keep them out. Walter wasn't sure, he knew how well rabbits could tunnel but he needed the work. He dug a trench and set the first layer of stones well below ground in the hope of dissuading them from burrowing underneath.

The morning sun lit the room and gave the tiled floor an orange tinge. A robin proclaimed his territory from the garden. A soft, summer breeze stirred the curtains and carried with it the scent of stocks. This should have been a quiet, peaceful day but Amy could see that her daughter was still in a highly stressed state. 'You're always worried and it's beginning to affect Michael. I'm sure you've noticed how quickly he gets out of the house. He hardly ever brings his friends here now. Come on love, tell me what's wrong. We can't go on like this.'

Kathleen knew that her mother was right; she *was* in a constant state of anxiety. The incident in the vestry had made matters worse and now she kept as far away from the curate as possible. They only saw one-another in the company of others: either when children from the Sunday school were there or at Church services. She was ashamed of her behaviour and wished to erase the moment from her memory and yet she had brooded on it because she felt the need to work out what had happened.

In his arms she had felt safe but there had been no sexual desire. He was an attractive man to whom she had been drawn, right from their first meeting, and she still remembered the extraordinary shock she had felt the first time their hands had touched. But, although she had admired him from a distance, like a silly teenager, when they were eventually physically close, her body relaxed but didn't respond. In some ways it was a relief; she craved his company but not his body. How could she explain this to her mother when she didn't understand it herself? I'm like two people, she thought; one, loyal to Jack, waiting and hoping for his return, and another experimenting with a relationship with another man. When I'm away from Mike, he doesn't signify but when he's there, this other woman emerges and feels the need to be close to him.

'Yes mam, you're right, I'm sorry. I'll try to cheer-up,' was all that she could muster.

'Tell me about the curate. Something happened between you two didn't it? You were upset. Did he try something?' Amy had been cool with Mike ever since that day, just in case he had acted inappropriately.

'No, no, nothing happened and nothing ever will.' Kath was adamant.

'Well listen Kathleen,' Amy only ever used her daughter's full name when she was about to deliver a sermon. 'Let me tell you what I think. For one thing, I know you're missing Jack, but more that that, you're worried that he might not come back at all…Also, you worry about your son; he needs a father. You're frightened that you might not be able to look after him properly by yourself… Then your home was destroyed around you and I don't think the shock of that has worn off yet. I hear you shouting in the night sometimes; you're calling out but I can't make out the words… I've got up and looked in on you and you've torn off all the bedclothes and you're thrashing about as though you're struggling to free yourself…' Kath opened her mouth to speak. 'No, let me finish or I'll forget something that needs saying... Another thing, like everybody, you worry about the war: what will happen if we lose and we're beaten by the Germans? I think that, subconsciously, you want to find a way to get rid of all these fears. Perhaps you saw Callthorpe as a safe place where your parents would look after you again. But your dad and me see you as an adult, as a woman, you're not our child anymore. It could be that you're looking for a sort of father figure because Walter is now more like a friend. The curate is a calm, stable character who could take charge; someone who might be able to make things right... What do you think?' She paused to weigh the effect of her words. Kath's face showed a mixture of surprise and anxiety. 'I'm sorry to go on so but sometimes a mum has to say things that no-one else would.'

Kathleen felt a mixture of amazement and frustration. She was surprised by the comprehensive manner in which her mother had covered her worries but also had a feeling of being controlled. She should have been able to perform her own analysis of these notions, which were entirely sensible and rational, she was, after all, a grown woman, but it had been left to her mother to articulate her daughter's personal feelings. Despite Amy's appeal for a response, she felt like a little girl again, unable to think of anything to say. Am I really looking for a father figure? She wondered. Is that what Mike is?

Seeing her daughter's hesitation, Amy was concerned that she had gone too far and tried to soften the impact of her words: 'don't be upset love, I may be completely wrong but sometimes it's easier for someone looking from the outside to see what's going on inside. You've had a lot to put up with in your young life; it's no wonder that you're having difficulty making sense of it all. We're all worried but you have more cause than most. But you must remember that we all love you, you're not alone although I know you feel to be sometimes.'

Kath looked into her mother's kind, grey eyes and read the concern etched on her face. What's the matter with me? She thought. 'You're right mam,' she said. 'Everything you say is true.

But I'm sure I don't love Mike, he just seemed so strong and calm ... I wanted someone to make it all go away... nothing really happened between us, he's a good man. There *is* something else though but I don't like to say it ... I worry that Jack might be badly injured... You hear of men returning with arms or legs missing, or with brain damage, or blind or, oh you know – not able to look after themselves... I know it's selfish but I don't know whether I could cope with that, I just don't know. I feel that I've let him down already and he's not even here.'

'Yes Kath, I understand that but it may not happen, and in the meantime, you have a son who needs you. He's growing up quickly and he will have his own worries. Who's helping him to make sense of this madness?...Think what he went through when the house was destroyed and the other day when the bomber crashed – how was he affected by those things? He seems happy enough but Michael keeps a lot inside you know. Did we help him to understand what happened or are we just thinking about ourselves?'

Using 'we' made it a shared problem but Kath knew that it was hers. She had to find strength within herself, it couldn't come from outside, from someone else. She paused before answering and then simply said: 'you're right ... thankyou.'

The two women sat holding hands, saying nothing. Kathleen reflected on the discussion, wondering if she had told the absolute truth: was she really indifferent to Mike? She shook herself, banishing the thought. The breeze had dropped, the curtains hung straight and still. They could hear the hens wittering to themselves.

Walter burst through the door. He was covered with stone dust, even his hair. He looked busy, workmanlike and smelled of fresh air. 'Hello you two, nothing to do? Run out of stone, on my way to get some. How about making a working man a cup of tea?'

*

There were no working parties today. The idleness of the day stretched before them. The summer sun warmed the air. Rodolpho and Leonardo sat on the wooden steps outside their hut, sheltered from the breeze that brought with it the scent of mown hay and farmyards. They smoked hand-made cigarettes and talked about Italy and their families. Other men were inside, either sitting or lying on their bunks, listening to scratchy records of Italian operatic music played on an old wind-up gramophone that had somehow found its way over or under the wire fence. Someone had managed to obtain, probably from one of the guards, a large coloured poster of the Coliseum in Rome and it was pinned up on the wall at the far end of the long wooden shed.

The two men outside had been together during their whole time in the army. They were both from a small village near to Genoa, and apart from when they passed through on their way to North Africa, they had never been to Rome. Nevertheless, the photograph and the music filtering through the doorway, made them feel nostalgic for their Italian countryside.

They had found the English winter very cold, and whenever possible crouched round the coal-fired heater in the middle of their dormitory. But much of their time was spent on Kruyff's farm. They liked to be out working because it took their minds off their situation. Some of their comrades refused to work properly and caused problems for the farmers but Rodolpho and Leonardo were used to farm work and they thought it was better to do the job rather than be left locked-up in camp all day.

They hated Kruyff because he was a bully who ordered everyone around, even the British guards. If their work didn't meet his expectations, he would shout and threaten them with the shotgun that he carried around. They also saw how Reuben and Mrs. Kruyff cowered before him. Rodolpho, like most Italians, was fond of children and hated to see a quiet, shy boy frightened to death of his own father.

'One day I'll teach that farmer a lesson,' he told his friend. 'I might have to kill him.'

'Oh sure. Then you'll get yourself in front of a firing squad,' answered Leonardo. 'And you'll never see Genova again.'

Although they had had little option but to surrender, the men, like Jack, harboured a sense of shame that they had allowed themselves to be captured. Rodolpho in particular, had discussed several possible escape attempts. They knew that they could escape, particularly when they were out working on the farms. It would be easy to overpower the guards, if there were any, and set-off across country but they were a long way from home and were daunted by the thought of traveling across England and then finding their way through war-torn Europe. Three of their number made a hole in the wire fence and escaped during one dark, winter night but they were soon recaptured and came back cold, dirty, hungry and thirsty having spent several nights hidden in a barn with nothing to eat or drink. They seemed almost relieved to be back in camp and vowed they would see out the war in Callthorpe Camp. But the two friends had a growing sense of dissatisfaction with their condition.

'We need to get out of here,' said Leonardo. 'I can't stand much more of this. We are no longer men; we are just slaves to do work for Kruyff. It would be better to escape and return to the fight, even if we fail, at least in the trying, we would feel like men again.'

Rodolpho agreed: 'but we would be better to escape at the beginning of the night, then we might have some hours before it was discovered. If we capture our guard or run away from the farm, they will know right away and will catch us quickly. If we can get out of the hut when it gets dark, we could dig quickly under the wire and be away before we are seen. We need to keep our plan simple and very secret and when we are ready, act quickly. The more planning we do, the more others will hear about it and they will talk and some will want to join us. Then it all gets too big and we will be lost before we begin.'

'We will need some food and different clothes and a map and compass if we are to get away from England.' Leonardo was the more practical partner in the scheme. Rodolpho was emotional and brave but needed the level head of his friend to curb his natural exuberance.

'I'd like to pay a visit to that bastard Kruyff before we leave,' he muttered darkly grinding his fist in the palm of his other hand.

'I also would like to give him something to remember,' said Leonardo. 'But we may not have enough time. Our main aim is to get as far away from here as possible before day breaks and before morning roll-call.'

'Yes, you speak the truth as usual my friend. But the main thing is: are you ready to take the chance?' Rodolpho looked directly into his friend's dark eyes and read his determination and bravery. He knew the answer before Leonardo nodded and offered his hand as a token of their shared intention.

'What are you two Genoans planning?' Guardi was a handsome Neapolitan. The northern Italians didn't altogether trust their southern comrade. He was a friendly, laughing character with a fine singing voice, who entertained the hut with his rendition of old Neapolitan songs. But he spent too much time fraternising with the guards and seemed to be able to obtain cigarettes and bottles of English beer. He was suspected of passing information about the other prisoners in return for these luxuries.

'We are remembering the oranges that grow on the trees in the main streets of Genova,' Rodolpho smiled as he answered.

Giuseppe looked at them quizzically, not sure if he was being deceived. 'We also have oranges; the finest in Italy grow near to Amalfi. Tonight I will sing you to sleep with a song of sweet oranges and sweeter women.'

As the men laughed together, the slight sense of tension eased. The day continued its lazy journey as more men came out to enjoy the summer day and dream of home and family.

*

Jack's condition appeared to improve daily. The medical officer was amazed at the therapeutic impact one letter could have. He asked the CO to remind the men to write home regularly as the episode convinced him of the importance for their morale of maintaining links with home.

He kept Jack in the 'hospital' as long as possible, but as soon as the Germans became aware of his improvement, they insisted that he become a member of the gangs that now worked every day outside the camp. It was clear that the work was important to the German war machine but Edward Johns was not brave enough to object to what was a clear breach of the Geneva Convention.

The men had to be on parade at five-thirty every morning so they could start work at six. The construction of factories demanded specialist skills and the Germans made particular use of anyone with a technical or engineering background. This was cleaner, less physically demanding work so the men, although reluctant to co-operate, were willing to do it in order to avoid the back-breaking labouring jobs. Jack's background in engineering resulted in him being employed in constructing the central-heating systems. This was different to anything he had done before but he decided that he would learn on the job rather than turn down the opportunity. Fortunately, he was sent to work alongside a slim, fair-haired Berliner called Wolfgang, who had been a boy during the occupation of Germany after the First World War. He had met some English soldiers, who treated him kindly, so he took a friendly approach to working with Jack and they formed an effective partnership.

When he first arrived at the site, Jack was amazed at the advanced state of the construction. The outer skin of the factory was complete and fitters of machinery were busy inside getting the place ready for the manufacturing process. The prisoners were not told what was to be made but the evidence of their own eyes and unofficial rumours suggested that it was something experimental, probably a weapon. The parts would be made in this factory, and the weapons almost fully constructed, before transport to the northern coast.

The place was a hive of activity. Through the open doors showers of sparks from welders' torches lit the interior and sounds of hammering, sawing and clashes of metal beams being moved around gave the appearance of a hellish inferno. Jack was alarmed, during his incarceration he had been accustomed to the sound of marching feet, barked orders and the noises of a prison. This was reminiscent of the old weaving sheds back home but without the stink of wool and grease. He was unnerved by the racket and purposeful organisation; everyone knew what they were doing, even the other prisoners went off to work with a clear understanding of their roles. His confidence failed, he felt weak and wondered where he would fit. In an instant the debility of his illness returned and he felt close to collapse.

'Come English, no time to stand looking, we have work to do. Come!' Wolfgang motioned for Jack to follow him into the bowels of the factory and before long was explaining how the heating units had to be connected to the pipes that would carry warmth around the huge area. The Englishman quickly forgot his uncertainty as he listened and watched the technical demonstration. Fortunately Wolfgang's English was good and he mimed where his vocabulary was lacking so that Jack came to an understanding of what was required and began working with obvious skill that pleased the German. This was the beginning of a working partnership and something almost approaching friendship.

In the final analysis, however, they were on opposite sides in a bitter conflict. At the end of the day, Jack returned to the prison camp with its inadequate food and lack of freedom, while Wolfgang went back to his wife and the warmth and comfort of his home life. On the one hand, bombing raids into Germany were increasing, while on the other, they were both aware that they were preparing for the construction of weapons to be used in an attack on Britain. Their relative status was also made clear by the fact that the German wore an arm band that signaled his role as guard over a prisoner of war.

Jack closed his mind to these uncomfortable notions. He was pleased to be busy and enjoyed the practical activity. To be using his hands and working with tools gave him satisfaction and was infinitely better than hanging around in the camps brooding about the lack of food and his physical condition, and worrying about Kath and Michael. He had enjoyed working with Bob Gunn at the farm but his memories of this were soured by his treatment at Dopplenz. This was different; here he had a clear role and he was using his skills. He felt he had an identity, the cadence of his life returned. For the moment he chose to ignore issues around patriotism and the nature of work that conflicted with his responsibilities as a soldier.

The very problems that Jack was denying to himself were crowding in on the consciousness of Edward Johns. He himself was not directly involved in the work at the factory but he was increasingly disturbed by the manner in which his men were being employed to prepare for the manufacture of weapons. He knew he should have expressed his objections in the initial stages and recognised his own cowardice. Now he couldn't escape from a mental dilemma: to raise objections at this late stage, or to adopt his customary posture of laissez-faire. At heart an indecisive man, his worries simply revolved in his head with no practical outlet.

There were other senior officers amongst the prisoners in Stalag X1BC and one in particular was unhappy with the CO's apathetic attitude to the employment of the British troops. His name was Alec Conroy, he was a major who had spent most of the war working in bomb disposal; organising the clearing of mines as troops advanced into territory previously held by the enemy. He was fearless and frequently led the way as his men cleared particularly difficult terrain. He hated the Germans because he regarded them as bullying aggressors and saw no reason for any form of co-operation. Physically, he was small but wiry, and the jut of his jaw gave away his strong will.

The Allied officers held regular meetings to discuss camp business and Conroy and the CO clashed frequently, particularly when matters relating to work parties were raised. Inevitably, the major had to obey his superior but ill-feeling simmered below the surface. Conroy considered the Colonel too conciliatory while Johns in turn regarded the Major as a trouble-maker who, if his confrontational approach were adopted, would probably have prompted an aggressive response from their captors. There was truth on both sides and the most productive approach probably lay somewhere in between their opposing positions.

The situation in the new camp was clearly resulting in British soldiers being employed to directly support the German war effort and Conroy found this intolerable. He determined to do something about it with or without the CO's permission. He saw no possibility of any formal agreement with Edward Johns so decided to use casual conversations as the forum for disseminating his ideas. It was with this purpose in mind that he spoke to Jack, Bob and some others while they were resting in their billet. They were surprised to get a visit, since it was unusual for an officer to mix casually with the other ranks, but as he spoke, they realised his purpose.

'I don't want to cause problems for you men but I need you to think about what you're doing in the factory every day. Most of us have been captives for a long time and it's easy for us to forget that we're part of an army that was raised to defend our country and to protect other countries that're suffering as a result of German aggression. I think we're becoming so concerned with our own circumstances that, maybe, memories of home are beginning to dim. I know some of you might be thinking that this is a war that we will not win but you need to be aware that some good news is filtering through. Also, that what the Germans tell us, you've got to realise, is probably coloured by their lying propaganda. In the end, though we're hundreds of miles from home, and apparently impotent, we're still British soldiers who have a duty to continue to fight in whatever way we can. I know that you'll take a pride in the quality of the work you do in the factory but you need to keep hold of reality - any weapons made could well be used to kill or maim people back home even, God forbid, our own families…'

'I know what you're suggesting but we're watched all the time sir.' Private Kelly's voice broke in. 'They'd just take us off the job if we wasted time or sabotaged the work.'

'Besides which,' Bob joined in, 'the CO says we have no option but to co-operate otherwise the Germans'll cut our supplies even more.' There was a murmur of agreement. They were all hungry most of the time and the coal supplies had been cut already so the hut was often cold, particularly in the early mornings. Many of the men were thin and weak after months of severe shortages and they didn't feel that they could stand any further privation.

'Yes, I know I'm asking a lot and it will be difficult. But I think it's possible to make small but vital errors that could cause problems later on when they start to produce these new weapons.'

Jack commented now: 'I'm helpin' to put up central heatin', I suppose they'd be cold in winter if it went wrong.' Someone laughed.

'Yes,' Conroy smiled. 'It sounds daft but even something like that could cause delays. If we work carefully, when we're not observed, little faults can cause big difficulties down the line. Look lads, I don't want you to get into trouble. I'm not suggesting wholesale, overt resistance, just minor, subtle sabotage, which if it goes unrecognized, can be more effective than open actions that are quickly identified and counteracted. Think about it. Remember those back home and see what you can do. Don't report to me, in fact, keep your actions to yourself. We all know there are some amongst us who talk too freely to the guards. I *can* tell you that there are already some men who are working quietly to delay the German effort. Just think about whether or not you can help. That's all I'm asking.'

With this he stood up and left. It had been well done; all the men recognised the truth of his words. Without saying much, they quietly acknowledged their support for his ideas. Jack felt that this was the kind of leadership they had lacked and was glad that the Major had decided to speak out. They all realised that his actions were brave because such behaviour could, at a later date, be construed as being in direct opposition to the orders of the senior officer, and as such, worthy of a court martial.

His intervention had a significant effect. From that day, the Germans found that progress towards completion of the factory and its subsequent operation were hampered by irritating, time consuming, minor problems.

*

Michael pedaled his bike up to Gant's farm. He found Thomas in the big barn feeding rabbits and scattering corn for the hens and geese. The heat of the day penetrated the walls of the barn and the smell of warm wood mingled with the scent of old hay to produce a soporific atmosphere. Michael threw himself on to a pile of hay and lay back. 'What'll we do today? I've got some lemonade from Grandma but nothin' to eat.'

'I could get some of mum's biscuits,' said Thomas. 'An' we could get some apples from the spare room.' A spare bedroom in the Gants' farmhouse contained an old dresser with several wide drawers that were used to store last autumn's apples.

'Yes sure you can. Take two each, they need eating up. I can only make so many apple pies.' Mrs. Gant was in the kitchen making huge cheese and onion sandwiches that she would take out to the fields for Mr. Gant and the land girls. They would need a 'middin on' at about eleven o' clock because they had been working since just after dawn.

The boys climbed the bare wooden stairs, their footsteps echoing through the old farmhouse. The room was permeated by the sweet, autumnal scent of fruit. They pulled out one of the huge drawers to reveal rows of russet coloured apples, kept separate by newspaper folds. They were too good to resist. 'Let's eat one now,' said Thomas. 'Then we won't have so much to carry.' This seemed an admirable idea so they sat in two arm chairs that were covered with dust sheets and sank their teeth into the sweet, wet flesh, laughing as the juice ran down their chins.

'Shall we go and find Reuben?' Michael suggested. The three had become firm friends in school, and although he was still reluctant to talk with other children and the teacher, Rueben was now beginning to trust Thomas. They often played together at school but only Michael was allowed to visit Kruyff's farm, and even then, only when Mr. Kruyff was out on business.

'What if old Kruyff's there?' Thomas knew about the limitation.

But Michael was feeling bold: 'oh, it'll be alright for once. We won't stay in the farm. We'll go over to the lake and watch the birds.'

'Some kids think Kruyff's a spy. They say he's not Dutch, he's really a German. An' he watches the bombers from Timpney and sends messages to Germany.' Thomas spoke with a mouthful of apple.

'Could be true. Remember, we saw 'im when the bomber crashed,' Michael agreed. 'Reuben won't talk about 'is dad an' his mum doesn't say much either. He lets the prisoners do all the work an' then shouts at them when 'e gets back. Rodolpho told me they hate him.'

'Well that's funny then. If he was a spy, they'd be on the same side an' he'd like the Italians and they'd like him.'

'Mebbe 'e shouts at them because they've been caught. Mebbe they don't know he's a spy. Anyway, I like Rodolpho and Leonardo, even if they are Eyeties.' Michael was confused. You were supposed to hate the enemy, he knew that, but the Italians were kind and friendly, much nicer that Mr. Kruyff, who was generally disliked around the village. He didn't know what to think.

'Tell you what,' he suggested, 'we'll do a spying mission on old Kruyff. Sneak up and watch what he's up to. See if he's a spy or not.'

This sounded interesting so Thomas agreed and the two set off across the fields towards the fences that marked the boundaries of the Dutchman's farm.

They skirted the edge of the big cornfield. Michael was looking forward to the next harvest, aware now of the importance of the event in the village. They examined the seeds copying Mr. Gant's method of breaking off a head and rubbing it between his palms. The seeds were still green and stayed fast. 'Not ready yet,' Michael intoned trying to sound like a knowledgeable country person. He still remembered his time in Stanbury and missed his friends, particularly Whacker, but he loved his new home and the countryside, and wanted to belong.

He often thought about his old friends and wondered what they were doing and if they were safe. He wished that he had kept up the letter writing. I could have written to Brian and Ernest as well, he thought. But he knew that neither of the boys was keen on written communication and the flow of letters would probably have gradually dried-up like it did with Whacker. He had no doubt, that were they ever to meet again, their friendship would very quickly be re-kindled. In his heart he was confident that the loyalty and comradeship of the Lucy Street gang was secure.

Rags appeared from the ditch that ran round the edge of the cornfield. He had grass seeds and sticky buds in his coat and his nose was muddy where he had been investigating the scents of passing creatures. He had given a desultory wag of his tail as Michael had left the cottage earlier but, unusually, had seemed inclined to stay on the kitchen floor. Sensing the boys coming down the field, however, he had decided to cross the lane and join them. Having made his presence known, he returned to his study of life in the ditch, marking each new discovery with a growl or a snuffle of pleasure.

They walked up the slight slope of the field to the top corner. Here the hawthorn hedge appeared dense and impenetrable but the boys knew of a hidden passage through to the next field that could be accessed by lying down and crawling on their stomachs. Halfway through they dropped into the ditch and then climbed up the other side. This was fine in dry weather, but during the winter, the ditch would be full of water.

Seeing Michael lying flat under the bushes, Rags decided that this was a game and jumped on the boy, giving his face a wet lick. 'Rags, gerrof!' Michael shouted but the dog was pleased that his master had decided to join him in exploring the wonderful world of a dry ditch, and proceeded to jump on his back and lick the back of his neck. Both eventually fell into the bottom, covered in dust and dried leaves, with Michael giggling and the dog barking with excitement. Thomas, crawling behind, decided to join in and slid down the bank, landing on top of his friend. They were now laughing uncontrollably.

'You look like a sweep,' laughed Thomas.

'You look like an Eyetie,' said Michael. This brought further gales of laughter which continued until they were exhausted. The sun sneaked through the dense bushes and produced little spotlights on the dirty, tear-stained faces of two scruffy boys and a ragged dog.

The next field was given over to potatoes. They could walk in the furrows between the rows of leafy plants without damaging the crops so the boys walked straight across while the dog pursued unseen quarry along the edge. Tiny, brightly coloured birds flew together along the hedge, moving in waves as if controlled by some invisible signal. 'Look, what are those?' Michael called.

'I think they're goldfinch,' answered Thomas, looking carefully. 'When they fly together like that they're called a charm.'

'A charm.' Michael rolled the word round his tongue. It seemed just right. 'There must be twenty at least - maybe more.' He was impressed by his friend's knowledge; it was part of the pleasure he found in their relationship.

A rabbit flew out from under the hedge with a bundle of rags in hot pursuit. In an instant they saw the creature's hind legs stretched to their limit as it reached top speed. Rags, still quick in his advancing years, accelerated, and was on the point of catching his prey when it turned sharply to the left and disappeared down a dark hole, leaving the dog to spin round on himself with a bemused look on his face. He scrabbled for a while at the entrance to the burrow, sending clods of grass and earth flying, but soon recognised the fruitlessness of his task and returned to the ditch, satisfied at least to have raised a quarry.

Rags had disappeared completely by the time they approached the common border between Gant's farm and the one belonging to Mr. Kruyff. The boys decided to become undercover agents. If the man actually was a German spy, they reasoned, it would be foolish to be caught observing his activities. They already had faces covered with dirt, and had leaves sticking to their clothes, but they added more dirt and broke off some branches that could be used as camouflage.

Looking from the hedge towards the farmhouse, they could see very little activity. The old house stood silent, baking itself in the sunshine. The windows reflected the bright daylight so that nothing could be seen in the dark interior. Apart from a few hens lazily pecking the dirt of the yard, there was no movement.

'Perhaps he's in his shed.' Michael suggested. To observe the shed meant getting to the other side of the farmhouse where there were no hedges to hide behind. They would have to cross the open farmyard and hide either in or behind the cow shed.

'Ok, we'll have to keep low and run as fast as we can. You ready?' Thomas's face was alight with adventure, he was enjoying the excitement. But Michael was more cautious because he had seen Mr. Kruyff in a rage and knew that they would not be made welcome if they were seen.

'Let's go further up the hedge and then we won't 'ave so much ground to cross,' he said. Thomas could see that this was a sensible idea. They would be able to get down the side of the cow shed and then creep down the back to get sight of the mysterious shed that Mrs. Kruyff had indicated as being strictly out-of-bounds.

With a nod they agreed and crept along the hedge until they were level with the cow shed and had only about ten yards of open ground to cross. The boys pushed through the hedge and carrying their camouflage branches, started to sprint but they had reckoned without the guard dog. Spying the intruders, it started to run towards them, barking loudly. Fortunately, the chain round its neck prevented the dog from reaching them and they kept running until they were behind the cow shed. The sheep dog recognised Michael as a regular visitor and wondered why he was behaving in this peculiar manner. Puzzled, it decided that its time would be better spent sleeping, so with a few desultory growls, it ambled back to its place in the sun feeling satisfied that it had done its job.

No-one responded to the dog's warning. The farm appeared to be deserted. The cow shed was empty because all the beasts were in the bottom pasture, near to the stream that ran through the land. A couple of wood pigeons burbled to one another and swallows tore out of the sky towards their nests in the roof of the old wooden building. Their fledglings, nearly ready fly, squealed for attention and thrust forward their wide open beaks ready to receive parcels of insects.

The boys crept along, keeping close to the wall. They had to clamber over a pile of old logs that were waiting to be chopped for winter fuel but otherwise they made easy progress until they reached the corner from where they could observe the shed. It stood in the shade formed by the farmhouse. Its roof was covered with tarpaulin and its wooden walls were stained dark brown. There were no windows and no handle on the door. It was just a shed, like thousands of others, but it seemed closed – impenetrable, with an air of menace about it.

'What now?' Thomas, the man of action, wanted to know.

'We have to watch – mebbe for a long time. You have to be patient to be a spy. Let's eat.' This seemed a good idea so they settled down, their backs against the cow shed, and bit once more into the juicy apples and drank cool, sharp tasting lemonade.

The drowsy summer afternoon wore on. The air was full of the scent of warm grasses and blue bottles buzzed their inconsequential explorations. A cock pheasant called from the woodland. Nothing stirred. The spies gradually became suspended in the stillness, absorbed by the atmosphere.

*

Who fell asleep first, they couldn't remember but they awoke together as Farmer Kruyff grabbed them by their shirt collars. 'Vot yous doing here?' He bellowed. Michael could feel the spit on his face. 'I tells you before to keep away from here.' Turning to Reuben, who stood behind his father's legs, he shouted, 'this your fault. I tells you don't bring boys here.' Before the boy could protest he received a kick on his backside and was knocked to the ground.

Thomas protested: 'it's not his fault, he didn't know we were here.'

'Shut your mouth, or you get same.' The farmer lifted both boys off their feet and pulled them towards the track leading out of the farm. Michael felt the fabric of his shirt collar tear as they were dragged along.

Mrs Kruyff appeared in the farmhouse door wiping her hands on her apron. 'Please don't hurts them. Oh Michael I tell you don't come here,' she cried, recognising the boy. She took a step forward as if to intervene but her courage failed her and she just stood, her face a mixture of anxiety and fear.

Suddenly, a small ball of ragged fury joined the proceedings; Rags, attracted by the angry shouts, and seeing his master treated roughly, attacked. He went head down, growling, towards the farmer's ankles but Kruyff was too quick and landed his boot into the dog's side, sending him flying. Winded but undeterred, Rags tried again and received the same treatment. 'Stop Rags, stop!' Michael called, worried that his friend would be seriously damaged. 'Stay boy!' The dog looked, puzzled, but obeyed and backed off, growling. The sheep dog was going frantic on the end of its chain but couldn't reach the action.

At the top of the track, he threw the boys forward as if they were chickens. 'Get away from here. I tells your father you trespass.' Michael almost shouted that his father was not there to tell but decided not to waste his breath when it was clear that Mr. Kruyff wouldn't be interested in such information.

They picked themselves up and joined by a limping dog, whose hackles were still raised, started to walk towards the lane that passed the bottom of the farm track. Michael looked back to see a picture frozen in time of a huge, angry, red faced man, a frightened woman and a skinny, tear stained, terrified boy. He felt angry and ashamed with himself for being caught like this and for the trouble that he had caused for his friend. He stopped and turned to walk back. 'I mus' tell you that Reuben didn't know we were here. Please don't hurt 'im.'

Kruyff turned and looked about, then walked to the grassy side of the track, where he found a piece of broken fencing. 'You don't tell me what to do. Get out of here or you gets this.' He was clearly beside himself with rage. Michael felt his hands form fists in frustration but there was nothing he could do.

'Come on, you'll make it worse,' said Thomas. 'You can't do anything, he's mad. We shouldn't have come.'

He was right and Michael knew it. They walked down towards the lane in a silence that was not broken until they reached Birch Tree Cottage, where they paused at the gate. Michael said, 'I'm goin' to find out what he's up to. Mebbe he *is* a spy an' that's why he keeps people away, we can't let 'im get away with it if he is.'

'Yes, well I don't like him either,' answered Thomas. 'An' I'm not afraid of him. We'll find out what he's doing but next time we have to make sure that we're not caught, because that gets Reuben into trouble an' that's not fair.'

They were agreed on this and having a sort of plan, made them feel better. Thomas set off towards his own farm wondering if Mr. Kruyff would really tell his father what they had done and how he would explain their exploit, while Michael pondered how to explain his torn shirt. Rags, still limping slightly, licked his master's hand. He didn't understand why he had been ordered to stop his attack but his loyalty was unquestioning.

Both boys decided that honesty was the best policy. They told their parents (and grandparents in Michael's case) everything that had occurred. Walter was inclined to visit Mr. Kruyff to protest at his treatment of young lads who meant no harm but Amy persuaded him to let the incident drop. She said that Kruyff was a strange man who was best left to get on with his life as he wanted and in any case, the boys shouldn't have gone to the farm without permission. They talked with Donald Gant, Thomas' father, and he said that he didn't want trouble with his neighbour who could be a difficult customer. Eventually they all agreed that the boys should be made to promise never to go near Kruyff's farm again and there in the customary, pragmatic way of country people, the matter was left to rest.

Michael and Thomas had no option but to promise but quietly agreed with one another that they still thought that Kruyff was a spy and should be exposed if the opportunity to do so presented itself. They saw Reuben at school during the remainder of the summer term but he wouldn't talk about what had happened. He said that he had been told not to play with them anymore and retreated into his shell, communicating with other people as little as possible.

*

The long holidays arrived and the two friends spent time together exploring the countryside but never went near Kruyff's farm. They thought about calling for Reuben but decided that they should try to keep their promise. The fields, woods and ponds, along with helping on the farm, provided plenty of entertainment and they blossomed into country boys with strong muscles and sun-kissed skins. Michael felt that he was in the right place. He hadn't forgotten Stanbury and often thought about the Lucy Street gang and Molly. He wondered what they were doing but had no wish to return to his old life.

CHAPTER 16

Winter 1943/44 Having surrendered to the Allies, the Italians now declare war on Germany. In November, the British launch a heavy bombing raid on Berlin. In January, Leningrad is relieved after a siege lasting 900 days. The monastery at Monte Cassino is bombed by the Allies.

Once again, winter fell hard on the small communities around Callthorpe. Snowfall was heavy and frosts lasted for many weeks. Pipes froze and even main roads were impassable. The residents of Birch Tree Cottage had to carry buckets of water to flush the outside lavatory. Inside the outhouse it was so cold that Michael feared that his bum would freeze to the seat.

Anna Newby managed to keep the school open but many children from outlying farms were unable to get through. Reuben appeared one day, looking cold and sad. The teacher went straight to him because he looked so forlorn and she was pleased to see him. The boy backed away as she approached and winced when she tried to put her arm round his shoulder. She immediately knew she had made a mistake; Reuben didn't like to be touched. 'Sorry love,' she said. 'We're glad you're here, come by the fire, you look perished.' The boy had only a thin woollen jumper and no topcoat. He went and sat by the fire next to Michael, who was busy with his sums.

'Hey, where've you been, we 'aven't seen you for ages,' he asked. But Rueben made no reply. 'Look are you still cross about us coming to your farm?' Michael thought this may be the reason that the boy had missed so much school and hadn't wanted to play with them.

Reuben spoke without looking: 'you shouldn't have come it made dad angry, I told you not to come.'

'No you're right we're sorry aren't we Thomas?'

Thomas nodded and said, 'we just wanted to know what goes on in that shed Reuben, why don't you tell us?' Reuben looked away and it was clear that he was on the point of tears.

Thomas glanced enquiringly at Michael, who shook his head with a look that indicated that they had better say no more.

After this, the boys tried several times to involve Reuben in their work but he showed no interest and just sat holding out his hands towards the warmth of the fire. Anna watched, unable to think of any way of getting through to him. She shook her head; it seemed to her that the boy had returned to his previous state, not prepared to talk to anyone, not even his friends. She was not surprised when, after that day, Reuben went missing from school, even though his home was not far outside the village. He had been a poor attendee in good weather and she was increasingly anxious about him, but so many country children went missing for long periods, that she just didn't have the time to visit all their homes to encourage the parents to send their children back to school.

Miss Newby was pleased that Michael and Thomas were good attenders because they were both bright students and were strong candidates to pass the examination that would provide them with entry to the grammar school in Seldown. This would mean traveling by the early bus and arriving home late in the evening but she knew that they would both benefit from the challenging level of the lessons.

The two friends, however, gave little thought to their future schooling preferring instead to play in the snow. They had built an igloo from ice bricks made by squashing snow into a wooden cement-brick mold provided by Walter. The sledge track, used by Michael and his grandad during their first winter together, had compressed to hard-packed ice under constant use by many of the village children, and provided an extremely speedy run. There was plenty to occupy the boys without the inconvenience of schoolwork. Neither of them was particularly keen to go to the grammar school; it was a long way away, and they suspected, would mean difficult lessons and considerable homework.

They did like Miss Newby though; by dint of providing interesting stimuli and modeling an enthusiastic approach to new ideas, she had the knack of motivating her charges to learn. So, the few children that attended regularly, spent their days engaged in acquiring a wide range of skills and understanding, while staying as close as possible to the wood burning fireplace at the back of the classroom. Naturally, because of the weather, their work focused on snow and ice. They looked, through magnifying glasses, at the patterns of snowflakes on black paper, weighed snow before and after melting, measured the speed of sledges on the icy playground, tested the melting speed of snowballs, observed why drifts collected in different places and collected information about the relative temperatures and climatic conditions of north European countries. They also agreed with the teacher, that one day, before the snow disappeared, they would test the strength of their igloo.

*

If Kathleen had been able with her mother's help, to rationalize her attachment to the curate, for Mike, the reverse was true: the more he thought about the incident in the vestry, the more muddled he became. To his surprise, desire had risen in his body when she was in his arms, but he had resisted any notions of furthering the relationship, waiting for some indication from her as to what the future might hold. He was well aware that she was a married woman whose husband was being held by the Germans, and that she had been bombed out of her home. Mike knew that she was likely to be in a disturbed state of mind, but despite his better judgment, he couldn't get the thought of her touch out of his mind. He wasn't sure what he wanted and knew that he should put all thoughts of Kathleen out of his mind but his thoughts kept wandering back to the moment in the vestry when her femininity had invaded his senses.

Since the incident all those months ago, Kathleen had given no sign that anything unusual had happened. She was polite and friendly when she discussed the progress of her Sunday school class but adopted a business like approach with no hint of warmth. This simply increased Mike's longing; he felt like a love-sick schoolboy admiring an unattainable woman from afar. Yet he couldn't bring himself to speak about his feelings; it would have seemed inappropriate and ungentlemanly. In any case, he was effectively Kath's spiritual guide; he shouldn't even have been entertaining these thoughts never mind acting upon them. So for almost a year, the curate had stayed silent, trying to push all thoughts of furthering their relationship to the deepest recesses of his mind.

Kathleen, although she had settled her own mind, was nevertheless aware that the business with Mike was unfinished. She knew she ought to speak to him but her natural diffidence prevented this. Also, she found it difficult to imagine that someone with his obvious education and position in the community could possibly be concerned about the nature of his relationship with a silly weaver-woman. Unable to summon either the courage or the words to broach the subject, she remained silent, hoping that the stream of time would wash away the incident and remove the need to speak about it. She didn't realise that this simply increased the man's sense of frustration.

*

It was after morning Sunday school. There were only a few children able or willing to get through the snow and the sky was darkening with the threat of another fall so Kath decided to cut short the session and send her charges home, with the instruction to walk with someone else or, if they couldn't do this, to wait for her. All of the children indicated that had a friend they could walk with, and Michael and Thomas said they would go home together.

Kathleen stayed behind tidying the small classroom and putting away the story Bibles that they used. Mike came in. 'Oh, Kathleen, I was coming to have a word with the children . . .'

'They've gone home, it looked like snow, so I thought . . .'

'Yes, yes, quite right, of course… I'll see them next time… I was looking for recruits for the choir… It's not a problem… You did the right thing.' He paused and then made a decision: 'Kathleen, I wonder if you've got a moment? There's something I've been meaning to ask you.'

She shuddered inside but tried to keep calm; knowing what was coming and determined that she wouldn't get upset. 'Yes?' Was all she could muster..

He stepped forward. Too close. She thought and almost stepped away. Now that he had started Mike didn't know how to continue. He realised that he should have rehearsed but it was too late. He took her hand; the contact helped, she didn't reject his touch. 'I just wondered … do you remember when the vase broke and …'

'Yes, yes, I remember. I know we should have talked. I'm sorry.' Kath fought the tears: I'm not going to cry, she told herself.

'Don't be sorry Kathleen, it's just that I wondered how you felt, er … how you felt about me?' There it was said. He had posed the question and felt relieved yet anxious. Now it was up to her and he might soon get an answer. But she looked in his eyes and remained silent, not knowing how to begin. He saw her anguish and misunderstood. He stepped closer and took her in his arms. He felt her closeness and bent his head to meet her lips. He thought they must be the softest things he had ever felt. She seemed to respond and his desire increased. But then she pulled away, her hands on his chest, pushing. 'No, no, I can't do this, I'm sorry, I'm sorry.'

Kath leaned against a table, she could feel her heart pounding. Mike turned as if to leave. 'No, please don't go, we must talk, I have to explain.'

He paused and then perched on another table, feeling a mixture of shame and frustration. 'No I'm sorry, I thought …'

'Yes, you were right to think what you did, it's my fault, I should have explained before, I just couldn't think that you were interested in a stupid woman like me.'

'That *was* a silly idea,' he said. You are not stupid, in fact you're one of the most attractive women I've ever met… I know that you're married and I shouldn't have touched you but in the vestry, I thought … well I couldn't help myself.'

'I understand,' Kath replied. 'You were very kind and I was upset. You're also very attractive you know. I liked you from the moment we met in the Minster and I did think at one time that I would like to be with you but I can't, you must see that, I love Jack… God knows what's happening to him, I couldn't betray him, and then there's Michael and my family you see… It's just impossible. Please understand.'

Mike could see the sincerity in her eyes. Feeling a deep sense of shame, he held out his hand and she took it without hesitation. 'Kath, please don't worry, I understand now. We're all the children of the war. None of us is normal at the moment, I don't know if we ever will be again. We were both looking for some comfort in the wrong place… Perhaps we can be friends?'

'Oh, yes. Please let's be friends, I don't want to lose you.' How inane, she thought. What a stupid, silly thing to say. What a fool he must think I am. But I need him for comfort and strength, not anything else. I don't want sex with him or anyone. She knew that some women had intercourse with other men while their husbands were away, but she didn't believe that it was what they wanted, she thought they did it because it was what the men wanted and they were not prepared to offer comfort if sex wasn't included.

Even as he spoke the words, Mike knew that it was a lie. Kathleen had awoken something inside him, and although he knew it was wrong, 'friends' was not what he wanted to be.

Outside, flat snow flakes fell quietly from the dark sky. Sounds were hushed. The fields and hedges slept under the deepening white blanket. Michael kicked his boots against the wall of the cottage and opened the door to the warm kitchen. Rags rose from the rag rug in front of the fire and wagged his way to his master. 'Where's your mum?' Amy asked.

'She's coming behind,' he replied.

*

While Jack's comment about the central heating system had been received as a joke, he had been raising a serious point. He felt that, in his position, there was little he could do to inhibit the progress of the factory. Nevertheless, impressed by Conroy's argument, he determined to search for information about the nature of the weapons that were to be produced, in the hope that he could find some way of disrupting their effectiveness. Towards this end he cultivated his friendship with Wolfgang. For some time the German resisted Jack's enquiries but one day, from their position on a gantry high in the roof of the factory, they could see the whole production line laid out beneath.

'This is impressive, you Germans are excellent engineers. I can see an area for engine construction, one for what looks like fuselage and another for wooden wing shapes.' Jack decided to present as much as he could understand of the layout in the hope that Wolfgang would feel that he already understood what was to be made. 'But I've never seen an engine shed like that one – it looks very special.'

The German looked at Jack in surprise: 'you are clever to see what is happening but I tell you, you have never seen an engine like this one.'

'What do you mean?' Jack's genuine interest lulled Wolfgang and he was also proud of German achievements.

'It will be a rocket. You see that man standing by the engine assembly, that's Herr Lusser, he is the designer.'

The news hit Jack like a smack in the mouth but he tried to speak calmly: 'a rocket? To carry men?'

'Nein, no, of course not it carries … we must work now, you ask too many questions.' Wolfgang suddenly realised the danger of talking too much and refused to answer any more of Jack's enquiries. But in many ways it was too late. The rocket was clearly intended as a bomb, a flying bomb. Jack now knew what

270

he and the other prisoners were helping to build and he was horrified.

In the evening after the prisoners returned to the camp, the atmosphere at the meeting with Major Conroy became increasingly tense as Jack outlined what he had learned. The short winter daylight meant that they started and finished work in the dark, returning to their billets more often than not exhausted by the day's work. Rations were still mostly limited to Red Cross food parcels, and soup, potatoes and bread provided by their captors. While this diet kept them alive, many were in poor health and could barely crawl into their bunks at the end of the day.

The discussion though prompted new energy and the group gathered conspiratorially under the light from the one dim electric bulb that they were allowed. Playing cards were scattered on the floor in case a patrolling guard became suspicious of the gathering. Small logs burning in the stove crackled and escaping smoke collected in the roof space. Other men joined in with comments about what they had seen and heard. Most agreed with Jack's conclusion that they were helping to produce a new kind of weapon which would soon be visited upon their homeland.

'We cannot allow this to continue,' Conroy spoke angrily. 'It's time Johns got off his arse and objected.' It was unusual to hear him speak in a directly critical way about their CO; it was an indication of his frustration. 'There is no way that we should be involved in preparing a weapon that will be used to attack our own people. It is clearly against the principles of the Geneva Convention and must be stopped.'

There were murmurs of agreement but Jack had another suggestion: 'I agree with you sir but maybe we should just 'old fire a bit. If we object an' they still make us work, they'll be on the lookout for men wastin' time or doin' a poor job. If we carry on as normal, they might not be so vigilant an' we could slow them down without them knowing.'

Bob Gunn was enthusiastic: 'That's right, mebbe we could try a bit of sabotage ... you know leave a bolt loose or a weld weak ... nothin' too obvious but serious enough to stop the bloody things flying straight.'

Conroy paused. He had little hope of Edward Johns mounting an objection that the Germans would take seriously. Perhaps this idea could be more damaging and it would avoid demonstrations of overt militancy that might give rise to German reprisals. They were in a vulnerable situation; it wouldn't take much punitive action from their captors to push many men closer to death.

'You could be right Gunn,' he agreed. 'But we need more information about how the things will work so that we can decide how best to affect their performance, you know, find out where their weak points are. How about it Spencer? Can you pump your mate for more information?'

'He's no mate sir but I can try, although 'e'll be on his guard. I think 'e knows 'e went too far today. Mebbe if I could take 'im a present. I know they're as short of luxuries as we are. You know, a sprat to catch a mackerel.'

'Good idea. We'll see what we can scrape together. I'll come again tomorrow, we need to get on with this, otherwise it'll be too late.' Conroy stood and signaled for the men not to rise. 'I'll be off. Keep this to yourselves; some of our blokes are loose tongued.' When he left, the usual fatigue settled on the men and they fell on to their straw-filled mattresses. As Jack lay back, waiting for sleep, he had a glimmer of light, a tiny kernel of optimism; maybe they might, at last, be able to rejoin the fight after years of impotence.

*

Thanks mainly to the efforts of the camp's unofficial quartermaster, Jack was able to hand over, one at a time, a pack of butter, a bar of chocolate and a packet of cigarettes. He staggered the presents over a few days so as to avoid seeming too generous, simply saying that they were items from Red Cross parcels that he didn't want. Wolfgang never visited the camp and didn't realise how scarce such commodities were. In the context of his own wartime privations, he was pleased to receive things that the German population found hard to come by. He began to regard Jack as a friend and went so far as to suggest that they might be able to get together when the war was over. His friendliness made Jack feel guilty about extracting information but this soon dissipated when he thought about the new weapons being used against his own family.

Major Conroy was pleased to learn more about the new weapon but increasingly horrified by its potential for devastating the lives of people back home. He couldn't identify how the prisoners might affect the working of the bomb without alerting the enemy so he asked the men to slow down their work as much as possible. In reality, however, they could only go so far. One of them, a corporal called Bentley, was taken off the work group because he was reported to be wasting time and working badly. This strategy was clearly not going to hamper production of the flying bomb sufficiently to create significant delay. Some other less obvious means had to be found. For several weeks it looked as though there was little the men could do and they became frustrated by their lack of success. Conroy began to think that they might have to raise the issue of the Geneva Convention and try to get the prisoners removed from the factory. At least that would mean that they were not directly involved in producing weapons to be used against their own people.

It was one of the RAF prisoners called Arthur Cleese who came up with a solution. He had served as a navigator on board a Shackleton bomber that had been shot down over Berlin and was one of the newer prisoners at the camp. He had been badly treated when captured and his face was still swollen from the punishment he received from the group of soldiers who pulled him out of his parachute harness. He said that he had believed that they were about to kill him, but an officer had intervened, ordering the men to take him prisoner.

Cleese studied the information that came from Wolfgang and realised the significance of the gyrocompass that controlled the direction of flight of the rockets. 'If we can destabilise this then the bomb will fly erratically and probably miss its target,' he said. 'Can you ask your contact how the gyrocompass is controlled?'

'I can try,' said Jack. 'But 'e might smell a rat if I get too technical. That's the sort of question someone who knows about aircraft would ask. I'm only a loom tuner who's 'elpin' fit the central heatin', I'm not expected to know about gyrowatsits.'

Cleese paused and rubbed his bruised chin. 'Ask him about the rudder then, that's not too technical and what he tells you might help us to understand,' he suggested.

At the next meeting Jack brought the information: 'Wolfgang told me that the steering depends on the Earth's magnetic field. I don't really understand that's all 'e would tell me an' I didn't like to ask more questions.'

'Oh, that's fine,' Cleese grinned. 'It means that the gyrocompass reads the magnetic field which keeps it on target. If we can find a way of disrupting this it will steer off course. Best way would be to introduce a small magnet into the body of the machine, or find some way of making one of the metal parts magnetic.'

This sounded plausible and others joined in, glad to explore the possibility of being able to sabotage these dreadful machines. 'Where'll we get magnets?' 'How do we get them inside?'

'They don't have to be very big, which is good because anything too large or too powerful would be noticed. There are magnets inside wirelesses if we can get some, then we can rub nails or screws till they're magnetic and that might do the trick.' There was a murmur of pleasure; the men forgot their tiredness and hunger and immediately began to dismantle the crackly wireless that they had managed to smuggle into the hut and kept hidden under a loose floorboard.

Over the next few days a surprising number of magnets were unearthed by people who could be trusted. They still had to be very careful about who was involved and so the supply was limited. While they were pleased with their success, there were nowhere near enough to cope with the number of flying bombs that the Germans were intent on producing so they gathered iron nails and screws from door frames and bunks and any that could be stolen from the factory. These they stroked repeatedly with magnets, following the same direction, until they became magnetised. The men were not sure how long the metal objects would retain their power but decided that they were better than nothing.

The next job was to find some way of introducing the magnets into the bombs and this was proving difficult, since none of the prisoners were allowed to work directly on the weapons. The work they did was peripheral: moving materials, cleaning up the work spaces, helping to build the factory structure or, like Jack, working in technical areas that were not linked to the bomb construction. Indeed, any attempt by a prisoner to get close to the key engineering areas was met by a barked reprimand from the armed guards.

It seemed that their plans would be thwarted and day-by-day they watched, with increased apprehension, as wings were attached and the destructive machines took shape. Even without taking into account their purpose, the flying bombs had a threatening appearance; the streamlined shape had a strange malevolent beauty. Just pausing to look at the weapon was discouraged so observations of the Germans' progress had to be covert: an occasional glance while carrying out their normal tasks or, in Jack's case, watching from high in the roof of the factory as he and Wolfgang attached the heating units.

He looked down one morning to see an almost complete bomb being lifted from the construction bed by a line attached to the upper fuselage. A shudder passed through his body; up till now the machines had been a conglomeration of bits, now this one looked ready for use. He pictured a flight of these pilotless beasts falling unexpectedly from the sky and wreaking blind, indiscriminate destruction on English towns. Fury rose in him. Jack also realised that the people at home were probably totally unaware of the impending danger. They had to do something. Either they had to find some way of sabotaging the bombs or they must at least send a warning across the sea.

Then he noticed something odd: the weapon was not balanced; the right wing hung lower than the left. He had only a limited understanding of the principles of flight but even he could appreciate that this would produce curving flight and must be corrected before the bomb could be launched. Jack watched as the workers fetched copies of magazines, and after rolling them up, pushed them inside a compartment in the left wing until the missile gradually achieved a balanced position; a simple, almost primitive approach but effective nevertheless. The men paid no attention to the contents of the magazines which they brought from cardboard boxes standing, unguarded, against the walls of the factory. He also noted that *prisoners* were carrying the boxes of magazines into the hanger from some outside store.

His mind raced: What if most or all of the flying bombs needed their static equilibrium stabilizing before launch? If magnets were secreted inside the pages of these magazines, could they then affect the gyroscope and produce erratic flight?

*

The Italian prisoners were as cold as their British counterparts. They huddled round the sooty, black stoves in their sheds, wrapping themselves in blankets, scarves they had knitted themselves, army coats and anything else that would keep the heat in and the cold out. There was little work on the farms at the moment so, apart from desultory games of football in the slush of the parade ground, they confined themselves to their barracks.

They had heard the news of Italy's surrender and wondered if this would mean their early release and repatriation.

276

The thought of returning to the warm sunshine of their homeland cheered them but hopes were dashed when the camp's commanding officer, Colonel Henry Chapman, explained that they were likely to remain at Callthorpe until the war finally ended. 'There are no plans for the release or swapping of prisoners,' he said. 'My advice is that you content yourselves with the knowledge that you are safe here. You have food and work and you will continue to be treated well. We are confident that the war will soon be over and you can rest assured that we will not keep you here longer than is necessary.'

'What is he saying?' Stephano Guardi, the dark skinned Neapolitan asked. Like many of the prisoners he spoke only a little English, just enough to persuade some of the camp guards to bring him beer or cigarettes.

'He says that we are stuck here for a long time to come.' Rodolpho had gathered the gist of the Colonel's words. 'You can forget about Naples and learn to live in this miserable climate.'

Like all the men, the inactivity weighed heavily on Rodolpho's spirits. He became morose and lost weight, even his beard looked lank and flecks of grey began to appear. Leonardo observed his friend's situation with concern. 'You are sad my friend,' he said. 'We must try to keep up our spirits – I feel that the war will soon be over and you will see Genova again.'

'I cannot stand this,' Rodolpho replied. 'What good are we here? We work for the bastard Kruyff, we sit in this hut. We should be helping our Country, we are Italians! We are not meant to be here in this freezing place. We must get out, we must!'

Leonardo was worried by his friend's mood. He knew that Rodolpho was a man of action with a big heart who might be driven to do something silly or dangerous for the sake of breaking the monotony. 'You must not even think about escaping at the moment. Look at the weather, the snow is deep and the frosts are cold enough to kill the vines in my father's vineyard. You would starve to death out there.'

Rodolpho scratched his beard and rubbed his forehead. 'Maybe it would be better to die trying to escape than sit here rotting,' he growled. 'Are you turning into a coward that you want to stay here?' He saw the hurt in his friend's face and immediately regretted his words. 'I am sorry Leo, I know you are as brave as anyone – forgive me, I am a fool.'

Leonardo laughed and touched his friend's shoulder. 'It is not a problem, I know how you feel and I feel the same, you know that. But we must be thoughtful. If we are to escape we must make sure that we have the best chance of success. I promise that, if you will wait for the better weather, I will go with you and we will try to get home together.'

'Leo, you are my good friend and you are right – to go now would be stupid. But you must keep your promise. In the spring we will go and if we die we will at least have tried.'

Leonardo looked into Rodolpho's deep brown eyes and saw there a mixture of desperation and hope. He realised that his friend was in earnest – he was making a statement of intent. He was going in the spring, by himself if necessary. The two shook hands solemnly. A pact was made.

CHAPTER 17

Spring – Summer 1944   War begins to turn in favour of the Allies. The German army surrenders in the Crimea and retreats after the landings at Anzio. The allied armies enter Rome and on June 6th the D Day landings begin. Also in June, the first V-1 rocket struck London and eight civilians were killed.

Winter didn't release its grip on Callthorpe until late that year. Even at the beginning of May there was a heavy snowfall. The countryside was an expanse of white and spring work on the farms was delayed. In the camp, Italian prisoners continued to be frustrated by inactivity and the cold weather. Walter had had a very quiet winter and needed to earn. Although Kath still received Jack's pay from the War Office and contributed to the family finances, this was barely enough to cover their basic needs. He was able to get some work refurbishing the stonework of the Minster in Seldown, and luckily, the local council, aided by a few farmers with tractors, had managed to clear the roads so that the bus could get through.

The walls of the ancient building were too icy and dangerous to work on so the masons, men to old to be called-up, worked in a tented area in the cloisters. Stonework and carvings that needed replacing had been measured and sketched during the good weather, so they were able to cut and carve pieces that would be fitted later. Although it was still cold in the tent, the work required physical effort so that this and regular mugs of tea, kept the men warm enough.

One Saturday morning, Walter took Michael and Thomas along to see the work in progress. They were fascinated by the skill of the masons particularly when they saw weird medieval gargoyles gradually emerge from blocks of ancient limestone. Naturally, the boys wanted to have a go at carving and the men, who were pleased to have young people interested in their work, let them use some old chisels on spare pieces of stone. Walter helped them, making sure that they held the tools correctly and chipped in such a way as to avoid flakes of stone shooting towards their eyes. They found the work difficult at first, but after and while, learned to maintain a regular rhythm and began to take pleasure in their developing skill. Michael's love for his grandfather was now enhanced by admiration of the old man's mastery of an ancient craft. He paused to watch as Walter worked, his white head bent over the work bench and his pink tongue protruding slightly as he concentrated on the curved, heavy eyebrow of an evil looking goblin.

'Why do they put such evil faces on the Minster?' Thomas wanted to know.

'They go back a long way,' said Walter. 'Some are put on water spouts – these are called gargoyles, others are just for decoration and they call them grotesques. But I think both types are supposed to ward off evil spirits.'

'Do you believe in evil spirits Grandad?' Michael joined in.

'No lad, I think there are some people who're evil but I don't believe in spirits.'

'What like Hitler an' the Germans? Do you think they're evil?' Asked Thomas

'Well, I think Hitler's an evil man, yes, but I bet there *are* some German folk who wish he'd never started this damn war.' Walter shook his head. He hated the war and what it was doing to families. He looked at the two boys and shook his head again. It wasn't fair that they were growing up in these times. Here was Michael only eleven years old, bombed out of his home, with a father he never saw and might never see again, and a mother who still cried out in distress during the night as she relived the nightmare of bombing raids.

'D'you think Farmer Kruyff's an evil man?' Michael interrupted Walter's thoughts.

'I don't know Michael. He's not very popular round 'ere an' I don't think he looks after his family and farm as well as he should but whether or not he's evil, I wouldn't like to say.'

'Well I think 'e's evil,' said Michael definitely.

'Me too,' Thomas agreed.

'Maybe you're right but you have to be careful about judging folk. One thing's for sure, you must keep away from his farm, we don't want any trouble like last time.' Walter looked straight into Michael's eyes to emphasise his instruction. 'Right you two?'

'Yes Grandad,' Michael agreed, with his fingers crossed behind his back.

*

Eventually the weather improved and this, along with good news about the progress of the war, made people feel more cheerful. In Birch Tree Cottage, they were listening to the news on the wireless; the reports they heard were more optimistic than they had been for months. It was early morning and Michael was just about to set off for school. This was the day of the tests for entry to the grammar school and he was reluctant to leave the house.

'Will dad be home soon then?' He was excited at the prospect.

'We don't know love we just have to wait and see.' Kathleen was pleased yet worried about the news that the war might be moving to a close. She wondered what might happen to prisoners. If the allied armies attacked the places where the camps were, might they actually kill their own soldiers in the process? And what about the Germans; would they let the prisoners go without a fight? And what if they let the prisoners out before the Allies arrived how would they live? Could they survive and find their way home? The whole situation was so complex that she didn't dare say anything optimistic in case the fates took revenge for her impertinence. 'You'd better get going, you don't want to be late today. Do your best in the test won't you?' The boy grimaced, accepted a kiss on the cheek and pulled open the kitchen door.

'Bye then – bye grandma,' he called across to Amy who was possing the week's washing in the aluminium tub. Steam rose around her and she paused to wipe her brow and called, 'bye, bye love – good luck.'

He walked down the path towards the gate and looked at the new growth in the garden. Remembering their first day at the cottage he looked for the sweet Williams and dog daisies but they weren't ready to show themselves yet. The lilac tree was in full bloom and the cherry still had some blossom but there weren't many flowers. It was a cool, spring day with a stiff, salty breeze blowing from the east coast. Michael wished he was going to the seaside instead of school. He enjoyed normal schooldays and learning new things but tests were different; everyone had to sit by themselves and work quietly and even Miss Newby kept emphasising how important they were. He really didn't want to leave Callthorpe Primary; it was so much better than his old school and he felt secure and safe with the teacher. Seldown Grammar would be big, with older children and teachers he didn't know. He knew that Thomas didn't want to go; what if he passed and Thomas didn't? Then he might have to go by himself. There was no way Reuben would make it and they were the only three in the whole class who were old enough to take the test.

With these thoughts running through his head, he arrived at the school door. No other children were allowed to attend on this day, which made it all the more threatening. The school that he loved took on a daunting appearance. He passed between the sandbags piled up at the entrance, placed his gasmask on the long wooden bench beneath the coat hooks and walked into the classroom. The furniture had been pushed back to leave three desks in the middle, in line behind one another. All the wall displays were covered and this, along with the paper crosses on the window panes took all the life out of the place. Even Anna Newby looked serious this morning but she smiled encouragingly and told him to sit at one of the desks until the others arrived. Thomas pushed through the door minutes later but Reuben, as expected, didn't arrive.

'We'll have to begin, I can't wait any longer,' said the teacher. 'I'll try to arrange for Reuben to do the tests later.' With this she placed the first paper on their desks and said, 'you've got an hour to do this one. I'll tell you when there are five minutes left. If you finish early, check back at your answers to make sure they're correct.'

Michael turned the paper over and looked at rows of sums with some written problems at the bottom. He picked up the pencil and wrote his name on the top and then sat, quite still, wondering what to do. After about fifteen minutes Miss Newby walked over: 'what's the matter Michael? Why aren't you writing? There's nothing here that you can't do.'

The boy looked down. 'I don't want to go to the grammar school, I want to stay here.'

For once his teacher's face looked stern and she spoke firmly: 'Michael, you need to understand that if you don't go to Seldown Grammar, you'll still have to leave here. They'll send you to Seldown Secondary Modern which is a good school but you'll do better at the grammar because they'll give you work that will suit someone as clever as you and you'll be able to get better qualifications and maybe go to university.'

'I don't want to go to university,' he replied. 'I want to stay here and work on a farm like everyone else. I'll just not go to school like Reuben.'

'You have to go to school Michael. Reuben's family will be in trouble soon if they don't send him. But you can still be a farmer if you want to, and if you go to university, you can be a better farmer and maybe get to be the boss and, who knows, maybe one day own your own farm. When the war is over, we'll need clever people to run the farms and help the country get back on its feet.'

At last the boy looked at her eyes and saw her concern. This made sense; he wanted the war to be over and for the

Country to be back to normal. If he could help, then maybe he should. 'Yes, I see,' he said. 'OK, I'll try to do my best.' Thomas had stopped working to listen but grinned at his friend and went back to the test. For the remainder of the morning they worked hard. At lunchtime they were free for the rest of the day. They agreed that the tests had been 'bum bloody awful' and spent the afternoon in Thomas's barn thinking up new swear words and shrieking with laughter at each invention.

*

Kathleen went into the village; there were several items they needed from the Co-op. Mrs. Crawshaw was the owner; a plump, talkative woman, whose husband had died several years before. She stood in her spotless, white apron, behind the counter and was chatting to Mrs. Hare from the big farm. They turned as Kathleen pushed open the door and caused the little silver bell to ring. The shop walls were lined with brown painted wooden drawers. These were meant to contain the wide range of produce that a country store needed. In wartime, however, most of them were empty and there were times when even essential foodstuffs were not available.

As she talked, Mrs. Crawshaw was winding the bacon slicer and allowing the thin strips of meat to fall on to the greaseproof paper that lay on the shiny, metal plate next to the spinning cutter. She lifted the paper and dropped it on the weighing scales. 'That's about eight ounces Mrs. Hare – alright?'

'Yes, fine,' said Mrs. Hare, passing over the money and her ration book. 'Hello Kathleen, how are you?' And, without waiting for an answer, 'how's Amy?'

'We're all as well as can be expected, thankyou, how are you both?'

'Mmm,' said Mrs. Hare. She was clearly not listening and had something else on her mind, revealed by her next question: 'you see the vicar - I mean curate, regularly, don't you? We were just saying that he doesn't seem himself lately. Any ideas why?'

Kath felt herself colouring and turned to examine a sack of onions leaning against the counter. 'Can't think,' she said, 'these are fine onions.' She started to select four big ones.

'We wondered if he was sickening for something – there's been a lot of flu about.' Mrs. Crawshaw said as she leaned over the counter to put the bacon into Mrs. Hare's basket. 'He seemed so happy here at first and now he's very quiet. We thought you and he were friendly, has he said anything?'

Kathleen turned and looked at them, knowing that her face was now bright red. 'He hasn't said…. I mean we're not fr….I don't know anything…. I'll call later.' She turned abruptly and almost ran out of the shop.

'What about your oni…. Well, goodness, what do you think about that?' The women exchanged meaningful looks as Kath disappeared, leaving the shop door swinging open.

*

She half-ran, half-walked towards the lane that led back to the cottage and then stopped. What a mess she'd made; behaving as though she was guilty of something. Those women would believe that she had something to hide. Mrs. Hare of all people - Amy's best friend! They'll suspect Mike and it's not fair on him. She turned and headed back to the shop determined to sort it out.

The Co-op door was closed again and the little bell seemed unnecessarily loud. The two women were still standing by the counter. They looked embarrassed as Kath entered and she knew that they had been talking about her. 'I just want to say something,' she said, looking straight at them. 'I had a problem some time ago and was upset by it and the vicar helped me so I got to know him a bit – perhaps more than most. When you asked me about his being sad, it made me remember the problem. Do you see – I mean, do you understand? I don't want you to get the wrong idea. It was to do with my husb… Jack being a prisoner.'

Mrs Crawshaw listened with pursed her lips and folded arms, looking judgmental. But Eileen Hare was a kind woman, and knew from Amy how unsettled Kathleen had been since arriving in Callthorpe. 'That's alright dear, we understand – we didn't think anything – please don't worry. But thank you for explaining – you didn't need to.'

Kath knew this wasn't entirely true but smiled. 'Thankyou – thankyou for understanding….. I'll call back later for my shopping,' she said and made a second, more dignified exit.

Outside the shop she breathed a huge sigh. She was pleased with the action she'd taken even though it may not have completely placed her beyond suspicion. But Kath knew how gossip spread in the village and Mrs. Crawshaw was known as a mine of information for anyone prepared to listen. She decided that she must speak to Mike so that he would be prepared for anything that might result from her behaviour.

She found him standing in the knave talking to the caretaker Mr. Collinson. Mike smiled as Kathleen walked in but the men continued their discussion about the state of the roof which had sprung several leaks during the hard winter. She went into the vestry and stood, waiting.

After a while she heard Mr. Collinson move off and Mike came in with a quizzical look. 'Hello Kathleen, something up?'

Now her determination failed. She intended to tell him about the events in the Co-op but they suddenly seemed silly and trivial. It was easy to deny her feelings when she talked with Amy or when there were others around or when he wasn't there, but alone with him, it was different. Doubts and guilt suddenly disappeared; she remembered the feelings of safety when she was in his arms. Why shouldn't I? She thought. Others do it, I'm no different – no better and no worse than them. He makes me feel better. I just want a bit of comfort, what's the harm? 'I need you to hold me,' she blurted and stepped towards him.

But Mike didn't respond, in fact he stepped back. 'It's no good Kathleen, I can't do this. I can't be friends one minute and more than friends the next. You must be aware that I care for you – more than I should – it may be love – I'm really not sure. But whatever it is, it's wrong. You come to me now and I see that you've changed your mind but tomorrow you'll change again because you want to be loyal to Jack. I would like to be with you but it's impossible. It would destroy us both and it would be a nightmare for the village at a time when the people here depend on me and the Church for stability in troubled times.'

Her face crumpled but she didn't weep. Now he was being strong in the other way; rejecting her because it was right to do so. In one way this was a relief – now there was no question, no uncertainty, she was alone and had to live with it. But suddenly he seemed more desirable; now that he was unattainable, the security of his arms was even more attractive. What's wrong with me? She almost spoke aloud. I'm two people, which one is real? Kath was silent for a while and then forced herself to speak: 'I know - I know, you're right but it will be so hard seeing you around ..... I......I'll have to stop doing Sunday school. I can't be near you, I'm too weak.'

At last he stepped forward and took her hand. She felt the same tremor as the first time. 'I've thought of that Kathleen. I've asked to go back to the Minster. They've found another vicar from Ludstow whose Church has been destroyed by bombs – he'll be coming here. I don't want to leave you but I must – it has to be done. I hope you understand.'

Kath was filled with anxiety tinged with resignation. She knew he was right. But there was guilt as well; by her silly, inconsistent behaviour she had disrupted this man's life and work. In her heart she wanted to beg him to stay or suggest that they leave and find a hiding place where they could be together. But now she felt she owed it to him to be dignified at least. 'I'm sorry Mike, it's all my fault. You shouldn't leave, the villagers love you, you've done such good work here'

'Kathleen,' he said, touching her face gently, 'it's no-one's fault. If you want to blame anyone, blame Herr Hitler. Without this war we probably wouldn't even have met. And, in the end, it's been good to know you. You've stirred something in me that

I thought was dead. So, let's move on and no regrets – yes? It will be good for my career to move on you know.'

Kathleen knew that this last was probably a lie but she didn't want to argue. She put her hand over his on her cheek. They stood for a while and then Kath looked into his eyes, smiled, then turned and walked away.

*

Colonel Chapman sat behind his desk in the prison camp office. He was an old soldier who had been involved, as a very young man, in the Great War. Remaining in the army afterwards, he had been keen to take part in this new conflict but those in power had decided that he was too old to fight. He hated his job as 'nursemaid' to a bunch of Italians for whom he had little regard. He believed that many of them had been all too ready to surrender and were quite content to sit out the war in the relative safety of Callthorpe Camp.

Now at last, there was something to get his teeth into: he had heard a rumour that some prisoners were planning an escape. The whisper had come from one of the guards who had heard it from that dark-skinned chap Guardi. He suspected that the big one, Rodolpho di Campo and his pal would be involved; they always seemed to be around when there was trouble. Well, if they thought they could put one over on Henry Chapman, they had another think coming. He was determined that there would be no escape from *his* camp. The camp guards were ordered to be particularly vigilant and extra patrols were organised to ensure that the men were fresh and alert at their posts. Work parties were allowed out to the farms but with extra guards who were more ordered to be more rigorous in their supervision of the prisoners.

The Italians, of course, noticed the increased security and knew that something had caused it but only Rodolph and Leonardo guessed the real reason. 'That bastard southerner must have heard us,' said Rodolpho. 'Maybe I have to slit his throat, the traitor. He betrays his comrades for a packet of cigarettes.'

'No, no, *I* will slit his throat,' muttered Leonardo. 'But I will do it slowly.'

The prisoners were working in one of Kruyff's fields weeding the rows between the winter wheat that was showing fresh green shoots through the black soil. In the past they would have been unguarded or the single guard would have gone to the farmhouse, to try to see what food or drink he could get from Mrs. Kruyff and they would have been left to their own devices. Today there were three guards, spread across the field, each with a rifle, unslung and ready to use.

Leonardo spoke again: 'maybe we have to wait and let things settle down.'

'No, I cannot wait, I will go mad here. I will go without you if you wish. We have a good plan and it will work, no matter how many guards they have.' Rodolpho was adamant. He had waited through the winter and could wait no longer.

Their plan was simple. While most of the repairs needed in the camp were handled by the prisoners, local workmen sometimes visited to do jobs that needed special equipment, for example; plumbing or electrical work. The electricity generator in the camp was old and often broke down. The two friends had noticed that the men who usually attended to this were similar in build to themselves. They were always dressed in blue overalls and were well known to the guards who just nodded to them as they opened the gate to let them enter or leave. In farmer Kruyff's barn, they had found a pile of his discarded old, blue overalls. They were torn and dirty but, with a little sewing and a wash, could be quite presentable. Two pairs of overalls, repaired and rolled up, were now hidden behind the cisterns in the camp's toilet block. The intention was to engineer a generator breakdown and substitute themselves for the two workmen.

*

Leonardo did persuade Rodolpho to wait for a few days to allow the guards to become relaxed when nothing occurred. They also decided to take no action against Guardi since this might increase suspicion that he had told the truth. They were, however, soon forced to initiate their plans because Kruyff had noticed the missing overalls and accused the whole work group, including the guards, of stealing from him. He was furious and threatened to use his shotgun on the culprits, whoever they were. When no-one confessed he became incandescent with rage and told them to clear off his land and promised that he would never let any of them back. Because he was now well known for his rages, the guards took little notice of his accusations, and simply marched the prisoners back to camp. But the two friends knew that someone might take it upon themselves to investigate the reported theft and the plan could be uncovered.

They chose a day when they knew that there would be no moon the following night, figuring that this would inhibit any pursuit, although hoping, with a bit of luck, that their absence would be unnoticed until the following day's roll-call. First, Rodolpho reluctantly shaved off the beard that he had had ever since he could grow one. It felt very strange to him and Leonardo was amazed at the difference it made to his friend's appearance. Their next task was to disable the generator. It was housed in a secure, concrete structure, inside the prisoners' compound but surrounded by barbed wire; apparently impenetrable. The power was then carried to the various buildings in the camp by underground cables. The weakness in the system was that the cables had to be above ground as they entered the rear of the prisoners' huts which were raised about a foot off the ground on brick piles. It was a simple task to drive an iron nail through the cable in order to create a short circuit. This caused the protective fuse leading from the generator to blow. The nail was to be removed afterwards to avoid arousing suspicion of a deliberate act of sabotage.

Kruyff's ban on work groups was fortuitous since it meant that they had all day to prepare. Also, since other work parties and guards were out of camp, there were no prisoners and only a few remaining guards who figured that the two men didn't need constant observation. They heard the generator slow to a stop as soon as the cable was attacked. The men returned to their billet and waited for action to be taken but no-one seemed to notice; the camp was quiet and no electric lights were turned on. It wasn't until Henry Chapman switched on the electric fire in his office that the situation was discovered.

The two electricians arrived in their old, rickety van and, after parking it outside, were allowed entry to the camp without a second glance from the sentries. They quickly diagnosed the problem, replaced the fuse, restarted the generator and began testing circuits in the huts to find the reason for the breakdown.

Leonardo and Rodolpho, already dressed in the stolen overalls, waited behind the door in their billet but they had overlooked one thing: the two men were accompanied by an armed guard. For a moment it seemed that their plan would be thwarted; they couldn't take on a guard. While they might be able to subdue him, his absence on their return to the gate would be noticed. Now though, they had the piece of luck that they needed; the guard said he would wait outside and have a fag while the electricians entered the hut to test the lighting.

Thinking that the hut was empty, the workmen were shocked to be grabbed from behind and told to stay quiet. They obeyed largely because of what they thought were knives held at their throats. These were in fact six inch nails that had been hammered flat at the ends to form rudimentary blades. Although these weapons were relatively blunt and would not have cut throats easily, the men had no intention of risking a test of their effectiveness.

Swiftly, the electricians were bound, gagged and tied to the toilets in the wash-house. 'If you make noise, we will come back and slit throats before we are taken,' Rodolpho snarled, 'OK?' The men, looking with big eyes, nodded their agreement. The Italians stepped into the main body of the hut and pulled up the collars of their overalls but then Leonardo paused; 'one moment my friend, he said and turned back to the washroom. He had realised that one of the men was wearing spectacles. They looked frightened as he returned but he simply took the spectacles off the smaller man and put them on. They had very thick lenses and his sight was blurred but it would have been foolish to take a chance so he pulled them forward on his nose and looked over the top.

'Ready?' said Rodolpho

'Ready'.

Feeling nervous, they pushed open the door and walked down the three wooden steps. The guard gave them a casual glance. 'OK?' He asked.

'Everything OK,' Rodolpho muttered. 'We go now.'

'Oh, you've finished then?'

'Yes, all OK.'

There was a moment's hesitation that seemed to last an hour. The guard paused as though he was going to question them further, which would have tested their command of English, particularly Leonardo's, but he appeared to decide against it, pushed himself off the wall, and started towards the main gate with the 'workmen' following behind.

Leonardo began to shake as they neared the gate and cold sweat beaded his forehead. He was sure that someone would notice but all the sentries saw was their colleague accompanying the two electricians that they had seen before. 'You goin' then?' One said. Rodolpho just grunted too nervous to trust his speech. 'Lucky buggers,' the sentry continued. 'Wish I was on me way 'ome.' The others laughed and opened the first gate. It seemed to move very slowly. The three walked into the area between the gates and waited while the first one closed behind them. At this point they were trapped. The Italians realised that if they were spotted now, there would be no escape. Time seemed to stop. No-one moved to open the second gate.

'Come on daft buggers,' the guard with them called. 'Open the bloody gate these lads want to get off.'

'Alright, keep yer 'air on,' someone shouted and the second gate began to move.

As they stepped out, Rodolpho suddenly realised with horror that there was a final problem. The electricians' van stood waiting but what if there was no key! They had forgotten to search the men's pockets. He paused and looked at Leonardo who returned the look quizzically, not appreciating the problem. Still, they had no option. They walked towards the van with Leonardo quickening his pace, wanting to get away. He went round to the driver's door and got in. Rodolpho stood outside the passenger door, looking in. NO KEY! He stared at his friend and then nodded towards the dashboard. Leonardo frowned and looked back, not understanding. Rodolpho tried again and this time his friend realised the problem. Strangely, he smiled and indicated that Rodolpho should get in the van. He then bent down and pulled at the wires below the dash, taking two, he rubbed the bare ends together and, amazingly, the engine fired. He twisted the wires together, grinned at Rodolpho and began to drive away down the track from the camp, grinding the gears as he did so.

'How did you do that?'

'I have a cousin from Torino, he used to steal cars and he taught me how.' Leonardo grinned again. 'Good trick eh?'

His smile disappeared as the camp siren started up. They hadn't even got as far as the main road.

*

For days the escape was the talk of the village and people kept near to their homes. Those who had shotguns made sure they were loaded and others put pitchforks and wooden cudgels behind their doors, ready for use if necessary. Through the village grape-vine, they found out who was involved, Michael said he didn't think Rodolpho would hurt anyone anyway but his mother made him stay close to home all the same.

There were soldiers everywhere searching gardens, fields and farm buildings but all they found was the electricians' van that had been pushed down a narrow track leading to a wooded area. After a while, it was decided that the men had probably left the vicinity and the search widened towards the coast because it seemed likely that they would try to get hold of a boat. This idea gained weight when Leonardo was recaptured hiding near the harbour at Kettlesea. He was weak with hunger and exhausted but wouldn't tell anyone where his friend had gone. He just told his questioners that they had become separated soon after the van broke down near Timpney and that was the last he had seen of Rodolpho. The search was then concentrated around Kettlesea and life in Callthorpe gradually returned to its usual leisurely pace.

*

'Do I have to go?' Michael was struggling to get out of Kath's grip as she combed his hair.

'Yes, it's Whitsuntide. You've got a week off school to play with Thomas. We're all going to Church, as a family.' The boy looked at the others standing in the kitchen. Amy had on her best hat and coat, despite the warmth of the day, and Walter was in his suit with a collar and tie, looking uncomfortable. He was tugging at the collar.

'I can't breathe in this thing,' he said.

'Dad, behave, set a good example for your grandson. Do you want me to comb your hair as well?' Releasing Michael, she advanced on her father waving the comb.

'OK,' he said smiling, pleased that his daughter was in a cheerful mood. She was surprised that he agreed but walked over and pulled the comb through his wiry, white hair, then kissed his forehead. 'Thankyou daughter,' he said. 'Come on Michael, the sooner we get there, the sooner it's over. After, we can go and watch the Morris dancers outside the Brown Cow if you like. We'll take some fruit and cake for our lunch.'

294

Michael accepted this and called to Rags who was outside glaring at the hens. If his master was going, then the dog went with them to Church but had to wait outside until the service was over. There were other, mainly farm dogs there. One was usually fastened to the railings that bordered the Church grounds, another sat in the farmer's trap while the pony munched on its feedbag. On this day, both were there when the family arrived. Michael looked Rags straight in the eye. 'Remember,' he said. 'No fighting and no chasing cats round the village.' The dog had been guilty of both these misdemeanors in the past. The worst of which had involved chasing a tabby tomcat through the tap room of the Brown Cow, upsetting a table with several glasses of beer on top and causing general disruption to the lunchtime drinking session. Rags put his head on one side, gave a single wag to indicate that he understood, and settled down in the shade provided by the lych-gate.

The family went inside and walked into their usual pew near to the back of the Church. Although Michael complained about having to attend, he liked the old building with its stone carved pillars, its roof made of mellow oak beams and the glowing stained glass. The place smelled of mature wood and furniture polish mingled with the perfume from the women in the congregation and the flowers round the altar. Other people were already inside, including Thomas and his parents. He turned and smiled at Michael who tried to communicate that he was going to see the Morris dancers afterwards. This was a difficult thing to mime, and after several abortive attempts, to which Thomas shook his head and shrugged his shoulders, Kathleen said, 'for goodness sake sit still.'

The service proceeded with Mike's clear, calm voice leading the congregation in their worship. In his sermon he told them about the origins of Whitsuntide. Michael didn't understand the Holy Ghost descending on the Apostles, and tried to ask Kathleen for an explanation, but was shushed and remained with a picture in his mind of a white sheet with holes for eyes coming from the sky to cover the heads of Jesus' disciples. Mike also told them that, in the past, people used Whitsun as an excuse for drinking to excess, and reminded them that, while drink in moderation was acceptable, becoming drunk was something that good Christians should avoid. In his parish notices, after the service, he mentioned that the Timpney Morris Dancers were in the village and that they would be happy if people went to see them. At this Thomas realised what Michael had been indicating and turned to nod his intention to go along.

The congregation filed out, blinking, into the bright, sunny day. They all paused to shake hands with Mike. Several, who knew his intention to leave, asked if he could be persuaded to stay because he had proved to be a popular priest but he declined to become involved in what might have proved to be a difficult discussion. Rags came wagging to be included but as usual, ducked away from any attempt to pat his head. Michael bent down and tickled the dog's chest and told him they were going to see the dancers. Rags didn't quite understand but gave a small bark of anticipation.

Outside the gate now, Kathleen, Amy and Thomas's parents left Walter and the two boys. A crowd was gathering outside the pub. The dancers were getting ready to perform on a flat area of grass in front of some wooden benches near the pub door. 'They're usually all men,' said Walter. 'But some women have had to join in because all the younger men are away in the army.'

'Is the boss called Morris, grandad?' Michael asked.

Walter smiled. 'No lad. I think that way back, they were black men who did the dance, and they were from Africa, so it was called the Moorish Dance. That's why some of them black their faces. But the dances have changed to make them more English so that there are characters like Saint George in the story and now they're called Morris dancers.'

The watchers stood or sat on the grass, leaving a space big enough for the dance to take place. There were people from Callthorpe and some had come from Timpney . Michael saw Maisie and he and Thomas went over to say hello. She gave them both a big hug and planted the usual sloppy kisses on their cheeks. 'I'm so glad to see you two,' she said. 'You've not been over to visit me though.' The boys looked at one another hoping that the other would speak but neither of them knew what to say. Maisie saw their confusion; 'oh, it's alright, I know young chaps like you are too busy to worry about an old woman, I understand.'

Michael was ashamed. 'We will come Maisie,' he said. 'We'll come in the summer holidays, won't we Thomas?' His friend nodded and smiled.

'Oh well we'll see. You know I'll be pleased to see you anyway. That's your grandad isn't it,' she said, pointing at Walter and waving. Walter waved back. He knew Maisie. Michael wasn't surprised. Since living here he had come to realise that, in the country, everybody knew everybody.

As the dancers, in their bizarre colourful costumes, began to get ready, the boys left Maisie and went to sit on the grass with Walter and Rags. The sun shone warmly on the scene and the old red-brick houses on the edge of the green seemed to lean forward protectively. For a moment, the war was forgotten and folk were relaxed, smiling and chatting with their friends, as they had in years gone by. Michael looked at the faces of the dancers, not expecting to recognise anyone, but two of them seemed familiar. 'Who're they?' He asked Thomas.

'It's Gert and Daisy,' laughed Thomas, recognising the land girls. 'You know they work on our farm and deliver the milk.'

'Yes, yes it's them!' Said Michael, excited. 'What're they doin' 'ere?'

'I told you, there aren't enough men to do the dance these days so they must've volunteered to help. Good for them,' Walter explained. The women saw that they were being pointed at and waved and bowed, blowing kisses at the boys which made them laugh as they waved back.

The dancers formed two lines ready to start. Michael got hold of Rags' collar in case he decided to join in the proceedings.

Some of the men who had been drinking in the pub came out on to the paved area outside and sat on the wooden benches. They saw that Mr. Kruyff was one of them. His face was even redder than usual and he was clutching a big silver tankard. The farm sheepdog followed him, cringing round his legs. He sat down heavily on one of the benches and nearly overbalanced, spilling some beer. Two men were with him but Michael didn't know them. They laughed uproariously together. 'Looks as though they've already had a skinful,' said Walter.

Three old men formed the band, playing a drum, a penny whistle and an accordion. They started to play with a cheerful rhythm and the dance began. The boys were particularly entertained by a young woman who danced freely around the others while they followed a strict pattern of movement. Dressed in a green costume with ribbons attached and a pointed hat with feathers, she had an inflated sheep's bladder on the end of a stick which she used to whack the other dancers. 'That's the fool,' said Walter. 'She has to be really clever not to get in the way of the others; otherwise she'd spoil the dance.'

'Who's that one?' Thomas asked, pointing at a dancer wearing a donkey's head.

'That's the beast – wait and he'll come and dance for you.'

As the dance progressed, the beast went to all the children and tried to make them laugh. He walked like a German soldier making the Nazi salute and doing the goosestep, then tripped himself and collapsed in a heap. Rags decided that this was a game. He broke free of Michael's grip and rushed to the fallen beast, barking and trying to bite the donkey head. The beast shouted, 'gerrimoff, gerrimoff.' The boys managed to get hold of the dog before he did too much damage and pulled him away, trying not to laugh as the beast tried to gain his composure.

They watched as different tunes were played and the dances changed to fit the rhythms until, after about forty minutes, the show ended. There was general applause for the performers and people threw pennies into the fool's hat as it was passed around. The cheerful crowd began to disperse. Michael watched as farmer Kruyff and his friends returned to the pub. He wondered if this might be the opportunity they had been waiting for. 'I've had an idea,' he whispered to Thomas. 'We could go up to Kruyff's farm while 'e's in the pub and see if we can get inside the hut. What d'you think?'

'I can't go,' said Thomas, 'My uncle and aunt are coming from Seldown, I've got to be there, mum said. An' I don't think you should go either, Kruyff's mad and you know what he said would happen if we were caught again.'

Michael was disappointed. He believed that Kruyff's farm, and particularly the shed behind the farmhouse, held a secret. He also felt that he and Thomas were the only ones who might be able to expose what might be hidden there. The rest of the country community appeared to be content to let matters lie; it was part of the country code to live and let live. But *he* knew in his heart that something was badly wrong and that that something, whatever it was, could explain Reuben's behaviour. He was clearly a very unhappy boy and it offended Michael's sense of right and wrong that nothing was being done to help his friend. He remembered when they had first started working on their farming project how after a while, Reuben had been pleased to explain what he knew about the subject and to show off his farm. But now the boy had gone back inside himself; no-one was able to reach him. Michael knew that Miss Newby had been pleased when he and Reuben had begun to relate to one another and he felt that in some way, he had failed both his teacher and his friend. He thought about Whacker and knew that he would never abandon a pal. He quite wished that his old friend was there because it was very possible, that between them, they would be able to come up with a plan to discover the secret hidden on Kruyff's farm.

As he pondered, Michael came to a realisation that he couldn't stand by and do nothing; whether Thomas went with him or not. He knew where farmer Kruyff was, and this was a chance that shouldn't be missed. He felt both nervous and excited by the prospect but the decision had been made; there was no going back.

Thomas stood up, thanked Walter for bringing them to the Morris dance and set off for tea with his relatives. Michael wondered how to explain where he was going and when his grandad started talking with Mrs. Hare and some other villagers, the opportunity presented itself: 'I think I'll catch Thomas and walk with him,' he said. Walter understood that the boy wouldn't want to hang around with the adults and agreed, saying that he would see Michael back at the cottage. Rags cast one last, longing look towards the donkey head that lay on the ground discarded by its owner, and followed behind.

He decided to follow the same route as on their previous visit to Kruyff's which meant cutting through Gant's farmland. There was a stile leading off the lane to Birch Tree Cottage, this allowed access to the correct fields without going near the farmhouse; he didn't want Thomas or his parents to see where he was going. As he clambered over the shaky wooden structure, Michael realised that he was dressed in his Sunday best clothes and the new leather shoes he'd got for his birthday. This was not appropriate attire for scrambling around fields and hedgerows; he'd have to try to keep them clean. The boy knew that clothing could only be obtained by using precious coupons and had to last for as long as possible so he took off his jacket and hung it on a lower branch of a young oak tree near to the style, intending to pick it up on his return to the cottage. He pushed his socks down as far as possible; better to get legs dirty and scratched rather than risk tearing new woollen socks. In the meantime Rags, in his customary style, had disappeared to investigate the rich variety of smells provided by the fields and ditches.

The boy reached the dense hawthorn with the hidden passage that led close to Kruyff's land; he had no option but to get on his knees to crawl through to the other side. He looked down at himself; the trousers looked reasonably clean but his white shirt was covered with grass stains and mucky marks. I'm going to be in trouble for this, he thought, but carried on, soon reaching the hedge that separated the two farms. He looked round but there was no sight or sound of his dog. Michael wasn't worried, he knew that Rags was hunting somewhere nearby and would turn up in his own time.

*

Rodolpho had seen everything: when the Home Guard patrol had spotted him, Leonardo had run up the steep, narrow, cobbled lane away from their hiding place, hoping to take the chase away from his friend. Then, when he was far enough away, he stopped with his hands in the air. The old soldier who got to him first held his rifle nervously and didn't speak. There was an unreal air about the moment; both men regarded the other with caution and a kind of shyness, neither able to think of anything appropriate to say. Then the others arrived and an officer took charge, ordering two men to get hold of the prisoner, while the others were told to continue their search for the second man.

The Italians had managed to reach the sea but getting hold of a boat had proved to be difficult, everyone had been warned about the escapees so vessels of any size were well guarded. They could have stolen a rowing boat but knew that to launch into the North Sea in one of those would have been tantamount to suicide. Leonardo was seen when he tried to find edible food waste in the bins behind a fish and chip shop. Rodolpho, witnessing the capture of his friend, had thought about giving up but although hungry and tired, he recalled his vow to himself that he would never surrender again. By keeping to the narrow alleyways and hiding in gardens when anyone approached, he managed to evade the searchers and get away from Kettlesea which was clearly becoming too dangerous. Now, exhausted and dispirited, he determined to make a final act before being recaptured or, at worst, killed. He had grown to hate Kruyff and particularly the way he treated his son. It was as though the man had come to represent the ultimate enemy. In his exhausted and befuddled state, Rodolpho felt that dealing with Kruyff could represent a last blast of defiance against a war that had destroyed his life and riven him from his home and family.

Traveling only at night and sleeping in hedgerows and deserted farm buildings during the day, he retraced his journey from Callthorpe. Since the search was now concentrated near Kettlesea, road blocks had been dismantled and he saw little evidence of military activity. The journey to the sea had been relatively easy: they simply headed east towards the coast but returning was more difficult because of the lack of signposts at crossroads and junctions. The eventual sight of the tower of Callthorpe Church gave him a strange feeling of euphoria; almost like returning home.

Through the still, warm air there were sounds of music coming from the village but the farm was quiet when Rodolpho arrived. Looking for a place to hide, he ran, crouching to the big barn, he knew that there was a disused hay loft at the back from where he could look through the cracked boarding to observe activity in the farmyard. The ladder to the loft had several broken struts but he managed to climb up and sank, gratefully into a pile of sweet smelling hay. Through the boarding he watched as Mrs. Kruyff came out of the house and emptied a bowl of water into a drain and then returned through the door. He could hear her talking to someone but couldn't make out the words. He was sure though, that Kruyff wasn't around and settled down to wait. He had no clear plan in mind; he simply believed that at some point in time an opportunity to take revenge on Kruyff would present itself.

He heard the distant music fade and the afternoon returned to the slumbering warmth of an early summer day; even the birds seemed to rest, only faint creaks from the planks of the old wooden barn and the occasional busy insect disturbed the peace. Time passed. Rodolpho's stomach grumbled and he wondered if there might be some eggs in the hen house. He looked out and saw a quick movement; a small shape disappeared behind Kruyff's shed.

*

Despite the warmth of the day, Michael was shivering as he reached the shadow of the shed. He had run as quickly and quietly as he could across the farmyard and believed that he had not been seen. He examined the wooden building to find a way in but it seemed impregnable. The door had a solid looking padlock and all the boards were securely fastened. He went into the narrow gap between the shed and the farmhouse and found that there was in fact, a small window, high up and just about big enough for a boy to squeeze through, and it was slightly open! But he couldn't reach it. An old milk churn behind the shed provided a solution. Although the lid of the churn was curved and a bit unstable, by standing on top of it he could just catch the window ledge in his fingers. He felt for the catch and managed to dislodge it; the window swung loose. Pulling with all his strength, the boy levered himself up and got his head and shoulders through the space, his legs dangling behind. He could see nothing, the bright sunshine made him blind in the deep shadow of the interior. Still, no turning back, he pulled his body through the window and allowed himself to fall into the void. He felt as though he had fallen on to a table from which he rolled and dropped to the floor of the shed. Something fell behind him. His head ached.

Michael's eyes gradually adjusted to the gloom. He was conscious of a mixture of rich red and black all around him. He gasped as he focused on the walls covered with huge flags bearing the awesome shape of the swastika. On newsreels, at the pictures, they were shown in black and white with crowds of people around and were just weird flags. Here, in the solitude of this warm shed, on an English farm, they were shocking, threatening and dangerous. The boy was chilled with fear; he felt to be surrounded by an evil force that enclosed him. It was like being back in the cellar of the bombed house: he was unable to escape a growing threat. He began to gasp for breath. There was more: he found himself staring at grainy photographs and saw the unmistakable figure of Adolph Hitler riding in a black, open-top limousine riding along a wet road surrounded by dense, waving crowds. In another, ranks of boys dressed in caps and uniforms with swastikas, stood with their right arms raised in salute. There were pictures of tanks and goose-stepping troops. Then he thought he recognised a face on one of the photographs and peered closer … yes, it was. Reuben standing like the boys in the other picture with his arm raised but strange, he had a shirt but no trousers. There were others; sometimes he had no clothes at all and was laying on a swastika flag. There were more of them and they were weird. He couldn't explain it but Michael suddenly felt nauseous, his heart beat wildly and his fear increased. It wasn't just being in the shed that was scary it was also the look of desperate loneliness and fear in his friend's eyes.

This is wrong, he thought, really wrong. He started to pull at the photographs. They tore in his fingers but he didn't care. He grabbed a loose fold in one of the flags and dragged it down from the wall with a ripping sound. Michael was determined to destroy this nightmare. He thought about Miss Newby's schoolroom and its displays; that's how walls should look, this was evil. He picked up the shotgun which had dropped off the table as he fell and started swinging the butt at the wooden walls of the shed, trying to break them down, beside himself with fear and anger.

In his frenzy he didn't hear Kruyff's approach but the light flooding from the opened door made him spin round to face the huge figure blocking the doorway. The boy glanced quickly at the window but it was too high, in his determination to erase this nightmare, he had smashed the table that had broken his fall.

The farmer didn't speak, he roared, and reached to grab the boy. Michael ducked and tried to get to the doorway but Kruyff was just too big and his hand closed on the boy's shirt collar. Twisting in the grip and hearing the familiar sound of his shirt tearing, Michael tried his usual mode of attack and attempted a punch to the point of the man's nose but he couldn't reach and the blow fell ineffectually on the huge chest. The boy felt helpless, impotent against the man's seemingly enormous strength. Another roar followed and Michael found himself held tightly and lifted off the ground. He could smell the sour beer on the man's breath as he spoke: 'So, you don't like my pictures,' he bellowed. 'Now maybe you be in my pictures, I show you now, I show you not to come to my farm. Now you never leave.' He tore Michael's shirt from his back and reached for one of the flags. 'I teach you to respect this,' he said, quieter now.

The flag was just out of reach and for a split second he relaxed his grip. The boy squirmed, kicked hard, broke free and burst through the door into the farmyard. He saw Rags careering towards him, barking loudly, and then felt his legs kicked from behind as he crashed to the hard earth, sliding along the gravel, banging his head and scraping his bare chest. The breath burst from his mouth in a groan as Kruyff's boot landed on his back. Rags attacked; his teeth sank into the farmer's standing leg but a savage blow from the butt of the shotgun sent him reeling. The dog tried to stand to return to the fight but his back legs wouldn't work properly; he couldn't move. He bravely tried to pull himself forward with his front legs but the damage was too severe and excruciating pain made him whimper.

*

Rodolpho was surprised when he saw Michael running across the yard. What is Michelangelo doing here? He thought. This was unexpected and might get in the way of his plans to wreak revenge on Kruyff. He waited, Michael didn't appear from behind the shed, the afternoon became quiet again. Then Kruyff arrived, Rodolpho tensed but waited. When, a few minutes later, he saw the boy trying to escape and being kicked to the ground, he decided to act. Regardless of the noise he made, the Italian threw himself down the old wooden ladder and out into the yard.

'Stop that - bastard,' he shouted in English as he ran towards the farmer.

Kruyff turned, his red face a mixture of anger and surprise, he raised the shotgun and called, 'I see you Eyetie coward, it is you who will stop.' Without hesitation he fired both barrels almost simultaneously. Rodolpho was deafened by the blast and felt as though he had run into an invisible barrier. He fell to his knees. At first there was no sensation and he looked down in surprise at the blood spurting from the front of his ragged overalls. The Italian, still full of anger towards Kruyff, tried to rise and continue his charge, he made a few stumbling steps and then collapsed roaring in pain and frustration. He managed to drag himself along the ground towards his adversary but Kruyff was in charge; he stepped forward and rammed the butt of the gun into the Italian's face. Rodolpho's eyes were filled with a myriad of searing colours then he stopped and went quiet, unaware of another, final blow delivered as he lay on the ground.

Reuben and his mother were horrified by the scene as they came to the door of the farmhouse. Mrs. Kruyff screamed. The boy shouted at his father, probably for the first time in his life: 'no father, no you've killed my friend, you've killed him!'

'Get inside, stay out of the way,' Kruyff bellowed. 'This is not for you to see, get back in the house. I deal with these two now. You will see, they not bother me again.' He moved threateningly towards his family and they fled into the darkness of the house, both sobbing. The man turned now to Michael and raised the shotgun with the butt aimed at the boy's head.

*

Michael, winded and concussed by his fall, was only vaguely aware of Rodolpho's attack. The noise of gunfire and shouting penetrated his consciousness and through his dazed vision he could see Rags on the ground whimpering and struggling to move but it was like a dream; as though he was watching from the outside of the action. He could hear another noise in the background; a harsh, hammering racket, but he couldn't identify it, he only knew that it was getting louder – deafening.

As the roar increased in volume, it began to take shape. Surrounded by a cloud of dust and moving quickly, Michael could make out spinning wheels and above them two figures, one with bright red hair. He was aware of a sickening thud and a screeching of metal as something heavy scraped along the hard packed farmyard, then the sound of running feet and more shouting, voices he knew - then blackness.

*

There was a grey light but his eyes couldn't focus. He made out a vague shape that appeared, disappeared and gradually turned into his mother. Michael was in his bedroom but it was daytime, the light flowed around the little room. He saw his books and the washstand. His head ached and his chest was in agony but the softness of the comforting sheets around him felt good. Kath looked at him. Her face was wet but she smiled. 'Oh, love, thank God,' she said. She stroked his hair and bent to kiss him. The boy wriggled. 'Mam!' He said. He had recently decided that kissing was soppy.

Kath laughed, 'he's awake,' she called. He heard running steps on the stairs and then the room was full of people. Grandma, grandad, Thomas and his parents, Mike the vicar and who are they? A man he didn't know and Whacker! But not Whacker, this boy was taller, but yet that same red hair? And then he spoke, grinning: 'Owdo pal.' Yes it was because that's what Whacker said – 'owdo?' That's what he always said when you met him. But how could it be?

*

Over the next hours the story unfolded. Whacker and Mr. Gunson had spent countless hours after school repairing the broken Triumph 250. They had visited local scrap yards for the parts after dismantling the whole machine and finding more problems in the engine. The project dragged on for months. It seemed that they would never succeed but they were both determined and three weeks ago, the engine had finally spluttered to life and they had been able to take it out on the road. As the Whitsun holiday approached, Whacker persuaded the teacher that they should make a surprise visit to Callthorpe. Mr. Gunson checked with Whacker's mother that the visit was acceptable and the plans were laid. Molly and the other gang members had wanted to be included, but with reluctance, agreed that there wasn't enough room for more than one on the pillion.

Having been lost several times because of the lack of road signs they had eventually found Birch Tree Cottage but no Michael. Walter directed them to Gant's farm, and there, with some reluctance, Thomas was persuaded to tell what he knew. After getting directions from the Gants, they had driven to the Kruyff farmstead.

The scene on arrival in the farmyard had astounded them both but seeing Michael clearly in imminent danger from the butt of the shotgun and responding to Whacker's urging, Mr. Gunson had ridden the Triumph straight into the huge farmer and felled him.

The Gants knew something was amiss and Walter, sensing that his grandson might be in danger, had arrived shortly after this event and found the teacher and Whacker sitting on Kruyff to stop him moving, with Reuben tending to Michael's wounds, while Mrs. Kruyff tried to staunch the blood coming from Rodolpho's chest. The badly damaged Rags could barely raise his head. He tried a bark but it came out wrong. There was no way he could stand up and had to be carried back home.

Michael listened intently while the tale was told and at the end, felt completely exhausted. His head sank back on the pillow and the room went quiet, waiting for his response… Suddenly he sat up; 'Where's Rags?'

'He's at the vets,' answered Walter. 'Don't worry we'll make sure he's well looked after.'

'Mebbe we can go an' see 'im tomorrow … if you're well enough.' Whacker's voice surprised everyone. He stepped forward and put his hand on Michael's shoulder

'Yes, OK, we'll all go tomorrow,' Kathleen agreed.

CHAPTER 18

EPILOGUE

The war in Europe progressed towards its conclusion. In August 1944, Paris was liberated. By the end of October the gas chambers at Auschwitz were turned off and by December, the Soviet army had reached Budapest. In January 1945, the Soviets reached Warsaw. The meeting at Yalta took place in February. Dresden was destroyed by Allied bombing. In April, the Allies liberated Buchenwald and Belsen. On 7th May the Germans surrendered unconditionally to the Allies.

In Birch Tree Cottage, at 7.40pm on the 8th of May, they listened to the announcement from a solemn, posh voice on the radio. 'Thank God, it's finished,' said Walter, quietly. Amy and Kath sobbed and smiled at the same time.

*

1995. Research shows that more than 100,000 people were killed in the Bosnian War. Both Serbs and Croats have been convicted of systematic war crimes. Thirty per cent of Bosniak civilian casualties were women and children.

We have learned nothing! As I drive through Timpney on the way to Callthorpe news of the ethnic war in Bosnia comes over the radio. In fifty years Europe seems to have forgotten the agonies that millions of people experienced and the countless lives that were wasted because of the evil prejudices of a small number of megalomaniacs. The horrors of Auschwitz are decaying in human consciousness; drifting away like debris on the tide of time. Now it may be happening again.

I haven't seen Callthorpe since Amy died. After that there was no reason to return. There are still people I know in the village, but without her or Grandad, the place just isn't the same. My mother and I are thankful that she lived to a good age and was able to look after herself until the final heart attack. For a long time I just haven't wanted to see the village without them around. I believe that Kath thinks the same, she has only been back to put flowers on their grave in the old churchyard. I missed grandad a lot at first. He helped me make sense of the war and taught me so much about country ways. I'm not even sure why I'm coming here now, something's drawing me. On my way to talk with some young farmers at a conference, I realised that I wasn't far from here. At first I couldn't find the road because there's a new bypass that goes round the little villages, you could easily drive by without noticing the signs. When I found it at last, my memory clicked into gear and every twist and turn in the lane, every farm track and all the little dips and rises were comfortingly familiar but somehow smaller than I remember. Familiar hedgerows fly past and a mixture of aromas filters into the car: hay, meadow sweet and honeysuckle mingle with fresh country air.

Memories crowd in; as I pass through Timpney with its village green and duck pond, I remember Maisie, her duck and the beautiful fruit cake. I can just make out where the airfield was. A huge, hedgeless field full of what looks like barley stands on the ground where the great planes rattled towards their take-off. I recall the early dawn and the bombers return, the chaos of the crash and the kindness of Sergeant Ferris.

The passing fields make me think of Thomas. I still keep in touch with him. With some financial help from his father, he now has his own farm and has settled in the south where he specialises in raising children and rare breeds of cattle. His mother died recently but old Mr. Gant is still fit enough to run his farm with the help of several farm workers and modern machinery. I could call on him but he would want me to stay and I haven't got time. The young farmers will be waiting to hear my talk about maximising wheat yields. We've learned more about this through the work of Norman Borlaug, and also when I worked in Africa, where they need to get the best return from their planting.

I'm happy with my life now and not looking forward to retirement. After university I felt a bit lost. Maybe my father's death upset me more than I knew at the time. When the allies finally reached Stalag X1BC, they found that the German guards had fled but left the camp gates locked and the inmates without food. Many of the prisoners, including Dad were in a poor state – undernourished and very ill. He was taken to hospital and for weeks, seemed on the point of death but he drew on some deep reserve of inner determination and made a slow recovery. Several of the prisoners were just too weak to survive and sadly, died before they could be repatriated. Dad lasted a few precious years but wasn't able to work. He and Mam became very loving when he returned. They found a house back near Stanbury but I stayed living with my grand parents so that I could go to the school in Seldown. Grandpa George lived long enough to see his son again and even the selfish sisters seemed pleased by their brother's return. Dad was so ill that he was awarded a disability pension which was just sufficient for the two of them to live on. He hated living on what he called 'charity' and got a job back in the same factory but only lasted three days before it became clear to everyone that he simply couldn't manage the physical effort. They offered him part-time work in the office but he was too weak even to manage that. He lived long enough to see me get to university. Mam nursed him tenderly during the last days but he died just before I got my degree. The lasting legacy of the men from his camp was the fact that only about twenty-five percent of the V1s hit their targets.

I can't help myself; I pull the car up at the bottom of the track to Kruyff's farm and look up it, half expecting to see him striding down towards me with his shotgun ready. Farmer Kruyff was arrested and eventually sent to an internment camp as an undesirable alien. He was not a spy but his extensive collection of photographs and flags indicated that he was a Nazi sympathiser and as such, a danger in time of war. Unfortunately, he was able to claim that he killed the fugitive Italian prisoner in self-defence and there was little evidence to suggest otherwise. When the conflict finally ended, he was deported and refused permission to re-enter the Country. He had clearly treated his son and wife very badly: both had suffered regular physical attacks, but although there was a strong suspicion that my friend Reuben had been sexually abused, he mutely refused to reveal any details.

As an undesirable alien, Kruyff's property was confiscated and handed, eventually, to Mrs. Kruyff but despite help from the villagers, she and Reuben couldn't manage to run the farm and it was bought by Mr. Gant so that he now owns the biggest farm in the area, much to the chagrin of Mrs. Hare. I'm sorry to say that even after all these years, I still see Kruyff in my dreams and wake up sweating, expecting to be prostrate on the hard ground of his farmyard.

Reuben was allowed to stay at the village school for an extra year and made up considerable ground in his learning. His confidence improved but there were times when he fell into black moods. At such times it was best to just leave him alone. We got together during the evenings and holidays but the relationship became difficult; it was as though he was ashamed of what had happened and in some way blamed himself. It would have been easy to end our friendship then but both Thomas and I felt that we wanted to help him to get over the events of that summer. We tried to reassure him that we still liked and respected him and I think he gradually came to believe us. After they had sold the farm, Reuben and his mother used the money to buy a house in Timpney. He found a job on a local farm and although still a very quiet and private person, he made an excellent farm worker and was accepted into the country community. We stayed friends till I moved away and then we lost touch. People said that he made contact with his father when Mrs. Kruyff died but when asked, Reuben wouldn't discus it.

Sitting here, my hand goes automatically to my chest where the skin was rubbed off as Kruyff kicked me to the ground and I feel a phantom of the soreness that left me long ago. I will never be able to repay the debt I owe to Whacker and Mr. Gunson. The teacher stayed for a few days until I had recovered and then he drove the old motor bike back to his home. Whacker's parents were contacted and he was allowed to stay for most of the summer holiday. There is no doubt that his presence helped accelerate my recovery and I recall the joy of days spent exploring the countryside with him and Thomas. We made Thomas an honorary member of the Lucy Street gang.

I still see Whacker regularly but I call him Andrew if we're with other people. After going to technical college to study motor engineering, he started his own business repairing motor bikes and became a star on the trials' circuit. He's kind of famous and important now but despite this, when there's just the two of us, we drop back to being like silly, scruffy kids again.

A dog barks up at the farm and my heart lurches but of course it's not him. Rag's right hip was shattered by Kruyff's blow. The vet in Seldown said it would be best if the dog was put to sleep but none of us were prepared to even contemplate the idea. We persuaded him to try an amputation. Afterwards, it took some time, but eventually the old dog learned to manage with three legs and went on to live till he was about sixteen as far as we could guess, since no-one, except perhaps old Tom Threlfall, knew when the dog had been born. He didn't wander the countryside as much after that and often stayed in the garden, much to the displeasure of the hens. My loyal old friend died in the autumn of 1947.

I start the engine. Stupidly, I feel hot tears filling my eyes – how ridiculous! I can't resist a glance at the cottage as I pass down the lane to the village. There's washing blowing on a line. The house looks much the same but different; the birch trees have gone. There's a white van parked outside the gate and it isn't our house anymore. I drive on.

The houses round the green, the church, pub and co-op look just the same. Parts of the village are locked in the past. But there are new modern houses in cul-de-sacs that didn't exist before. To me they seem totally incongruous. Stupidly, I want things to be exactly as I remember. I'm even annoyed that they've taken the sandbags away from the entrance to the school and what stupid person put that ugly mobile classroom in the old playground? I wonder what became of Miss Newby and Mike the curate. In the middle of the green is the war memorial. I pull up and walk across the grass to read again the little plaque at the bottom, separate from the other names:

> *To remember, with thanks, the sacrifice of Rodolpho*
> *Antonio Bocelli, 1918 – 1944*

Dad once told me that he met an Italian prisoner in the desert and he thought that *his* name had been Rodolpho but it couldn't have been the same man could it?

FOOTNOTE

* A Child's Garden of Verses   R L Stephenson   Longmans,
   Green and Co. 1904

ACKNOWLEDGEMENT

Whilst the story line and characters in this book are works of fiction, some events are drawn from the memories of family and friends who lived through the Second World War as both civilians and forces personnel. Particular thanks are due to my father John and Uncle George along with Jack who was a prisoner of war. Also, a particular mention for Arthur, my friend who served in North Africa and Italy; he helped with many revealing first hand recollections. GM

BIBLIOGRAPHY

Wartime Britain 1939 – 1945 by Juliet Gardiner   Headline
Publishing 2004